Joan Byrd

Also from the
All My Tomorrows **series**
by Joan Byrd
From Indigo Sea Press

A New Beginning

indigoseapress.com

Love Finds a Way

Book Two of the
All My Tomorrows
Series

By

Joan Byrd

Star-Crossed Books
Published by Indigo Sea Press
Winston-Salem

Joan Byrd

Star-Crossed Books
Indigo Sea Press
PO Box 67201
Winston-Salem, NC 27114
This book is a work of fiction. Names, characters,
locations and events are either a product of the author's
imagination, fictitious or used fictitiously. Any resemblance
to any event, locale or person, living or dead, is purely
coincidental.

For information regarding bulk purchases of this book,
digital purchase and special discounts, please contact the
publisher at indigoseapress@gmail.com

Cover design by Pan Morelli
Manufactured in the United States of America
ISBN 978-1630664800

I dedicate this book to:
My husband, Ray Byrd,
who gave me support and time to write;

My niece and little buddy, Dene Murrell,
who was my dearest friend when I wrote this book in the 70s;

And Patrick, my guardian angel.
Without him and his outstanding gifts of storytelling, there
would be no book.

I will love you throughout all my tomorrows.
—Joan Byrd

Joan Byrd

Chapter 1

TarSa 1973-1974

Gene Scott sat quietly thinking in the Crain's living room. He and Susan had a giant-size problem. But they did love one another, he thought to himself. And Edna walked in and sat down next to him. She patted his hand.

"Hey, Gene, where is your mind?"

"Can't you guess?" He stood up and walked over to the window. "Shit, Edna! Why can't two people in love just live happily no matter what the rest of the world thinks?"

"I'm sure there's a way you and this mystery woman in your life can work things out, Gene." Edna looked down at her hands and bit her lip. "Gene, I've been putting two and two together. What I have come up with . . . well, if it's what I think, you have a big problem."

"What is it you have come up with?" He turned to face her.

"I think I know who the girl is, the one you're in love with." She stood up and walked over to him. "It's Susan Andrews, isn't it?"

He took hold of her shoulders. "Yes, and how did you come up with it?"

"Oh, Gene, that's what I was afraid of. She turned and walked back to the sofa. "I figured it out by the things I saw: the looks between the two of you; her wanting to come visit the children because you were going; her calling you Gene instead of Reverend Scott. Not to mention your getting jealous over David."

"Was it that obvious?" He joined her on the sofa.

"You really do love her very much don't you, Gene?"

"Very much, Edna? We love each other very much." He buried his face in his hands. "What are we going to do?"

"Oh Gene, how could it possibly work out? She is only seventeen to your thirty-six." She touched his shoulder gently. "Your daughter, Tracy, would have been her age if she had lived. Maybe it's the daughter you lost that you love and not really Susan."

"No, Edna, it's not that simple." He stood up. "I love Susan and if I thought it could possibly work, I'd marry her this very day."

"But, Gene, what about the Andrews? They would never allow Susan to marry you. And how can you be so sure she loves you.

1

Young girls at that age are always falling in love with older men. When I was seventeeen, I was deeply in love with my history teacher." She felt her heart breaking for her friend. "Okay, Gene, at least think a great deal about this before you do something you might regret the rest of your life."

"I have been thinking, Edna. Thinking and thinking. But when I see Susan, I know I don't want to live without her." He turned when he heard a noise behind them. David was standing at the door. "Well David, home so soon?"

"Yes. I came to tell you, you had a telegram from Pogo. He'll be arriving tomorrow afternoon." He walked quickly to the steps.

"David, what's wrong with you?" Edna walked toward her son.

"There's nothing wrong with me, Mom." He stared at Scott. "I'm not the one who has a ridiculous problem." He turned and ran up the steps.

Edna looked puzzled as her son disappeared behind his bedroom door. "Now what do you suppose is wrong with him?"

"He must have been listening to our conversation, Edna." Scott stood. "I think he likes Susan very much. I'm afraid David's not going to have much use for his old pal Gene anymore."

"Come on now, Gene. David will get over this little pouting spell. He could never stay mad at you for long."

"I'm not so sure of that. I've known best friends to break up and do terrible things to each other because of a woman." He stood next to her. "Maybe it would be for the best if I just moved into a hotel room."

"Nothing doing, Gene Scott. Other friends may break up and do stupid things, but I won't allow it in my house. David will just have to learn to understand things don't always go his way." She slapped his shoulder. "Now come help me in my garden. We'll work something out for you and Susan. If it's love between the two of you, then that's what I'm for. You can count on me doing my part to help you both."

"Oh, Edna, I love you." He grabbed her and swung her around. Let's go ho-ho-ho for a while. They laughed as they walked out to the garden.

"I'll solve your problem," David whispered softly to himself as he watched them from his window. "I'll solve both our problems, and good."

The doorbell rang as the Crains and Scott sat down to eat supper. David jumped up.

2

"I'll get it. Don't eat everything, Scott," he laughed as he ran to the front door.

"See. Gene. I told you everything would be alright." Edna handed him a piece of bread. "See how easily the young forget."

He looked up from his plate when David stepped back into the kitchen calling his name.

"Gene, it's for you, special delivery." David handed the telegram to Scott.

"Who's it from? Pogo?" Edna tried to read the telegram through the envelope.

"No." Scott glanced up at David. "It's from the bishop."

"Weber?" John sat up straight and took the paper from Gene's hand.

"How on earth did he know you were here?" Edna asked, setting down her fork. "You didn't tell him, did you?"

"No, I didn't tell him." Scott gazed at David, who stared at his plate.

Edna followed Scott's gaze and her eyes rested on her son. "David, did you tell Bishop Weber Gene was here?"

"Me? No, why would I." He kept staring down at his plate.

"Maybe because you don't want me around, so you can have Susan all to yourself." Gene stood. "Well, David, I'm ashamed of you for trying something like this."

"David, did you inform Weber that Gene was here?" John Crane grabbed the boy's arm. "Answer me!"

"Alright! So maybe I did!" David glared at Gene. "He wanted an answer to his problem, so I fixed it."

"You really fixed it alright." John rose angrily. "And if this place where Weber is sending Gene is dangerous, why I'll—"

"Dangerous? Sending?" Edna got to her feet. "David, where is he sending him?"

"Somewhere in Bolivia I've never heard of: SanReVillage." John frowned at his son.

"What exactly does the telegram say?" Her hand shaking, Edna poured herself another cup of coffee.

"It says, 'Scott, good to hear assignment completed. Sending you next to SanRe Village, Bolivia. Some danger involved. Job is to build church to replace old one. Good luck, Henry Weber. Gloria sends her love.' And that's all it says."

"Oh Gene, I'm so sorry. I wish there was something I could do." Edna took his hand in hers. "What are you going to tell Susan?"

3

"Nothing." He walked toward the door. "I'll prepare to leave as soon as Pogo gets here."

"Gene, what do you want us to tell Susan. She'll want to know," Edna said, reaching for his arm.

"Please tell her nothing." He pulled away and walked quickly from the room.

Edna burst into tears. "Oh, David, how could you have done this terrible thing to Gene?"

"Mom, I thought he . . . a . . . well, maybe getting away from Susan was the best thing for him."

"For him, David, or for you?" She walked out the door calling over her shoulder, "You can wash the dishes, David. That will do for a start on your punishment."

David turned to his father and said, "Dad, I never meant to—"

"Just do as your mother said!" John snapped and followed Edna out, leaving David alone.

Gene walked along in his typical long steps as Pogo raced beside him, trying to keep up.

"Are you sure you want to go, Pogo? I'm told it could be very dangerous."

"Look Scott, I came over here to be with you, and if it means going to Bolivia, then that's where it will be." He stopped to watch as a lovely blonde twisted by him.

Scott yanked his arm, pulling him along. "You really don't have time to watch the women if you're going with me."

"I haven't found a woman yet, Scott. I figured maybe I could if I was to hang around with a good-looking man like yourself, who always has women hanging all over him."

"That's what you get for thinking, Pogo." Scott stopped when he reached the ticket counter. "When's your next flight to Bolivia?"

"Bolivia?" The agent, a pretty brunette, gazed unabashed at Scott's handsome face.

Standing behind him, Pogo leaned around to stare at the girl who was waiting on them.

"Yes, that's right." He glanced at Pogo. "What are you doing?"

"Me?" Pogo chuckled sheepishly. He stepped out from behind Gene and leaned on the counter, smiling at the agent. Conspiratorially, he whispered to Scott, "Now she's kind of cute, isn't she?"

The agent, who heard him, shook her head and smiled. "There is a flight going out tomorrow morning."

"Good. I'd like two tickets please." Scott pulled the money from his billfold and paid her. He stuck the tickets into his pocket. "Come on Pogo, let's go."

"Thank you, sir." The girl behind the counter smiled at Scott. Pogo waved at her and she gave him a knowing smile. "So long, kid." Shaking her head, she turned back to her work.

"Shit," Pogo muttered as he ran to catch up with his friend. "What's it with you, Scott? They melt when they talk to you, but me, how they freeze up."

"Pogo, your problem is that you try too hard." Scott nudged him with his shoulder and they walked from the airport.

Edna stared at Scott with tears in her eyes. "Gene, aren't you even going to call her?"

"No, Edna. If I hear her voice, I might break down and tell her and that would be the wrong thing to do." He picked up his suitcase with a solemn expression. "I know Susan. She would just try to follow me. I don't want her getting into danger because of me. Not to mention that she keeps putting me in tough situations."

"Oh, I wish I didn't know where you were going." She flopped down on the sofa. "What if I break down and tell her?"

"Edna, you can't. You just can't." He sat down next to her. "Promise me you won't tell her where I've gone."

"I'll try, Gene. Honest, I will." She glanced at the wall clock. "Oh! You'd better run before you miss that stupid plane." She hugged him. "Be careful will you?"

"You bet I will." He kissed her forehead and walked to the door. "If you will, see that Susan's happy. Check up on her once in a while, will you?"

"Oh, of course, Gene." She watched him walk through the yard and waved as she closed the door behind him. Edna shook her head slowly. "Why should he always have to suffer over the ones he loves?"

As he sat with Pogo waiting for their flight to be called, Gene kept eyeing the payphone on the wall. He scooted around in his seat and finally stood nervously.

"There's one phone call I forgot to make, Pogo. Will you stay with our things?"

"Sure thing, Scott." Pogo couldn't take his eyes off the ticket counter brunette.

Smiling, Scott picked up the receiver and slid a dime into the slot. Slowly he dialed the Andrews' number. It was answered instantly and he recognized Jobi's voice on the other end.

"Jobi, this is Gene Scott."

"Oh, hi, Reverend Scott." He began to whisper, "Susan's not here right now, but she should be back in about ten minutes. She went to pick up some cleaning. You want to talk to me that long or to have her call back."

She must have told Jobi about us, Scott thought as he gripped the receiver. "I really don't have time to hold on, Jobi. And I know I probably won't get another chance to call back any time soon."

A voice came over the airport loudspeaker: "Everyone going to England should be at gate I2, ready for departure."

"I have to go pretty soon, Jobi."

"Go? Go where?" Excitement rose in the boy's voice.

"Uh . . . a . . . to a meeting in the church." He tried to laugh normally. "Tell Susan . . . well . . . tell her . . ."

"Go ahead. You can say it, Reverend Scott." Jobi laughed. "I know what you're going to say."

"Well if you know what I was going to say, then I don't have to say it."

"Go on. Just say it. I want to hear you say it." He waited to hear Gene say the very thing Susan had also said. "Go on, Reverend Scott, don't be chicken."

Gene swallowed. "Tell her I love her." He looked down at his shoes, suddenly very sad and lonely.

Pogo slapped him on the back. "Come on. The board says the flight to Bolivia is loading."

"Oh. Okay," he muttered. "Jobi, I have to go. Take care of Susan for me."

"I will." Instantly the line went dead, surprising Jobi. "Scott? Scott?"

Jobi's eyes got big as he saw Susan step through the door. "You're too late, sis. That was Scott calling for you."

"Jobi, why didn't you tell him I would be right back." She tossed the dry cleaning aside.

"I did! He was in a big hurry."

"What sort of hurry?" Susan plopped down in a chair beside her brother. "Tell me, Jobi, is something wrong?"

"I don't know, sis. I just don't know."

"Well tell me exactly what he said to you." She stared at him impatiently.

"When I asked him to call back, he said he had a meeting at the church. Said he didn't have time to talk. Only, from the commotion in the background, I'd say he was at the airport."

"The airport!" Susan felt her heart jump to her throat. "Did he say anything else?"

"He said he loves you and he told me to take care of you for him."

"Oh, Jobi, something's wrong!" She bit her lip. "Hand me that phone book, I'm going to call the airport and have him paged."

Susan found the number and dialed it quickly. The airport operator paged Gene, but there was no response.

When she came back on the line, she said, 'I'm sorry, miss. If Reverend Scott was here, he must have already departed."

"Can you tell me how I can find out where he was going?" She couldn't keep the anxiety from her voice.

"I'm sorry, miss. Airline policy forbids us from giving out personal information. And, unless you know what airline he was flying, we wouldn't be able to find that out anyway. Perhaps there is a common acquaintance who could help you."

Susan nodded. "Okay. Thank you very much." She hung up the phone and jumped to her feet. "Jobi, I'm going over to the parsonage to talk to John and Edna. They have to know where Gene is."

"But sis, you'll be giving away your secret." Jobi grab his sister's hand.

"I don't care, Jobi. I just have this feeling that Gene may be in some sort of danger. I know I have to go help him."

She dashed out to her Corvette, Jobi right behind her.

"I'm going with you, sis." He jumped into the passenger's seat. I'm supposed to be watching you for Scott remember?"

"Okay, okay."

She drove a little over the speedlimit on the way to the parsonage and raced to the front door and rang the bell.

"Oh come on. Somebody answer this stupid door!"

Edna opened the door, slowly, her face anxious, biting her lip. "A . . . Susan . . . Jobi. What a nice surprise." She motioned for them to come inside. "John. David. Come see who came to visit us."

"Good!" Susan exclaimed. "I want you all out here when I say what I'm going to say." Susan swallowed her fear and stood straight as David and John came into the living room.

"Susan . . . has something to say to us. Won't you sit down children?" Edna motioned toward the sofa.

Susan turned to her brother. "Go ahead and sit down, Jobi." The rest of you need to sit down too. I think . . . I will remain standing." She took a deep breath. "Now I realize that you must think I'm a child and that you would probably never believe what I'm going to tell you could possibly be anything but a schoolgirl crush. But I can assure you all, that assumption is completely wrong." She licked her dry lips. "I love Gene Scott with all my heart and he loves me too. We've spoken about getting married to one another and believe it or not that is my only wish for my life."

"Susan dear, don't you think—" Edna stopped when Susan held up her hand.

"Please, Edna, let me finish! I can see why you want to protect Gene. He is your friend and I respect your feelings. Really I do." She felt the tears welling in her eyes. "I know something's wrong here. Gene has gone away, hasn't he?" Her lips quivered. "Please, oh please, tell me what it is."

"Susan." Edna got up and put her arm around the girl's shoulders. "You really do love him, don't you dear?"

"Oh yes, Edna, yes I do." Tears begin streaming down her cheeks. "If anything were to happen to him, oh Edna, I just want to die."

"There, there, Susan. Gene is a very strong and smart person. He can do things most people can't. He'll be back before you know it." She bit her lip. "Oh me and my big mouth."

"I knew he was gone! I could feel it! Oh where? Where? You must tell me!" Weeping, she pleaded with Edna.

"John what should we do?" Edna looked to her husband for help.

"Gene is depending on us, Edna." John's eyes were full of sadness as he gazed at Susan.

"I'm so sorry Susan. John's right. We did promise Gene we wouldn't tell you."

"Then, then you knew about Gene and me." Susan tilted her head. "Oh please—Edna, John—please tell me!" She buried her face in her hands sobbing.

"It will be alright, sis." Jobi went to Susan and threw his arms around her. "Please tell us, Mrs. Crain. Reverend Scott might need us."

"Jobi, I can't tell you. If you and Susan went there, you might be in danger too." Instantly aware of what she had said, Edna glanced at her husband and closed her eyes.

"Danger?" Susan sat up straight. "Is Gene in danger? Edna, you just have to tell me."

David, who had been standing silently and listening, went to Susan and bent down to her. He lifted her face with his hand. "You really love Gene, don't you?"

"Oh yes! David, will you please tell me." She looked deeply into his eyes. "Please, David."

He gazed to his father and mother.

John smiled at Edna. ..Gene never made David promise not tell, did he?"

Her face brightening, she replied, "No! No, John. He didn't."

"Then I can tell you," David said firmly. Susan listened eagerly.

"After all," David continued, "it was all my fault in the first place." His face dropped. "I phoned the bishop and told him that Gene was here. He immediately sent Gene a telegram assigning him to his next mission."

Susan gazed at him. "Where, David?" she asked softly. "Where?" She covered his hand with hers.

"SanRe village in Bolivia." David looked into her eyes. "Will you ever forgive me? I was a stupid, jealous creep, who had no right to be jealous in the first place."

She smiled and kissed his cheek. "I forgive you, David . . . . If I'm going to make Gene a good wife, I have to be a good Christian first, right? We have to forgive each other."

"You are a good Christian, Susan, you are," Edna said, nodding. She hugged the young woman. "Whatever you do now, you must be careful."

Susan felt herself choking up with joy and gratitude and feared she would not be able to speak. "God bless you all," she managed.

Getting to her feet, she hurried to the door, where she stopped and sighed and turned back to the Crain family.

"I'll have to think of something good to tell mom and dad. Well, goodbye and thank you so much."

"Goodbye, Susan," Edna called. She took John's hand as the door closed behind her. "Oh, John, do you think we've done the right thing?"

"Well," he responded slowly, "she's a very determined young lady. I don't think she would have given up until she found out where he went whether we told her or not." He hugged Edna. "I'm sure, once she gets to Gene, things will work out alright."

"You mean, once he gets over being mad?" Edna picked up her knitting. I'm just glad I'm not going to be there when he sees them."

9

Chapter 2

Susan and Jobi Andrews sat staring out the airplane window.

Jobi smiled at his sister. "You know, sis, I think that 'school tour of Bolivia' was a great idea. Dad really bought every word."

"Why wouldn't he? I think it sounded pretty convincing." She smiled coyly.

"Yeah. 'Dad,'" Jobi mocked his sister, "'there's this preschool tour going to Bolivia for a few weeks. It sounds terrific and it's a good chance to meet new friends.'"

"Alright, Jobi, that's enough." She looped her arm around his neck and rubbed the top of his head. "It got us here didn't it? That's all that matters."

"Yeah, I guess you're right." He dropped his eyes to the booklet on Bolivia in his lap. "Just as long as they don't find out we lied to them."

"Yeah, well let's hope they don't find out." She laid her head back and closed her eyes, imagining Gene's face in her mind.

"And I bet Scott will be pretty surprised to see as, huh?"

"Oh yeah!" Susan swallowed. "He'll probably feel like killing us." She glanced at her brother. "Still, he had no business running off like that without telling me."

"Keep on, sis. Maybe you'll convince one of us anyway that this little caper is perfectly reasonable."

He laughed and shook his head just as a woman's voice came over the intercom. "Please fasten your seatbelts. We are about to land in Bolivia."

"Well, we shall soon find out how Gene feels about our coming." Susan hooked the seatbelt around her waist. "But I'm sure I can prove to him that his little visit here will be much better with me along."

Scott and Pogo walked down the street of SanRe village. It was a dirty town, with children playing in the side ditches where pigs lay sunning themselves. Pogo frowned at Scott and wiggled his nose.

"This place really stinks." He nodded toward the children. "You can hardly tell the children from the pigs."

"I wonder where their mothers are." Scott pushed his way into the SanRe hotel. "They should be horse whipped for letting them play in such filth." He slapped his hand down on the bell at the desk.

A sleepy looking man came running from the back room. "Why did you ring, senor? Can you not read the sign?"

He rubbed his sleepy eyes as he pointed at the sign which read: "Come back later. Taking my siesta."

"Look, I've got too much work to do to worry about your bad sleeping habits." Scott sat his luggage down and pulled out some money. "I need a room for my friend and myself. I'm not sure how long we will be staying."

"It's only fair to warn you, senor. The people here no like strangers."

"That's tough. Real tough." Scott snatched the room key out of his fingers. "They'll just have to put up with us." He turned, and taking three steps at a time, walked up the stairs to their little, hot hotel room.

"Boy! Now this is what I call luxurious!" Pogo sat down on the lumpy bed. "And this bed? No wonder the kids play with the pigs."

"Pogo, stop complaining, will you?"

Scott gazed out of the dirty window. At the far end of the village he noticed the ruins of the old church.

"I wonder what really happened to the church. It looks as though it was set on fire."

"Maybe some of the friendly village people will tell us," Pogo snickered as he stretched out on the bed.

"Yeah, I get it, Pogo. Hopefully not everyone is as 'hospitable' as the hotel clerk." He took Pogo's arm and pulled him to his feet. "Let's go have a look around. Maybe everyone in the village isn't hostile."

"Scott, we just got here. Can't we rest a while? That bus ride here was no picnic."

"That's why moving around will be good for you. It will loosen up your joints." He pushed him toward the door. "And besides, I don't think lying on that bed is all that conducive to your health."

"Yeah maybe you're right." Pogo rubbed his back end. "I believe that dumb bus driver hit every hole in the road."

Scott chuckled as they made their way down the village street. Children stared at the two strangers as they walked past them.

Pogo bumped Scott's arm and pointed out a scene taking place down the street from them. Two young men held a young girl, trying to kiss her as she struggled to get away. A younger boy tried valiantly

11

to push them away from the screaming girl. One of the rough men slapped the weak boy down.

Instantly Scott ran toward them, Pogo close behind him. Scott grabbed both men with one motion and sent them flying on the ground. One yanked a knife from his shirt. With a kick of his left foot, Scott sent it flying through the air. The man gripped his hand and screamed. The other one leaped toward Scott, flying backward as his face crashed against Scott's fist. The attacker flew backward into the mud-filled ditch.

Pogo helped the little boy to his feet and put his arm around the girl's shoulder. "Are you alright, miss?"

"Yes, *señor*, thanks to you and your friend."

The little boy ran to Scott and threw his arms around his hips. "You much strong! Rodriguez pray for you to come." He breathed heavily, as though each breath was a struggle.

Scott smiled at the sickly child. "Where do you live, son? I'll take you home. I think you've had too much excitement."

"I'll show you friend . . . friend." He smiled at him broadly. "What friend name?"

"Oh. I'm Scott. Reverend Gene Scott. My friend is named Pogo."

"I see! God send man of God. Pretty smart, huh, my sister." He smiled at the girl.

"My little brother, he have big imagination. Sometimes he get very sick. Have much fever. Mama say that's why he speak such foolish words."

"Not foolish this time, my sister." He took Scott's hand firmly in his tiny grip. "You come help my village people, no?"

"That's right Rodriguez. I came to build you a church." He gazed after the two attackers as they retreated down the street, looking back at him. "And to clean up around here."

Scott lifted the boy and put him on his shoulders. "How about you riding?"

"Great!" He laughed, his face full of joy. "See, my sister, what did I tell you and Mama?"

"Rodriguez," the girl replied, frowning, "you must not keep getting up your hopes. Our new friends are in much danger if they try to help our people. Jose, he will not like."

"So who is this Jose?" Pogo could not resist smiling at the beautiful, raven-haired girl. "Why should we be concerned about him?"

"Oh, he nobody important, my friend Scott," Rodriguez assured with a smile. "He think he a big man. He think he can tell everyone in the village what to do."

"He very mean, my friends," the girl said anxiously. "He may try to kill you like the others." Fear showed in her eyes. "Please, you must leave SanRe at once."

"So what is your name?" Pogo asked, smiling.

"Maria." She blushed, her eyes falling to her hands. "My brother and I live alone with our momma. Our Papa, he was killed and by that villain Jose."

"Well that creep won't scare Scott and me." Pogo looked at the tall man standing beside him, seeking assurance. "Will he, Scott?"

"I came here to do a job," Gene said simply. "And I won't leave until it's done." He patted the boy's small legs. "Now which way, buddy."

"That blue house, my friend Scott." Still elated, the boy laughed between heavy breaths. "Where you stay? At crummy hotel?"

"Yeah, you can say that again," Pogo said, shaking his head. "It's no Hilton, I grant you."

"There room at our house. You stay there. Food much better and cleaner place for my friend to sleep."

He wiggled to get down and Scott lowered him to the dirt street. The small boy opened the door and called for his mother. A woman appeared as they entered the house, looking like her daughter apart from abundant wrinkles and grey hair.

While she had no idea who these strangers were, she clearly grasped the need for hospitality. "Welcome to our home." She motioned for them to sit down.

"Mama, this is my friend Reverend Gene Scott. He big man."

"Much big, my little son." Her smile revealed abiding weariness in her eyes. "And small man? What name?"

"Oh. Just call me Pogo." He smiled, his eyes drifting back to Maria.

"And I am Anna Latabio. You welcome to eat with my family, friends Scott and Pogo. But you must leave village to protect yourself."

Scott shook his head. "My dear Mrs. Latabio, I didn't come all these many miles to turn around and run like a coward." He kissed her hand. "We would be grateful for a decent meal before we return to our room."

"No! Mama, I told friend Scott he stay here." The fragile child tugged at his mother's sleeve. "Please, Mama! He came to help our village. We can not let him sleep at lazy Pedro's dirty place."

"Mama, little brother is right! They save me from two of Jose's dogs outside a while ago." Maria pressed against her mother's side. "Please. He come to·rebuild our church!"

"I . . . do not know if it be wise to let strangers—"

"I understand your fear of these villains, Mrs. . . . . may I call you Anna?"

She gazed at Scott. "My children, they trust you *señor*. You come to help us. I would like you to stay here. Please to call me Anna."

"We wouldn't want to bring you any trouble by staying here." Scott smiled at the loving family. "Thank you anyway for asking. You were the first to care what happens to us."

"There are many who would friend, Scott. They just afraid of Jose and his dogs." Mrs. Latabio began setting the table. "You get your things. You stay here. Please, you do this. You be closer to the building of your church here."

Pogo pulled at his sleeve. "She's right, Scott. I'll take any chance I get to get out of that dump."

"Are you really that interested in getting out of that place," Scott whispered, "or is it being closer to that cute little Maria that is making you want to move out."

"Come on, Scott. You know perfectly well this place is twenty times better than that funky hotel." Pogo glanced at Maria. "Not to mention there is a lot more beauty here to enjoy. Sorry to say, but you're not all that good looking to me."

Gene sighed and stood. "Alright. Anna, we've decided to take you up on your offer, if you're sure it's alright."

"Never before have I met anyone like you *Señor* Scott. Go get your things then we'll eat."

"We'll be right back." Pogo winked at Maria. "Save me a place, will you?"

She smiled shyly and looked down. Scott yanked Pogo out the door after him.

"Pogo, this is no time to be getting involved with a girl."

"Ha! Just because a girl falls for me instead of you doesn't mean that I can't be interested." He scurried along, trying to keep up with Scott. "And don't tell me I shouldn't think about women. Speaking of which, who is 'Susan?"

"Susan? Why do you ask?" Scott kept his eyes straight ahead, trying to avoid Pogo's.

"Well, at the airport I heard you mention Susan. And then on the plane and on the bus you called her name in your sleep."

"Oh? Well. People are always talking in their sleep." He made his way up the steps to their room.

"Come on, Scott, come clean. You can tell me. I'm your friend Pogo, remember?"

"Get your stuff together, Pogo, and stop annoying me with stupid questions." Scott picked up his suitcase.

"I don't think they're so stupid, Scott. I think there's something going on, and I think someone named Susan is very much involved."

"Yeah, well listen, I don't need a mind-reader at the present. It wouldn't help." He averted his eyes again and walked out of the room, Pogo right behind him.

"Look, Scott, if you got a problem with this chick, I'll understand and I can help. I'm kind of an expert on these girl-guy problems."

Scott turned to him with an expression of disbelief. "Pogo, if I want man advice, I'll get it from someone who doesn't have so much trouble holding onto a donut-selling Girl Scout." He shook his head and chuckled as he made his way quickly down the street.

Pogo ran alongside him. "Very funny, Scott. It may surprise you to know I might be able to solve your problem a lot easier than you can."

Gene shook his head. "No thanks. I have had one young mind try to solve it, and he screwed up everything."

Scott knocked on the Latabio's door. Maria opened it smiling. "Where do we put these bags?"

"Up in the loft. You and Pogo, that where you stay." She pointed at the ladder. "Not much room, but clean and fairly cool."

"Thank you, Maria."

Pogo couldn't hold back his smile as he followed Scott up the ladder. "She's about the cutest thing I ever saw. Don't you think, Scott?"

"She's very pretty, Pogo." Scott had to bend over at the waist in the little loft room to keep from bumping his head. "Well let's go down and eat. We got to turn in soon. Tomorrow is going to be a busy day for us."

Pogo slid down the ladder after Scott. "You suppose we'll get any help from the people in the village?"

"I guess we'll find out tomorrow." Scott smiled at Anna Latabio. "Are you ready for us, Anna?"

"Of course. Please sit down. I pour you drink." She filled their glasses with a rich red wine. "Tastes pretty good, no?"

"Tastes very good, Anna. Did you make it?" Scott licked his lips.

"Mama, she make wine all time. From grapes I grow at back of the house." Rodriguez said with a proud smile. He patted Scott's hand. "Rodriguez help Scott tomorrow, yes?"

"Rodriguez, I'd love to have your help." Gene could almost feel the agony the little boy must be going through with each breath he took. "I certainly need a small boy to bring me water in that hot sun." He glanced at Anna." Do you think any of the village men will help us build the church?"

"I know not, friend. You could ask early in morning." Her jaw tightened involutarily. "Jose and his dogs sleep most of the day."

Rodriguez got up and kissed his mother. "Rodriguez go to bed now, Mama. Must get sleep, so I'll be strong in morning to help friend Scott."

"Goodnight, my son." She returned his kiss.

"Goodnight my friend, Scott. See you in the morning, yes?"

"You betcha, buddy." Scott stood and put his hand on the boy's head gently. "Come on, Pogo. We've got to get some shut-eye too."

"Go ahead, Scott. I'll help Maria with the dishes." Pogo began picking up the empty plates. "I'll be up soon."

Scott gave him a wary look. "Okay, Pogo, but don't be goofing off. We've got a lot of work to do around here."

Scott climbed slowly up the ladder. He took off his pants and shirt and stretched out on the bed. Closing his eyes, he pictured Susan in his mind. Her warm face melting his heart and making him want to embrace her, kiss her, tell her how much he cared for her and loved her.

"Oh Susan, Susan," he whispered in the dark little loft. "Susan, I miss you so much."

Finally, after what seemed like hours of tossing and turning, he drifted off into a restless sleep.

The sun came streaming into the little window onto Scott's face. He blinked his eyes and turned his head. Pogo slept silently beside him. Scott sprang to his feet and slapped Pogo heartily on the rear.

"What the shit!" He looked at the smiling face above him. "Oh, it's only you." He slumped back down. "I was dreaming of somebody else. Wake me up later, will you?"

"Nothing doing, you lazy missionary," Scott said as he pulled on his clothes. He took Pogo by his feet and dragged him onto the cool floor. "Let's move that lazy ass!"

"Oh shit, Scott! That floor is cold on my butt." Pogo jumped up and bumped his head on the low ceiling. "Boy, I'm really starting this day off with a bang. If this is an example of the rest of my day, I think I had better go back to bed."

"Quit prattling, Pogo. Get up and get a move on."

Gene made his way down the ladder. The table was laid out with food and Maria was sipping on a glass of milk.

"Good morning, young lady."

"Good morning, *Señor* Scott." She smiled shyly. "Please sit down and eat before you begin your work."

"Thank you." He sat down and filled his plate. "Where's Rodriguez this morning? Still in bed?"

"No. He has gone out to round up some of the people in the village." She smiled when she saw Pogo sit down next to Scott. "Good morning, Pogo."

"Good morning, Maria." Somehow he managed to fill his plate without taking his eyes off the girl.

"Where is he having the people to meet us, Maria?" Scott drank the rest of his milk and stood.

"At the old church, *señor*."

"Hurry up, Pogo. I'm going to talk to whatever workers there are. Then we'll get started, if the lumber and hardware get here like it's supposed to."

He walked from the small blue house and joined Rodriguez at the church site. The boy sat on the steps of the burned out building, a proud grin on his face as several dozen citizens of SanRe stood silently, expectantly watching Scott approach them.

"Well, Rodriguez, you certainly have been a busy little beaver this morning." Scott smiled at his small friend.

"Yes, my friend Scott. Rodriguez thought Scott would like me to do this yes?" He took a deep breath.

"Oh yes! I'm very glad to have such a smart young man at my side." Gene laughed, enjoying the boy's great smile. He gazed out over the silent gathering before him. "Well buddy, they don't look as happy as we do."

"They much afraid, my friend Scott. You talk to them. You convince them to help." Rodriguez motioned with his hands to get the crowd's attention. "Please listen to my friend, Scott."

Gazing at their faces, Scott realized the boy was right. In every face he saw reluctance, uncertainty and outright fear.

"I've come here to help you build your church," he said. "Now the Latabio family has told me all about the threats of this man Jose, but it won't stop me from doing God's work. I can get it done much faster if I have your help, though. If each one of us, working together does our part we can build your church and clean up your streets."

He looked at the dirty children on the outskirts of the crowd. "Do you know your children can catch diseases from playing in the mud with the pigs? Look at them. Some are already puny and look at the sores growing on their skin."

"If they died, señor, it will be a blessing for them instead of living in this stinking lousy place!" A stringy-haired woman spoke loudly, gesturing with both hands. "And you aren't going to pay us. Why should we work and slave in the hot sun for nothing?"

"For nothing? Woman this is your church, the place where you meet with God, who hears and answers all prayers. So why shouldn't you help build it?" Scott's hand went to his hips. "And you men—if you can be called that—what sort of work do you do?"

"Work?" The woman started up again. "They no work! They just lay around, make babies and get fat!"

The other women in the crowd began to laugh.

"Oh no," Scott said. "Now look at you women. You aren't doing so much for God or for your village, are you?" Scott's voice grew louder.

The expression on the face of the outspoken woman changed instantly. Her eyes widened and she stomped her foot. Her husband laughed loudly.

"Scott," the husband called as he walked toward Gene, "Pedro, he help you."

"Good for you!" Scott responded, smiling gratefully. He looked across the little group of villagers. "Well? What about the rest of you?"

"Teresa is right, *Señor* Scott. If we build this church, Jose and his dogs will tear it down or burn it to the ground." The man who spoke was among the oldest in the crowd. "I can remember when SanRe was a quiet gentle village and no man was afraid to leave his house at night."

Gene nodded. "SanRe can be that way again *señor*. If all you people stick together and help each other. Help me do what I came to do—which is to help you. We can do this! Trust me!"

He smiled and pointed to the wagon of lumber and supplies

coming down the street. "Here's your chance to start over again. Only you have to work together."

"I say we give it a try," Pedro said boldly.

"Pedro is right, my friends!" Rodriguez said loudly between labored breaths. "Scott, he come very long way to help us. He get nothing for what he do, but still he do it! What do we have to lose?"

"Our lives, maybe?" Teresa Lucas spoke up and the other women shouted their agreement. "And what of our children. We must think about them."

"It's about time!" Scott shouted. "You can't be happy with the way they are living now. Now listen to me, all of you. Jose and his creeps are just a handful of men. I say we build the church. If there's any trouble, we take care of it as it comes. Let us work together and do this!"

"*Pronto*! Let's build the church now!" Pedro pointed for everyone to go to the supply truck.

Moments later Scott had them clearing away the remains of the old church. It was only then that Pogo joined him.

Scott stared up and down his friend in disgust. "Well, your highness, did you finally decide to come and help?"

Pogo shrugged. "Looks like you have everything under control, Scott." He helped Scott unload the lumber from the wagon.

After they had pulled the supplies from the wagon, Scott got the driver's attention. "Now go back and bring us the rest of the materials and tools as quickly as you can."

The driver smiled broadly. "Alright, you're the boss!" He laughed, showing his broken front tooth. He climbed laboriously onto the wagon and picked up the reins. "Alright you lazy bunch of critters, get up!"

"Boy, Scott, that driver is about one ugly fellow!" Pogo said under his breath.

"Well, Pogo, beauty isn't everything. Being good looking is sort of wasted on you, isn't it." Scott slapped his friend on the shoulder and went to work on building the church.

Susan and Jobi got off the old run-down bus and stretch their tired muscles. They looked around at the dirty surroundings that stretched out in front of them. They could see the village in the distance.

"Oh wow, you mean we have to walk to that village?" Jobi set down on his suitcase. I'll bet it's two miles."

"Well, compared to the wonderful transportation we just came on, I prefer the walk."

Susan picked up her luggage and started walking down the narrow little road. Jobi lazily picked up his and followed along behind her.

"Look out, Jobi!" Susan pulled Jobi over in the ditch as the supply wagon went flying by. "Why don't you look at where you're going, you creep!" Susan yelled as the wagon sped out of sight.

"Corne on, sis, save your energy. We're almost there and I've got a feeling when Reverend Scott finds out we will need our energy to run away." He laughed as he kicked at a stone.

"Oh, Jobi!" Susan punched her brother's arm as she stepped under the rundown sign. "*Bienvenido a SanRe*." Susan looked up as she translated the words. "Well this is it, Jobi, our destination."

"Doesn't look like much, does it?" He turned up his nose as the stink filled his nostrils. "Yuck! Can't say much for the smell either."

"Yes, I know what you mean." She coughed.

Hearing someone clear his throat, she turned around. A shaggy-haired man sat leaning back in a chair on the porch of a shack. His eyes searched Susan's body, causing her limbs to grow stiff involuntarily.

"Could you please tell me where the hotel is?"

"It would be my pleasure, *senorita*." He stood lazily and spat out the weed he had in his mouth. "Please to follow me."

Jobi tugged on his sister's arm. "I don't know whether I want to follow him or not, sis. He looks shifty."

"By the way this town looks Jobi, they're all pretty scruffy."

"Yeah, I know what you mean. Everything just sort of fits into place."

Susan laughed quietly and shrugged.

At last they found themselves entering the lobby of the SanRe Hotel.

"I hope none of this place rubs off on us."

They giggled and the shaggy haired man turned to see what the Andrews kids were laughing at. They forced a smile toward him.

He smiled at Susan and called over his shoulder. Hey, Tabelio! Get your lazy self up here. You got some business!"

"*Si*, Jose, my good friend Jose." He tried to laugh without showing his fear. "What can Tabelio do for you?"

"My friends here would like a room. See that they get a good clean one, yes?" He kept his eyes on Susan. "We don't want our little friends to think that our lovely town is not friendly."

"*Si*, Jose, always right." The little man behind the desk ran around to where Susan and Jobi were and took their luggage. "Please follow me."

"Hey, sis, everyone around here speaks alike," Jobi whispered loudly as they walked up the steps behind the fat man. "Always wanting us to follow."

"Well, the less I can see of that Jose creep, the better off I'll feel." Susan handed Tabelio a tip and shut the door. "Boy, Scott can pick some of the cheapest places to stay!" She flopped down onto the bed. "The only thing that could take my mind off these lumps at night would be Scott."

"Gross! Better watch that kind of talk, sis." Jobi laughed as he looked out the window. "I bet Scott is down there working."

Susan hopped up and looked out the window at the little gathering of people who were busy rebuilding the church. She tried to make out Scott among the workers.

"Darn. It's hard to see through this dirty old window," she mumbled.

Jobi ran a comb through his dark hair. "Shall we go and have a look around? You know he's going to see us sooner or later."

"Yes, let's go." She walked to the hazy mirror. "How can anyone see in this thing."

"Sis, you look great. At least compared to the rest of this village!"

"Thanks a lot, Jobi!" She laughed and pushed him out the door.

They made their way quickly down the village street. Susan spotted Gene up on a beam. Her heart began to pound rapidly as she slowly made her way up the ladder. She slipped up behind him and put her hands over his eyes.

He jumped lightly as he reached up and his fingers felt those hiding his sight. In that instant, Gene realized who was behind him. He swallowed, his heart pounding as well. He pulled his hands down slowly and whispered, "Susan."

He rose slowly, turned and stared into her eyes. His first instinct was to grab and embrace her, but his anger at the thought of her being in danger fired in his brain. His fingers bit into her flesh as he grabbed her and gritted his teeth.

"Damn, Susan! What in the devil are you doing here?"

"I'm the one who should be mad, Gene Scott!" She closed her eyes to hide the pain she felt in her arms. He must have sensed it, for his grip loosened. "Running away like that and not telling me. Is that how you treat someone you love?"

"Susan, I had no other choice, believe me." His eyes burned into her eyes. "Why are you always making more trouble for me?"

"Trouble! Is that all you can think of? Gene, aren't you even just a little bit happy to see me?" She gazed at her hands. "I thought that I could help you. Otherwise I would not have come."

"Help me? By getting yourself—or me—into danger." Looking down, he saw Jobi smiling at him. "And why did you have to bring Jobi. Don't you think I have enough to look after?"

"No one is asking you to look after us!"

She started to climb down the ladder when Scott pulled her back to him. "Susan, don't go getting on your high horse. I only meant, well . . ." He pointed out to the village. "Just what do you and Jobi think you can do here?"

"At least as much as any of these skinny, fat, lazy looking people! Again, I'm sure there's something we could do." She wrinkled her nose. "This place could use a good cleaning up."

". . . And you intend to do that, do you?" His voice softened. "Sure, why not. Those children could sure use a good bath. Why it's a wonder they're still alive."

She took his hand. "You must have seen them playing in the mud with those dirty pigs."

"I saw them." He frowned at the women working slowly below him. "It seems as if the mothers could care less."

"Well I care! Where can I take them to bathe them, Gene?" She stared intently into his eyes.

He smiled as he touched her cheek gently. "I'll get someone to help you." He called to Rodriguez. "Hey, pal, would you take this pretty girl and her brother to your sister Maria?"

"You bet, my friend Scott. I take." He smiled at Jobi. "What name, boy?"

"Jobi. What's yours?"

"Rodriguez. What pretty sister name?" He looked at Susan.

"Susan. She is Scott's girlfriend." He put his arm around the puny boy standing next to him. "They make a great couple, don't they?"

"Oh yes, very good together." He looped his arm around Jobi.

"Scott pretty smart to choose young woman."

Pogo stood behind the two boys, smiling at the scene in front of him. He made his way slowly up the ladder, chuckling to himself.

"Well, so you are Susan," he said when he reached the top. Susan turned to him and smiled. "Scott sure thinks about you a lot," Pogo said. "That is, if you're the same Susan he dreams about."

"Oh!" She smiled coyly at Scott. "Am I the Susan you dream about?"

"Okay you two, we got work to do." He gave Pogo a glare of disgust. "You start hammering. Susan, follow Rodriguez. He'll be a good helper to have with you."

"All right, but first answer my two questions." She smiled into his eyes. "Is it me you dream about?" Her tongue slid across her lips. "Are you happy to see me?"

"Yes. And yes." He helped her down the ladder. "Now go, before I give you a spanking for wasting my time."

She waved and walked happily away beside Rodriguez.

Chapter 3

Anna Latabio looked up from her sewing and smiled as Scott pushed himself away from the table.

"Scott work very hard today."

"Well, we got a lot done." He returned her smile. "Supper was very good."

"Many thanks." She set her sewing down and began clearing the table. "Your Miss Susan, she's very smart girl. Her and my Maria become good friends."

"Oh? How did they do with the children?"

He started to help her clear the table and she pushed his hand away. "Scott done enough for one day." Her tired eyes smiled. "They do very good with the children. All came in dirty little piglets, left clean like little angels."

"Ha. I wonder how long they will stay that way." He sat down in the chair and closed his eyes.

"Your Miss Susan, she tell the women, 'You better keep your kid clean, or I'll send Scott to straighten you out.'" Anna laughed. "She little, but can be pretty tough."

Scott nodded and smiled. He looked up as the door opened.

Susan and Maria stepped in, laughing. Each had a suitcase.

Scott stared at Susan. "Where are you going?"

"Where does it look like. Here!" She sat down on his lap. "Maria said I could share her room. Jobi is sleeping with Rodriguez."

"She can no stay in that crummy hotel, Mr. Scott," Maria said, waving her hand. "It's not fit for mad dog."

"True. Can't disagree there." Scott stood. "Think I'll go down to the lake and have myself a bath. He sat Susan down easily. Be back soon."·

"Are you sure you don't want me to give you a bath?" Susan ran her fingers through his hair. "I've become an expert at it."

"You might go into shock, sweetheart, when you see that my bottom doesn't compare with the little ones you've been washing." He caressed her blushing cheeks. "Now if you will excuse me."

Pogo came in the door with Jobi and Rodriguez as Scott walked out. He turned to face Scott.

"Hey, where are you off to?"

"To wash off some. Remember, I worked a little later than somebody I'll not mention."

"Very funny, Scott." Pogo crammed his hands in his pockets. "I don't see how you can stay out in that sun all day. I thought I would die."

"Well sure. I'm not going to argue. I'm going to have a bath."

"You want me to come with you?" Pogo started to follow.

"No, Pogo. I think I'm capable of washing myself, despite what you and Susan think."

Susan turned to avoid Pogo's smiling eyes.

"Oh she offered too, did she?" He laughed. "Pretty cool chick. Young and Sassy. Bet that's what you go for, huh, Scott? Or is it that sexy body? Wow has she got one sexy body!"

"Listen, for a fellow who's about to get his mouth busted, you sure keep running it." Scott stormed out into the darkness.

Pogo smiled to himself. "Boy," he said, "old Scott is really hooked on Susan. It must be love." He twirled around in the door.

Everyone in the house began to laugh and he blushed. "I think I'll go to bed." He scooted up the ladder and closed his eyes. Oh shit. Why am I such a show off?"

Scott climbed out of the water and put his clean clothes on. He didn't see Jose and three of his pals walk up behind him, so when a twig snapped under one of their feet, he twirled around.

"Oh sorry, *Señor* Scott. We didn't mean to frighten you." Jose smiled, revealing a gold tooth.

"You must be this Jose I've been hearing so much about." Scott continued to get ready as though he could care less that these four were probably up to no good.

"I'm flattered." Jose laughed loudly. "How did you recognize me?"

"Well, it seems to me most reptiles creep or crawl up on their prey."

"Huh!" Jose exclaimed as he gritted his teeth and slapped his laughing partners. "Think you're pretty tough man, Scott? Come to my town and think you can do as you please?" He looked at his men and laughed. "Pretty funny, no?"

"*Si*, Jose! Funny, very funny!" The toothless freak walked up to Scott. "Jose, want to see just how big man Scott really is?"

"Yes, and the whole town too maybe want to see." Jose smiled grotesquely. "Let them see that the man they think will help them is a coward, just like the rest of the Gringos." He clicked his finger and his men produced their guns and knives. "Now, *Señor* Scott, big man, take off your clothes and let's have a good long look."

"Jose, you bastard, you can scare everyone else with your stupid childish games, but I'm not one so easily frightened off." Scott stared into Jose's eyes.

"Oh, listen to the big man talk!" Jose spat at him.

Scott looked him up and down with disgust.

"Now, big man, take off those pants or I'll take them off for you."

"If you think you're man enough, go ahead and try." Scott didn't budge.

The youngest of the group spoke up arrogantly, "Go ahead, Jose, show him! Let him see a real man in action."

"Shut up Billy!" Jose's eyes burned on Scott. "Do as I say!"

"Go ahead, Jose, show me. I'm waiting!" Scott remained relaxed.

"Let him feel the bite of the knife." Jose smiled into Scott's eyes. "See how he holds up to pain."

A man on Scott's left whipped his knife through the air and the blade bit into Scott's upper arm. He grabbed the knife instantly and slung it into the lake, along with the man who had thrown it. With his right foot he dropped the man on his right with a single kick. Unconscious, the man lay in a heap. The brash, younger man turned and ran, leaving Scott to stare at Jose.

"Well Jose," Scott said calmly, "What are you waiting for? Come and make me drop my damn pants. Come on."

"Now come on, Scott. We were only fooling around. No harm meant." Jose backed up as Scott came toward him. "It was just a joke."

"You're not scared, are you, Jose?"

Jose turned around quickly to see many people from the village standing behind him, smiling and laughing.

Teresa Lucas waved her hands as she said, "Big man, huh? What's wrong with you, Jose? You're no more than a chicken."

"Yes and there were four of you against one Scott," another voice came from the back.

Their laughter rose in the night, as Jose turned quickly and ran from the scene. The crowd gathered around, pressing against Scott as he walked through their midst. Gentle hands caressed him quietly.

"See you in the morning, Scott," one voice called.

"Yes!" came another. "We work very hard. Maybe get finished."

"Yes, Scott responded, nodding, "that would be fine." Scott waved goodnight as he stepped into the blue house.

The first thing Susan saw as she looked up was blood on his shirt. She let out a surprised scream and ran to him.

"Oh, Gene, you've been hurt!" She turned to Anna who had hurried over. "Anna, get some water and bandages and some alcohol if you've got it."

"Yes, Miss Susan. I go get."

She raced from the room and came back with medical supplies. She and Susan dressed his wound and wrapped it neatly.

"There. Now Scott be just like new."

"Thanks, ladies. I really appreciate all that attention." He smiled at Susan. "You're a real angel."

"Who did this, Gene." Susan bit her lip. "And why? Why would anyone want to hurt you? You're here to help these people."

"It was that Jose, wasn't it?" Maria spoke up. "He and his pack of wild dogs."

"Yes, they thought they could play a little game with me." He laughed softly. "They never figured it to backfire."

"Jose?" Susan stood up. "Is he the one with shaggy black hair, green eyes and a gold tooth?"

"That's the one all right. How the hell do you know him?" Scott rose and took her in his arms.

"He helped Jobi and me find a room when we arrived." She swallowed. "That's all really."

"Miss Susan, he man you better stay away from. He evil and a murderer!" Anna picked up the extra bandages and pan of water. "I go sleep now. See my friends in morning."

"Goodnight, Mrs. Latabio." Scott turned to Susan. "And goodnight, Susan. Please do as Anna says and stay away from that creep."

"Alright, Gene, if you like." She put her arms around his waist. "Kiss me, handsome!"

"Susan!"

He smiled sheepishly at Maria, who smiled broadly.

"It all right, Scott. Susan, she told Maria all about your love." She laughed sweetly and walked into her room. "Leave you alone to kiss goodnight. Much better, yes?

"Yes, thank you Maria." Susan nodded to her. "'Well, what are you waiting for now huh?"

"Not a damn thing." He grabbed her and kissed her passionately.

His lips blew a warm feeling into her ears. "Susan, I love, you," he whispered tenderly.

His lips parted and gently covered her lips. She sighed as his tongue embraced her mouth and his arms tightened around her body.

"Oh, Gene, don't ever leave me again. I thought I would die if I would have never seen you again." She held onto him tightly. "I love you so much."

"Better get some sleep now." His fingers gently caressed her face. I love you." He kissed her and walked her to Maria's bedroom. "Sleep well, baby doll."

"Dream about me." She released his hand slowly and slipped into the bedroom.

Intoxicated by her embrace, Scott climbed up the ladder slowly and fell into bed with a smile.

"I love her. She loves me. We must work it out. I know now, life without her is out of the question."

He closed his eyes and drifted off to sleep.

Susan watched Scott walking to the church. She felt proud that he belonged to her and that she was the one he loved. She felt a tug on her arm and turned to smile at Rodriguez.

"Oh, I'm sorry Rodriguez. Are you ready?" She looked back toward Scott. "I had my mind elsewhere."

"Yes, Rodriguez see!" He laughed and punched Jobi's arm. Don't we, my friend?"

"Yeah, my sister has a one-track mind these days. Reverend Gene Scott."

"Yes Rodriguez see how Miss Susan be in love with him. He most wonderful man."

Susan couldn't resist a smile. "You can say that again!" She rubbed his little head. "Well, I guess we start on the houses today."

"Sis, you can't just go into somebody's house and start cleaning it up." Jobi stared at his sister. "That's, well that's . . . it's stupid!"

"Oh good grief, Jobi. These lazy people would eat it up with a spoon." She looked at Rodriguez. "Nothing personal, Rodriguez. Your family is an exception."

"*Si*, my mama and my sister, they good clean women. He took Susan's hand. "But you are right. They more like eat it up with a shovel."

"Oh!" Susan and Jobi laughed. "Here comes Maria and your

mama. They said they would help and get some of the other women too."

Susan turned to her brother. "Jobi, you and Rodriguez start checking for houses we can work on."

"Okay, sis. Let's go Rodriguez."

The two boys started knocking on doors and checking out the houses. Jobi was somewhat surprised that each of the families he approached was glad to have them come to clean.

"Thank you," he said to the woman he spoke to at the third house on the street, "they'll be here soon."

As they walked down the street, Jobi turned to his new friend.

"How old are you Rodriguez?"

"Why friend want to know?" He drew a deep breath.

"Well, you look so little, you know, young. But you seem to be very smart and, you know, sort of grown-up." Jobi kicked out at a stone.

"Rodriguez much small for his age. I twelve. Soon to be thirteen." He looked down. "I hope."

"Hey, you will live to be 100." Jobi patted his little friend's back.

"Say, this is a strange-looking house." He turned up his nose as the garlic smell filled his nostrils. "Yuck! It really stinks bad."

Rodriguez' tiny arm shook as he pulled Jobi. "Please do come with me! We must stay away from that house!"

"Hey what's with you, Rodriguez?" Jobi tried to see in the window. "What's in there you're afraid of?"

"Please, must go on with our job, friend Jobi. Must not stay here!" His voice grew shaky as he struggled to breathe.

"Come on, Rodriguez. Susan said check every house. Well this is a house isn't it?" He knocked on the door.

"To the people of our village, this house does not exist. It evil." Rodriguez sat on the ground.

"No one seems to be here. Who lives here anyway?" Jobi stared back in the window.

"Please my friend, believe me. This place is evil. We leave now."

He stood and pulled at Jobi's arm. Please come. Please to come with me."

"Not until you tell me who lives here." Jobi pulled his arm loose. "You're acting as though a little vampire lives in this old run-down house. Come on. Stop shaking and tell me."

"Just an old woman. She live there alone after her son, he . . . I cannot tell. It will bring out the evil that lives in there." His breathing deteriorated even further, coming in short bursts. "Please let us go on."

29

"Hey, are you alright?" Jobi stared at his companion.

"'I no feel too good, my friend."

"Come on, Rodriguez. I'll take you home." Jobi put his arm around the boy's slim shoulders. "After you lie down a while, maybe you'll get to feeling better."

Rodriguez smiled at Jobi. "You are a good friend. I like very much." He leaned his head onto Jobi's shoulder. "I like you very much."

"Just hang on, pal. I'll have you home in no time."

He opened the door to Rodriguez' room and helped him to bed.

"Just lie still there. I'll go find your mother and be right back."

"Thank you, my friend." He smiled weakly." My friend, please stay away from evil house. Please." His weak fingers gripped at Jobi's arm.

"I will. Just rest and I'll run get your mother."

Jobi ran quickly from the house and found Anna. He told her to go care for her son.

Susan stared at Jobi. "What happened?"

"He got upset, sis. Over this dumb house the village is afraid of."

"Why? Is it supposed to be ghostly and haunted?"

"I think they're superstitious, sis. He said something evil lives inside it and it stunk. Boy did it stink."

"Which house is it, Jobi?" Susan looked down the street from the window of the house she was cleaning.

"That one over there, sitting up the street."

"The one with all the old trees around it?" She swallowed. "It does look kind of scary."

"Oh, come on, sis!" Jobi forced a laugh. "Just some poor old woman lives there. He said she had a son that something happened to. He froze up when he was trying to tell me."

"Oh, that poor old woman." Susan was suddenly filled with an overwhelming feeling of compassion. "I bet no one will have anything to do with her."

"Probably not." Jobi wrinkled his nose. "And if she smells anything like that house, I don't blame them."

"Jobi!" Susan pinched his arm. "Let's go over and pay a visit to the poor thing."

"She's not at home. There was no one at home when I was there just a few minutes ago," he said as he walked quickly alongside his sister.

"Well maybe she's back now." She stopped at the door. The odor burned her eyes. "Garlic! This place must be covered in garlic!"

She choked and rapped lightly on the door. No one came so she knocked louder. There came a creaking noise from within the house. "She must be in there. She probably can't hear very well. If she's there, maybe the door is unlocked."

Susan tried the knob and it turned in her hand. "What do you think, Jobi? Should we go on in?"

"Might as well," he said softly. "If your curiosity is anything like mine—and I'm sure it is—we won't be satisfied if we don't."

"You're right. Let's go!" She held her brother's hand and slowly opened the door.

Inside, the house smelled even more heavily with garlic. The room was empty except for a few heavy pieces of old furniture and a large silver crucifix hanging on a large, heavily bolted door. Susan's eyes met Jobi's. He forced a smile.

"Sort of reminds you of one of those horror movies when someone is trying to ward off something evil, like vampires and werewolves," he said

"Yeah! I certainly am glad I know there are no such things." She giggled nervously. "This place could make one's imagination run wild."

A sudden noise from behind them caused both kids to jump.

"It came from behind that door, Susan." Jobi swallowed. "It sounded like chains rattling."

"Yeah, that's what I thought it sounded like too." Holding Jobi's arm, she backed toward the front door. "I think maybe we should go tell Scott."

"Yeah, that sounds like an excellent idea." Jobi turned and raced out the door, followed immediately by his sister.

Gene looked down from the open rafters of the new church when he heard Susan call his name. She wore the unmistakable look of concern. He came down the ladder quickly and took her by her shoulders.

"What's wrong?"

"Gene, could you come with us for a minute. We have something we think you might like to see."

"Hey, Pogo," Scott hollered up into the rafters. Take over for a while. I'll be back shortly."

Pogo grinned at the little group below. "Take your time, Dynomite!"

"I'll Dynamite your ass!" Scott took Susan's hand. "Which way?"

31

"This way." Susan looked up at Pogo and smiled. "He's cute."

"He's going to think he's cute if he keeps cracking those smart remarks." He glanced at Susan. "And what do you mean you think he's cute?"

"Just what it sounds like. I think he's cute." She laughed and squeezed his hand. "Jealous?"

"I' m not jealous."' He kept his eyes straight ahead. "This better be important, kids. The church is almost finished, but they goof off when I'm not there to keep them hopping."

"Slave driver, are you?" Susan exchanged a glance with him. "Are you going to make me a slave when I'm your wife?"

"Only in bed." His face turned red when he saw Jobi smiling at him. "Uh . . . how much further?"

Susan stopped in front of the house. "Here it is." She smiled at Gene's expression. "Stinks, doesn't it?"

"Stink isn't the word." He wrinkled his eyes. "Well?"

"There's something strange going on here, Gene. Something is in there, locked behind this heavy door. We heard the chains." Excitement crept into Susan's voice.

"Yeah," Jobi said. "And there's garlic all over the walls and a large silver crucifix hanging on the bolted door." He swallowed, remembering what the house was like on the inside. "Everybody in the village pretends this house doesn't exist."

"My, my, aren't we full of mystery." Scott chuckled. "And next I guess you're going to tell me a witch or a vampire lives in there."

"Gene, this is not funny and we are not joking." Susan opened the door abruptly and pulled him inside.

"Susan, we can't just walk into someone's house without their permission."

Scott's eyes took in the room. It was just as they had told him. The noise came loudly from behind the door—a moaning sound followed by a growling noise greeted their ears. Susan and Jobi moved to Gene and pressed against him.

Jobi's voice was low and halting. "What . . . what is it?"

"I don't know Jobi, but I intend to find out."

Scott walked toward the door. Susan grabbed his arm.

"Gene, what are you doing. You can't go in there!" There was fear in her voice as she held on firmly to his arm. "Please, Gene, darling don't go in."

"Susan, somebody is in there and they may be hurt. We need to find out." He lifted the heavy crucifix from the door and handed it to

Susan. "Here, hold this if it makes you feel any safer."

He yanked the bolt. It was made secure with a big lock. Scott searched the room with his eyes. "Help me find the key."

"Gene you were right. We shouldn't be in here. Please, let's get out!" Susan follow him around the room as he searched madly for the key.

"Susan, if you're not going to help me find that key, just stay out of my way." He scooted her aside gently.

She grabbed his arm. "Please Gene, let's go."

"Go if you like. I understand. I'm staying here until I find out what's behind that door." He picked up the crucifix as Susan set it down.

"Leave you here! Nothing doing, Gene Scott." She drew close to him again." What are you going to do with that?"

"Just stand back. I'm going to knock the lock off the door."

"It won't work, Gene. You could never knock that big lock off with that cross." She pressed her hand against her stomach. "Be careful!" she yelled as he slung the crucifix around and the lock went flying off the door.

Susan caught her breath. "You did it!" She was astonished.

"Why did you have any doubts?" He lifted the bolt out of the way. "Now you can stand back."

"Gene, be careful."

Susan went to Jobi, took his shoulders and moved him back. Scott started to open the door when a noise came from behind them. They turned to see a tiny, ancient woman glaring at them.

"What are you doing?" Her voice was firm, but feeble. "Get away from that door!" She came toward Scott. "Are you mad? Are you insane to do this?"

Scott's voice was calm as he responded. "Who is in there? Why do you have them bolted in like an animal?"

The old woman's eyes fell. "Because, in its own way, it is an animal." She drew a sad breath. "Please, you must leave at once."

"Not until you tell me who's in there." Scott stood staring at the woman, compassion in his voice. "Please."

"It is what is left of my son. He is mad and helpless and . . . and . . ."

"And what?"

"He is a werewolf." She closed her eyes.

"Wow, a real werewolf?" Jobi's eyes grew large. "Wow!"

Susan squeezed his shoulders when Scott glanced at him.

Gene's voice was gentle but firm. "As hard as this is for you to believe, what you are saying is a lot of superstitious nonsense." He went back to the door.

The old woman grabbed his arm. "Please, *señor*, it's true! Four years ago SanRe was a quiet, beautiful place. Then they came." Her eyes brimmed with hate. "The girl and that Jose. She no-count woman! She made passes at every man in SanRe, including my son Donrogus. He good boy, no like devil woman. She was murdered one night. Jose, he say it was my Donrogus!" She looked up pleadingly into Scott's eyes. "My son, he was innocent. He could not hurt bird, much less no-count girl. They got my son. Took him to the old witch in the cave. She do this to him. She make him into werewolf."

She walked slowly to a box from which she took a gun. Then from her pocket she produced a silver bullet. "I had this bullet made from my wedding ring and my mother's necklace. I try hard to kill the beast which is taking over my Donrogus. But I cannot bring myself to use it."

"Gene, what do you make of it?" Susan stared at the old woman sadly. "You don't really suppose—"

"That her son is a werewolf?" Scott looked at the door. I'm not sure what the answer is yet. But there's got to be a logical answer somewhere. I intend to find out just what it is."

He opened the door. The thick odor poured out of the room. The old woman reached out to stop him, but Susan took hold of her.

"It's all right. Scott knows what he's doing. Please trust us." She felt the old woman relax in her grasp. "That's it, just try to relax. Everything will be alright, you'll see." She closed her eyes and thought, "I hope."

The room was dark. They heard the squeaking of rats scurrying from the light. Moaning came from one corner. Looking through the darkness, Scott could make out the remains of a frightened madman. His eyes blinked at the light as he tried to cover them. Chains were·wrapped around his hands and feet and he jerked wildly at them.

Scott gritted his teeth. "Damn, no wonder the poor fellow is mad. Being shut away in this dark, rat-infested pit of hell." He calmed himself as he turned and spoke to the old woman. "Your son needs help, woman. I'm taking him where he can get it."

He went to Susan and spoke softly. "Go up to where my things are in the loft where I sleep and bring me my medicine box. Okay, love?"

"Yes, of course." They exchanged a tender look before she ran from the house.

"Jobi." Scott bent down to his young friend. "Go get Pogo and that Pedro fellow. Bring them here."

"Okay, Scott. Be back in a jiff." He tore out the door.

The old woman was trembling as Scott took hold of her shoulders. "It's going to be alright. I'm going to send your son to a hospital near here where they can help him."

"Do, do you think they can help?" A tear ran from her ancient eyes. "My dear God, what a blessing, what a miracle it would be."

"I have a friend working where I'll be sending your son. He's very good at this type of case."

Susan appeared at the door, carrying the medicine box. Jobi and Pogo were close behind her.

"What gives?" Pogo stared at the room, his eyes adjusting to the darkness. "Yew. What's that smell?"

"Pogo, I need your help." Scott motioned him over to the door where they could speak confidentially. "This woman's son is in that room. He's mad and I want to give him a shot to put him to sleep."

"Gross! No wonder he's mad. God this place is terrible." Pogo wrinkled his nose. He glanced around Gene and his eyes fell on the madman in the corner. "That's . . . that's what we've got to give a shot to?"

"Yes, Pogo. Together we can do this."

Scott prepared the injection and handed it to Pogo. "I'll grab him and you let him have it with a needle."

"Scott, are you kidding? That is no normal everyday person standing over there." Pogo's hand shook as he gripped the syringe.

"I know. That's why I said I'd grab him." He moved over slowly to the man in the corner. "Be ready with that needle."

"Scott, I think you're as mad as he is." Pogo swallowed.

"Shut up, Pogo, and do as you're told." Scott turned his attention to the man in chains. "I'm not going to hurt you, Donrogus. Trust me. I only want to help you."

"Oh boy, Scott, that's real funny," Pogo groaned. "A big man like you walking toward him, me standing over here ready to let him have it with this ugly needle and you telling him to trust you."

Scott turned to frown over his shoulder at Pogo. "If you would kindly shut up, Pogo, and be ready. I'm about to go . . . now!"

He grabbed Donrogus, pinning his arms to his sides. Pogo ran to them, then stopped to stare.

"For God's sake, Pogo, stick that damn thing in him!"

"Where?" He looked helplessly at Scott.

"In his arm, his stomach, anywhere! Just do it!" He grunted as the wild man fought to free himself.

"It might hurt him . . ."

"Not like I'm going to hurt you if you don't do it! Go ahead!"

Pogo jabbed the needle in Donrogus' arm and ran back toward the door. Scott felt the man go limp in his arms.

"Alright, Pogo, help me get these chains off of him."

"Are you sure he's safe?" Pogo made his way slowly over to them. "I mean he's pretty strong."

"Trust me on this, Pogo, you have a lot less to fear from this poor fellow than you do from me if you don't shut up and help me like I asked you. Just wait until I show you how strong I am when I get mad." Gritting his teeth, Scott yanked the chains from Donrogus' feet.

He blinked his eyes as Scott and Pogo helped him into the other room. Susan grabbed Jobi and pulled him out of the way.

The old woman stared at her son weeping. "My poor Donrogus. These friends, they help you."

He tilted his head and stared at his mother. She caressed his cheek. "You be good boy."

Scott looked around the room. "Where is Pedro?"

"He waited outside. Said he wouldn't be caught dead in this place."

"Oh he did, did he?" Scott stuck his head out the door. "Hey Pedro, you coward, go bring a wagon and make it snappy!"

"But, Scott why?" he stuttered.

"Just do as I say!" He turned back to Pogo. "Didn't you wear sunglasses today?"

"Sure. Why?" He reached into his shirt and pulled out his sunglasses.

"Put them on Donrogus. The sun will hurt his eyes."

"Where are you taking him?" Pogo slipped his glasses onto the madman.

"I'm not. You and Pedro are taking him to the next town. Take him to the clinic of Dr. Roy Sawyer. He's a good friend of mine. He'll know what to do for Donrogus."

"But . . . but you expect me and that scaredy-cat Pedro to take this mad man all alone?" Pogo swallowed.

"You can take the syringe, now that you know how it works."

Gene grinned at Pogo. They heard Pedro drive up. "Okay, let's get him out to that wagon."

Pedro started to jump down and run away when he saw Scott leading Donrogus to the wagon.

"Where do you think you're going, Pedro?" Scott called. "Your job is to drive this wagon to Dr Sawyer's clinic. I know you've heard of it."

"No, *Señor* Scott! It's not safe. The devil, he is in this man. The moon, it come out and he—"

"Keep talking, Pedro, and you'll bring out the devil in me." He spoke with complete authority. "There is nothing wrong with this man. He's sick and needs help, that's all. Nothing more about this werewolf nonsense."

Scott turned to Pogo. "Pogo, if Pedro gives you any trouble and tries to jump off and leave you tell me first thing. He'll have me to answer to."

Pogo's eyes grew wide. "Pedro, my friend, I think you better play it cool and drive me to the next town. Your life will be much safer with this madman than with Scott if you make him angry."

Pedro looked into Scott's furious eyes and back at Pogo. "*Si, Señor* Pogo. Pedro see what you mean. We go. We go!" He lashed the horses and the wagon pulled away.

Scott looked at the old woman. "Which way to the witch's cave?"

"Oh, please my friend, you must not go there." Her voice quivered. "You will be in great danger."

"Gene, she's right," Susan spoke up. "You saw what the old witch did to her son." She took his arm. "Please let it go."

"Susan, there are a lot of questions I have and the answers I need are with that old bat in the cave. I'm going. Now which way?" He set his hand on the old woman's shoulder. "You do want your son's name cleared, don't you?"

"Yes but . . . I don't want you to be hurt."

"Actually I have a pretty good history of dealing with unpredictable women." He glanced at Susan. "I think I'm capable of handling an old woman." He smiled at the mother. "Now where?"

"Take that road winding off into the woods. About two miles you'll come to a fork in the road: Take a right. You will know when you reach her cave. Everything is dead. Nothing grows."

"Thank you."

Scott turned and walked out of the house, Susan right behind him.

"I'll be back soon."

"If you're going, so am I." She clung tightly to him. "I won't let you go out there alone."

"And what can you do exactly?" He grinned at her.

"I don't know, but believe me if someone is trying to hurt you, I'll do plenty of something!"

Gene laughed and drew her into his arms. "Susan, my sweet Susan." He kissed her. "Stay here. I won't be long."

"No! Gene Scott, I'm coming with you."

"No, you are not, Susan Andrews. And that is final. Do you think one time you can listen?" He turned and walked away.

Chapter 4

Scott held the reins tight in his hands as he stared straight ahead. "I don't know what's wrong with me. I've never let a woman tell me what to do before."

"It's because you love me." Susan moved closer to him.

"I would have felt better if you had stayed back at the village." His eyes met hers. "It could get pretty rough."

"Well I'm not going to sit around worrying about what happens to you. If anything does, well . . . it can just happen to me too!" She rested her hand on his leg. "I wouldn't want to live without you."

"You might have to someday."

"And what is that supposed to mean?" She took his arm. "Gene?"

"Well, let's face it, I'm a lot older than you, sweetheart. So I'm sure to go first." He caressed her cheek gently. "But you'll probably want to get rid of your old man before then."

"Never, Gene Scott! I love you with all my heart and the only way I could ever stop loving you is through death. But then—even then—I would love you. For my love has grown for you to such an extent that even through death I would love you, only you.

"Susan, how did I become so lucky as to find you and your love?" He put his arm around her. "Hey there is the fork in the road."

He turned the wagon to the right. The further along the road they traveled, the deader things looked.

"Everything's dead, just like Donrugus' mother told us." Susan gripped Gene's hand nervously. "The old woman was right, Gene. This place looks gruesome."

"It does look a bit morbid." Gene stopped the wagon just outside the old cave. "Well, this is it." He climbed off. "You stay here."

"Nothing doing, Gene Scott! You're not leaving me out here alone." She held out her hands and he helped her down.

"All right, let's go," he said, his voice full of resignation.

He looked into the cave entrance. There was a door and what looked like a window. He glanced at Susan before knocking twice loudly on the door. It opened slowly revealing no one.

"How did that door open by itself?" Susan's voice shook as she watched it close automatically behind them. "And close all by itself?"

"There's got to be a logical explanation."

39

Scott walked over to investigate the door. His fingers slipped across the top and his lips melted into a smile as he jerked out a wire.

"Here's your mysterious opener."

His smile vanished as he caught sight of an old woman standing in the doorway at the other end of the room. "Well I see you decided to come out."

Susan twirled and saw the shaggy gray-haired woman staring at them. She felt her heart beating in her throat. The eerie feeling that came over her caused her to step behind Scott.

"How dare you come here uninvited?" Her words were powerful, loud and drawn out. Her voice was an ancient croak. "I order you to leave my home at once!"

"Not until you answer a few questions, old woman." Scott edged closer to her.

"I'm warning you, young man. Get out before I put a curse on you!" Her arms waved through the dank air of the cave, revealing long fingernails, sharp and pointed. "Not one more step, do you hear .me?"

"Now listen, you old hag, I'm not one of those cowards in the village you can scare off so easily with all your witching talk." He studied her closely, his eyes full of suspicion and disgust. "It's time for you to cooperate with me before I lose my temper. I've got a job to finish and you had better not waste any more of my time."

"Oh!" She backed away from him and called loudly, "Tarree! Tarree!"

Instantly a ragged wolf appeared from the back of the cave, it's teeth bared, snarling.

"Attack, Tarree!" the woman shouted. "Attack!"

The wolf lunged at Scott. Susan screamed in horror as Scott tangled with the wolf in mortal battle. With a powerful, swift movement, Scott managed to get both hands around the wolf's throat, squeezing and twisting until slowly the life ebbed out of the wild predator and it slumped to the floor.

Equally amazed, Susan and the old woman stood silently staring at the lifeless wolf. Lifting her eyes to Scott, the woman turned abruptly and tried to run away, just as Scott reached out and grabbed her.

"Let me go!" she screamed, only this time not in the voice of an elderly woman but of a much younger one. "No! Please don't hurt me."

Scott's right hand kept a tight hold of her while his left hand clutched her gray hair and pulled it off, revealing long, thick, black curls. He yanked her around to face him.

She began crying softly and pleading with him. "Please, you're hurting me." Her face was full of remorse and fear as she said, "Please he made me do it. He made me."

"Who made you do it? Jose?" Scott stared at her, unsmiling.

"*Si*. It was Jose. He—he evil. He want the people of the village to be scared so they no come out at night." Her voice shook. "He no want no one to get suspicious."

"Suspicious of what, of his stealing?" Scott loosened his grip slightly. "Is that why Donrogus was framed for killing his girlfriend? He got wind of what was going on and Jose had to shut him up?"

"I don't know, *señor*. I only do as he tells me, so he no kill me." She swallowed. "Honest."

"Honest my ass!" Scott tightened his grip again and pulled her to him. "In truth you are Jose's supposedly dead girlfriend, sent here to make these superstitious villagers think there's some supernatural force, some witch causing evil in the place."

"No! No! That is not so," she pleaded. "No!"

"Oh yes it is, damnit! Admit it!"

She withered and writhed in pain as he twisted her wrist.

"And this whole plan was probably your idea, wasn't it?" he said between gritted teeth. "You came up with it, didn't you? Because, let's face it, Jose just isn't smart enough to conceive of all this."

"Gene, for God sake!" Susan shouted, "You're breaking her wrist!"

"Stay out of this, Susan," he said calmly and then put his face next to the dark-haired woman. "Are you going to tell me or do I have to beat it out of you?"

"Alright! If you let me go, I tell you, you—you pig!"

He released her and she wept for a moment, holding her throbbing wrist before her. Defiantly she looked into his eyes.

"This stinking village is full of stupid, ignorant people. Jose's crazy aunt live here in cave. Everyone already think she is witch. So I thought it would be perfect place to hide the stuff."

"The stuff you stole, right?" Scott's gaze was icy.

"*Si*, you smart ass!" She tilted her head in insolent pride. "Then that Donrogus, he get wise to our game. So we fix his wagon."

"By driving him out of his mind and making everyone think the old witch cursed him?" Scott looked around the interior of the cave. "Where is Jose's Aunt?"

"That crazy old hag, she dead. Jose, he strangled her with her own hair. She was no use to us."

"Oh how cruel!" Susan exclaimed in horror. "You can't have any heart to kill a poor crazy old woman like that."

"I didn't. I would have let my wolf eat her." She laughed loudly.

Instantly Scott drew back his hand and slapped her. She sailed across the room and crumpled unconscious on the floor of the cave.

A victorious laugh escaped Susan's lips. "Oh my! I can't believe I enjoyed that as much as I did. But I have to admit, she did have it coming." She turned to Gene. "Way to go, Samson." She threw her arms around him in joy and relief. "So now what are we going to do?"

"We're going to take her back to the village and hide her somewhere safe. Somewhere Jose can't find her."

"What about that room Donrogus was caged in?" Susan said excitedly. "No one would expect her to be there."

Scott nodded. He held Susan tightly. "Pretty smart thinking there. I've got one smart woman."

"Well I'm glad you think so. Let's get this—this—" Susan turned up her nose. "This witch to her pit of horrors."

She giggled as she opened the door for Gene. He carried the unconscious girl to the wagon, laid her in the hay and concealed her with a blanket. Quickly they turned the horse and headed for the village.

Pogo was waiting for Scott when he and Susan entered the Latabio's house. "Where have you been?" he asked anxiously.

"Out rounding up spooks," Scott replied, gently slipping his arm around Susan's shoulders. "How did you do with·Donrogus? Manage all right?"

"Sure. It was a breeze. No thanks to that scared Pedro." He chuckled and shook his head. "I had to bend over backwards to get him to lift one little finger to help me."

"Think you could find the way back to that town in the dark?" Scott dipped himself a cup of water. "I want you to take a message to the authorities there."

"Sure I can find it, but . . . but what gives?" Pogo stared at his friend, puzzled. "Are you expecting trouble?"

"I want you to tell them I've captured the leader of a gang of thieves and murderers." He set the cup down and whispered to Pogo, "Jose and his creepy thugs are part of it and we don't want to arouse their suspicions. Got it?"

A broad smile crossed his face. "Got it!" Pogo slugged his friend's shoulder. Shit, when do I leave?"

"Have you had your supper?"

"Yeah about half an hour ago," he said, pulling out a chair to sit down.

Scott lifted him back to his feet. "Then what are you doing sitting down? Get going. He patted his friend on the behind. "Be careful and hurry back."

"I'll be careful. You don't have to worry about that." He smiled at Maria, who had been listening to the conversation in silence. "Care to go with me to saddle my horse?"

She smiled down shyly at her hands. "I go."

She followed Pogo out the door. Scott chuckled and patted Susan gently on her back end.

"Sit your sweet butt down. Let's eat. I'm starved." He piled his plate full and smiled at Anna Latabio. "Anna, you're a doll. Fixing all this good food." He winked at her as she returned his smile.

Rodriguez made his way slowly into the room and put his slender arm around Scott. "Rodriguez glad friend Scott got back. Rodriguez got present for Scott."

"A present? For me?" Scott looked around his little friend. "What's the special occasion?"

"You my friend, my very special friend. You build church for my people. Now Rodriguez have someplace beautiful where to be buried."

Scott felt a lump grow in his throat. Susan gazed down at her plate to hide the tears that came to her eyes.

"Hey, what kind of talk is this young man?" Scott stood up. "Let's have a look at that gift you made."

Rodriguez took his hand and led him into his room. He motioned to his bed, where Jobi sat reading.

"Please to sit beside friend Jobi and close your eyes, please."

"Oh. Gladly." Gene scooted Jobi aside, sat down and closed his eyes. "All closed. Let's have it."

Gently Rodriguez placed a cross into Scott's hand. Gene's eyes moved across the beautiful handiwork that he held. He thought of all the love and hopes of this small, dying boy that had gone into this cross. It was painted intricately with a glowing white paint. Scott's eyes grew misty with sympathy. His heart weighed heavy within his chest as he hugged the frail, tiny body.

"Rodriguez, this is truly the most beautiful present anyone has ever given me."

Rodriguez beamed joyfully. "My friend Scott really like present, yes?"

"I love it, son," he replied solemnly. He stood admiring the cross. "And I know exactly where it should go."

"Where?" Rodriguez laughed with giddy excitement. "Where, my friend Scott?"

"On the very top of the church, of course. That will be the first thing people will see when they come to SanRe."

The little boy nodded. "Rodriguez thought my good friend Scott would do this. That why Rodriguez smart and paint with shining paint of my father." He put his arm around Scott's neck. "It lead people to God, even in the night."

"Rodriguez, I know God is very proud to have you as one of his children." Scott set him on his knee. "You see, the cross is a symbol of what Jesus has done for us. Jesus was the light of men and his life was an example of how he wants us to live. What you have done, my little friend, is to make a beautiful reminder of both. The cross is a reminder that Jesus died for our sins and the light that is everlasting."

"And the light shines in the darkness and the darkness comprehended it not." Rodriguez quoted the scripture with a smile. "Rodriguez want good friend Scott to say some words over his tired body when he go to live with Jesus. Yes?"

The request stopped Gene cold. After he composed himself, he replied, "Rodriguez, you'll probably outlive me." He tried to laugh.

"No, my friend. Rodriguez no strong like friend Scott. I'm glad I live long enough to see church built. Now my poor sad Mama have place to go and pour out her sorrows."

Jobi choked back the tears as he watched Scott holding tightly to the weak body of his new little friend.

"Oh God, if there was some way I could give you some of my strength." Scott bit his bottom lip. "God that I could."

"No, my friend. God made you for much help. He take Rodriguez soon." His frail, thin fingers wiped away the tear from Scott cheek. "Must not cry. Must stay strong."

"In your own way, my little friend, you are the strongest of any of us."

Scott stood and lifted Rodriguez to his shoulders. He reached down to take up the cross. Let's go put it on the church.

"Me too?" Rodriguez asked excitedly.

"Who do you think is going to put this cross on the steeple?"

Scott patted the boy's leg and carried him out the door toward the church. Susan, Jobi, Anna and Maria followed closely to observe.

"Hold tight around my neck. Here we go."

Scott made his way up to the cupola. Rodriguez held the cross tightly in his trembling fingers.

"All right, now I'm going to lift you up and you slide the cross into the slot we prepared for when the church could afford a cross."

Rodriguez smiled brightly as he slid the cross into place. Scott let him down slowly. Once on the ground, he grabbed Scott around the neck. The little group stood together, admiring the boy's glowing handiwork.

"Thank you, Rodriguez," Gene said quietly, "for making such a great present. It's one that can be shared with anyone."

"It look pretty good, huh?" Rodriguez laughed and hugged Scott around the waist.

"That's the best looking cross I've ever seen. It really sets off the whole church." His arms around the boy, Scott squeezed him gently.

"It's really beautiful, Rodriguez." Susan choked out the words. "Don't you think so, Jobi?"

"Yes . . . yes, it's . . . it's a very special cross." He swallowed back the tears.

"Mama, you like?" Rodriguez breathed heavily.

"Yes, my sweet son. SanRe will always have a part of you in that cross you make." She took him up into her arms. "Now, better tell your friends goodnight. Need much rest."

"Yes, Mama." He looked at Scott and winked. "Rest no help, but—I know that must keep Mama happy. Goodnight my good friend, Scott."

"Goodnight, my little friend." He forced a smile. "Rest well. It will be good for you."

The boy told Susan and Jobi goodnight and his mother took him into the house. Scott gazed sadly at the shining cross. His heart was filled with pain for the little friend he had grown to love so deeply.

Susan took his hand. "I wish there was something we could do. He's . . . he is . . ." She lay her head on Scott's chest and wept.

Gene folded his arms around her as he held back his own tears. "Susan, we must stay strong, if for nothing more than to comfort his mother and sister when he goes." He glanced at Jobi, who stared at the cross, tears streaming down his cheeks. "Susan, take your brother in and put him to bed. Everything has its way of working out." He walked with them to the blue house.

"Aren't you coming in?" She took his strong hand in hers.

"Not right now. I want to be alone for a while, to sort things out."

"Alright, Gene." She gently ran her fingertips against his cheek.

"I love you."

"And I love you." He kissed her on the lips before he opened the door for them, then walked slowly back to the church

Scott looked at his watch. It was nearly 10 p.m. He had been at the church for almost an hour. He stood and stretched and walked to the door. As soon as he opened it, a bottle crashed against the side of his head. Stunned, he fell to his knees.

Jose spoke in a quiet voice to his men. "Chain him to the post in front of the church. We will give our overly smart people something to remember." He laughed and walked toward the Latabio's house. He knocked loudly on the door. Anna opened it and screamed as a big hand fell across her face.

"Help strangers, will you?" Jose pushed his way past her. "Where is the Andrews girl?"

"What do you want of her? She no cause trouble!" Anna's voice shook in terror.

"Listen, you old bean bag, get her before I cut your worthless throat."

Susan burst into the room. "How dare you say that to Mrs. Latabio!" Her eyes burned with rage. "Who do you think you are, barging in here like this?"

"Talk pretty brave for a girl who is about to make love to Jose." He laughed wickedly and stuck a piece of broom straw in the comer of his mouth.

"I would rather be dead than make love to a pig like you." Susan quivered at the thought of the creep touching her. "Gene will kill you if you lay so much as one lousy finger on me."

He broke into laughter. "Oh! What a trick that will be-seeing how he's all tied up at the moment."

Susan gasped. "What? What have you done with Gene?" She tried to push past him out the front door.

"Calm yourself down, beautiful." His hands gripped her firmly around the waist. "He ain't dead, yet. If you want to keep him alive you better cooperate with me."

"What have you done with him? Tell me!" She grabbed his arm, pleading, "Please!"

"Just come with me. His life is in your hands, sweet one." His eyes roamed her body. "So just do as I tell you and he will not get hurt, very much."

"Oh, Gene!" Susan screamed when she saw him chained to the post.

Scott looked up at the sound of her voice and saw her held tightly in Jose's grip, the thug smiling triumphantly. Scott made a fist and gritted his teeth.

"Damn!" he mumbled as he struggled against his restraints.

Jose motioned for his youngest helper to round up the villagers to watch the game he was about to play. His men stood near him, their guns ready in case someone got brave enough to want to stop them. Jobi, Anna and Maria stood helplessly watching.

Scott's eyes blazed with a rage beyond anything he had ever felt as Jose put his hand on Susan's breasts. She shut her eyes and felt sick. Scott pulled against the unyielding chains.

"Take your hands off her, you bastard!" he shouted.

Jose responded with calloused laughter. "Now is that very friendly, Scott?" He ran a hand through his hair. "She is so very nice. So much a woman to be so young. And I bet Jose will be her very first, eh?"

"I'm warning you, Jose, if you try anything with her, I'll kill you and send you straight to the devil!" The metal of the chains bit into his skin as he struggled furiously.

Jose roared with laughter. "Big man," he mocked. He took his knife, long and menacing, and began cutting the buttons off her gown one-by-one. "Let's see what I'm about to enjoy." He licked his lips as he cupped one hand across her breast.

"Gene!" Susan cried, trying to push his hand away. "Help me!"

"Yeah, help her, Scott. Where's the big man now?" Jose taunted him. He waved the blade through the air as he gazed about at the silent people of SanRe. "You see, he's not so big. Any wild animal can be trapped and tied down."

Caught in a rage beyond any he had ever known, Scott jerked the chains with all his strength. He felt no pain even as the heavy steel tore his flesh.

"Break, damn you, break!" he called, looking at the earth beneath him.

Jose strolled casually to where Scott struggled and spat on him. "And now, before I take your woman's innocence in front of you, I will warm up this place so she won't get cold. Seeing as to how she will be naked."

For an instant Scott stopped and glared in hatred at Jose.

"What's wrong, Scott? Giving up so you can enjoy the show?" He motioned to his men. "Pour gasoline on the church. We're going to have a holy bonfire."

47

Instantly the men complied. Jose laughed as the building was soaked and the rich smell of petrol saturated the air.

"No!" Rodriguez broke away from his mother and ran toward the building. "You bad villain, Jose. No burn church!"

Jose watched without concern as the boy threw himself against him, wrapping his puny arms around his leg. "This poor, weak brat, he is the bravest one in the village." He kicked Rodriguez out of his way. "Go die and get out of my hair, you sniveling brat."

Scott's voice took on a strange power and calmness. "When I get loose, Jose, you'll wish you had never been born."

Jose sneered as Jobi ran over and helped Rodriguez back to the porch.

Jose struck a match and lit his cigar, then smiling at Scott, he tossed the burning match onto the steps of the church. Instantly the building burst into flames.

"Now to ease my desires of the flesh." He went to Susan, grasping her gown to rip it off as she tried to pull away again.

"Take your hands off now!" Fury erupted in Scott throat as he surged forward and the chains snapped away from the post.

A wild look of panic flashed across Jose's face as he called out to his men, "Grab him!"

Scott slung the chains around, knocking all of Jose's dogs to the ground. The village descended on them, seizing their weapons. Scott grabbed Jose in his arms and carried him to the fire. He lifted him up to throw him in.

"Have mercy! For the sake of God, don't kill me!"

Scott's voice was cold fury. "Mercy? Did you have mercy on a dying child? Did you have mercy on an innocent girl?" His hands dug into Jose's flesh. "Did you have mercy on your own aunt when you strangled her?" Scott closed his eyes tightly as he felt the heat against his body and prepared to throw the whimpering man into the fire.

"Please, I don't want to die! I don't want to go to hell!"

"Your aunt, did she want to die?" Scott shouted.

"She was old and crazy. She knew nothing." Frantic terror filled his voice. "Please I'm afraid of fire! Don't burn me!"

"You might as well get used to it. You'll be living in it for the rest of your eternal life." Scott's temper was exploding within him.

"Gene, don't kill him! Gene, the law will take care of him!" Susan screamed as she pulled on his arm. "Gene, you won't be able to live with yourself if you kill him."

Slowly Scott's eyes rose to the cross atop the burning church. He turned and threw Jose to the ground.

He yelled over his shoulder, "You men, tie up that bastard!"

Jerking the chains from his wrists, he searched for a way through the flames to the church.

Standing behind him, trying to avoid the terrible heat, Susan called, "Gene what are you doing?"

"I'm going to get that cross."

Without another word he started climbing the outside of the building, which was nearly engulfed in flames.

"Gene, please! You might get burned!" Susan held her stomach, doubled over in a fear beyond what she felt moments before when she had nearly been raped. "God, please, please don't let him die!"

Somehow in the smoke and darkness, his hands found the cross and he lifted it out of the cupola. He turned and began to make his way back through the heat and smoke. The cross scorched his hand as he descended and realized how close it had come to catching fire.

A dozen feet from the ground, Scott leaped down and rolled away from the raging fire. He got back on his feet next to Susan. She grabbed him and pulled him away from the falling and exploding timbers, all that remained of the church.

"Gene."

He turned to her. Tears made sooty tracks down her cheeks.

"Don't ever do that to me again." She clutched him tightly.

He caught his breath for a moment, then asked, "How's Rodriguez?" Scott's eyes burned from the smoke. "Can you see him?"

"He's been taken back to the house." She grabbed his hand. "Come on, let's go to Anna's. There's nothing more we can do until tomorrow."

Quietly they went into the blue house. Scott placed the cross gently on the table. His hands ached with pain from the burns. Susan took them gently and rubbed lotion on them. His eyes met hers and his hands circled her waist as his lips gently pressed against hers.

"What would I do without my wonderful darling Susan?"

"You would be miserable, wretched, extremely unhappy and probably get yourself killed." She sighed and kissed his lips sweetly. "We will build the church back won't we?"

"You bet we will, Susan. You bet we will." He held her against his chest. "You're the most wonderful thing that's ever happened to me. I love you more than I could ever begin to tell you."

Happy that, at last, she felt so warm and protected in his strong arms, Susan closed her eyes as she whispered softly, "Let's get married."

He nodded. "Soon, very soon." His hand went to her chin and lifted her face so his lips met hers, and they exchanged a passionate kiss. "We better get some sleep now. Got a lot to do if we expect to get that church rebuilt."

"I hope we get it finished before . . . before . . ." She swallowed back the tears. "Oh poor little Rodriguez."

"Susan, we must keep hoping. We can't give up. We can't." Scott squeezed her tightly. "There's always hope."

"Maria told me that a big shock could weaken his little heart enough to kill him. Seeing all those dreams, all his hopes going up in smoke wasn't easy on him."

"Not to mention that bastard Jose's knocking him down and saying those terrible things." Gene stood up and looked through the window at the smoking ashes. "We just have to build that church as quickly as we can. If it means working night and day, I intend to give Rodriguez his dream." Scott moved away from the window and picked up the cross. "And he will lift the cross back on top, just as he did tonight for the first time."

Susan burst into tears. Scott turned to her and took her in his arms.

He bit his bottom lip to hold back his own tears.

His voice quivered as he whispered in her ear. "God will give us the strength we need, my darling. We must get it done. We have to." He closed his eyes tightly. "We must!"

Chapter 5

Scott had the village people working day and night on the new church. Rodriquez' health was failing fast and Scott was overrun with the obsession to finish so his little friend could see it as it was before. At long last the final nail was driving into place. Scott walked quickly to the blue house and bent down by Rodriguez' side.

"Are you asleep, buddy?" He rubbed through his wet hair. Rodriguez' eyes opened slowly as he smiled up at Scott.

"Not asleep, my friend Scott." His voice came weakly and he took short breaths between each word. "Just very tired."

"Save your strength, buddy." Scott held up the cross. "The church is all ready and I want you to put the finishing touch on it. Will you do this for me?"

"Rodriguez would like very much to do this thing for my good friend Scott, but Rodriguez too weak to walk. Cross be much too heavy to lift." He closed his eyes and smiled. "Rodriguez very sorry. He's not strong like good friend Scott."

"I will help you. I'll carry you up and help to lift the cross into place." He swallowed back the lump in his throat. "Well, how about it?"

A feeble hand reached out and grasped Scott's strong one and he sat up slowly.

"Rodriguez say yes. He liked working with friend Scott. We can do it together." He slipped his arm around Scott's neck as Gene lifted him up from his bed. "My friend, you can be the strength I need, and I will supply what little love I have."

Scott could feel his eyes burning as he'd tried to hold back the tears.

All the people of the village stood silently watching as Scott made his way to the steeple. Scott held onto Rodriguez tightly with one hand while he used his free hand to help put the cross into place. Rodriguez smile through his tears as his eyes looked deeply at the cross.

"Do you see Jesus, my friend Scott? He is here to light the cross I make to guide his people safely home to him."

"Do . . . do . . . you see him?" Scott closed his eyes as his heart was breaking in two.

"I see him, yes, my friend. He smiles from the cross." His weak little hand caressed Scott's face. "Remember, my friend, say the words over my body. I go to live with Jesus now. He closed his eyes and his hand fell slowly from Scott's cheek.

Scott bit his bottom lip and it quivered. "God! Oh my God!"

His tears fell gently on the smiling lips of his little friend. He made his way slowly down as everyone watch silently. Scott's eyes fell on Anna Latabio, who stared at the little body limp in his hands. "He has left us, hasn't he?" She choked back the tears as she took her son's body from Scott's strong arms. "He loves you very much, my friend. I'm sure he died bravely in your arms."

"He . . . he was an extra brave little boy Mrs. Latabio." Scott swallowed. "I've never met anyone quite as special and loving toward everyone as he was."

"I take his body into my home to prepare it for burial in the morning."

She walked slowly toward her house, Maria close behind her.

Susan and Jobi ran to Scott and wept heavily in his arms. When he raised his head at last, Gene realized the whole village was mourning the loss of Rodriquez, their silence and their tears speaking for their heavy hearts.

Unable to sleep, Scott built the casket for his little friend.

When the time came for the service to begin, he stared down into the peaceful face, then gazed up at the church, full of worshippers. He could barely see the congregation through his misting eyes. He cleared his throat.

"There is little need of words to express the feeling we all had for our little buddy lying here. His warmth reached each of our hearts and grew to a friendship we can cherish and remember forever. We know that his short life on this Earth was full of suffering and pain. But no one would ever guess the depth of pain he must have been going through, for his feeling for others seem to come before his own needs."

He looked down and swallowed back the lump in his throat, then continued. "He was not strong with physical strength, but he possessed a rare and special kind of strength. The strength of faith and. love. I have been deeply blessed to have known him and to have been his friend.

Scott's eyes filled with tears. The . . . world . . . has been blessed for twelve short years by his life. . . I dedicate this church to him and hereby name it the 'Church of the Little Saint Rodriguez.'" He looked up and cleared his throat. "Let's sing 'The Church's One Foundation' as our memorial to him."

When their voices began the hymn weak and shaky, Scott stopped them before they begin the second verse.

"Rodriguez will think his church is dead with singing like that. Let's open those mouths and sing. He's with God. He's happy and out of pain."

He opened up and sang loudly and the rest of the congregation joined in as the church rang with their voices.

Susan leaned her head wearily on Scott's shoulder as the plane took off from Bolivia. They were all exhausted from rushing to finish the church.

Scott's fingers gently ran through her hair as he spoke softly. "My girl tired?"

"Your girl is very tired." She smiled at him. "And my man, he looks very tired too." She gently touched his face. "Aren't you, love?"

"Physically and mentally." He smiled and kissed her nose. "But I'll survive. Somehow we always do."

"Poor Rodriguez. If there had only been some way to help that poor little boy." She lay her head back on Scott. "At least he got to see the church standing tall again."

"Yes, it was as though he held on to life just for that purpose." Scott closed his eyes to shut off the tears. "He really meant something very special to me."

"Yes, I know." She took his hand and kissed it. "Do you think Pogo will get over Maria?"

"Pogo? Sure. He falls in love with every pretty girl he meets." Scott laughed. "First it was his first grade teacher. Then it was this tomboy who played baseball with him. Then a Girl Scout who sold donuts, and then Maria and probably many, many more." He laughed and pointed at Pogo who was busy talking to a stewardess. "See, scarcely off the ground and he is already making passes at another woman."

Susan laughed and bumped Scott's arm. "Hey, you're not going to forget me that easy, are you?"

"Well, there are a lot of pretty women in the world," he teased and she punched his arm. "Calm yourself, honey. There may be a lot of pretty women in the world, but I have chosen the one I want. Remember—for all my tomorrows. "

"Oh Gene, I love you so much." She snuggled into his arms. "My big, strong, beautiful man."

"And what kind of fib did my sweet, little, beautiful woman tell her parents before you left?" He caressed her shoulder. "Well?"

She laughed softly. "Well, it was a good one. I told them the school was sending a group of kids to Bolivia to study history. They thought it was a good idea, you know, meeting some new friends and all that stuff parents think about." She squeezed her arm around his waist. "When in truth, all I wanted was this. Being in your arms, kissing you and being with you."

"Well supposing they ask you a lot of questions about the historical things you were supposed to have seen." He kissed her head.

"Oh, that's the easy part." She laughed and clapped her hands. "Jobi and I got all sorts of pamphlets about Bolivia. Isn't that brilliant?"

"Oh yeah." He laughed slyly. "Suppose I tell them the truth?"

"Gene Scott, you wouldn't!" She sat up. "Then they might get ideas about us and you know we have to keep this a secret until we find an easy way to tell them the wonderful news."

"But still, they are your parents."

"And they would ground me for weeks if they found out I lied to them." She grabbed his arm, imploring. "Gene, darling you must not tell them."

He smiled at her and shrugged, rolling his eyes up toward the ceiling. "I'll have to think it over."

"Gene, if you love me, if you want to see me! I mean I can get out of the house to meet you anytime now the way things are, but if you go run your big trap . . ."

"Alright, alright!" He laughed and hugged her. "I was only teasing."

"Gene Scott, you're just a big tease." She laughed and laid her head back on him. "I feel so good here."

"Why don't you try to get some sleep? We've got quite a bit further to go and if you're as tired as me you could use it." He·caressed her head lightly and closed his eyes as he drifted off to sleep.

The stewardess shook their shoulders gently. "Please fasten your seatbelts. We are about to land in Tarsa."

The bright afternoon sunshine shone brightly against the crystal blue sky as they made their way off the plane. They picked out their bags and headed toward the airport exit. Scott flagged down two cabs and they all climbed in, Pogo in one to the parsonage, Scott and the Andrews in the other one.

"Well, I'll take you kids home first." Scott touched the driver's shoulder and handed him the address. "Did you get all rested up?"

"I did!" Jobi laughed and stretched. "Those airplane seats are pretty comfortable when you're bushed."

"Yes, the body I was leaning on while I slept on was even better." Susan smiled at Scott.

The driver's eyes sparkled as he stared in the mirror at her. Scott poked him in the back. "Just keep your eyes on the road, buddy." He took Susan hand. "When can I see you?"

"Let's see. Today is Wednesday. At least by Friday. I don't think I can wait any longer." She touched his cheek. "Will you call me tonight though?"

"I don't know, Susan. Suppose your mom or dad answers?"

"Susan or I can grab the phone first. We're pretty fast compared to the rest of the household." Jobi said. He smiled broadly as the car pulled to the stop in front of the Andrew's home. "Well, see you Scott," he said as he climbed out."

"You bet, partner." He smiled at Jobi and turned to Susan. "Try to be a good girl, will you?"

"Just for you." She kissed him quickly and jumped out. "I love you."

"I love you too, sweet doll." He waved and shut the door.

The cab driver cleared his throat. "My, my. You certainly have done it up right, mister." He chuckled. "How in the dickens did a man your age hookup with a pretty young chick like that?"

"Your job, mister, is to drive me home. So I'd suggest to start doing it before I show my temper." Scott sat back and closed his eyes. "Sand Palms Methodist Church, please."

"Feel the need for prayer, huh?" He clicked his lips. "Well I wouldn't worry about it none, pal. You hear tell of people robbing the cradle all the time. I'll say one thing for you, when you robbed the cradle you really got one sexy living baby doll."

Swiftly, silently, Scott took a tight hold on the cab driver's shoulder. "Now listen, I'm going to the church because I live at the parsonage. If there's any praying to be done, it better come from you because if you keep running your big mouth about my personal life, I'll knock you flat on your ass. Got it?"

"Ouch! Sure sure!" His brow furled with the pain. "Boy, buddy, you sure are touchy on the subject of that chick. And your grip is pretty good too."

Scott let go and sat back. When they reached the parsonage, he climbed out wordlessly and paid the driver.

Edna ran up to meet him. "Gene you're home! Thank God you're back in one piece."

He turned to get his luggage and saw the cab driver shaking his head as he watched Scott embracing Edna. The cabby was muttering something about multiple women.

"You can leave anytime, brother."

Scott slammed the cab door and walked with Edna into the parsonage. "Who told Susan where I was?"

"Now Gene, having her around wasn't so bad, was it?" Edna consoled him, patting his shoulder.

"Well if you think my nearly killing a man all because of her wasn't so bad, then I guess it was alright." He plopped wearily onto the sofa.

"Oh geez, tell me you're joking." Edna turned white. "Well, she came over crying and pleading with us to tell her. She looked so torn up and unhappy."

"I understand that, Edna, but you and John promised me that you wouldn't tell her."

"We didn't, Gene."

When she walked into the kitchen, Scott hopped up curiously and followed right behind her.

"David was the one who told her. He never promised you anything, remember?"

"David! I might have known. First he does one thing, then he turns around and does something else." Scott picked up an apple and bit into it. "I think he would have been the last person to tell her, seeing as how he wanted her to himself."

"Oh no. You see, David knew true love when he saw it, and he knew he couldn't stand in the way." Edna set a plate of food on the table. "Sit down and eat, dear. I bet you're starved."

"Well, now that you mention it, I am rather hungry." He sat down and began to feast on the delicious food. "Edna, you're an extra super cook. Old friend John is one lucky man."

"Yeah, I keep telling him that." She chuckled and sat beside him. "Tell me the truth, Gene. Weren't you really glad to see Susan?"

"Sweet, inquisitive Edna. Always a romantic at heart, aren't you?" He touched her cheek. "Yes, Susan was a wonderful sight to me. Oh Edna, I love that girl so much it's frightening."

"I wonder what the Andrews would think about all of this," Edna mused and smiled. "I can just see Shirley's face now."

"Well, we don't intend to tell them right away. Not until we come up with the right approach. This is a very delicate situation and a lot of people could get hurt if we handle it poorly."

"Of course you're right, Gene." She rose and refilled Scott's coffee cup. "Are you two planning to get married anytime soon?"

"Well it's got to be pretty soon, Edna I'm not sure how much longer I can . . . restrain my affection for her, if you know what I mean." He took a sip of coffee. "Every time I'm with her, the desire to express my love for her fully grows. It's really embarrassing when I . . . show·just how excited I am."

"Oh!" Edna's face turned red. "Well, you just have to hold out, Gene. That's all there is to it."

"Somehow I must," he said, shaking his head. He sighed. "I think I'll go unpack."

"Alright. Just put what clothes need to be washed out in the hall with Pogo's. I'll pick them up on my way."

"You're an angel." He kissed her cheek and walked to his room.

Susan and Jobi stared at each other, struggling to respond to what their mother had just said.

"You mean both Aunt Joan and Aunt Jewel are coming to live here?" Susan asked, sitting down on the sofa.

"Yes, dear. They'll share the apartment upstairs. That's why your father built it. We knew it would be a nice surprise." Shirley Andrews looked from her daughter to her son, smiling. Owen and I thought it would be nice to have a little party to help them get to know some of our friends here. I especially want my sister Joan to meet Reverend Scott."

Jobi and Susan looked at one another in shock.

"Why?"

"Oh, I think they would make a beautiful couple. Joan is so sweet and I know how much you kids would like to have Reverend Scott in the family."

"Mom, don't you think Reverend Scott should have a little something to say about who he marries?" Susan stood and walked to the window. "He . . . he may already have someone he's deeply in love with."

"Well, as close as you are, I'm sure if he had, you two would know all about her." Shirley got up and clapped her hands happily. "I think our Reverend Scott would like Joan very much."

"I hope not," Susan whispered to herself, then said, "When is this party going to be? I will call Reverend Scott and ask him if he can make it."

"Saturday night. Your aunts are out shopping now. You know how they are both always trying to outshine each other."

"I sure do," Jobi said as he rose and went to Susan. "I don't think either of them is right for Reverend Scott."

"Me either, Mom. The way Reverend Scott, talks, he already has his eye on somebody else."

"Well I think perhaps you're both just afraid he might take to your aunts and ignore you. Perhaps you're just a little jealous."

"It's not that, Mom. He practically told us he had a thing for someone." Susan swallowed. "Don't you think he's capable of choosing for himself?"

"You're absolutely right, dear." Shirley patted her daughter's shoulder.

"If he chooses Jewel instead of Joanie, well . . . I'll just have to accept it." Owen came into the room and Shirley smiled at him. "Hello, dear."

"I just told the children about our new house guests."

"And I bet you were overjoyed. Am I not correct?" He glanced at Susan.

"I'm . . . overwhelmed with joy, Dad." Susan feigned a smile.

"Well I'll let you visit with your father a while. I have to talk with Mildred about the refreshments for Saturday night." She smiled and hurried to the kitchen.

"Your mother always get so excited about parties," Owen laughed as he pulled Susan onto the sofa beside him.

"Yes, I know." Susan bit her lip. ". . . Dad, would you please talk to Mom about pushing Joan off on Gene. I think it would be a bad mistake."

"You are so right, my dear." He kissed his daughter's cheek. "I'm with you. I think that my darling sister Jewel is the right one for our friend Scott too."

"I never said that, Dad!"

"I know you didn't, sweetheart. It's just like you, too. Never want to hurt anyone's feelings." He laughed. "Oh Joan is sweet in her own way, but when it comes to matching up the best one for dear old Scott, well it's definitely Jewel.".

"But, Dad!" Jobi grabbed his father's arm. "You can't expect Scott just to fall in love with either of them."

"Oh, Jobi." Owen Andrews patted his son's head. "When you grow up, you will think differently about men falling in love with women." He shook his head, laughing as he got up and climbed the stairs to his room.

"Oh, Jobi, what am I going to do? Gene will simply die when Mom and Dad start playing their matching games with him."

"Why don't you tell him not to come?" Jobi picked up a handful of candy and popped it in his mouth.

"Because they will expect me to be here, and I want to be with him." She paced up and down the room. "Oh Jobi, why can't people just leave each other alone?"

"Don't know how, I reckon." He took his sister's hand. "Hey, sis, it will be alright. Scott loves you. No matter what they do, it won't change that."

"You're absolutely right, Jobi. He does love me and if Aunt Joan or Jewel so much as touch him, I'll explode!"

"Well, better try and control yourself. Wouldn't want anyone getting suspicious , would we?"

"No." She went to the telephone. "Well here goes."

She picked up the receiver and dialed the parsonage and recognized the voice of the pastor's wife on the other end.

"Hello, Edna. Is Gene there?"

"Oh, hi, Susan. Yes, he's here. Just hold on there." She called up the Gene's room. "Hey, Gene, there's a very beautiful girl on the phone for you."

Scott stuck his head out his bedroom door. "Did you say Susan was on the telephone?"

"That's right, Susan."

He flew down the stairs three at a time and snatched the phone from Edna's hand. "Thanks, Edna." He kissed her on the cheek. "Hello, Susan. Couldn't you wait for me to call you?"

"My mom wanted me to call you, Gene," she whispered loudly. "Oh, Gene, my parents are giving, a stupid party for my two aunts and they want you to come."

"A party?" He wrinkled his nose. "Do I have to come, Susan? I mean, parties I can do without."

"Gene, sweetheart, if it wasn't for my not wanting to be alone at the stupid thing, I'd say don't come and gladly. But you wouldn't want to spend your Saturday night without me, would you?"

"Hmm. Well, maybe we could split the party when no one is looking." He smiled at the thought. "Maybe take a ride to the beach or something."

"That sounds heavy. I hear the beach can be a very romantic place at night." She pictured herself in his strong arms standing on the soft sand, looking out over the moonlit ocean. "Oh, take me up in your arms, sweep me off my feet, carry me to your bed and make love to me." she said dreamily.

"Much more talk like that, young lady, and I'll be afraid to be alone with you on the beach," he replied softly.

"Sorry. Well, a little sorry, maybe." She laughed quietly and cleared her throat. "Just don't pass out when Mom and Dad start making over you in front of their sisters."

Puzzled, he asked, "What do you mean?"

"They're each going to try and sell you on their sisters. Mom thinks her beautiful, bleached blonde sister Joan is for you. Dad thinks his delectable Jewel is just what you need."

"Lord, that's all I need." Scott slumped down in the desk chair. "What do you think about the situation?"

"I think I'm what you need," she whispered into the receiver.

"I don't think—I know you're what I need," he whispered back. "When does the matchmaker party start?"

"Just one second, I'll find out." She covered the phone and yelled to her mother, "Mom what time is the party Saturday? I've got Scott on the phone."

"Tell him 7:30, baby," she called from the kitchen.

"She said, '7:30, baby.'" Susan wrinkled her nose and giggled. "Didn't I say that sexy?"

Scott laughed. "Oh, extremely! Well, I'll come prepared for anything Saturday night."

"Won't I see you Friday?" She bit her lip. "I mean, just because you're going to see me Saturday doesn't mean you can't see me Friday too."

"You know I'd like nothing better, honey, but it might be a little late."

He looked down at the calendar by the phone. "I have a talk to give around 7 Friday evening for a church group . . . but if you can meet me afterward."

"Just name the time and place," she whispered. "I'll manage somehow."

"How about The Malt Shop around the corner from your house? About . . . 8:30?"

"That's great! I'll be there waiting." She closed her eyes in delight.

"Good. I'll see you then." He blew her a kiss over the phone. "That will have to do until I see you."

"And here's yours." She kissed the receiver loudly. "How's that?"

He rubbed his ear. "Boy, I almost felt that one." He laughed. "I love you, you know."

"That's good, because . . . I love you too." She said just thinking how lucky she was. "Well, Goodnight, darling."

"Goodnight my love." He spoke softly and romantically.

Susan felt her heart racing as she hung up the receiver. "Oh Gene, Gene, Gene." She twirled around and flew up to her room.

Susan turned every time the soda shop door opened to see if it was Gene. She fumbled with the straw in her soft drink. Looking at her watch, she knew he would probably be on time. Just because she had come early didn't necessarily mean he could, she thought to herself.

A tall boy came to her table and sat down. His eyes were trained on her low-cut blouse.

"Waiting for me, beautiful?"

"No. Not hardly." She scooted her drink closer to her."

"Now that's not very friendly." He scooted his chair closer to her. "I can show you a really good time, baby."

"No thanks." She moved away from him. "Go find someone else to show your good time to." She gazed at the door, hoping Gene would come walking through it.

"I rather fancy you, honey lamb."

He moved next to her and put his arm around her shoulders. She pulled to get free, but he held her tightly.

"Now just try and relax. Old Freddy here ain't going to hurt you none." His hand went for the front of her blouse as he tried to kiss her. "Come on. Quit fighting me. Give Freddy a little loving."

"Here's you some loving, fellow." Scott yanked the boy to his feet and flung him like a rag doll across the floor.

"Gene!" Susan grabbed him around the waist. "That creep was trying to . . . to touch me."

"I saw him." Scott's eyes burned coldly on the boy who stared up at him from the floor in shock. "Get up, kid."

"Now—now wait a minute, mister! This is between me and that chick." His voice shook. "You just stay the hell out of it."

"Watch your filthy mouth, freak." Scott yanked him to his feet. "Nobody talks to my woman like that, let alone any of that hanky panky you were trying to pull. I suggest you get out and go home to your momma."

"Well . . . okay." He tried to free himself from Scott strong grip. "Let me go, mister."

Scott gritted his teeth. "First, apologize to my woman."

"For what?" The boy's forehead wrinkle from pain and confusion.

"For putting your filthy dirty hands on her. . . . Well, what are you waiting for. Apologize."

"Alright!" he yelped in pain. "I'm sorry, sweetheart."

Scott threw him aside. "All right. You apologized, kind of. Now get lost." They watched silently as Freddy slinked out the door. Scott's took Susan's hand gently.

"Let's get lost too. I think we've given these folks enough to talk about for one night." He turned from all the staring faces who had watched the scene in awe and asked the waitress, "How much does she owe you?"

Smiling broadly, she replied, "It's on the house, doll. That was the best thing I seen in ages. Finally old Freddy Parker got what he deserved."

"A troublemaker, huh?" Gene gripped Susan's hand.

"Troublemaker is right. He thinks he can pick up every girl he chooses. Most boys are afraid to tangle with the creep." She patted Scott's arm. "But not you, handsome. That was worth my working the late shift."

"Thanks so much for the drink." Susan tugged on Gene's arm. "Let's go, darling. Your wife needs a little attention."

"Wife?" The waitress shook her head, disappointed. "Darn, can't the good ones ever be single."

Scott chuckled as Susan pulled him toward her door.

"Boy," she said in exasperation, "why do all the waitresses have to get hooked on my man?"

"What other waitresses are you referring too? The one on the ship?" He laughed as they stepped out into the fresh, air. "I didn't realize I belonged to you back then."

"It just goes to show how unobservant you are." She put her

hands around his neck. "For your information, Gene Scott, I fell in love with you the first time I set my eyes on you."

"I think it happened to me that way too. Although I tried to make believe it was something else." He looked at his car, then hers. "Which car?"

"Take your pick." She held out her keys. "Only, you drive."

He laughed and took the keys to her Corvette. "Hop in and I'll show you just what your baby can do."

The motor roared to life and they sped away.

"Better watch that lead foot, sweetheart. This thing practically goes by itself." Susan scooted over as close to him as she could get. She noticed the speedometer read nearly 80. "Hey, handsome, slow it down."

He glanced down and his eyebrows arched instantly. At the same moment, he caught sight of the flashing red lights in the rearview mirror.

"Great! Just hang on, Susan. I'll lose them."

He floored the gas pedal and Susan twirled her head around as she felt herself pushed back into the seat.

"Gene!" she laughed. "You better stop. You're going to kill us!" Then she closed her eyes so she wouldn't have to see whatever was going to happen next.

She did not see Gene switch off the Corvette's lights and slid to a stop on a side road. The better part of a minute passed before, slowly, she opened her eyes again.

"Are . . . are we dead?"

He leaned over to her and kissed her gently. "Does that feel like you're dead?" He smiled at her and leaned his head back in his hands. "We'll just sit here until they get tired of looking for us and clear the area. Wouldn't want to go to jail and miss that great party tomorrow night."

"Hey, that wouldn't be a bad idea," Susan teased. "That way Joan and Jewel wouldn't try to snare you."

He brushed his fingertips across her cheek. "Of course you would be spending Saturday night alone if I went to jail. What about that?"

". . . That's a really bad idea." She slipped her arms around his neck. "Why, Reverend Scott, I just don't know what to think about a preacher man taking an innocent girl down a dark lonely road at night."

A wry smile crept across his face. "Where do you think they got the old saying about backwoods preacher?" He took her in his arms.

"How about giving your old man a kiss?"

"I'd love to give my man a kiss."

She kissed him tenderly. He pulled her closer and returned it passionately.

"Oh, Susan, I can't take this."

He turned his head away, only to have her pull it back to face her. "Gene, please darling. I love you." She kissed him gently on the neck.

"Kissing . . . is . . . better . . . than . . . nothing."

She moved her lips slowly back to his parted lips and his tongue found the inside of her mouth. Her hands moved slowly down his chest as his breathing deepened. She took his hand and moved it gently to the opening in her blouse. His fingers found their way quickly to her breast where they encircled it with maddening slowness. She slid her hands down the front of his pants deliberately. His heartbeat wildly in his throat as her fingers went around the hardness of his erection. Quickly he pulled himself free from her and climbed from the car, gasping for breath. He closed his eyes tightly and gritted his teeth."

"Damn!" He hit the hood of the car.

Susan climbed out, tears streaming from her cheeks.

"Oh, Gene, I'm . . . so sorry. I just want you and need you so badly." She fell to the ground on her knees, covering her eyes with her hands. "I love you so very, very much. I . . . I can't help my emotions."

He lifted her, taking her tenderly into his arms. "I know, Susan. Believe me, I know. I feel the same way. I love you so much and my willpower is getting weaker each time we are alone." His hand beneath her chin, he lifted her face to his. "I guess to be on the safe side, we had better get married pretty soon."

"Oh, Gene!" She grabbed him around the chest. "Soon, soon, soon!"

He sighed. "Well, young lady, I better get you home before your dad sends out a search party."

He helped her into the car and they drove back to the soda shop. She smiled at him and he smiled at her as he took her hand.

"See you tomorrow. Let's not hang around too long. Parties and man-hunting women are not my idea of an enjoyable night."

"Mine either. Especially when it's my man who's being stalked." She laughed softly. "And by my own aunts at that."

"Well," he rubbed his chin, "what do they look like? Maybe it won't be so bad," he teased.

"Listen here, Gene Scott. You can just put a cork in that kind of talk right now." She leaned over and kissed him. "I'm the only member of our family you can have any romantic interest in, understand?"

"Well, that's all right by me. If the rest of your women folk are as tempting and sinful as you, I'm better off leaving them alone." He drew her to him and kissed her. "My little Delilah is all the woman I need." He kissed her nose. "I love you. Drive carefully and don't be picking up any Freddy's along the way."

She laughed. "Well don't you be picking up any waitresses."

"Don't worry about that. I think I've got more woman than I can handle now." He kissed her one last time and climbed out of the car. "Leaving you gets harder and harder."

"Yes. That's a feeling I well know." She smiled, her eyes on his. "Don't come dressed so damn good-looking tomorrow night, hear?"

He laughed. "So now you've taken up swearing?"

"Well I can't help it. My dear sweet husband to be says it all the time and he's supposed to be setting examples."

"You know it's not befitting to a wife or a mother." His eyes glimmered.

"Do drive carefully honey. Goodnight."

"Goodnight, my wonderful sexy man." She cranked up the motor and drove away.

"Damn!" he exclaimed. "I love that woman." He laughed as he headed home.

Chapter 6

Gene Scott knocked on the Andrews' door. He had meant to arrive on time, but he didn't anticipate the flat tire he had while driving over. Mildred opened the door, smiling.

"Good evening, Reverend Scott. I'm sure glad to see you." She took his arm and pulled him inside. "They has been beside themself in there waiting your arrival. My lady, she has her precious Joan standing by the door ready to grab you whenever you walk in. And Mr. Owen, well he has been standing by his lovely spoiled sister, keeping one eye on the guests and the other eye on the door."

"What about Susan? Where is she?" he asked as he nervously fixed his tie to let some air pass through.

"She just sits and stares at the door. Miss Susan looks pretty bored about the whole party." She giggled and took his hand. "She don't know the surprise she going to get tonight."

"Oh? What sort of prize?" Scott gazed at Mildred curiously.

"It's an early birthday party for her. Her one and only sweetheart is coming tonight. Only she don't know it." Her head jiggled with laughter. "Sometimes I just don't understand my lady and her husband. I mean, they were against Miss Susan and Peter going together from the start."

"Who is Peter?" Scott's eyebrow arched upward.

"None other than Peter Simus, Susan's long-loved high school sweetheart. I never know why they invited him to the party, seeing as to how they stopped the two younguns from running off and getting themselves married."

"Married!" Scott was surprised at the sound of his own teeth grinding together. "How old is this—this Peter?"

"Oh, I'd say he's eighteen, same as Miss Susan will be." She grasped his arm. "'Enough talking. If'n my boss lady knew you were here and I was the responsible party for holding you up, she would have my job."

She strolled him lazily to the door, where the party was in full swing. Scott looked around to see where Susan was sitting. He saw her through the crowd at the far end of the room. Their eyes met and Susan sat up and smiled. Scott stared back, unsmiling. Shirley appeared beside him and took his arm.

"Reverend Scott, we've been waiting for you to come." She laughed girlishly and pulled her sister up beside them. "I want you to meet one of the sweetest girls around, and available. My sister Joan. Joan, this is Gene."

"Gene, I've heard so much about you. I really have been looking forward to meeting you." She tossed her blonde curls. "Do you like living in TarSa?"

His eyes remained on Susan, even though he felt Joan touch his arm.

"I . . . ah . . . said, do you like living in TarSa?" She glanced at her sister with an uncertain expression and shrugged.

He turned to her and smiled. "TarSa is a very beautiful place, but I don't exactly live here," he said. "I should ask you how you like it here. You'll be making this your home, I hear."

"Yes, oh yes. My dear sister Shirley insisted that I and Owen's sister as well come here to live. It's such a lovely place." She attempted a casual laugh. "I plan to join the church real soon."

"Well that's nice." His eyes wandered back over across the room. "Sand Palms, where your sister and brother-in-law attend, is a lovely church."

"Oh yes," Shirley interjected. "And my sister wants to become a Sunday school teacher as well." Shirley slipped her arm around Joan "Don't you, my dear."

"Oh? Oh yes! I've always loved working in the church." She took his arm again, this time a bit more firmly. "You know, it may sound funny," she said with a laugh, "but I've always wondered what it would be like to marry a preacher."

A flash of despair and humor widened his eyes. "Oh, now that is funny." He leaned back, tilting his head to the side to get a full view of her. "I would have thought, since you're a very attractive woman, you would prefer—and be much happier—with a wealthy businessman; maybe a prominent member of society."

"Oh, Joanie is very conservative. You might even say a homebody type," Shirley said, feigning a laugh. "Aren't you dear?"

"Oh, yes! Yes!" She returned her sister's faux smile.

"You don't say?" Scott rubbed his chin skeptically. "I wouldn't have thought that, given the lovely, expensive evening gown you're wearing."

"Oh, this old thing?" She flipped the fine lace fringe. "I've had this for years. It's just something I keep around for special occasions like this."

During their conversation, Susan had made her way over to where the three were standing. She smiled and cleared her throat. "Oh, Aunt Joan, I love your new dress. That is one of the ones you bought yesterday, isn't it?"

Her aunt's eyes grew wide as she stared at Susan. "No, Susan, dear." She giggled anxiously. "I've ... had this ... a ... old dress for years." She gazed back to Scott, smiling broadly.

"Are you sure, Aunt Joan?" Susan's voice was full of curiosity and dripping with childish innocence. "I could swear that's one of those you modeled for Mom and me yesterday when you bought all those other outfits." Susan bit the inside of her lip to keep from smiling.

When Shirley Andrews realized her sister was speechless, she glared at her daughter and said, "Joanie rarely ever buys herself anything new, Reverend Scott. But, well, tonight was so special, she ... uh ... well she wanted to look extra nice." And when she saw that Susan could not resist smiling, she said curtly, "Susan, dear nothing is funny."

"Sorry, Mom." She took a deep breath and turned to Gene. "Care to dance with me, Reverend Scott?"

"Oh," he said casually. "I'd be delighted." He took her hand and smiled at Joan, saying as he stepped away, "Seriously, Joan. If you like the idea of being a minister's mate, I think I might be able to help. I have a preacher friend back in the states. He is just dying to find a godly, beautiful woman to take care of him. When his first wife walked out on him, he got stuck raising their five kids by himself." At that point Susan had pulled him far enough onto the dance floor that he could no longer converse.

Joan's shoulders sagged. She looked at her sister. "That did not go the way I intended. I think I goofed badly." She gazed after him. "You're right, though. He is gorgeous."

"Well, don't give up just yet, Joanie. It takes time to convince a happy bachelor that he needs a wife." Shirley patted her sister's arm. She squinted at her daughter on the dance floor. "I'll have a little talk with Susan as well. She seems to have a certain amount of sway over the good reverend. I'm sure she will come around to my point of view that you're far better suited for Reverend Scott than Jewel is."

Susan stared curiously into Gene's eyes. "Hey, you haven't said hardly anything to me. What did I do?"

He gazed at her for a moment, wondering if he should bring up the name of the person who was supposed to be her big surprise.

Gene realized he simply had to ask about him.

"You failed to tell me about Peter."

She caught her breath. "Peter? Peter Simus?"

"Yes," Gene replied, a little more loudly than he intended. "Remember him, your long-time love, whom you were going to run away with and get married? Him."

She smiled at a guest who turned at the sound of Gene's words. "I didn't say anything to you about him because he isn't important. That was only a school girl crush, nothing more."

"You were planning to marry him." He loosened his grip when he realized he had unintentionally tightened his fingers on her arm.

"Thanks to Mom and Dad, I didn't make that mistake," she said tersely. "Gene, you can't be upset about that. It was just a childish mistake."

He sighed, glancing about the room. "And . . . perhaps you're wanting to marry me is just your latest childish mistake." He looked down at her elegant, perfect face. "I'm sure you really thought you loved him . . . . Perhaps you just think you love me too, like it was with Peter."

Tears welled in her eyes. She could not believe he would say such hurtful words. "Gene." Her lips quivered "That's just not true. Look at me." Now she was the one grabbing his wrists and stopping him. "I love you. I really, really love you," she whispered. "You must know that." She sighed. "Oh, let's go to the beach now, where we can talk freely."

"That suits me fine, but what about Peter? We don't want to disappoint him." Gene looked around the room. "A bit late, isn't he?"

"Gene, honey, what are you talking about?" She shook her head. "Peter's not coming here."

Scott leaned down to her and said softly, "Yes he is, Susan. Mildred told me. It's supposed to a big, secret surprise for you—I know it was for me. Your parents invited him to come for your birthday!"

Her cheeks flushed instantly in shock and anger. "Oh my god! They would do something stupid like that!" She stopped dancing immediately and gripped his hand. "Let's go, maybe we can get out of here before he shows up." As she spoke, she saw her father approaching, accompanied by her other aunt. "Ought-oh. Don't look now, but I think you're about to meet Aunt Jewel."

"Shit!" he muttered, then turned when he heard Owen call his name.

"Gene, I want to introduce you to my wonderful, charming,

sweet, lovely, Christian sister Jewel. Jewel this is that great fellow I was telling you about."

"Hello. So nice to meet you, Jewel." Gene realized he was still holding Susan's hand and he squeezed it.

"The pleasure is mine, Reverend Scott or may I call you Gene." She looked shyly down at her hands.

Susan laughed and Owen Andrews cleared his throat.

"Oh, by all means," Gene replied, ignoring the young woman who gripped his hand so tightly. "Please call me Gene. Susan was telling me how much she enjoyed the extensive shopping excursion you all took yesterday."

Jewel glanced up at her niece. "Oh, she did?" She gave Susan a poisoned smile. "Sweet little Susan. Well like most women, there are occasions when I get the urge to buy something new."

"Oh Gene," Owen laughed, "you know how women are, always wanting to look pretty for us men. My sister is a knock out, isn't she?"

"Yes." He nodded, "I was just thinking that she is very attractive."

"Oh Owen," Jewel frowned in mock humility. "What sort of thing is that to say? What was Gene supposed to say once you asked him that?" She leaned toward Scott. "That was very kind of you, Gene."

Owen shrugged. "Well I'm a man who is very proud of his beautiful sister." He thumped Scott on the back. "You don't blame me, do you?"

Gene's eyes grew wide. "Of course not. For responding to undeniable beauty in a lovely young woman? How could I?" He glanced back at Susan helplessly.

Quietly Jobi had joined the group, holding a plate of h'ordeuvres and listening to the conversation, waiting for the perfect moment to speak up. "Yeh, for someone who loves to eat like Aunt Jewel, I guess you could admire her looks too."

Susan gasped and laughed aloud. Jewel stared in shock, first at Jobi and then Owen.

When he realized everyone was looking at him, Jobi shrugged and said, "That's what I've always admired about her. She can eat rings around the rest of us."

"Oh Jobi, you know good and well it was Joan who had three pieces of that chocolate cake when I only had two little pieces." She swallowed nervously.

"Really," Jobi replied thoughtfully. "Oh, I remember now! The pieces were different sizes. Joan cut off three slivers and you had two slabs—well, plus that third piece you snitched in the kitchen last night, right?" He winked at her.

Jewel's face turned a deep red and her mouth dropped open.

It was at that moment Mildred appeared at the door with Peter Simus in tow. He spotted Susan and walked straight to her. A great smile spread across his handsome, youthful face as he turned Susan toward him and put his arms around her shoulders.

Scott had an instant taste of brass in his mouth, but calmed himself. He put his hands, which had of their own accord doubled into fists, into his pockets as he stared nonchalantly at the well-dress young man.

Susan laughed self-consciously. "Oh Peter, what a pleasant surprise."

"Susan, you don't know how good it is to see you." He held her at arm's length, like someone admiring a painting. "Stand back there and let me have a good look at my favorite girl."

If Scott had ever doubted the depth of his affection for Susan Andrews, it was clear to him in this moment as never before. He pushed back the temper building inside him, reminding himself that Susan had to be the person to decide ultimately whom she loved and truly wanted to be with. Still, he was astonished at the raging jealously he felt, beyond anything he ever experienced.

He turned quickly to Jewel. "Would you care to dance, Jewel?"

Susan glanced over her shoulder at him in dismay and to his surprise spoke out plainly. "Make it fast, will you, reverend. Remember you promised you would help me with this little problem of mine."

"Oh, Susan dear, this is no time to burden Reverend Scott with silly, little personal issues." Jewel smiled at her and caressed her cheek with her fingertips. "Why don't you run along with Peter? You two get reacquainted and have a good time."

Susan shook loose of Peter's grasp and stood, determined, hands on hips. "My problem may seem little and silly to you, Aunt Jewel, but to me it's quite serious. Don't you agree, reverend?" She stared at him fiercely.

In that instant he recognized beyond all doubt that Susan indeed loved him as much as he loved her. And he realized that whatever had transpired between her and Peter was little more than puppy love.

"Of course, being a minister, I can't divulge the nature of the concerns Susan has discussed with me and asked me to help her with. But I did promise her, Jewel." He touched Susan's hand in a pastoral way, his eyes blazing with restrained passion. "Well talk soon, Susan. I guess you have other things to attend to."

"Susan," Peter interjected anxiously, "we've got so much to catch up on." He grabbed her arm just above the elbow. "'Let's go in to the next room and talk privately."

Susan returned Scott's gaze with her own smoldering stare and replied without looking at Peter, "It wouldn't be polite for me to walk out on our guests, Peter."

"Now Susan," Owen Andrews put his hand on his daughter's shoulder, "it's alright dear. No one begrudges you a little privacy if you want to catch up with your friend. Peter came all this way just to see you. I'm sure your mother and I, along with your aunts and all our guests, are happy for you." He winked at Peter "Now you two just run along and enjoy yourselves."

"Thank you, sir." Peter turned Susan and led her out the room.

Scott watched them disappear behind the door to the library. His arms hung loosely at his sides, but his fists were still balled tightly. He heard Jewel giggle and felt her hand on his wrist.

"Hey, how about that dance?"

He forced a smile. "I don't think I can dance to this tune. Is it okay if we just sit down and talk?"

Her expression brightened. "Oh yes. I would like that very much." She motioned toward a love seat next to the fireplace. "How about over there?"

"We won't be able to hear ourselves in here," he said. "How about, I don't know, the library."

He started toward the door when she grabbed his arm. "We can't go in there, Gene. The children are in there and I don't think they want to be disturbed." She tried to guide him toward the loveseat, but he was steadfast, his eyes on the library door. "Now Gene, I'm sure you remember how it was when you were young and in love."

"I do, actually. It seems like only seconds ago." He could not avert his gaze from the library door. "Really, I don't think Susan would object if we just slipped in there to sit and chat for a moment. After all, this music has given me a headache."

"Oh no! I'm sorry, Gene. Maybe we should go outside for a walk . . . or something."

When Jewel started for the patio door, Gene walked straight to the library and opened the door. Susan looked up from the sofa where she was sitting and instantly gave him a sweet smile.

"Reverend Scott." Her voice was full of joy and relief. "I didn't introduce you to Peter properly, did I?"

"Peter Simus, I believe." Gene shook his hand.

Peter's expression was one of resignation and sadness. "Yes, Reverend Scott. Susan has been telling me a great deal about you. I know she admires you deeply." He swallowed and for a moment Scott thought he was going to start crying. "I guess I'm not so lucky as I thought."

The library door opened again, Jewel Andrews entering and closing the door behind her. Immediately she said, "Why Peter, is something wrong between you two love birds?"

She took a seat next to Peter. Susan took Gene's hand and pulled him down beside her.

"It looks as if the fair love bird flew the nest, Jewel." Peter's eyes dropped to the floor. "She . . . she said there is someone else."

Jewel's jaw dropped as she looked at her niece. "Susan, you never told us there was someone else. When and where did you meet this mysterious man?"

"Several months ago, Aunt Jewel." She reached her hand back, out of the view of the others, and took Scott's hand. "He's the most wonderful person I've ever met."

"Well, why in heaven's name didn't you tell us, or bring him home to meet the family?"

"I will, when I think it's the right t ime." She thought quickly to change the subject. "What made you two decide to abandon the party?"

"Gene got a headache from the music. I suggested that we go outside, you know, the fresh air bit." She smiled sheepishly. "But he just insisted on coming into the library."

"Oh." Susan glanced over her shoulder at Gene. "Any . . . certain reason you picked the library, . . . reverend?"

". . . Well. For one thing, I heard so many nice things about your friend, I didn't want to leave the party without having the chance to meet him." He smiled grimly at the boy. "And I wanted to see if you were ready for our little talk, you know, before I call it a night."

"Now, now, Gene." Jewel stretched over and patted his knee. "Susan can't leave poor Peter feeling so broken-hearted. Why don't we just sit here and talk a while as this poor young man recovers from his shock."

"Well alright," Gene said earnestly. "What should we discuss, Jewel?" Scott leaned his head back on the sofa.

"You!" She could not conceal the excitement in her voice. "How did a good-looking man like yourself remain a bachelor all these years."

Gene tried not to look at Susan. Even someone as oblivious as Jewel would surely see the passion between them if their eyes met.

"I haven't been a bachelor all my life. I was married and had two beautiful children. I lost them three years ago in a car accident." He glanced at Susan then, waiting to see how she would react.

"Oh Gene." Tears filled her eyes. "Why didn't you tell me?"

"I suppose I would have, eventually, Susan. If the right time ever presented itself." He smiled at Jewel and Peter, who stared in bewilderment. "That's the thing about this Susan of yours," he said. "This little gal here is always wanting to know everything about everybody."

"Yes, well most women are inquisitive at times." Jewel nodded and laughed "How old would your children be Gene, if they were still alive?"

"Aunt Jewel! I'm sure Reverend Scott would rather not discuss this with us." Susan's hand, unseen, squeezed his tightly. "I understand . . . that might be a very sensitive, painful subject for you."

His expression melted into a smile. How wise and tender was this young woman he loved so much.

"I don't mind, Susan. My son would be twelve and my daughter would be Susan's age."

"Seventeen? Oh my." Jewel patted his knee. "Well, no wonder you feel so close to Susan and Jobi. I can see how they would remind you of your own children."

Susan stared into Gene's eyes. The inevitable question, voiced so clearly by Jewel, created an irresistible longing. Scott realized Susan wanted to know if he saw her as a daughter to replace his own—or if he truly loved her as his life's mate.

"I think it's time Susan and I went for our talk. "Scott stood up and motioned for Susan to follow him to the exit. "Will you excuse us?"

"Sure, Reverend Scott." Peter got to his feet, smiling "Maybe you can convince her that this other man is not the one for her, but I am!"

Susan looked up at him. "Is that what you're going to try to convince me of, Gene?"

Gene shrugged. "Peter, I haven't known Susan all that long, but I can tell you that, once she makes her mind up about something, it's pretty much impossible to change it." They started toward the door. "Excuse us."

They made their way quickly past the other guests until they reached the entrance to the hall. Gene breathed a sigh of relief when they got out of the house unseen by Susan's parents.

"Let's take my car."

He helped her in and drove toward the beach. Neither of them spoke.

Susan climbed out as soon as Gene pulled his car to a stop. She walked quickly toward the water. Gene grabbed her arm and turned her around to face him.

"Susan, it's not what Jewel said. I love you. Not as a replacement for my daughter. I've told you this before. I love you as a woman! I want to marry you."

For an instant she studied his face in the moonlight reflected off the sea. Then she grabbed him, her arms around his chest, and cried out, "Oh Gene, I love you so very much."

"Susan, my sweet, sweet Susan." His lips parted gently over hers as his tongue found the inside of her mouth.

"Oh Gene, Gene!" She breathed heavily. "We must get married soon. I can't take much more of this torture. I want you completely."

"Susan, I know that feeling all too well. You can't imagine what agony I go through when I have to pull myself away." His powerful arms encircled her, pressing her against him. "I promise, honey, we will be married soon—very, very soon."

"I know you must've loved her deeply, didn't you?" She pulled herself away and sat down on the soft sand. "What was her name?"

"Do you mean my wife?"

She nodded.

"Faye. And, yes, I loved her. She was a very special sort of person and a wonderful mother to my children." Gene recognized the emotions rolling behind Susan's eyes. "Honey, I did love them, all of them. Very much. But they're gone now. It's all the past. You can never have it back and if you want to live the life God wants you to live, you have to realize that and embrace those who God brings into your life now. . . . What I have now—with you—I never had before. What I feel for you, I never felt for anyone before." He took her face in his hands. "I've never loved anyone like I love you, Susan. I've never loved anyone as much as I love you."

She closed her eyes as the tears flowed from them. "Oh Gene, my darling, Gene. I don't deserve such wonderful love. I . . . I feel so terrible, being jealous over a memory. Over a family. I know you loved with all your heart." Her fingers gently traced the contours his face "I know you're capable of loving many. I'm just thankful you fell in love with me, only if it were but just a little bit, because your love is so pure and strong."

"A little bit? Oh Susan, how can I tell you, what words can I say that will make you believe that I love you more than I have ever loved before or will ever love again?"

His kisses burned with passion on her lips. He slowly moved his kisses down to her neck. Their breathing grew heavier and their bodies grew ever closer, yearning to become one. His lips found hers again and his tongue went inside and moved slowly around. He slipped closer to her and she could feel the irresistible swell of his erection even through his slacks and her dress. Her heart beat wildly in her throat as he blew tenderly into her ear.

"Susan, I think I have found the words." His ragged breathing against her neck made her desire, grow all the more as her fingers slid beneath his shirt, moving up and down his back.

"What my darling? What are they?"

He pulled away and stared into her eyes. "You stole into my heart, locked the door and threw away the key."

She gently touched his face and wiped away a sudden tear.

"Oh Gene, that's beautiful." She looped her arms around his neck. "I love you so much, so very, very much."

"Well, enough of this beach play, young lady, before I succumb to the wiles of my wonderful sexy Delilah." He stood and brushed off his pants.

She held her hands up to him and he pulled her gently into his arms.

"It would be so easy to let myself go with you."

"I'll not stop you." She smiled coyly.

"I know. That's what I'm afraid of." He patted her on the bottom. "Now get your sweet butt into that car."

"Whatever you say, Samson." She climbed in, sliding over as close to him as she could get. She began to caress his ears. "You better marry me pretty soon, if you plan to stay sinless."

"And what is that little threat supposed to mean?" he asked with a laugh.

"As you remember, Delilah kept trying until she broke Samson down. I'm sure if I keep trying, I'll find out just the right little thing to do to make you give in."

"Susan, you're cruel!" He put his arm around her and pulled her against him. "I'm going to have to marry you soon to make a good Christian girl out of you."

"I'm going to make you a good wife, Gene. I promise." She snuggled up next to him. "I'll give you children, lots of children. Maybe ten or twelve."

"Hold on there, girl. I'll settle for five. I think five examples of our love running around will be plenty for us to keep up with." He stopped the car in the shadows of the house and pulled her into his arms. "Besides, your old man will want most of your attention for himself. Especially at night."

"We will make sure our bedroom is off limits to our kids, fair enough?" She reached up and kissed his cheek. "What mom and dad do behind that door is strictly their own private business."

"And I can assure you, there will be plenty going on." He returned her kiss with loving passion.

"Call me soon, will you?" She held onto him tightly.

"I will, honey, soon as possible." He got out and helped her out. "I may call you about a blood test and a physical too. You are turning eighteen. It will be perfect!"

"To get a marriage license! Oh Gene!" She grabbed him. "Anytime. I'll be ready."

"Good girl."

He walked her to the front door. Mr. Andrews was showing some guests out.

"Hello, Owen. I see the party is breaking up."

"Oh yes, Gene." He glanced at Susan. "Jewel told me you were going to help Susan solve a little problem. Were you able to help her?"

"I think we're making a great headway to solving it." He smiled at her "Would you agree, Susan?"

"Oh yes, I do." She walked through the doorway, turning back toward her father to say, "Reverend Scott has solved my biggest problem and in a few weeks—maybe days—I shall be the happiest girl in the entire world." She winked at Scott. "Goodnight."

"Goodnight, Susan." He smiled broadly and waved over his shoulder at Owen Andrews. "Sleep well, Owen. Be talking to you."

"But . . . but, what did you mean? I don't understand." Owen watched Scott climb into his car laughing and drive away.

As Gene Scott drove toward the parsonage he said smiling, "Someway, somehow, I am going to take my girl and get hitched, and there will be no one, Jobi or Pogo, tagging along to mess up our honeymoon!"

Chapter 7

Reverend Gene Scott looked up from his report he was trying to finish for the church meeting. His attention had been drawn to the loud thunder that seem to rock the church office's foundation. In the distance he heard a siren and said a quick prayer for the person who may have gotten hurt.

He resumed his report, but only briefly, for a bright flash of lighting dimmed the desk light. It was followed by an even louder clash of thunder. There was a sudden burst of rain; it fell in torrents as it beat up against the office window.

The sound of another siren drove him to his feet. Something felt wrong as his eyes fell on the desk clock. He could hear the church secretary's phone suddenly ringing. He walked over and looked out the window. The rain was pelting down so heavily he could not make out the parking lot just outside the window.

The sound of quick footsteps pulled his eyes toward the door as it opened and Mrs. Barber, the church secretary stared inside, eyes wide with concern.

"What is it Beverly?" he tried to keep calm, but his heart was pounding in his chest.

"It is Memorial Hospital, Reverend Scott." her voice trembled. "They need to speak with you, sir."

Nervously he lifted the receiver up to his ear "This is Reverend Scott."

"Reverend, we need you to come to the emergency room at Memorial just as soon as you can. There has been a terrible accident, please hurry. We are so sorry." The phone went dead.

Gene stared at the phone still in his hand. Sweat was running down his face as he grabbed his car keys off the desk and raced out the door.

He could not remember driving to the hospital and he felt as though he was running in the emergency room in slow motion. Someone stopped him and took him inside a room where three beds were lined next to each other. The bodies in the beds were covered with white sheets.

"I'm so sorry, Reverend. Your wife's car was completely mashed. There are no survivors."

"What . . . are you saying?" Gene felt the room spinning "Are you saying Faye and the kids are. . .?"

"All dead, I'm . . . terribly sorry."

Gene Scott sat up in bed, dripping with sweat and tears. It had been a dream, a very horrible dream. He managed to slide, to·the side of the bed.

His thoughts difted back to the party at the Andrews the previous night and Jewel wanting to know how he remained a bachelor all his life. He had not told Susan about Faye and his children. He had pushed them inside until last night when he revealed he had been married and told them about the tragic accident that took his family from him.

His fingers brushed through his hair as he stood up and walked to the bathroom. He looked at himself in the mirror.

"I guess I should be ashame for not thinking about Faye or the kids since I left for the mission to Africa. My thoughts have been consumed with Susan."

He closed his eyes a vision of her perfect face coming into his mind.

"Dear God, you know how much I love Susan. Is it so wrong for her to take up the best part of me? Second to you, Lord, there is no one I love more than her. I don't need to tell you how much I cared for Faye and how much I loved and adored Tracy and Billy."

Gene Scott finished getting dressed and felt some what better after talking it out with God. He walked over and looked out the window. The first rays of daylight were bringing out Edna's rose garden below.

"Roses?" He walked quickly from his room and peeked inside of David's. Both young men were fast asleep. Gene walked and tugged lightly on Pogo's arm.

"Hey buddy, wake up. I need to talk to you."

"It's early Scott. Is anything wrong?" Pogo tried to open his sleepy eyes.

"Nothing bad, pal. I just need to ask you a question," Scott whispered. "Meet me in the kitchen. I'll go start the coffee if Edna is not up yet."

Pogo sat up and yawned. "Be down in ten minutes."

"Grab a cup and sit down Buddy." Gene pulled out a chair next to him and waited for Pogo to get settled down. "The roses, Pogo? Is anyone putting roses on Faye and the kids' graves?"

"Oh crap! I forgot to tell you, didn't I?" Pogo looked over sheepishly. "Why did you wait so long to ask me?"

"My, mind has been preoccupied." Gene rolled his eyes up. With a certain girl."

"Yeh, I can see that, Scott." Pogo winked and took a sip of coffee. "Hazel Purit."

"What about Hazel Purit?" Gene Scott frowned at his young friend.

"That's who is taking care of the graves for you. Her and the other women in her group from church." Pogo laughed. "You know how they all admire you Scott."

"At least those ladies know how to work in flowers." Scott poured himself another cup of coffee. "Remind me to send them a thank you card."

"They will probably frame it." Pogo teased and stood up.

"Hey pal, where are you going?" Gene looked up.

"I thought I would fix us some breakfast, I'm starved." Pogo started to walk away and Scott pulled him down in his chair.

"Hey, what gives?"

Look, Pogo, when you are staying with the world's greatest cook, you wait patiently for her to come down and fix breakfast."

"Gene, Pogo?" Edna walked into the kitchen smiling. "Did I hear 'breakfast?'"

"We would love some of your wonderful breakfast; wouldn't we, Pogo?" Gene put an arm around his quiet friend.

"Is anything wrong, Pogo?" Edna put her apron on and looked from Pogo to Gene.

"Gosh no, Edna. You are the best." Pogo forced a smile. "I'm still learning."

"Oh, I get it." She threw Pogo an apron. "Put that on and come help me. I will teach you just how simple making breakfast can be."

Pogo jumped up laughing as he looked back at his big friend "What are we doing today Scott?"

"Going shopping." He smiled at the two cooks, who suddenly turned to stare at him. "Nothing big. I just have an item I need to pick up, that's all."

"Boy, you had me going there for a while Scott." Pogo let out his breath "We are going to the hardware store or auto department! Right?"

"Neither one pal, but you're close." Gene smiled at the plate of bacon and eggs set down in front of him. "Let's eat then we can go shopping."

Susan had gotten up early, too excited to sleep after Gene had told her he would be calling her to go down for a marriage license. Sitting at her desk, she reached inside her locked drawer and pulled out her art diary. Being born a gifted artist, she could draw or paint the close image of a person. She had been drawing her memories with Gene Scott ever since she returned from Africa. She found it helped her when she was not in his presence.

Opening it to the first drawing, she sighed softly. It was her first glimps of the man she gave her heart to and longed to spend the rest of her life with.

"I will never forget looking into your eyes for the first time. You were so handsome, you took my breath away. Something inside me changed the moment we looked into each other's eyes. I knew I loved you."

Standing on the deck of the big ocean liner with her brother Jobi, saying goodbye to their parents as they traveled to spend some time with their grandfather in Africa, she had turned to see Reverend Gene Scott for the first time.

Smiling, remembering all their words, looks they had shared with each other on their four-day voyage, Susan turned each page over lovingly. The first sight of him on the first morning in the dining room, him playing shuffle board, him sitting next to her at the pool where Jobi introduced them. From his sermon in the open air church service that led the brother and sister to follow him into the jungle to help out with his mission and all the way through how close he had come to kissing her in the moonlight. Getting to the back of the diary, she smiled at the photos they had taken on the ship. Her heart was filled with butterflies just looking at the face she loved so much. Lifting it to her lips, she kissed it.

A sudden knock came on her bedroom door. She quickly slid her precious drawings and photos back inside her desk drawer and locked it.

"Yes, who is it?" she stood up and made her way over to the door.

"It's your mother, Susan dear," Shirley Andrews spoke softly. "May I come in?"

Susan opened her door and smiled at her mother "You're up early, Mom."

"I see you're dressed already. Got plans today, dear?" Shirley held onto some brochures.

"Sorta, nothing final yet, Mom." Susan noticed the brochures "Is that for me?"

Shirley held them out. "Yes dear. They are loaded with information to some of the colleges you were interested in."

"College?" Susan had not given school any of her thoughts. The last thing she wanted was to go off to some college away from Gene. "Mom, I'm not sure I want—"

Her mother cut her off. "Now Susan, dear, I know your father and I said you would not have to move away again—and please know this will always be your home—but college is something you have been working for. Both Yale and Princeton have accepted you, Susan!"

"Mom, my priorities have changed. I want to remain in TarSa!" Susan grew excited "Yale or Princeton don't interest me anymore."

"But Susan dear, you are such a brilliant student, your grades were always perfect, all A's, darling." Susan's mother touched her daughter's face lightly "You were so excited about the art courses offered at both these prestigious universties. What has changed your mind, dear?"

"The size of a school does not make it always the best one mom, at least not for me. There are far better art schools, perhaps the college right here in TarSa."

Shirley laughed and handed Susan the bottom brochure. "Here darling, TarSa College! I must admit your father and I was hoping you might choose to remain on the island. Since there are not many dorms on campus most students remain at home and drive to school each morning."

Susan opened the small book showing a beautiful building surrounded by huge old oaks.

"Isn't it lovely dear? Much warmer than a huge university." Shirley reached her arms around her daughter and gave her a loving hug "Mildred will have breakfast ready soon. See you in the morning room."

"I will be down soon." Susan watched her mother leave and her brother slip in behind her looking down. "What gives with you Jobi?" She saw the paper in his hand. "Let me guess, Mom has spoiled your morning too. News about good old TarSa School, right?"

"Yeh, what did she give you?" He started to flop down onto her freshly made bed.

"Oh no you don't, little brother. I just made that bed!" Susan pulled his arm toward the door. "I got out of going to Yale or Princeton, but to satisfy mom I told her I would prefer going to TarSa College." Susan made a face. "At least we won't have to move anymore and I will be able to run off with Gene, then think of some reason to delay college."

"Susan! Jobi!" the distinctive voice of Mildreld called from the foot of the stairs. "Come down and eat your breakfast for it gets cold on you!"

"Breakfast?" both Andrew siblings made a face at each other then laughed.

Chapter 8

"Susan, I thought if you and Jobi did not have any plans today, we could visit both your schools." Shirley smiled over her coffee. "Your dad says he might be able to take a few hours to go along with us."

"That is very sweet, Mom, but could we plan that for another day?" Susan patted her brother's hair. "I promised Jobi I would take him shopping for some school clothes."

"Shopping?" Jobi looked up at his sister, bewildered. Then saw he had his mother and aunts' attention. "Oh yeh! Shopping! There are some really neat shoes I've had my eyes on."

"Shopping sounds like a splended ideal kids!" Jewel smiled at Shirley's sister. "What do you say, Joanie, care to tag along with the kids?"

Susan and Jobi looked at one another for a way out of this one.

"If we wouldn' t be interfering with the children's plans." Joan looked at Shirley.

"I'm sure Susan and Jobi would love to have you join them, is that not right children?" Shirley stood up smiling "You can take my car Susan dear. Your little car is much to small for all of you."

"You can say that again!" Jobi frowned at his sister. "What if Jewel and Joan want to shop longer than we do?"

"We could spit up, darling, when we get to the shops." Jewel patted Jobi's cheek "We have no reason to shop in the kids and teens department. You children will not be bothered with us at all."

"Aunt Jewel, I am not a child and I wish everyone would stop referring to me as one!" Susan stood up to leave "If you are going with me you had better move it!" Susan winked at her brother "I am going to roll wheels!"

"Hey Scott, these shops are all dress or shoe shops!"

Pogo stared at his big friend as they made their way down the row of shops. Pogo noticed a bright blue shirt in one of the men's store windows and stopped. "Check that out! I think I would look pretty cool in that!"

"You are not a shopper, remember pal." Scott continued until he stopped in front of a jewelry shop. "Here we are."

Pogo looked in for a minute then it dawned on him why his friend had chosen this particuiar store. "Scott, you son of a gun" Pogo teased. "You are here to get a ring for Susan, aren't you?"

"Now look, Pogo, you can not tell a single soul about this buy." Gene Scott took hold of his young friend's shoulders "It could get back to the wrong person."

"My lips are sealed, Scott." Pogo smiled slyly. "Are you going to get her an engagement ring?"

"Diamonds on my salary?" Scott punched his arm lightly. "I think my girl would be happy with a nice gold wedding band to seal our marriage."

"I thought all girls liked diamonds, Scott." Pogo followed behind his best friend. "You know, diamonds are a girl's best friend."

"Look pal, I'll 'best friend' you if you don't stop quoting from movies!" Gene looked over the big selection of gold wedding bands. He turned to Pogo and winked. "Besides, why would my little Susan want a silly shiny expensive rock when she has this rare gem of a man?"

"Couldn't she have both, Scott?" Pogo avoided looking at his friend as he gazed over the shiny diamonds lining the glassed-in case. "She gets a 'girl's best friend' diamond plus the gem she has been digging for and loosening him from his secure bachelor life."

"What the shit does that mean, digging and loosening me?" Scott nodded to the clerk for help. "Just because I was afraid of my own feelings for a seventeen-year-old girl?"

"Lighten up, pal. I only meant making the poor thing wait so long to know how you felt about her, that's all." Pogo put some chewing gum in his mouth. "I just look up to you, man. It's not like you to be afraid of a woman."

"Listen, Pogo, I am going to say this one time! You and David can stop discussing my love life with each other! I am not afraid of Susan or any woman, get it?" Gene Scott smiled at the nervous clerk who had heard the last part of their conversation.

"How did you know it was David that told me?" Pogo had not noticed the clerk until he saw Gene smiling. He looked around and offered his own shaky grin. "Hi there, do you have any cheap diamonds?"

"Cheap diamonds?" His eyebrow went up. "I beg your pardon?"

"Please forgive my young, inexperienced friend, sir. This is his first time inside of a beautiful jewelry shop." Gene's smile was brilliant. "I am looking at these two matching wedding bands. Would they be something you recommend for me·and my very dainty fiancée?"

"You, sir, have excellent judgment." The clerk smiled at the tall, handsome man. "The gentleman's ring is beefy enough for your big hands and the lady's gold band can be made to fit a small beautiful hand, just as you described your fiancee." The clerk pulled the rings·out and laid the boxes on the counter. "You may try the man's, sir, and if you know your lady's size I can get it sized in an hour." He smiled broadly.

"She wears a size 6 on her perfect finger." Gene winked at Pogo as he showed him the flawless fit on his finger.

"Scott, how did you guess size 6? What if you go to put it on her perfect finger and it doesn't fit?" Pogo's eyes were wide in wonder.

"It will, pal, trust me." Gene laughed. "I asked Mildred."

"Mildred?" Pogo watched the clerk take the ring to have it measured for size. "Scott, Mildred may be a house keeper-slash-cook, but that does not mean you can trust her with your secret!"

"Trust me, buddy, I know what I'm doing here."

"But Scott, Mildred is a woman. Women cannot keep a secret no matter how much you trust them!" Pogo watched as the clerk came out of the back room carrying the ring for Susan. "Scott, woman are born to gossip, she will blab her big mouth and the gig is over!"

"Will you relax, I've got this covered!" Gene smiled at the clerk as he rang up the two rings. "You can put this little ring on that bill as well." He smiled at Pogo who was looking at him with dismay.

"They are sweet little pinky rings. Good buy too." he rang up the sale price "This is your lady's birthday, sir?"

Pogo looked even more perplexed as Scott spoke to the sales clerk.

"It will be tomorrow. I noticed my gal likes rings on her little finger." He looked at his friend. "I thought she would love this with her birthstone on it, don't you buddy?"

"Birthday? Oh I get it! You told Mildred you were getting her a ring for her birthday!" Pogo blew out his frustrations, then he noticed the clerk watching him closely. "Was it a 6?"

"I beg your parton young man?" He looked confused.

"The wedding band, does it need to be sized?" Pogo shrugged his shoulders at Gene.

"The band, yes, it is a size 6." He handed the preacher the bill. "I thought you were referring to the wee ring."

Scott pulled out his checkbook and wrote out the check as he shook his head. After paying his bill, the clerk handed him the fancy bag containing the three rings. Gene Scott thanked the clerk and turned to leave when he spotted Susan, Jobi and her two men-chasing aunts getting out of Shirley Andrew's BMW.

"Damn! I can't let Susan see me coming out of here, not with those two aunts of hers! They might get the wrong impression, think I'm shopping for one of them!"

"What are we going to do? Buy something else in here?" Pogo smiled to himself "Like an engagement ring?"

"Pogo, just pretend you found something you're interested in." Gene got down and pretended to be looking inside the glass case, afraid that someone outside might spot him. He reached up and pulled Pogo down next to him. "Get down here before they see you!"

"But I saw a really cool watch up there I was checking out." He started to get up when Scott yanked him back down. "Hey, you wanted me to check out the merchandise, didn't you?"

"Pretend, Pogo, I want you to pretend you are checking out the merchandise!" Scott gritted his teeth "Start pretending down here!"

"Do you fellows see something else you would like to purchase?" The salesclerk had made his way over to the odd-looking pair.

Pogo jumped up and pointed at the watch he had spotted earlier. "Yeh, how much for this watch?" he smiled at his big friend who was staring back angrily.

"It is fifty dollars, sir." The clerk checked the tag and looked from the window "But if you are going to buy it, please hurry, there are three ladies and a young boy about to come in the shop."

Gene closed his eyes as he stood up and crammed the fancy bag inside his jacket pocket. "He will take the watch. After you ring it up can you wrap it. It's a present." He watched the clerk go to the cash register then whispered to Pogo, "You have been spotted pal! We have been busted. Let me do the talking if you want to be able to eat your supper today."

Scott walked over quickly and pulled out cash to pay the bill.

"Just forget the giftwrap, we are supposed to meet those ladies and kid you spotted." Gene grabbed the bag, smiling at the confused clerk "If any of those ladies come in here, don't tell them about the rings. It's a surprise."

"Yes, I understand, sir. Your secret is safe with me." He watched Scott move swiftly toward the younger man, grab his arm and dash out the shop door.

Chapter 9

The group of four jumped back out of the way when Gene and Pogo pushed open the door and walked out.

"Reverend Scott, Funny finding you shopping!" Susan teased. "I thought shopping wasn't part of your favorite things to do."

"Just when it's necessary, Susan." He winked at her "My pal Pogo needed a new watch after he accidently drove over his in the driveway."

"How did it get on the driveway in the first place Pogo?" Jobi looked at the fancy bag clutched in Pogo's hand.

"Probably when I was washing Gene's dirty car." Pogo peeked inside the bag and saw the box. "Hey Scott, that clerk forgot to wrap it!"

"Why on earth would he wrap it if it wasn't a gift?" Jewel laughed.

Gene frowned at his young friend then forced a laugh "It is a gift, Jewel, an early birthday present for the boy. Pogo's never grown up when it comes to gifts. He loves to open presents, but time did not allow for wrapping when I spotted you lovely ladies."

"Christmas isn't very far away, Pogo dear. Maybe Gene will give you an extra present to make up for your birthday gift." Joan smiled warmly up at the handsome minister.

"Yeh Scott, two gifts, maybe three or four." Pogo pulled the box out.

"Maybe a sock filled with coal, buddy, if you keep pushing my buttons!" Scott feigned a smile at Joan, then turned to Susan. "What are you out shopping for Susan?"

"School clothes, Reverend Scott." She made a face." Jobi and I were reminded by my mom this morning that both school and college start in a few weeks."

"Our Susan is a very smart girl, Gene. A straight A student." Jewel patted her niece's head "She has been excepted in both Yale and Princeton. Is that not wonderful news?"

Gene looked down at Susan, questions filling his blue eyes. "Susan is a very remarkable young woman, Jewel." He took Susan's hand lovingly. "Which university did you choose Susan?"

Her eyes looked deep into his. "I chose neither, Reverend Scott.

I will be attending TarSa College this fall."

A look of relief fell on his face "I hear TarSa is a wonderful college."

"Hey Pogo, off of the school topic, can I see that new watch?" Jobi wanted to change the subject.

"Sure kid." Pogo opened the box and smiled to himself. It looked even better in the sunlight. "Isn't it fine?"

"That is one cool watch, Pogo!" Jobi stared with wide eyes. "I may let mom buy me one!"

"No luck, kid. This was the last one." Pogo closed the lid and looked at Susan's aunts. "What are you ladies shopping for, bargains?"

"I came along just to check out the latest fashions. I won't be buying anything." Jewel smiled at Gene.

"Yes, we only intend to browse around in a few shops while.the children—" Her eyes fell on Susan's frown. "While Susan and Jobi shop for back to school clothes." Joan rolled her eyes toward Gene.

"Aunt Jewel, Aunt·Joan, when you both finish buying everything that draws your eye, we will need to say a silent prayer to get everything to fit inside Mom's trunk." Susan tried to hold in her laughter from the looks both women were given her.

Jewel glanced down at her watch then up at the preacher. "Gene darling, I know it's only eleven o'clock, but my very small breakfast—" she frowned at the Andrew siblings. "Is about to give out and I thought how lovely it would be to invite you to lunch, my treat."

"Now isn't that a coincidence." Susan moved next to the man she loved. "I was just thinking what a grand idea it would be if I could treat you to lunch."

Gene smiled down into her eyes then glanced over to Jewel.

"Ladies, that is a very sweet offer, but I find it impossible to accept either one of you. To choose one I would hurt the other one's feelings."

"Then let me give you a solution, Gene dearest." Joan looped her arm in his. "I will treat you to lunch."

"You? I ask first! Of all the nerve!" Jewel glared at Shirley's sister.

"Well, he's my friend! I have known him the longest!" Susan put her hands on her hips. "Just because you were brazen enough to ask my friend first doesn't give you any rights!"

"Frankly, I think I should be the one to treat Gene!" Joan spoke.

"You both are acting like spoiled children." She laughed sarcastically "Ha! Susan is a spoiled child! Children, children, children!"

"Ladies, ladies, there's no need to get so upset over this," Scott laughed "I cannot possibly choose among you. I would gladly take all of us out for lunch but I am running a bit low on funds at the moment."

"I say we go dutch." Susan gave Gene an "I'm sorry" look. "What do you all say to that? I will get Jobi's and mine."

"Sounds like a great solution, Susan." Gene winked at her, then turned to Pogo. "I will get yours, buddy. How 'bout that little sandwich cafe across the street?"

"I've heard the food is very good, Reverend Scott and the outdoor seating looks very popular." Susan noticed several customers seated under the vine-covered trellis. "Oh, in the far corner is a table for six. If we hurry we can sit together."

"If it gets taken, I'm sitting next to Gene at one table." Jewel tried to get next to Scott, but he had grabbed Susan's hand and started to walk swiftly across the street straight toward the round table in the corner.

The server smiled at the handsome man and said, "Welcome to the Trellis. You are in luck today. This table isn't reserved until twelve."

Susan tried hard to iqnore the flirty waitress as she sat down on the back side, Jobi next to her. Jewel hurried over while the woman was handing Scott the menus and sat down next to Susan. Joan left an empty chair for the good reverend and motioned for Pogo to sit beside of her and Jobi.

As Gene looked over the situation, Susan punched her brother's leg. Jobi saw what had his sister upset, so he pushed his chair back and stood. "Reverend Scott, would you mind sitting next to Susan, The sun is shining down low and it will be in my eyes before my food arrives? You're tall, so it won't hit you in the eyes."

"Sure thing, little buddy."

Gene Scott winked at him and sat between Susan and Pogo. Sliding his hand under the table, he took hold of her hand. Susan smiled and looked into his eyes, unspoken words of love between them.

Jewel broke the silence. "I cannot decide which one of these decadent entrees I want. They all sound so tempting and delicious." She glanced at Gene with flirting eyes.

"Don't you think they look tempting, Gene?"

"Tempting and delicious!" He squeezed Susan's hand as he thought to himself, "That is my little sexy Susan: tempting   and delicious."

"Order everything on the menu, Aunt Jewel." Jobi kept his eyes on his menu as he spoke. With your appetite, you can put it away no time flat."

Susan laughed softly as she tried to·speak. "I think the blackened chicken sandwich is my choice, with a nice glass of red wine."

Everyone eventually placed their orders. After small conversation the meal was finished. Gene patted Susan's knee and stood.

"If you would excuse me, I need to visit the john."

"I'll walk with you, Gene." Jewel rose, smiling at Susan. "I need to pay the ladies room a visit as well."

She took his arm and pulled him inside the cafe. She stopped him just outside the restrooms.

"Gene, tell me the truth. I think you were shopping for ·something besides that watch for Pogo."

"What else would I have been looking for, Jewel?" he asked casually, knowing what she was hinting at.

"An engagement ring, silly." She touched his hand lightly. "We are not getting any younger."

"Jewel, I must be perfectly honest with you." Scott looked around and saw they were alone in the dark hallway "I met someone this summer. I am very interested in her. As for you, I hardly know you, so I think it's for the best that you look elseware for a mate Jewel. I"m not that man."

"I won't give up on you that quickly Gene." She smiled seductively into his eyes. "I think we would make a lovely couple."

She went slowly into the ladies room while Gene rushed inside to finish quickly before she returned.·He met Pogo at the men's room and grabbed his arm.

"Is Joan still out at the table?"

"She accompanied me to go to the ladies' room." He looked at his friend. "Susan and Jobi are waiting with everyone's bills."

"Listen, pal, I'm going to grab Susan and take off before those man-chasing women come out from primping." He pulled out some money. "Pay our bill and Susan's. Tell those flirts I have taken Susan to help me pick out a gift for someone, got it?"

"Got it. Just go!" Pogo laughed. "Man, I wouldn't know how to feel with three women chasing after me."

"Trust me, pal, it can be hell!" Scott patted his shoulder. "Wait for me, buddy. I'll be back after I've had some time with my girl!"

Gene rushed outside and grabbed Susan's hand then turned to Jobi. "Jobi, I'm going to steal your sister away for a little while. Pogo has the money for both our bills. Stay with him until I return. He can fill you in if those two aunts are not around."

"Better run then. I see Pogo and Jewel coming through the cafe!" Jobi's eyes were big as he watched Pogo trying to stall for time. "Just take sis and run!"

Gene and Susan took off down the sidewalk. They went to the far side of the park to be free of foot traffic. He looked around to make sure they were alone, then pulled her into his strong arms and kissed her with passion.

"Mumm" Susan smiled into his eyes. "I am glad I did not order dessert, this is far sweeter."

"I've been wanting to kissed those gorgeous, luscious lips from the moment I stepped outside that shop." He gently rubbed her neck. "God, I love you Susan Andrews."

"Reverend Gene Scott, I love you, my darling, handsome man." She wrapped her arms around his neck. "Care to kiss those 'gorgous luscious lips' again. They belong to you."

He smiled down at her lips "Gladly will I kiss you, darling." Again their lips met, this time in a firey kiss. They were lost in their embrace for a minute until they heard someone clear his throat.

Susan and Gene turned quickly to see who had caught them kissing. An elderly man had stopped his stroll to watch the two love birds.

"Ah, young love, how beautiful." His smile was warm and genuine. "To be young and in love again." He tilted his cane in approval, then winked at Scott. "Don't let me disturb your romance. I shall resume my walk and leave you to it." he walked away whistling.

Gene laughed out "Boy, he was a catbird!" He nodded toward a park bench. "Better watch our moves out here, little darling. The next person could be someone who knows us."

"You are right, it was too close for comfort," Susan said, still holding Gene's hand. "That old gentleman was so sweet and precious. He never saw you as the older man and me the younger woman. Just two people in love."

"I got something for you." he reached inside his pocket and

pulled out the fancy bag. "Call it an early birthday present." He handed her the small box from the bag.

She smiled as she opened it and saw the pinky ring with her birthstone. "Oh Gene, it is darling, I love it." She slid it on her small finger.

"You're not disappointed it wasn't an engagement ring?" he watched her reaction closely.

"Of course not, Gene. I've got the most precious stone I could ever wish for, my wonderful darling." She looked back down at her gift from Scott, a beautiful smile stretched across her face.

"There is something you need to know. But don't fly off the deep end." He could see her eyes cloud over as she looked up "When your aunt escorted me to the restrooms, she asked if I had bought an engagement ring."

"The very nerve! Did she assume you were getting her an engagement ring?" Susan practically jumped out of the seat.

"Susan, calm down, darling." He took her hands in his. "She said we, meaning she and I, were not get any younger, and she thought that we would make a beautiful couple." He touched her lips before she could speak. "I told Jewel I had met someone this summer and that I was very interested in her. I told your aunt I hardly knew her and thought it best that she look elseware for a mate." Gene looked into Susan's eyes. "I said, 'I'm not your man!' Susan, you know my heart belongs to you and only you. I am your man, Susan, now and for always!"

"Knowing Aunt Jewel she won't give up that easy." Susan hugged him.

"But she is wasting her time, and she is not as young as she thinks—her own words!"

Susan admired her ring one more time then slipped the empty box inside her purse. Her eyes fell on the fancy bag still clutched in Gene's hand. "I was wondering when my girl was going to notice I hadn't put the bag away." His eyes twinkled with laughter. "There is yet another surprise inside this little bag that might make you even happier."

"Tell me please, Gene!" She sat up, her face alight in total joy. "May I see the surprise now?"

"You will see it later, when I slip it on your beautiful hand." He carefully slipped the package back in his jacket.

"A wedding band!" She hugged him. "Oh gee, I need to shop for yours darling." She lifted up his hand. "What size do you wear?"

"The one inside this bag fits perfect and it is exactly my size." He pulled her into his arms. "I wanted our symbols of love to match. I can tell you this much, they are·gold, a paycheck perfect and the never-ending circle describes our love for one another, never ending, for all my tomorrows remember?"

"Gene? You spent all your paycheck on those beautiful rings?" Susan had tears in her eyes. "Let me help you, sweetheart. Let me pay for yours!"

"Nothing doing, young lady. Now that we are getting married everything I have will be yours. Besides, I'm not without money, little darling. I have a savings account and a checking account that's not too shabby."

"I love you, Reverend Scott!" She hugged him again then sat back and smiled. "How did you know my ring size?"

"Mildred, that's how." He held up his hand to stop her from speaking. "And before you start worring about Mildred knowing our secret, I told her I wanted to give you some kind of birthstone ring for your birthday. You are marring a clever man, Susan. Mildred was more than happy to tell me your size."

She laughed softly. "Then tell me, my clever husband-to-be, what will my aunts think about you wisking me away?"

"Got that covered, little darling." He winked at her. "They think I borrowed you for a while to help me pick out a gift for someone."

"I see." She looked up at him as if she had him trapped. "So Mr. Clever Scott, where is this gift we went to find?"

"On your beautiful finger. Ha ha, thought you had me, Susan." He helped her up to start back to the village. "I will tell those man-chasers I wanted to surprise you with an early birthday present. They will buy it knowing what good friends we are."

"I'm sure your winning smile will win them over, Gene darling." She squeezed him, strong and lovingly. "I know it melts my heart."

"If I hadn't spot our group ahead, I would lay a big kiss on those lips of yours." He touched her lips tenderly. "I will have to wait for that kiss later."

"Not too much later, I hope." She noticed Joan look their way. "We have been spotted. When can I see you again, Gene?"

"Hopefully tomorrow for your birthday, darling. I've promise John I would help him with a church project tonight." He heard a woman's voice call his name and saw Joan Rogers waving them over. "I will be making a fast get away when we cross the street."

"That will leave me with mixed emotions, Gene." Her eyes were on the stoplight that held them on the opposite side of the street from her flirty aunts. "I will be extremely sad to see you go, but overjoyed you won't be here for those two to make over my man!"

The light changed and they began walking across.

"Just remember that, darling. I am your man, for all time!" He stopped speaking and looked at the packages in Jewel and Joan's hands.

"Ladies, I see you have been busy shopping."

Jewel looked down at the two packages in each hand. "Oh these two buys." She tried to laugh "FiAnnes Ladies Shop, an 80% off sale, it was too good to pass up, right Joanie?"

Joan pulled her three bags up next to her chest, trying to minimize their large size. "Oh yes Gene, top name designers rarely ever sale this low."

"How about all those other packages Jobi and I took to Shirley's car to store in the trunk so you could move more freely shopping? Were they on sale too?" Pogo gave the two aunts a big smile.

"Yeh Aunt Jewel and Aunt Joan! We had to take two trips to carry them all!" Jobi blew out like he was out of breath. "Wooh, what a load! Better not buy many college thing, sis. We're running out of trunk space."

Susan laughed at her aunt's shock expression. She winked at Pogo for bringing up the touchy subject.

"I promise I will restrain myself from buying everything I like." Susan tried to keep a straight face.

Jewel spoke up as she looked from Susan to Gene. "It would appear we are better at shopping than you Susan."

"I beg you pardon, Aunt Jewel. What is that supposed to mean?" Susan locked eyes with her outspoken aunt."

"I am merely saying, if Gene went looking for a gift, you, my dear, were of no help." She looked to be quite proud of herself. "Don't look .so innocent, sweetie. I've got eyes and I can see neither you or Gene is holding any bag. No bag, no gift!"

"Now that you mention it, Joanie, you are very correct!" Jewel stopped, looking embarrassed, and patted Shirley's sister's hand. "Little Susan was no help whatsoever, Gene darling. Let me go with you and pick out that perfect gift."

"That is a kind offer Jewel but the gift has been purchased and the receiver is very please with it." Gene smiled at Susan. "Isn't she?"

"She certainly is!" She caught her aunts by surprise. "If you must know, there is no bag because I wore the gift out of the shop!" She smiled triumphantly. "Reverend Scott bought me an early birthday present, to a dear friend from a dear friend." she held out her hand and the small stone shone brightly in the sunshine.

"Oh it's—" Pogo caught Scott's angry glare. "It is absolutely breathtaking! It almost left me speechless!" He feigned a laugh.

"You should have bought it in here where you purchase the kid's watch." Joan tried not to laugh at the small stone, although it was very nearly perfect on Susan's little finger. "You are a good friend, Gene. I am sure our sweet Susan will cherish it forever. I know I certainly would."

"I think it's adorable Gene, perfect for a teenager." Jewel feigned a smile at Susan. "Even I would love to receive one of those precious pinkies."

"You don't say. You would never guess based on those rocks both of you are wearing." Scott's smile was innocent with a hint of mischief.

"Fake! This is just a good copy of the real deal, Gene." Jewel tried to smile normally. "I would never waste money on real gems."

"Aunt Jewel, didn't dad give that ring to you last year for Christmas?" Susan asked innocently.

"It sure looks like the same ring, sis!" Jobi smiled at his sister "I remember mom telling dad he spent far too much money on that ruby."

Jewel glared at the Andrew siblings. "Well maybe Owen bought me the real thing, but you would never find me wasting good money on costly jewelry!"

"Oh, Reverend Scott, I'm so glad I spotted you." The Diamond Gallery's clerk stepped outside his shop waving a piece of paper. "You forgot your receit for the young man's watch." He handed it to Gene "I hope you did not mind me addressing you by your name, sir, but it was on your check."

"Gene, please forgive me but how did you write that check so quickly after you jumped up and raced over to the counter?" Jewel could tell by everyones' eyes on Scott that they too wanted to know how he managed it.

"Well frankly, at first I thought he and the young man were hiding from you lovely ladies when the the boy hopped up and ask about the watch." The clerk turned his attenting on Jewel. "Oh, Miss Andrews? Among all this confusion I almost did not recogize you my dear."

97

"That is quiet understandable, Mr. Monroe." She laughed nervously from the saleman's acknowledgement of her. "So, what you are saying is Gene stooped down behind the counter to write the check?" She wanted to divert the attention from herself.

"The check? You see Reverend Scott—"

Gene took a tight grip of his shoulder and the clerk anxiously remembered he had a secret to keep. "A—yes, the check. It would appear the good reverend had everything written out on his check except the amount!" He looked hopefully in Scott's eyes, receiving a wink of approval.

"Jewel, it appears you know Mr. Monroe, I believe?" Scott's eyes twinkled with mischief. "I think you might have told us a wee little fib just now about expensive gems."

"I can assure you, Reverend Scott, if Miss Andrews gave you any advice on the perfect gem—ruby, emerald, diamond, even silver, gold, and platinum—you'd better take it." The clerk smiled at red-faced Jewel. "My dear, we have just received a new shippment of perfect stones! Do come in and check out everything!" His eyes lit up, then his attention turned to each woman, wondering which was the lucky one to receive the gold band from the preacher.

Gene watched him closely as he turned smiling. "It could not have been easy," the clerk thought. He winked. "My congratulations to your happiness." He turned to go back inside his shop. "Coming, Miss Andrews?"

Her eyes were on Gene Scott. "Later Mr. Monroe, I may come back to browse." She heard the shop door close, then stepped closer to the handsome preacher. "Tell us, Gene, why was Mr. Monroe congratulating you?"

"I'll tell her, Reverend Scott." Susan caught Gene by surprise. "He just received a big raise in his pay for doing such an excellent job on his missions!" she took his arm and squeezed it in a friendly manner. "That's why he wanted to buy Poge and me gifts. I'm so proud of you, Reverend Scott. You are the best!"

"And thoughtful, that's Scott!" Pogo joined in on the farce as he patted Scott's back. "Yeh, one terrific guy!"

"Let's not get carried away here." Scott looked down at his watch, then his eyes fell on Susan, "I will leave the shopping to you now. I've got to run."

Jewel grabbed his arm as Susan lifted her eyebrow angrily.

"Gene, dear, I was hoping we might go out somewhere tonight for dinner or a movie?"

"Aunt Jewel, I asked Reverend Scott earlier if he could come over for dinner tonight with the family, but he has got obligations at church."

"Jewel, Susan is right." Gene motioned to Pogo. "In fact, I'll be tied up all week. Perhaps I can have dinner at the Andrews next week."

"Then I suppose we must wait." Jewel sighed.

"See you later, Reverend Scott." Susan's eyes were fiery with passion, and Gene's eyes returned it.

"You bet, Susan." He grabbed Pogo and walked quickly away before the other two women could speak and distract his last thoughts from the girl he loved.

Chapter 10

Gene Scott walked lazily in the kitchen and slipped up behind Edna. He grabbed her from behind and she jumped, letting out a little yip.

"Oh Gene!" She slapped his arm. "You big tease! Sit down and I will fix you a plate."

"Sounds fair enough!" he laughed and pulled out a chair "Where's John?"

"The last time I saw him he was fast asleep in bed." She started scooping scrambled eggs into Scott's plate "How many do you want?"

"Just one. Susan." He smiled shyly.

"Oh Gene, really!" She slapped his shoulder. "Eggs, how many?"

"Oh, about three." He poured himself a cup of coffee and smiled down at the scrambled eggs. "How do you know there are three eggs there Edna?"

"If you have been a cook for as long as me, Gene Scott, you would not need to ask." She sat down next to him laughing.

John Crain walked into the kitchen yawning.

"A-ha! Caught you! I knew I would catch you two alone, sooner or later." He laughed as he sat down and winked at Edna. "Alright, Gene, confess! What have you been doing with my wife?"

"John, my friend, I have been making passes to her over the scrambled eggs." He pushed the empty plate away and stretched. "I believe I have got a painting job waiting for my attention."

"Yes, and remember, it is the three classrooms in the left wing. I painted the three across the hall last week. So if yours looks as good as mine, it will be expertly done." John smiled as he took a big sip of coffee.

"John, old boy. I will make your job look like some child did it." Gene stood and patted his friend's back. "Gotta go and find that Pogo. He said he would give me a hand."

"He and David had breakfast right before you came in, Gene. I think I heard them say something about going for a swim." Edna cleared the dirty dishes from the table.

"Swim his ass!" Scott walked over to the door "He knows better than to run off to play when he has got work to do!" Scott walked outside yelling "Pogo! Where the devil are you?"

Pogo slapped the paint brush in the empty can and looked around smiling at their well-done job.

"You know Scott, we could aways go into the painting business. I think we did a great job!"

A car pulled to a stop in front of the parsonage.

"Alright, Rembrandt, see who just pulled up out there." Scott stacked the empty cans in a box.

Pogo grunted as he stared from the window at the unexpected visitors. "Oh God! Scott!" he turned to face his friend "You will never believe it!"

"Come on Pogo, who is it?" Gene Scott said, disgusted as he sealed the box shut and walked over to the window. "Weber! Shit!"

"All of the Webers, Scott. Gloria is up at the door already with Karolyn." Pogo moved so Scott could see the front door of the parsonage. "Can you see them?"

"Who could miss that red hair?" Scott hit his fist on the window sill. "I wonder what they want?"

"I don't know but I bet we soon will find out." Pogo pointed at Gloria Weber running across the lawn to the church, calling in her baby voice. "Gene! Gene, darling!"

"Doesn't that bring back warm, beautiful memories, Scott?" Pogo laughed.

"Shut up, Pogo. Just shut up!" He walked swiftly from the room, Pogo close behind him.

When Gene stepped outside, Gloria ran up and grabbed him. He pushed her away.

"Gene, is that any way to treat your future wife?" she whined, then smiled at him.

"I don't treat my future wife like that." He began walking toward the parsonage. "What does your father want?"

"Then it is true, what David told father. Are you seeing another woman, Gene Scott?" She took a tight hold on his arm.

"Every chance I get." He jerked his arm away. "And I am sure she would not want you handling her merchandise."

"Oh Gene! What could this woman have that I don't have?"

"Brains for one thing." Pogo slapped his friends arm. "Right Scott?"

Gene laughed and Gloria groaned.

"Just be quiet, Polard. No one asked you for your worthless

remark." She gazed at Scott, laughing sarcastically. "I hope daddy sends you far, far away from this—this whore who is running after you!"

Gene Scott jerked Gloria around, his strong grip bit into her soft arms. "Now you listen Gloria, I don't ever want you saying anything like that about my girl again! Is that clear?" His eyes burned into hers. "Well, answer, damn it!"

"Alright Gene. Why are you so hung up on this woman?" She rubbed her arms when he turned loose.

"I love her and I intend to marry her." He pushed her aside and made his way into the parsonage.

Gloria ran in behind him. "Gene, you will see she is wrong for you—and that I am the only real woman for you!" she snapped. "Don't forget daddy listens to me, Gene!"

Seeing her father sitting on the sofa, Gloria walked over and joined him. "David was right, Daddy. Only our Gene thinks he is in love with the mysterious girl."

"Love? Oh Gene, how utterly ridiculous." Henry Weber motioned him down. "Sit down and take the load off your feet."

"I do not care how ridiculous you think it is, sir. I do love her. Believe me, what you and your family think about my personal life makes little or no difference to me." Scott sat down across from the Webers.

"Determined to be bull-headed and a jackass, are you?" Weber's tone grew harsh.

"You should know what one is like, sir! You have been one ever since. I've known you!" Scott practically shouted.

"Gene?" Edna feigned a laugh as she took a firm hold on Scott's shoulder. "Gene is such a big tease."

"Edna, you do not have to defend me!" Gene patted her hand. "I meant what I said, Weber. I guess you are planning to send me away again, am I not correct?"

"If I remember correctly Scott, you put in a request to become a missionary." Weber opened the candy dish sitting in front of him and selected a big piece. "Mummm! Edna, this is very tasty. Did you make it?"

"Yes, yes I did." She bit her lip to keep from saying something she might regret later. "Karolyn, would you or Gloria care for anything?"

"All I want is that stubborn Gene, Edna dear." Gloria smeared on a sweet smile. "He is so mean to little bitty me. I just cannot understand it."

"Oh shit!" Scott mumbled to himself and rubbed at his fresh

headache. "What is it you want me to do Weber?"

"First of all, I want you to go to Hawaii for me and pick up some very important papers. They are extremely confidential, so no peeking. You are to pick them up at the First United Methodist Church on Four Palms Street."

He laid his head back and closed his eyes. "When do I leave?"

"You leave here late Thursday and should arrive Friday morning. You may stay for the remainder of the weekend if you like." Henry Weber reached for more candy "A small vacation before I send you off again."

"Thanks!" He stood. "I will go and get my ticket for Hawaii then." He walked toward the door, Gloria chasing after him.

"Gene, wait darling! Don't you want to take me with you?" She batted her false eyelashes.

"I think I can find the airport without your help. Besides, I want to be alone." He opened the door to the Crain's car.

Gloria turned up her nose at the Crains Chevy. "Gene, I meant take me to Hawaii with you, silly. We could have a very interesting time under the palm trees and the warm romantic moon."

"Any romantic games I play, Miss Weber, I will play with my woman, not you." He started up the motor "Better move back before some of this car's beauty rubs off on you."

She jumped back as he drove quickly from the parsonage.

Gene pulled the car to a stop in front of a pay telephone. He got out and dialed the Andrews' phone number. Mildred answered and within seconds his heart melted at the sound of Susan's voice.

"Susan, it's Gene."

"Gene! Hello, darling. I wasn't expecting to get such a wonderful surprise so early in the afternoon."

"Are you free for the remainder of the day honey?" His voice made her heart beat loudly in her throat.

"Yes Gene, for you, I am always free." She spoke softly to prevent anyone from hearing her conversation. "What did you have in mind?"

"Can you meet me at the malt shop?"

"In five minutes! Will that be soon enough?" she whispered loudly.

"Don't drive fast, sweetheart. Just meet me there as soon as you can. We are going to get that marriage license." He swallowed "Now hurry."

"Oh Gene! Gene, do you mean it?" She grew excited.

103

"I will tell you everything when I see you, little darling. Now go, hurry!"

He hung the receiver up and headed to the malt shop two blocks away. Gene found a table in the far corner and ordered a cup of coffee. He checked his watch then looked out the window as Susan pulled into a parking place and jumped out. She made her way quickly into the shop and spotted Gene.

"Oh sweetheat, I'm so excited!" She slid in next to him "My heart is beating a thousand times a minute!"

"You really do need a physical then, girl." He laughed and took her hand under the table.

"Gene, why did you decide all of a sudden? It was so fast, I didn't know whether or not you were joking." She tilted her head as she stared at the man she loved. "Gene, do not keep me in suspense another second!"

"The Bishop is sending me to Hawaii for the weekend. He wants me to pick up some important papers for him." He squeezed her hand "I thought it might be the perfect place and time for us to get married. Do you think you can get away?"

Susan could not contain her emotions. "Oh Gene! Hawaii for a honeymoon!" She closed her eyes dreamingly "I will get away somehow. Don't you worry!"

He paid for the coffee and they walked slowly to his car. He helped her inside then slid behind the wheel. Susan pulled his arm tightly around her shoulders.

"Oh Gene, I cannot remember when I've ever been this happy! This is the happiest moment of my life!"

"I'm too nervous to know how I feel. honey." he laughed softly as they made their way inside the courthouse.

They walked from the license office laughing. Susan held tight to the long-awaited marriage license.

"Isn't it beautiful!" She kissed it "Everything went so smoothly. The physical and the blood test, not to mention the fact that I just turned eighteen two days ago."

Gene leaned down and kissed her tenderly, then smiled broadly. "I didn't think I was going to hold up in there when that clerk said in his nasal voice, 'been counting the days for her birthday, Reverend?' What a hoot!" He wrapped his arm around her small waist. "And thanks to that modern way of getting a quick blood test and returns all in the same hour."

"Yeh, that was real heavy!" Susan laughed as she squeezed Scott's hand tightly. "I thought it would take days to complete all we did in just less than two hours."

"We have one more stop to make before we can go home." He held open the car door for her. "The airport. Can't go to Hawaii without tickets."

"Gee, now why didn't I think of that?" she teased and moved over close to him. "How did I get so lucky to find such a smart husband-to-be?"

"I guess the same way I got lucky enough to find such a beautiful young bride." He stopped at the airport and climbed out, Susan right behind him.

"I think I will go shopping tomorrow. There is so much I need to get before Thursday evening." She held his arm as they made their way to the ticket window.

The girl behind the window reconized Gene from his last flight and smiled up at him.

"May I help you, Reverend?"

"I would like two tickets to Hawaii, Thursday evening flight."

Susan·smiled at Gene, then turned to the girl at the window. "Make that two romantic seats please. We are on our way to get married."

"Married? Oh!" the girl ruefully. "Why do all the best ones always get grabbed?" She handed Scott the tickets. "Good luck to you."

"Thank you." Scott smiled at Susan. "Well darling, that's got everything."

"Oh Gene, I cannot help feeling I am dreaming this whole beautiful thing." She lay her head against him. "I wish I could yell it to the world!"

"Me too, honey, but for the time being we had better hold it happily within us." He touched her face lightly "Right?"

"Right!" She climbed into the Crains' Chevy and kissed Scott as he got behind the wheel. "I love you, Gene Scott."

"I love you, Susan Andrews." He returned her kiss and started up the motor. Driving slowly, he went back to the malt shop where Susan had left her sportscar. "Well, here we are beautiful."

Susan looked at her yellow Corvette and turned back to the man she loved. "Will I see you before Thursday sweetheart?"

"There is a lot I have to get done between now and then, honey. If I see I can't get away, I will call you and let you know where and when to meet me Thursday. Fair enough?" He smiled at her.

She gently caressed his face. "Fair enough." She pulled herself up to meet his lips and he kissed her passionately. "Oh Gene darling!" She took a deep breath "I cannot wait till Friday night."

"I'm kinda looking forward to it too!" He laughed slyly and reached across her to open the car door "Now go home before I say something stupid."

"Like what?" she asked with a laugh.

"Be prepared for anything Friday night, little darling. I may decide to keep you up all night, and I don't mean up, up. I mean in bed, up and awake!"

"Mummm!" she sighed "Your making love to me will be worth staying up all night—and half the moirning."

"The way I've been feeling lately when you arouse me, darling, I just may go that long." He laughed and gave her a light push out the door. "I have said enough, you wonderful nut. Now go home."

Susan walked around to the driver's side and he rolled the window down "Alright, I am going." She leaned in and kissed him. "Goodbye, you sexy devil you."

"Goodbye, you luscious sexy lover." He watched as she left, waved and drove off laughing softly "Hot and sexy! Friday night, old Gene is going to let the covers fly and, pretty Susan, watch out!"

Chapter 11

Gene picked up Edna and twirled her around. "Edna, you wonderful, sweet, beautiful woman!" He laughed and sat her down. "Better go get my suitcase and go to the bird of paradise."

"Gene, are you feeling alright?"·Edna watched him happily run up the steps to his room.

He glanced down over the banister, smiling broadly. "I have never felt better in my life, Edna, you wonderful sexy doll." He turned and disappeared behind the door.

"Do you see, John, exactly like I told you." Edna looked at her husband, who sat staring up the staircase. "He has been acting overly happy and a little wishy-washy all·day. Do you think it is safe for him to go to Hawaii in this condition?"

"Now Edna, he's probably just trying to make the most of this little short vacation Weber has given him." John lit his pipe. "The thing I do not get is how he can be so happy about leaving Susan."

"I thought of that too, John. I wonder if he has told her yet." Edna looked up when she heard Scott's bedroom door open and close. His smile was brilliant as he made his way down the steps. "All ready, Gene?"

"Yeh, I sure am." He set down his suitease. "Well, wish me luck."

"On getting those papers for the bishop?" Edna smiled as she gazed into his sparkling blue eyes. "Gene, with all the things you have been through, I should think this little chore would be a snap."

"Sure, the papers will be easy enough to get." He took a small box from his pant's pocket and handed it to Edna. "Look at this and see what you think."

Her eyes grew wide as she stared at the wedding band. With tears in her eyes she took Gene's hand. "Gene, you and Susan?"

"Yes, we are going to tie the knot, sometime tomorrow. What do you think?" He smiled at his friend on the sofa.

John shook his head and laughed. "Gene, you old rascal!" He got up and hugged him. "Well no wonder you are so blame happy."

"Oh Gene, I think it is beautiful." Edna reached in her apron pocket and pulled out a tissue. "Darn, I hope I don't see Shirley. It is so hard to keep a big secret like this."

"But you will try very hard." Scott took around her. "We would not want Shirley and Owen to undo what we are about to do, would we?"

"Don't worry, Gene. I will keep a sharp eye on Edna." John laughed and patted Scott's shoulder. "Wow! Getting married!"

"Hey Scott, better go before Susan leaves without you." Pogo called from the porch. "Or maybe I should go in your place."

Scott said his goodbyes and hurried to the porch. "I think maybe you're asking for a swore jaw, buddy, ole pal." Scott threw his suitcase in the back seat and climbed in behind the wheel.

"Sure you don't want me to drive?" Pogo climbed in beside Scott. "Bridegrooms are known to be pretty shaky on the eve of their wedding night."

"And I am no exception pal. I am scared shitless!" Scott stopped for a red light. "Come on! Hurry up and change!"

"I wonder if I'll be all this shook up when I decide to get married?" Pogo blew a bubble with his gum. "Shit, Scott, just think what you have got coming tomorrow night. Damn!"

"That's right, buddy, and I have waited for it long as I could." He stopped the car in front of the TarSa Airport. "Well, this is it."

"Yeh, the next time I see you Scott, you will be an old married man." Pogo slapped his shoulder, felt the pain and made a face as he shook out his hand. "Shit, solid steel! Susan has got quite a bit coming too."

"She sure has, little buddy." Scott laughed coyly as he pulled his suitcase out. "See you when I get back; and if you buy any doughnuts, do not forget about the holes."

"No comment! Better go or Susan will give up on you and then you will be looking for a doughnut, with all the sex energy you have been building up." He laughed and slipped behind the wheel as he watched his big friend dash inside.

Over his shoulder, Scott called, "Pogo, get going!"

Long steps carried him into the airport waiting area. Susan stood up, looking relieved, and waved him toward her.

"Where have you been, Gene? I was scared you wouldn't make it!"

"Thought I had chickened out on you, huh?" He took her hand as they heard their flight being called. "Never in a million years!"

Gene Scott stretched his arm around Susan's shoulders as the plane lifted off the runway. He smiled and leaned his head against the headrest.

"Scared Susan?" He turned to face her.

"Maybe a little." She smiled and looked down at her hands. "Maybe a lot. Are you?"

"I guess everyone gets a little nervous on their wedding day. It's a big step. But after you finally make that step and you are in each others' arms, it's well worth the sweat." He took her hand "What did you tell your folks this time?"

"I told them I was going off for the weekend with Jackie and Ali. They're covering for me." She took a deep breath "They could not believe my good news."

"Susan, you mean you told them we were getting married?" He sat up.

"Sure, Gene, why not? They are my friends and, besides, I had to tell someone besides Jobi. My insides were bursting with excitement." She smiled at his anxious expression. "Relax sweetheart, they promised they wouldn't tell anyone, not even Michael or James. Jackie and Ali think the whole thing is beautiful and romantic."

"Okay. honey, but if they let it slip. . . " He leaned his head back and closed his eyes. "Better try and get some sleep, darling. We will probably be up pretty late tomorrow night." He grinned, despite himself.

Susan bit her lip and stared from the window as she thought, "Yes I better because I think I'm in for quite a treat tomorrow night." She let her head rest on the seat as her eyes drifted lazily into a deep sleep.

The loud voice over the intercom brought them both out of their restful sleep.

"May I have your attention please. We are about to land in Honolulu. Would you please sit forward and fasten your seatbelts? Thank you for flying Hawaiian Royal Airlines. We hope that your flight was enjoyable."

"Relaxing anyway!" Scott stretched his long arms over his head and patted Susan's knee "Right?"

"I slept like a baby." She looked from the window and saw the island below them. "Oh Gene, it is so beautiful."

He looked at the girl he loved·so deeply and smiled. "Yes, it is so very beautiful."

"How do you know?" She laughed softly. "You haven't even looked out. Come over and see."

"I am looking at the most beautiful sight in my world." Her eyes met his. "Susan, I am such a lucky man."

"I'm the lucky one, daring." She touched his face lovingly. "Lucky you even looked twice at me, much less ask me to be Mrs. Gene Scott."

The brilliant sun danced through the open doorway. Scott held Susan's hand tightly as he led her down the aisle. He smiled down at the stewardess as Susan walked down before him.

"We hope you and your daughter enjoyed your flight." She smiled.

"A—yes, thank you." He followed Susan quickly down the steps, where they were greeted by friendly native girls. They drapped a reef of flowers around each passenger's neck as they welcomed them to the island.

A raven haired Hawaiian woman waved at Scott and walked up to them smiling.

"You must be Reverend Scott. You fit the description by your six foot-seven inch height and those strong muscles."

Gene laughed and put out his hand for a shake "Yes, I am Reverend Scott. I did not know the church would be sending someone to meet me." He glanced toward Susan "This is Susan Andrews. She made the trip with me."

"Welcome both of you to Honolulu. I hope you can stay long enough to enjoy. our beautiful warm home." She motioned to a white car parked in front of the main entrance. "Just follow me please."

Scott easily picked up the luggage and followed behind Susan and the the friendly Hawaiian lady. She turned to them smiling.

"I'm sorry. I never introduced myself. My name is Tehani. I am the secretary at the church. Reverend Tilman sent me down to pick you up."

"That was very thoughtful of Brother Tilman." Gene helped Susan slide into the back seat, then put their bags in the trunk before getting in beside her. "I guess Weber informed him about sending me."

"Yes, Reverend Scott, Bishop Weber called and said you would probably like to stay at the parsonage."

Susan looked into Scott's eyes. "Gene? What are you going to tell him?"

"I don't know yet, sweetheart, but don't worry. I am not spending my honeymoon in a parsonage." He squeezed her hand. "I will think of something."

Tehani smiled at the two lovers behind her. "I'm sorry, but I could not help but overhearing. Are you two secretly married?"

"No, not yet anyway." Scott wrinkled up his forehead, wishing he hadn't spoken so loudly. "We were planning to get married today, secretly."

"How beautiful!" Tehani pulled her car to a stop in front of a modern church. "Reverend Scott, Susan, my family is having a Luau tonight on the beach. If you like, you could come and celebrate with us."

"Oh Gene, what fun! Let's go! I have always wanted to go to one! It will really make our visit perfect here!" Susan looked pleadingly at him. "And maybe Tehani would like to be a witness at our wedding."

"Susan, I'm sure Tehani is very busy and would not have time to—"

"Have time? Ha! I will take the time." She hugged Susan as they climbed out of the car. "Susan, you certainly have landed one nice groom."

"Yes, believe me, I know." She smiled at the man she loved. "Well, are we going to the Luau, darling?"

"I certainly would not want to upset my bride on our wedding day." He pulled her into his arms. "And I think it was mighty sweet of Tehani to ask us."

"I know how important wedding days are, Reverend Scott. There should be much laughing and singing. My husband Marama will be overjoyed to have you. He loves people." She walked up the steps toward the church office. "And do not worry about what to tell Reverend Tilman. Mrs. Tilman has been worring herself sick about her houseguest. I am sure if you tell them you had other plans, it would be accepted very well."

Scott received the secret documents from Reverend Tilman and offered his regrets, saying he had made other plans for his stay in Hawaii. As Tehani had predicted, neither Tilman nor his wife were too upset about Scott not staying with them.

They stepped back out into the sparkling sunshine. Scott held the papers for Weber in a briefcase under his arm.

Tehani smiled at her new friends. "As expected, Reverend Tilman has given me the rest of the day off. I called Marama and told him to meet us at the Justice of the Peace's home office."

"Great!" Scott swallowed as he felt in his pocket to make sure the rings and marriage license were still safe. "We will grab something to eat after the ceremony."

"Who can eat?" Susan cleared her throat "I feel like there is no more room left in my stomach with all those butterflies fluttering around."

"Just try to relax, honey." Scott slipped his arm around Susan as they made their way up the walk way to the judge's home. "He said he would be at home today. I bet he stays as busy in his study here marrying couples as he does in his office downtown."

"Oh he does indeed, Reverend Scott." Tehani laughed "He married me and Maroma here about a year ago."

"I called him from TarSa on Tuesday to make sure he could take us." Anxiously, Gene rang the doorbell. "He said come anytime Friday."

A short, heavy set lady opened the door and smiled at the three visitors. "Yes, may I help you folks?"

"Yes, we are here to get married." Scott's voice cracked from nerves and Susan laughed softly. He made a face down at her then turned to the friendly woman "Is the judge in?"

"Always on Fridays, young man." She winked and motioned for them to follow her. "It is good to see you again, Tehani. I take it you are friends with the happy couple here?"

"Yes, Mrs. Shields, I am." She patted Scott's arm. "Relax! My husband is on his way over to be a witness too, Mrs. Shields."

"Oh, good, excellent." She stepped behind a piano. "Would you like the wedding march, my dear?"

"No thank you, Mrs. Shields. Getting Gene is enough for me." Susan gripped Gene's hand. "There is enough music going on in my head."

Tehani patted Susan's shoulders gently and motioned toward her husband as he came through the door.

"You are a beautiful bride, Susan." She smiled at the jittery bride and took her husband's hand. "This is my Marama. Honey, these are my friends from the island of TarSa, Gene Scott and Susan Andrews."

"I am very happy to meet you, Marama. Your wife has been very sweet to us ever since we arrived in Honolulu." Scott shook his deeply tanned hand.

"We are really looking forward to the party tonight."

"Just happy you could join us." He smiled broadly "I know what you must be going through right now, Scott. I was so nervous on my wedding day I passed out. Remember, Tehani?"

"Who could forget, Marama." She laughed and smiled at the

judge as he walked toward them with brisk little steps. "Good evening, Judge Holland."

"Good evening, young friends." He fumbled with the small white book in his hands. "Alright, let's see here, which of you two are getting married?" His small eyes peered over his wire rim glasses. "Humm?"

Scott pulled Susan up front, took her hand and smiled nervously down at the skinny little judge as he cleared his throat.

"We are, your honor."

"Oh? I see, mummm!" He rubbed his chin and slapped Scott's back. "Done it up right, didn't you my friend?"

"Ah—yes! I think I done very well for myself, sir." He pulled nervously at his shirt sleeve.

"Yes indeed, I would say. The young ones last the longest." He laughed. "But of course that means you have to hold out longer too though." He clicked his tongue "Oh, to be young again."

"Yes, yes! Can we please get on with this?" Scott's hand moved nervously in his pant pocket.

"Of course, I understand, waiting can be torture." He winked at Scott, who glanced away impatiently. "Dearly beloved . . ." Judge Holland drew out each word until finally he finished with "And now I pronounce you husband and wife." He winked at Susan. "Now Reverend, you may kiss your bride."

Taking Susan's face in his hands, Gene gently kissed her lips as everyone began congratulating the nervous couple. The judge and Marama kissed Susan while Scott was being kissed by fat old Mrs. Shields and Tehani.

After getting in the back seat of Tehani's car, Gene put his arms around Susan and whispered in her ear. "I love you, Mrs. Scott."

"Oh Gene, that sounds so beautiful! Mrs. Scott! Mrs. Gene Scott! Susan Scott!" She laughed and let her head fall back against his strong chest. "I am so happy! I love you, Gene Scott! I could shout and sing!"

"Shout and sing? You can do both at the family Luau, Susan." Marama smiled at her in the rear-view mirror. "Maybe you can learn the hulla."

"You really think I could?" she asked excitedly as she kissed her ring, shining on her left hand. "And Gene darling, you can learn the hulla too!"

"Susan!" he squeezed her shoulders "I would look pretty ridiculous doing the hulla!"

"Gene is right Susan." Marama laughed out at the thought of a man doing the hip-moving dance, much less a man built like Gene Scott "Better leave the dancing to the women."

"Gene could try the rhythm sticks." Tehani smiled back at him "It takes lots of concentration, but I bet you could master it."

"Tehani, is that where two men slap sticks together and then they jump in and out?" Susan pushed back her hair.

"That is one way of putting it." Tehani laughed "How 'bout it, Gene?

Marama can teach you the skills of stick dancing. He is the best in our family."

"Why not, might as well give it a go." Scott rubbed Susan on the top of her head. "All I can do if I make a mistake is get a crushed foot."

"Not on our wedding day you don't, Gene Scott!" Susan elbowed him.

"I don't think a crushed foot would stand in my way with what I have planned for tonight, little darling." He cleared his throat, noticing Marama's big smile in the mirror. "Besides, if our friend Marama can jump those rhythm sticks, so can I."

"And you are correct Scott, you wont' be using your feet all that much tonight." Marama laughed slyly. "Just be sure not to fall and get something else crushed between those sticks."

"Marama!" Tehani slapped her husband's arm and laughed. "Susan and Gene will think you are terrible."

"No, he is right Tehani" Scott patted the handsome Hawaiian on his back. "I will be extra careful and make sure I do not lose my footing, if I get brave enough to try those sticks."

Chapter 12

The Luau got into full swing at around seven o'clock. The food was prepared in true Hawaiian style and everything tasted wonderful to Gene and Susan. The newlywed couple fit right in with Tehani and Marama's family. It was a large happy group that seemed to get along very well. Marama kept filling up his and Scott's glasses with the pineapple-berry wine his mother had made and bottled for many years. The effects began to work on Gene as he watched, with great interest, as Susan mastered the art of hulla dancing.

"Ummm, damn!" Scott slapped Marama's back playfully. "Boy, don't I have some sexy woman? Shit! I cannot wait to get that little gal in bed! Hmmm-weeee!" he laughed.

Marama stood on shaky legs, laughing as he pulled Scott to his feet. "Come on, Tiger, let's try that rhythm game while we are still sober, alright Rev?" Marama laughed as he drank the rest of his wine, and closed his eyes smiling. "Hummm! That mama of mine can really make a great little glass of wine."

"Yes, you can say that again." Scott slapped Marama's back nearly knocking him down. "Bring on those damn sticks!" Scott shouted and put his arm around Marama's unsteady shoulders as he smiled at the other men happily watching "I want to show my friend here—" he patted Marama on the head. "That daredevil Gene can master anything he attempts to do!"

"Well, you must be pretty sure of yourself daredevil!" Marama laughed. "I mean a man your age marring up with a young thing like Susan—" He winked at the men taking in their conversation. "You must really be sure you can sat—ah—satisfy her needs." He fumbled with the sticks.

"Are you kidding!" Scott laughed loudly. "My friend, I'll have you to know I am one of the hottest lovers this sweet little world has ever had." His eyes fell on Susan and he smiled. "My little woman will never go hungry for love, gentlemen. I can guarantee her that!"

Even high on Pineapple-berry wine, Gene quickly mastered the sticks as he did any other sport he tried. After getting a thumbs-up from Susan and high fives from the men watching, Gene turned his attention back to the woman he loved.

Marama followed his gaze and smiled. "I will say one thing for you Scott, you—you sure are a big man, one hell of a man!" he slapped at Scott and missed, nearly falling. "Aren't you afraid you are a little too much man for that little bitty girl?"

"Naw! I'll just take it nice and slow at first, you know, break her in easy like." He wrinkled up his eyes to focus on Susan. "I'm going to have to leave pretty soon. I think Susan is getting drunk!" He thumped Marama repeatedly on the back. "She is swaying back and forth." He made his way slowly to Susan, swaying from side to side. She frowned at him.

"Oh Gene, honey, are you getting drunk?" She pulled him down beside her. "Tehani, could you please bring me some nice, strong, hot, black coffee."

"Yes Susan, I see what you mean." She smiled down at Scott. "Got to get you all sober so you will remember your honeymoon night."

He laid his head down on Susan's lap and smiled shyly up at her. "Has Gene been a had boy?"

"Yes, very!" she leand over and kissed him. "But if you are a bad boy in bed, I want you to know about it."

"I'm not that drunk!" he sat up and rubbed his hand through his hair "I still know everything that is going on Susan."

"Are you afraid of little me?" She ran her fingers down his chest.

"I'll show you just how afraid of you I am, young lady, when I get you in bed." He pulled her head to his and parted his lips over hers in a tender kiss.

Tehani cleared her throat. "Drink your coffee so you two can hurry and be off to your love room." She handed Scott the steaming coffee "Don't burn your tongue, it's hot."

"God forbid! I use it too much to go and burn it." He smiled at Susan's blush. "What's wrong honey, you are not afraid of little big me, are you?"

"Oh Gene, don't be silly!" She twisted at her wedding band nervously. "I am not afraid of my husband."

"Good!" he took a few sips of the coffee and stood up pulling Susan up with him. "Let's go then! I think I have waited long enough."

"Ah—sure Gene." she swallowed and waved at Tehani. "Wish me luck."

"You've got it, Susan!" she laughed "Just enjoy yourself. I know you will!"

"You said it, sweetheart!" Scott called over his shoulder. "I have been holding out for this night a long time and I intend to turn hog loose and run wild!"

Susan's heart beat in her throat as the elevator made its way up to their hotel room. She could feel Gene's fingers gently on her shoulder and she knew what lay ahead was a totally new experience for her. "Oh God," she thought, "let me be a good lover for him. I have just got to satisfy him."

"A penny for your thoughts." He took her hand and led her slowly down the hall and stopped in front of room 112C. "Now, no secrets from your husband."

"I hold no secrets, darling. I was just thinking I am a very lucky girl, Gene Scott."

"And I am a very lucky fellow, Susan Scott!" he put his arms around her. "I am madly in love with my wife."

"Oh Gene, I love you so much!" She looked at the door and swallowed. "Let's go inside and see our first room together."

"You bet!" He unlocked the door and set the suitcases inside the room, then he gathered Susan up into his arms and carried her through the door. With his foot, he shut the door and with his lips he kissed her passionately. After locking the door securely, he laid her gently on the bed and bent down beside her.

"Need to do anything before we crawl under the sheets?"

"I would like to go the bathroom first please." She bit her bottom lip anxiously.

"Okay, beautiful!" He helped her to her feet. "I think I could use it too."

"Oh? You go ahead first." She sat back down "I'll wait."

"I bet you are gonna put on some sexy little nightgown to turn me ape with, right?" He ran his fingers through her long black hair "Be right out, sweetheart."

"Take your time," she swallowed and closed her eyes when he disappeared behind the bathroom door. "Pull yourself together, Susan," she whispered to herself. "This is the night you have been dreaming about so do not goof it up."

She jumped quickly to her feet when the bathroom door opened.

Gene had taken off his shirt and she stared dreamingly at his strong chest "All—all finished?"

"All finished!" He smiled down at her. "Okay, okay! Let's move that sweet butt!" He winked and she smiled sheepishly as she quickly walked into the bathroom and closed the door.

Scott took a deep breath as he removed everything else but his pants. He sat down nervously on the edge of the bed and ran his hand along the sheets. Hearing the door open, he looked up and noticed

Susan still had on her dress. She smiled shyly at him.

"I—I guess you are wondering why I am still wearing my dress."

"Well, I sorta was expecting to see my sexy wife walking out in a nighty." He stood up. "Is something wrong honey?"

"Ah—well, no, I just thought you may like the honors of undressing your sexy wife." She glanced down and laughed softly "But if you rather I put on my—"

"No, Susan!" He went to her and lifted up her face, then kissed her forehead. "I would love to do it for myself." His fingers gently undid the buttons on her dress and slid it to the floor. After removing her slip and hose, his eyes fell to her black underwear. A smile of approval came on his lips as he slipped his hands behind her back and undid her bra. Gene's lips met Susan's as he slowly pulled her panties down until they fell at her feet. She stepped out and let her fingers glide down his chest until they came to rest on his zipper. Gazing deeply into his eyes, she unhooked his pants and pulled the zipper down.

They fell to the bed, their bodies embracing for the first time as man and wife. He began kissing her passionately, his tongue slipped inside her mouth and hers found his. Gene's hands gently moved over her breast and down her stomach. His lips moved slowly down her neck and found her small, round nipple. As he slid his tongue over it his breathing became heavier.

"Oh Gene, Gene!" Susan also breathed in and out with hot desire as her fingers wrapped around his hardened erection. "Boy, my man sure has one hell of a baby-maker!"

"And it is all yours, darling." He took a deep breath and kissed her stomach. "I love you, Susan, I love you!"

"Gene, my darling, if it is mine, take off thoses boxers and let me have it! Now Gene!" She bit his ear lightly as she stuck her tongue in it. "Please, don't tease me anymore!"

"I won't my wonderful sweet, Susan." He yanked his shorts off as he gazed lovingly into her eyes "Now sweetheart, you know I am a big man and you are a delicate young lady. I am going to put it in slowly so I will not hurt you."

"Gene, couldn't you give it to me all at once, you know, get it over with?" Susan blinked, her eyes wide.

Gene laughed softly. "Trust me, Susan, it will be better slower." He started inside her slowly and gently, his heart pounding with desire. As he moved forward, he felt Susan's body tense up as she moaned in pain. Then her face relaxed as she sighed in relief. Gene knew at that moment he had broken Susan's virginity.

He smiled to himself as he thought, "I am the first to have her." Gene moved deeper and deeper. It was hard for him to hold back, but for Susan he knew he must. He watched her close her eyes as he made it in completely.

"How does that feel Susan? It is all inside you now."

"Gene darling!" with a big smile and breathing heavy, she said happily. "It's a perfect fit!" He laughed as she spoke in his ear. "I love being connected to you like this, darling."

He started moving his hips up and down slowly. Susan smiled and picked up the rhythm. The more they moved, the more Susan's passion swelled. She could feel something, something new and exciting was about to happen.

"Gene? Gene—what I feel—oh God!"

"Just relax darling.: His breathing was hot in her ear. "I feel it too sweetheart! We are going to our—own—paradise! Yes! Oh God, Susan!"

Gene and Susan reached their dynamic climax at the same time. Gene lay on top of Susan for a few seconds then rolled off, taking a deep breath. "Damn Susan, that was the best sex I have ever had!"

"Reverend Scott, that was the only sex I have ever had and it was—wow, fantastic!" She rolled over on him and kissed him. ''I knew it was going to be good. I just never dreamed it could feel that wonderful!" Susan rolled out of the bed smiling "Excuse me, Mr. Scott. Mrs. Scott has got to use the bathroom.

Gene laughed and folded his hands behind his head as he watched her walk naked to the bathroom. He smiled to himself. "Gene Scott, you are the luckiest damn man around. Shit, Susan has a sweet butt."

She came out smiling, her round breasts glowing in the lamp light.

His eyes fell down her body and he could feel himself getting aroused again. "Damn, this has never happened to me before!"

"What has never happened to my wonderful husband before?" Susan walked over to the bed and looked seriously at her man.

"Come here, darling." He reached for and pulled her into his arms. "I will show you. Just look what you do to me."

Susan's eyes searched his face, fell to his chest, then Gene's erection, "Oh? Isn't that normal, sweetheart?"

Gene laughed at her innocence and pulled her closer. "Susan, I have never gone twice this quickly, but I have been waiting and wanting and hurting so long, needing you like this, I guess it's payback!"

"Or your reward for waiting."

Susan smiled as he pulled her beneath him and slid inside her, moving in expert rhythm. Once again Susan felt herself reaching ecstasy as she clutched tightly to Gene.

"Gene—I can't—hold back.:

"Don't hold back, Susan. Just enjoy it, my love."

After she had let out a long sigh, Gene kissed her neck "Good girl, keep pumping darling."

They continued to move and got faster and faster until Gene gripped Susan's shoulders tightly feeling himself about to reach his own ecstasy.

"Damn! Susan, are you—about to—"

"Yes, oh yes, darling! Just let it go—now!" She moaned happily as once again they reached their heights together.

"Shit, Susan, I am yours forever and ever!" He kissed her tenderly "I will never ever let you go!"

"Good!" She yawned. "Because I am yours forever, Reverend Scott!"

"Let's get some rest now, sweetheart." Gene put a protective arm over her stomach "Tomorrow, we can start all over again."

Susan smiled "I will hold you to that, Mr. Scott." She snuggled close to Gene and they finally fell asleep as the sun was slowly slipping over the blue water.

Chapter 13

Susan opened her eyes slowly and looked around the sunlit room and heard the gentle waves in the distance. She propped herself up on her elbow and smiled down at her new husband.

"My sweet wonderful love," she whispered to herself. "Poor thing, so tired and exhausted after all that good loving he gave me last night." She gently ran her fingers through his hair. "Mummm Gene, you are such a good lover, damn good!" She giggled softly. "I only hope I was as good for you."

Susan let out a little scream when Gene grabbed, her laughing. "If you had been any better, I do not think I could have stood it!" He pulled her down and kissed her tenderly.

She sat up. "Gene Scott, how long have you been awake?"

"Long enough to know what you think about your husband!" He laughed, reached around her and slapped her naked butt. "Now, how about a nice, big breakfast!"

"Now? Can't we just lay here a little while longer?" she climbed up on top of him and lay full length on his body. "Mummm, you sure feel good, Mr. Scott."

"You don't feel none too bad yourself, Mrs. Scott! Down right sexy!" He put his arms tightly around her back. "I guess I am about the luckiest preacher in the entire world!"

"I know I'm the luckiest girl in the entire world." She kissed his nose and laughed softly. "What are we going to do today, Reverend Scott?"

"Much more of this type of lying around and I can tell you what the morning will be filled with." He smiled at her slyly. "I thought it would be fun to take a boat over to Havaiki. Catch some sight seeing and take a few pictures of my new bride."

"Oh Gene, you don't want any pictures of me, sweetheart." She wrinkled her nose.

He leaned up and kissed it. "Oh but yes I do, darling. I have to have something to look at when we are seperated."

"Gene, don't mention that!" She dropped her head against his chest. "Let's just pretend while we are here that we are like any other married couple."

"Susan darling, I wish I could shout our beautiful love to the world. I wish I could proudly say, folks, this is my wife, the love of my life, Susan Scott! I wish I could tell Weber to get lost along with his darling daughter Gloria."

"Oh yes, Miss Gloria Ann Weber, the red headed witch who is trying to steal my husband!" Susan frowned at Gene. "And why didn't you ever tell me about her?"

"It seems as if you know plenty already." He chuckled. "Who gave you all your information?"

"Let us just say I have friends who keep me well informed on what my man is up to and who is after him." She smiled at him. "The Bishop had better keep a chain on that daughter of his if he wants her in one piece."

"Oh ho! My wife sounds like the jealous type!"

"No more than my husband. Don't you think I could tell you did not have any love for my dear friend Peter."

"Dear? You had better watch that kind of talk young lady!" He rolled her over and began tickling her waist. She began laughing and kicking.

"Gene! Stop it!"

"No wife of mine is going to talk sweet about another man!" He laughed mischievously as his hands slowly moved to her breasts. "For a little girl, you certainly are built well."

"Do you like what you possess, Reverend Scott?" She smiled wickedly up and took his errection in her hand. "I certainly like my possession!"

"Only like?" His eyes stared seriously into hers.

"Love! L O V E love! Every sweet sexy wonderful inch of my man!" With her free hand she pulled his head down so that their lips met in a fiery kiss. "Oh Gene, after last night, I became a complete woman and I love you darling, so very very much!"

He kissed her again, letting his tongue slide into her mouth. Their breathing became heavy as their bodies connected in a hot, loving game that sent them soaring into a paradise all their own.

Gene rolled out of bed rubbing his back. He walked lazily to the bathroom and cut on the shower.

"Whooo weee! That feels great!" he shouted as he stepped into the steaming water. "The second best feeling I've had all day!"

"And what was the first?" Susan called from the bed.

"You and your sexy little body, little darling!" he called back, laughing as he walked from the bathroom with a towel wrapped around his hips. "Alright lazy, haul that sweet butt out of bed and go get a shower. We've got all that beatiful sunshine just waiting for us."

"Alright, if you say so!" She climbed quickly out of bed and raced off to the shower.

"Hey girl, what' s the rush?" he laughed. "For someone who was taking your sweet time, you certainly did get in a hurry."

"Sure, why not?" She stepped into the warm spray. "I must learn to hop when my husband says to hurry."

"Oh boy, I wonder how long that will last?" he mumbled to himself and slipped his arms into his white turtle neck. "She'll probably be trying to give me orders before long."

"Are you talking to yourself honey?" She slapped him on the behind as she walked by him. "Hey you, standing over there at the mirror!"

He looked at her through the mirror and pointed to himself.

"Yes you, handsome! Hand me my suitcase and, when you get finish there combing those sexy curls, go wash the dust off my shoes."

"Boy, it's already happening," he mumbled as he sat the suitcase on the bed in front of her. "Already giving me orders and we are still on our honeymoon."

"Come now, lover boy, don't look so surprised. I might as well break you in right from the start." She slipped into her yellow underwear set. "I think I will wear my yellow pant suit today. How does that sound, darling?"

"You would look beautiful in anything, sweetheart." He picked up her shoes and carried them to the bathroom. "You'll probably just get these shoes dirty again today. But, to satisfy my blushing bride, I'll wash them."

"At least they will look nice when we start out." She smiled from the bed when he handed her the shining, clean shoes. "Oh Gene, they look so much better. Thank you, darling." She blew him a kiss and he pretended he was falling backward.

"Boy, what powers you possess, you wicked little Delilah." He helped her to her feet and started for the door. "Let's go. I'm starving!"

"You mean all my love does not fill up your big appetite?" She looked in the mirror and combed through her hair.

"As far as my sex life is concerned, all your love fills it up to overflowing. But being the big eater that I am, I still need my daily amount of actual food." He put his arms around her when she joined him at the door. "But between my two appetites, I prefer my appetite for you."

"That's good, my darling husband." She took his arm. "Shall we quench your second-best appetite?"

"You are on!" He opened the door and checked his watch. They walked arm in arm to the elevator. "I am so hungry, I could eat a horse."

"Any certain kind?" Susan laughed as she stepped off the elevator and walked beside him to the cafe.

"Who cares what kind, as long as it is well-cooked and seasoned properly." He laughed at her expression. "Sit down, Mrs. Scott, I'm sure they have something more appetizing on the lunch menu."

"I certainly hope so!"

She smiled at the waitress, who seemed to be more interested in her husband. Susan stared at her thinking she looked rather dumpy in her short, blue uniform, and her dyed hair was growing out from the roots. The flirty waitress chomped loudly on her chewing gum as she tilted her head to have a closer look at the handsome man.

"Yes sir, what would you like to have?"

"Susan, have you made up your mind yet, honey?" he touched her hand and she glanced down at the menu.

"I have not decided. You go first." She felt her blood burn when the waitress winked at Scott.

"I guess you go first, daddy." She nodded toward Susan. "You sure have a cute kid, handsome."

"What? I beg your pardon!" she practically shouted. Everyone eating turned to see what was going on.

"Susan, sweetheat, calm down." Gene gently took her hand. "I will have the fried chicken dinner with coffee please." He smiled at Susan. "What for you, Mrs. Scott?"

The waitress' mouth dropped open. "You—you're married?"

"Yes-I-am!" Susan spit out each word "And I will have the same thing as my husband, the fried chicken dinner with coffee."

"Ah—yes, very well." She grabbed the menus, smiled sheepishly then hurried away to the kitchen.

Susan's eyes followed her until she disappeared behind the swinging door. "The nerve of some women! Just come right up and flirt with my husband and call me his kid!"

"Now come on, honey, you might as well get use to that sort of thing." He touched the back of her neck. "People are going to find it hard to accept a man my age being married to someone as young and beautiful as you."

"Gene Scott, stop making it sound as though you are an old grandpa and I am a baby still cutting my first tooth." She took a sip of water then made a face. "You know good and well I am a complete woman. It's obvious you are nowhere near being over the hill!"

"Susan, Susan, Susan."

He leaned over and kissed her. Their eyes met in a burning passion as their lips melted together.

The red-faced waitress cleared her throat. "Must be newlyweds, huh?" She popped her gum as she sat the plates in front of them. "I can always tell newlyweds. They can't seem to keep their hands off one another."

"Well, lady, if you can tell so good, why did you think I was my husband's daughter?" Susan forced a smile.

"I guess it's because you look so much younger, dear." She brushed a curl from her eyes. "I will say one thing for you, dearie, you certainly do have yourself one heck of a man there."

"Yes, I am well aware of that." Susan laid the napkin carefully on her lap and noticed the waitress was still observing Gene. "That will be all, dearie."

She frowned. "Yes, of course." Her eyes turned to Scott. "If you need anything, just call me." She smiled and lowered her voice. "Anything at all."

She turned and twisted off toward the kitchen. Scott smiled and Susan slapped his arm.

"What are you smiling at, Gene Scott?"

"I am a happy, friendly man, Susan. Why shouldn't I smile?" He patted her knee and started to take a bite.

Susan cleared her throat. "Aren't you forgetting something?" She tilted her head, waiting for him to answer. "Well, preacher, think!"

"My prayer, yes." He took her hand and said grace. "I am so mixed up, it's lucky I even put my pants on right this morning."

"The way some of these women keep staring at you, I am beginning to think you didn't." Susan took a bite of her crispy chicken, then glanced toward at Scott's pants.

"Susan?" Gene saw several people watching her smiling "What are you doing?"

"Looking to see if you got your trap shut." She giggled when the old lady sitting across from them snorted at her words.

"It is shut, for God's sake! Just eat, will you?"

"Am I embarrassing you, darling?" Susan gently touched his face. "I am sorry, really I am. People should not be so interested in someone else's business though."

"Yes honey, I know!" he reached for a piece of bread "Hey, woman, you never did tell me who told you about Gloria."

"Gene!" She glared at him. "Did you have to ruin my lunch?"

"Oh Susan, come on now. Was it Edna or David?" He smiled over his coffee cup.

"Both!" she laughed "They said the wonderful sweet spoiled Gloria Ann Weber tried to make you marry her. Some nerve of that—that Woody Wood Pecker."

Scott burst into laughter. "Susan, you are priceless!" He motioned for the waitress. "Would you like anything else, honey?"

"No, thank you." She smiled up at him. "Not to eat anyway."

"Mummm hummm!" He raised his eyebrows mischieviously. "We will have our bill now, please."

"Honey, I'd give you anything you ask for." The waitress smiled broadly at Gene.

"Well, honey, he asked for the bill!" Susan stood with her hands firmly on her hips. "So kindly hand it over!"

Scott took the bill, stood and took Susan's arm and led her to the check out. He paid silently and, without speaking, walked from the dining, room, pulling Susan behind him. She gazed up at him when they stepped out into the bright sunshine.

"Are—are you angry with me?" She bit her lip when he remained silent. "Gene, say something!"

He grabbed her and began to laugh. "Had you scared for a minute, didn't I, hon?" He kissed the top of her head.

"Gene Scott, don't you ever do that to me again!" She kicked at his leg "You big meanie!"

He turned about and spotted a drugstore down the busy street.

"Come on. Let's go invest in a camera." He took her hand and headed across the street. "I might as well go all out and buy a good one. Hell, you only get married once—or twice in my case—and it's for life, right?"

"Right, Gene. But, honey, I have two cameras at home, expensive cameras." Susan smiled at the clerk behind the counter. "There is no need to spend alot of money."

"Susan, did you bring one of those expensive cameras with you?" He glanced at her.

"Well, no but—"

"I want one of your Polaroid jobs. Better throw some film in the bag too." He pulled out his wallet. "Just whatever it takes, drop it in."

"Gene honey, those cameras are expensive. Why don't you buy a regular camera?" She smiled sheepishly at the clerk who was listening to their conversation.

"No Susan. It's not that much more. He winked at the clerk. "Some of the type of pictures I have in mind a drug store would not develop."

"Reverend Scott! Really! I bet my mom and dad would not have let me assist you on this trip if they knew what you had in mind." Susan looked down at her hands to keep from laughing at Scott's funny expression. The sales clerk's eyes grew wide and he started stuttering.

"Ah—ah—Reverend—would you still like to purchase the Polaroid?"

"That's what I asked for, wasn't it?"

The clerk turned to get the camera and film. Scott grabbed Susan's wrist.

"What's the big idea?"

"Idea, Reverend?" she spoke loudly. "It was your idea, not mine. But my folks did tell me to listen to you and do exactly as you said."

"Susan!" Scott squeezed her hand as the clerk choked from swallowing his gum. "Stay still!"

"That will be—$31.95—ple—please." He smiled nervously at Scott.

A disgusted look on his face, Gene handed him two twenties.

"Out of $40." He rang open the cash register and handed Scott back his change. "Sir? It—may not be—any of my business, but don't you think you had better not do anything—ah—you know—seeing as to how her folks do trust you—and all."

"Don't worry, sir!" Gene frowned. "I won't lay one finger on her for the remainder of the trip!" He turned and stormed out the door, Susan chasing after him.

Chapter 14

"Hey Scott! Can't you take a joke?"

She caught up and ran alongside him. He remained silent as he kept walking straight ahead.

"Gene, stop acting like a spoiled little boy. Say something."

He stopped and stared down at her. Looking around and seeing a bench, he went to it and sat down. He took the camera from the bag and loaded it. Susan propped her chin on her hands and stared down at her feet.

"Silence. I am surrounded by silence," she said softly as she kicked at a rock. "Gene, did you really mean it when you said you weren't going to touch me for the remainder of the trip?"

Scott glanced at her and stood. He headed toward the boat dock. A look of dismay on her face, Susan followed along behind him.

"I married a big mouth who turned into a mummy! Gene Scott, will you say something! I hate the silent treatment!"

Susan stood watching him pay for a ride across to Havaiki. He took her hand and pulled her on the boat.

Gene sat down next to an old grey hair woman who smiled at him with approval and cleared her throat. "This your first trip to Hawaii?"

"Yes. Yours?" He smiled at her while Susan feigned shock because he had begun to speak again.

"Yes, as a matter of fact, young man. This is our second honeymoon, Fred and mine." She patted the knee of the bald-headed man sitting silently beside her. "I'm Tootie Reinworth."

"It's nice to meet you, Mrs. Reinworth. Gene Scott."

She shook his outstretched hand. Gene reached across and took her husband's hand. "Nice to meet you too, Mr. Reinworth."

"Same here." He mumbled and turned back to his newspaper.

"Say, Mr. Scott, that is a mightly pretty little girl with you. Is she your daughter?" Her fat cheeks jiggled as she spoke.

"Yes, this is my daughter Susan Scott." He grinned at Susan's unsmiling face. "Now Susan, be friendly and tell Mrs. Reinworth hello."

"Alright, 'daddy,' if you like." She forced a smile. "It is a pleasure to meet you, lady." She giggled. "I bet you like to eat, don't you?"

"Susan?" Scott laughed sheepishly. "My 'daughter' is a bit naughty at times, Mrs. Reinworth. She is always trying to embarrass her old man."

"Well, children will be children, Mr. Scott." She patted Susan's cheek. "I was always like that myself growing up."

"Well, you are certainly right about the way children act." He took Susan's hand. "Even though my little Susan is eighteen, she is very immature for her age."

"Oh!" Susan gritted her teeth. "Now daddy love, you certainly don't believe that of me when we are in bed, do you?"

Scott's mouth flew open and Mrs. Reinworth let out a gasp.

"Oh dear, dear me!" She turned to her husband. "You meet all kinds, Fred, when you take vacations! That is why I wanted to stay home, so I—I would not be confronted with this sort of thing!"

"If you wasn't so nosey, Tootie, you would not stick yourself in such situations." Her husband spoke lazily as he continued to read his paper.

Susan patted Scott's arm as he glared at her.

"Better tell Mrs. Jelly Roll the truth honey," she whispered. "We would not want her going about spreading sick rumors, would we?"

"No, I guess we wouldn't." He turned to the shaken woman. "Mrs. Reinworth, may I explain this little misunderstanding?"

"Well, young man, it would be interesting. I mean, it would be less confusing if you can explain what she meant."

"Let's just start over then, shall we?" Gene cleared his throat "I am Reverend Gene Scott and this is my pretty young wife Susan."

"Oh!" her fat cheeks broke into a big smile. "And I bet you just got married, didn't you?"

"Yes we did, Mrs. Reinworth, and we are sorry we played that little trick on you." Susan's smile was genuine. "Everyone makes the mistake because I look so much younger than Gene, so we just play along."

"Yes, but dear—"

Fred interrupted his wife. "Tootie!" He smiled at Scott "Pretty smart there, son. Yeh, if'n I had it to do over again, I would pick a new model too."

Tootie Reinworth hit her husband across the head with her pocketbook. "Very funny, Fred!" She patted Scott's knee. "Then that means you two are on your honeymoon too. Isn't that a co-incidence?"

"Yeh, I guess it is at that Tootie." Scott laughed and stood as the captain told everyone to go ashore. "It was nice meeting you both. I hope you have a fun filled honeymoon."

"It sure want be as exciting as the first one, Reverend, but you two can make enough loving for the both of us while we just eat and enjoy the scenery." Fred chuckled as he helped his jolly wife off the boat.

Susan took Scott's hand and they walked along the beach of Havaiki. He took several pictures of Susan standing by palm trees with the surf in the background or in front of ancient ruins. Scott noticed two Hawaiian girls coming down the beach toward them and ask them to take their picture with him. Smiling at the strong handsome man, they happily agreed, their giggles filling the air.

Susan groaned as she looked through the lens at Scott hugging the girls, his smile stretched across his face. She snapped the button and feigned a smile at the three.

"Okay ladies, you can let go now." She set the camera for sixty seconds and started walking down the beach. She smiled to herself when she heard Gene running to catch up with her.

"Hey, were you trying to get away from your old man?" He bent down and kissed her lips lightly. "How was that shot? It felt like a good one."

She stared at him angrily. "What do you mean, 'it felt like a good one?'"

"Well, you know, Susan," he motioned with his hands, "you can sorta tell when something is going to turn out good."

"Oh really?" She pulled the bright, clear pieture from the camera. "And it did, tiger!" She handed him the photo and sat down on a fallen palm tree. "Hey, here comes four Hawaiian fellows. I wonder if they would take a picture with me?" She jumped up and waved them over. "Oh guys, could you come here a second?"

"Susan sweetheart, why don't you just make it with two of them." He looked at the four boys running to answer Susan's call. "I mean, there may be too many for the shot."

"Gene, don't be silly, darling. You can get a lot of people in a photo." She smiled at the heavy-breathing fellows in front of her. "Hi fellows, I'm Susan Scott!"

"Hi Susan, I am Teror. These are my friends, Mato, Kelolo and Tamatoa. He was named after one of our kings."

"Oh? How nice." She smiled sweetly at the well-tanned young man. "Are you all from this island?"

"No, my pretty friend." Teror smiled broadly at the beautiful girl, his white teeth glistening in the sunshine. "My friends Mato and Kelolo, they live here on Havaiki, but Tamatoa and myself live on Bora Bora."

"I have heard that is a beautiful place." Scott gazed through the camera to focus it.

"Yes, Bora Bora is very beautiful, sir." Tamatoa smiled at Susan "Is this your father?"

"No! I am not Susan's father!" he practically shouted. "I am her husband!"

Susan drew close to Gene and whispered, "Darling, why did you let them know in such a hurry? Jealous maybe?"

"I just do not want to try and explain anything else when it is not necessary, that's all." He looked at the surprised faces of the four boys. "Would a couple of you fellows stand on either side of Susan so I can get a picture here?"

All four boys surrounded Susan. Two hugged her around the waist on either side, while the other two got behind her and looked down over her shoulders. Gene grunted to himself as he focused in the little scene. "Hey, could one of you boys in the back come around and squat down in front of her?"

Kelolo ran around in front of Susan and stared up at her. Her halter top hung loosely and Kelolo's eyes grew big as he spoke. "Yes, this is a much better place to be."

Scott walked over and jerked him to his feet. "On second thought Kelolo, go back behind her. I think it looks better."

"Not from my view!" he laughed.

"Well I'm the one with the camera! Now move!" He gave him a push and Susan cleared her throat.

"Gene darling, please take the picture and stop making a big fuss." Susan put her arms around Teror and Mato. "Anytime honey."

"Okay. Everyone hold still." He snapped the button and set the timer. "Alright, you guys can release my wife now, I've got it."

"Too bad, I was just beginning to like my position." Mato laughed as his eyes lit up with an idea. "Say, why don't you both come to my house just over the hill, for a cool drink."

"Oh Gene, that really sounds heavenly. I am burning up out here and a cool drink would hit the spot."

"Just over the hill, huh?" Gene checked his watch to see if they had the time. "Are you sure it won't be any problem?"

"No problem, sir. My sister Keoki makes very good mango lemonade and will be happy to prepare it for us." He took Susan by the hand and pulled her up the green hill toward a small white house, motioning to Scott. "Please follow us, sir."

"Sir!" Scott mumbled to himself and he followed behind the group of fellows surrounding his wife. "Me and my bright idea—coming to Havaiki."

Keoki came running from the house waving "Aloha! Aloha!"

"Aloha!" Susan smiled down at the raven-haired girl. "If it won't be any trouble for you, Keoki, your brother said we might get a cool drink."

"It will be no bother." She smiled at the handsome, tall stranger who had stepped inside the cool hut. "Please, come in. I just made a large container full of my mango lemonade, spiked with a good vodka"

As the group enjoyed the very refreshing drink, they struck up a friendly conversation.

"It must be rewarding work you do, Reverend Scott." Teror smiled. "I often thought about becoming a missionary."

"Is that right!" Scott's eyebrow went up into a smile. "I'm sure the Lord can always use another brave soldier, Teror."

"Didn't your people use to worship idols?" Susan set her empty glass down as she waved away Keoki' s offer for a refill.

"Many years ago, my people did worship false gods." Teror held his glass out for a refill. "They were not all stone idols, those like Kane and Kanaloa who controlled the waters or the great volcano gods." Teror laughed. "But thanks to men and women like your husband, we know the true God today."

"Well, I have really enjoyed your hospitality, the great mango lemonade." He winked at the shy girl. "And I would love to talk all day, but—" He checked his watch. "Our boat heads back for Honolulu in about twenty minutes." He stood and helped Susan to her feet. "Again, thank you for everything. You have made our trip special."

"Thank you for coming into our home as a stranger and now true friends." Teror walked them to the door "If you ever come to Bora Bora, please look me up."

"Thank you. Glad to." Scott stepped out into the fading sunlight. "If you and your friends are ever in TarSa, an island not too far from here, drop by the Sand Palms Methodist Church."

"Yes, I will. Aloha my friends!" Teror waved as the rest joined him at the door, calling to the couple as they made their way down the hill.

"Aloha!" Susan waved over her shoulder. "Aloha! Such a beautiful group of people."

They smiled at one another in the elevator as it climbed it's way up to the sixth floor. Scott stepped out and picked Susan up, then twirled her around in the air.

"I love you Mrs. Gene Scott!"

"And I love you, Mr. Gene Scott!" She hugged him tightly around his neck as he made his way quickly down the hall. "Hey slow down! We've got all night."

"And that is it for a while, honey." He held on to her with his right arm while he fished in his pocket for the room key.

"Hey, don't drop me!" she laughed as she hung on to him.

He laughed and pushed the door opened. "Never would I drop you beautiful!" He walked to the bed "Except, maybe on the bed!" He laughed softly, then his eyes grew serious as his lips slowly went down to meet hers. He patted her lightly on the behind and dropped her across the bed. "Mummm! you look very inviting down there."

"You don't require an invitation, you know." She smiled and slowly licked her lips.

"I'm well aware of that."

He stared down at her, his heart pounding as he felt himself hardening. He sat on the side of the bed and removed his shoes and socks. Susan raised up and started playing with the curls on the back of his neck.

"Honey, did you know that when you really get excited and hot, these sweet little curls really curl up."

"Well, I am sure before long, they will be up to that little trick again!" He patted her leg and stood, undid his pants and dropped them to the floor. Quickly his fingers pulled the turtle neck over his head and he fell back on the bed in his underwear.

"Now, that is as far as I go until I get my girl ready!"

Slowly he reached up and unbuttoned her top. She ran her hand slowly over his bare chest.

"Gene, why did you say, that is it for a while, at the door?"

"You know, baby doll, it's going to be hard to get together when we return to TarSa." His fingers guided her pants to the floor and went back up to her bra. "We will be lucky if we get to be together over the weekends."

"Oh darn, Gene! It's just not fair!" She lay her head on his chest. "Now that I really know what it is like being your wife, I don't ever want to be seperated again from you!"

"In time, Susan my darling, we will work things out where we never need to be seperated again."

Finally removing the rest of their clothes, Gene rolled over on top of Susan. He kissed her on the nose, then his lips parted over hers. Throughout the dark hours of the night, their bodies shared a deep, moving romantic longing that reached out secretly for them alone.

Chapter 15

Gene opened his eyes slowly and looked at Susan. She lay fast asleep on his arm. "For a little woman, she sure has one hell of a body," he thought. "I am so darn lucky."

He smiled as he slid silently out of bed and got the camera from the dresser. His fingers gently pulled back the covers, barely leaving her breast covered. He focused in for a good shot, reached over and pulled the sheet up revealing her shapely legs, then pressed the button. As the flash went off, Susan sat up in shock.

"What was that?"

"Nothing to get uptight about, honey doll." He counted out sixty seconds and pulled out the freshly made picture. "Mummm! That is what you call good photography!"

"What—what did you take?" Susan pulled the covers over her quickly, blushing.

"Let's just say, those playgirl bunnies have nothing over my wife."

"Gene Scott, you didn't!" She stared, wide eyed.

"Yes Mrs. Scott I did! Stop worring that pretty little head over this beautiful work of art. It's not provocative, nor is it a complete nude shot—although I was tempted. Then to play it safe in case it should get in the wrong hands, I would make it cheesy enough for your old man, but not tempting to any other man." Gene laughed and pulled her out of bed "Now to the bathroom young lady. We've got to get a shower and pack up. Our plane leaves at noon."

"Oh darn! I don't want to go back now!" She followed him into the shower. "Hey, husband, wash my back."

"Gotcha. Turn around." He lathered the washcloth and began scrubing her back. "How's that?"

"Hey, not so hard, Mr. Scott. Use your hands." She sighed softly as his hands began touching her lightly. "Mummm. That's much better."

"Could prove dangerous too." His hands moved slowly to her breast. She took a deep breath as he gently rubbed them. "You feel so good, honey."

"So do you." She could feel him pressing up against her. "Do we have the time?"

His breathing was heavy as he turned off the shower and pulled

Susan against him. "We better. I'm taking it!"

He picked her up and carried her to the bed. She rubbed her fingers through his wet curls.

"Gene, honey, we'll get the bed wet."

"That is the last of my worries." He laid her down and eased onto her. "Besides, sweetheart, they expect anything from newlyweds." His lips parted over hers as their bodies knew one another again.

"Got everything?" Scott stood at the door waiting for Susan to follow. "We've got fifteen minutes to make it to the airport!"

"I know. I'm coming." She took one last look around the room. "I will never forget you, you beautiful room." She gently took Scott's hand as she shut the door and picked up the room key in her spare hand. "I think I'll keep this for a lovely reminder."

"Alright, but let's hurry."

They walked quickly to the elevator and rode down to the lobby. Scott paid the bill, flagged down a cab and they reached the airport just in time.

Hawaii seemed to grow smaller as the giant bird soared higher into the blue afternoon sky. Susan played with the room key as she looked from the small window.

"Suppose we can come again and visit Hawaii?"

"We can sure put an effort at it!" He laughed and took the key from Susan's hand. "It certainly was a great vacation! Boy, if old Weber only knew how good my little vacation was, he would probably hate himself."

"He's not planning to send you away again, is he?" Susan looked at Gene with a serious expression. "Is he Gene?"

"Now sweetheart, just relax. If Weber is sending me on a mission, I will let you know." He took her hand. "It's a promise Susan."

"And you will take me with you, right?"

"Susan, college will be starting soon and you know how we committed to keep all this a secret." He kissed her. "It's for the best, Susan, that I take my missions alone."

"No! You are my husband. My place is with you. I love you, Gene. I want to be with you." She threw her arms around his neck. "I don't care what people may think or what they might say. I just don't care!"

"Susan, honey, we talked this all over before. If we tell your parents about us now, they might try to have our marrage anulled.

Don't you see?" His hands held hers tightly. "I know what you are thinking. You're eighteen and by law you have the right to marry, but, Susan, you're still their little girl in their eyes. They see you as just starting your life, going to college like all young girls your age. They could say that I took you just as soon as you turned eighteen— a man who soon will turn thirty-seven. Those few days could make a case for them, they could have me locked up for taking you."

"Oh, they wouldn't do that!" Susan's tears filled her eyes as she turned to Gene. "They really love you, darling."

"But honey, they could never understand my marrying their little girl. It would hurt them very much." He touched her cheek with his fingertips. "In time we will find the right way to tell them and hope we get their blessing."

"Alright, we shall keep it a secret, but I still can go with you, Gene. I can always make somthing up. Please, Gene, you will take me with you. Promise me you will take me."

"I cannot promise, honey."

"Why not? Don't you want to be with me?" Her lips quivered.

"Susan, of course I do, but there are times when it's not safe for you to be around." He looked at his hands. "I would certainly die if anything was to happen to you."

"And you think I wouldn't if something happened to you?" She gently touched his leg. "I would kill myself if anything did."

"Susan, don't say that! Don't ever say that!" He took a firm hold of her shoulders. "If you did and went to hell and I was in heaven, I would probably put in a tranfer just to be with you!"

"Oh Gene!" she hugged his neck "Do you love me that much?"

"More, much much more!" His hand touched her leg as his lips parted over hers and his tongue found her tongue. "I wish I did not have to be seperated from you ever Mrs. Scott."

"When can we be together again darling?" Susan held him tightly.

"I'm not sure, honey, but I will call you just as soon as I can come up with something." He laid her head on his shoulder and leaned back onto the head rest. "Just be standing by with a good excuse to get out of the house."

"I will write up a list of excuses," she laughed softly. "I will be using them quite a bit. "

The parting at the airport was almost unbearable for Gene and Susan. She walked quickly away, tears streaming from her eyes.

Scott slowly picked up his suitcase and made his way back to the parsonage in a taxi. Pogo came running out to meet him when the cab pulled to a stop.

"Scott, how was the honeymoon?" He slapped his back carefully as not to hurt his hand. "You look like a new man!" Pogo noticed his unsmiling face. "Not very happy though. What happened?"

"Nothing happened." Scott·paid the cab driver and headed for the porch.

"You mean there was no honeymoon?" Pogo walked quickly to keep up with his friend.

"It was a terrific honeymoon." Scott smiled to himself. "It's leaving Susan that's tough. I wish I could keep her with me forever."

"You can in time, Scott!" Pogo laughed. "How was she?"

Scott frowned at his inquisitive friend. "That's for me to know, Pogo." He walked into the house and shouted. "Where is my favorite cook?"

Edna came running from the kitchen laughing. "Gene, you're home!" She grabbed his hand. "How was the honeymoon?"

"I certainly do have a lot of inquisitive friends running around." He patted her on her back side causing her face to turn red. "My honeymoon was extra wonderful and my little bride is a great, wonderful, sexy lover. I would not trade her for all the women in the world!" He winked at Edna and smiled at Pogo. "Does that answer all your questions?"

"All but one." Edna pulled a note from her apron pocket. "Are you going to tell Susan about this mission?"

Scott grabbed the note from her hand and read it aloud.

"Scott, I hope you got rested up."

Pogo laughed and Gene glared at him.

"Chuck it, Pogo!" His eyes fell back to the note. "Your mission is to rescue Reverend Martin from the desert rats. They are led by a man named Jesse Stevens, a thief and a murderer. Brother George was captured while on a church building mission in Israel. I will come by to fill you in on the details, Weber." Scott slapped the paper in his hand. "That George Martin! Might know he would go screw something up."

"Boy, the way he talked, you would think he was tough as an old shoe." Pogo flopped down on the sofa. "When do we leave?"

"Oh no Pogo, this is my baby. You stay here!" Scott walked to the staircase. "I don't want you getting yourself hurt."

"Yeh? Well what about you? Somebodies gotta protect you."

Pogo climbed the steps behind Scott.

"And you think you can?" Scott laughed and sat his suitcase on the bed.

"This is not going to be a picnic, Pogo. I have heard some things about this Stevens guy that would make your hair stand on end." He pulled out his dirty clothes and threw them on the floor. "Stevens and his rat pack go into little towns and wipe them clean, killing men, women, and children—except women they can use."

"Use? For what?" Pogo's eyes grew wide.

"They rape them, Pogo, make them become slaves to them. Then when they're tired of them, they kill them." He stared at the camera in his hands. "I hear it is no pretty sight what those devils do." Scott picked the photos up with his clean underwear and put them in his top dresser drawer.

Pogo's eyes fell on the camera. "Hey, what kind of pictures did you take with this?" He picked it up to examine, then smiled Scott. "A Polaroid huh? Where are the pictures?"

"Wait until I put them in a book." Scott tried to avoid his friend's smiling eyes. "I'll put them in order as to the things we did."

"All the pictures for all your events?" Pogo sat down on the bed. "All the pictures, Scott?"

"Alright, I get your point!" Scott jerked the camera from Pogo's hand and put it on the closet shelf. "All but my private collection."

"Oh gee, Scott, they are the best," Pogo mumbled. "Are you going to tell Susan about our mission?"

"My mission! I thought I would write her a letter." Scott's eyes wandered around the room. "She can not know where I am going, Pogo. She will try and follow me and I could not take her being anywhere near that Stevens."

"But if they are as dangerous as you say, Scott, you could be in a lot of danger." Pogo got up and gripped his friend's strong arm. "Let me go with you!"

"Nothing doing, Pogo, and that's final!" He looked out the window when he heard a car pull up. "Shit, it's Gloria."

"That figures," Pogo mumbled. "She's been calling all morning to see if you had returned."

"Oh great! That's one broad I would like to tell I'm married!"

He and Pogo turned to face the door when it opened and Gloria Ann Weber stepped in.

"Gene darling." She ran across the room and grabbed him.

He pulled away and gritted his teeth. "Miss Weber, do you

always go running into men's bedrooms without knocking?"

"You ran into mine, darling." She smiled shyly. "Remember Gene?"

"Who could forget being on Mars," he laughed.

"Very funny," she snapped. "Daddy sent me to fill you in on your little old mission to save George."

"That's just great. I hope you remember everything." He walked to the door "Come on down to the study. We can talk down there."

"I kinda prefer your bedroom, darling, if Polard would kindly get lost." She sat down on Gene's bed. When he yanked her to her feet, she whimpered, "Must you be so rough, honey?"

"Come on. Let's get this over with!" He led her out the door. "Can you make it down the steps or do you need a little push?"

"Oh!" She marched quickly down the stairs. "I can manage! Thank you!"

Gene sat down behind the desk in the study while Gloria took the seat in front of him. He pulled some paper from the desk drawer and looked up at her.

"Alright, what exactly am I supposed to do?"

"You are to go to a little village in Israel named Rajila. It is surrounded by desert. George went there to build a church. The authorities sent us word that Jesse Stevens and his naughty old men raided the village, stealing their few valuables. They captured George along with four young girls."

"Why in the devil did they take George?" Scott stared at her, puzzled.

"They didn't exactly take George, Gene. George was out of the village buying supplies the day they raided. The villagers sent poor George to bring the girls back, but alas, dear, George never returned."

"What makes your father think he's still alive?" Scott dropped his pencil on the desk.

"Well, Gene darling, Daddy does not know for sure. The villagers people think it's the church's fault that their village was raided."

"A scapegoat." Scott stood. "The village is too cowardly to rescue their women, so they turn it over to someone else. Too bad for them it was Martin."

"Well, like it or not, darling, it's your job now." She rose. "How is the mysterious woman taking the news of your departure?"

"I haven told her yet."

"Better tell her soon. You leave Saturday morning—very early." She went to the door. "I'm sorry I can't feel any pity for her." She shrugged. "If I knew who she was, I would laugh in her face."

"That is enough Gloria." Scott took her arm and led her out the door. "Goodbye! Tell your old man I will bring George back if he is alive."

"Just bring yourself back darling." She headed down the walk toward her car. "Like my new sports car?"

"It's just what you need: the only thing you can turn on." He turned away, stepping back inside the parsonage.

Gloria climbed into her car angrily and sped away.

Chapter 16

The days seemed to run in circles around Scott and Friday morning burst upon him with brilliant sunshine. He walked quickly into the kitchen and grabbed Edna's arm.

"Come with me." He led her to the study. "I need you to do me a big favor."

"Sure, Gene? What is it?" She gave him a puzzled look. "If I can, you know I would be more than happy to help you."

"Good! You know once you said you would do any thing to help Susan and me"

"Of course I remember, Gene." She took his hand. "And I meant it. What can I do? Just name it."

"Call Shirley and tell her you want Susan to come over and help you today. I'm sure you can think of some good reason." He smiled. "You can tell her it will be late before you're finished with her. To keep her from driving home late, you recommend that she sleep over here."

"Well here goes." She picked up the phone. "Don't just stand there and listen. Go eat your breakfast."

Scott kissed her cheek and laughed. He hurried off to the kitchen. He only put small portions on his plate. His appetite vanished at the thought of having to leave Susan. He stared at the food, his heart breaking within him.

"How can I tell her, Lord? What words can I say?"

Edna walked through the door.

He looked up. "How'd it go?"

"Lying certainly comes easy doesn't it, once you really get going." She pulled her chair up next to Scott. "Susan will over in about an hour."

"Great!" A smile stretched across his handsome face. He picked up a fork and began forcing down his food. "Now don't mention my leaving to Susan. Understand?"

"But, Gene, you are going to tell her, aren't you." Edna put her hand on his arm. "She is your wife, Gene. She has a right to know where her husband is going."

"I will tell her, Edna, somehow. Only I do not want her to know where I will be going, get it!" He stood and walked quickly to his room.

In less than an hour, Susan's yellow Corvette parked in the parsonage driveway. She jumped out and raced up the walk to the door, which burst open. Scott pulled Susan inside and into his arms.

"There's my girl!"

"Oh Gene, here is where I belong and have longed to be all week! I have missed you so very much darling!" She felt so safe and protected in these strong arms that held her so passionately. "Did you miss me?"

"Only every second I breathe." His lips met hers in a burning kiss.

"Who thought of Edna calling Mom and telling her she needed me?" Susan put her arm around Scott's waist as he led her to sofa. "Was it my loved-starved husband?"

"Pretty clever idea, huh." Scott laughed. "I came up with it last night while lying in bed."

"Bed! That is such a wonderful word." Susan lay her head on Gene's shoulder. "Don't you think bed is a beautiful word sweetheart?"

"Only if you are in it with me, little darling." He slowly wagged his tongue at her.

"Hey mister, don't stick it out unless you plan to use it!" She smiled coyly.

"Glad to!" His lips parted over hers as his tongue moved slowly inside her mouth. "Oh Susan, Susan, I love you so very much."

"And I love you, Gene darling." She draped her head back on the sofa and took a deep breath. "Much more of that, Gene Scott, and I will drag you up to your bed."

"Our bed and that will be alright by me, Susan Scott." He touched her face tenderly.

Edna walked in the back door smiling, her basket full of fresh vegetables just gathered from her garden. "Hi Susan, I see you forced yourself to come over to help me all day."

"Forced? I know you're kidding!" Susan laughed. "Mom told me at nine and I was ready to leave in ten minutes. She insisted that I eat some breakfast or I would have been here fifteen minutes sooner."

"You certainly deserve some time together." Edna went into the kitchen. "I think I'll start lunch."

"Need any help?" Susan called.

"That's sweet, but no thanks. This is your and Gene's day to spend together."

"She is so thoughtful and sweet, isn't she?" Susan put her arms around Gene's waist. And I love you! I love you! I love you!"

"Hey, I think I am loved!" he laughed and kissed the top of her head. "Love·is what I feel for you too, Mrs. Scott, love, love, love and more love!"

"Wow, I must be in the world of love!" Pogo laughed as he walked lazily down the steps. "That's the impression I get with that word 'love' floating around."

"Alway the comedian, huh, Pogo?" Scott sat up on the edge of the sofa. "What are you up to today?"

"Nothing much." He opened a cabinet and took out a baseball and began tossing it up and down in his hand. "Catch, Gene!" The ball sailed across the room and luckily Scott's big hand captured it before it broke anything. "Way to go!"

"Never miss!" Scott laughed and Edna stuck her head around the kitchen door. "Alright, you two, if you are going to play ball, you can just go outside. I kinda like the way I have things arranged in here without you fixing everything your way."

"Okay, you two, you heard Edna. Out!" Susan stood and pulled Scott to his feet. "You overgrown boys can go outside to pitch the ball. I will help Edna in the kitchen."

Scott bent down and kissed her gently. "You're on." He patted her on the seat and walked out the front door, calling over his shoulder, "Alright slugger, get a move on. I'll show you a fast ball!"

"I know your fast balls, Scott, ole pal!" Pogo laughed and stood with his back against the church. "Let the old gal fly!"

"Well, for heaven's sake, don't miss it!"

Scott sent the ball soaring to Pogo. He caught it, then quickly yanked his hand from his glove, shaking it.

"Shit, Scott baby, that hurt!" He made a face as he slid his glove back on and narrowed his eyes. "Get ready, Scott. This is going to be a bomber!"

"Let me have it then, baby. I'm ready." Scott laughed as the ball landed neatly in his glove. "You call that a bomber?"

"Hey, I thought that one was really good and fast." Pogo slapped his glove. "Admit it, Scott!"

"Sure thing, Babe Ruth! Get ready, pal. Here comes the bomber!"

Scott threw the ball toward Pogo. Thinking the ball was going to hit him, he reacted by ducking and the ball crashed through a church window.

"Shit Pogo! Why the devil didn't you catch that?"

"It was going to splatter me! I am sorry Scott. I guess that one really was a bomber, huh?" Pogo forced a laugh as Scott looked him up and down with disgust. "I think I'm ready for the axe."

"Stop with the dramatics, Pogo. We're not getting anything done standing here looking at our little accident." He glanced toward the house to make certain no one had observed the event. "We can go to the hardware store and pick up a new pane before somebody finds out. We will never hear the end of it if they know about it."

"Right. Let's go!" Pogo raced over to where the Crain's car was always parked and realized John had taken it out earlier. "Good Lord, Scott, what do we do now? No wheels!"

"Relax, will you. I guess we take Susan's car. She won't mind loaning it to her old man." He walked quickly up the steps. "Get in. I'll go get the keys and be right back."

Susan looked up from the potatoes she was peeling when she heard the kitchen door open. Scott smiled at her sheephishly.

"Could I borrow your car, sweetheart? I need to go pick something up at the hardware store."

"You don't have to ask me, of course you can, Gene. What's mine is yours." She stood and pulled the keys from her pant's pocket. "Here you go."

"Why don't you ride along with him?" Edna picked up the bowl of potatoes and began washing them off. "There isn't much to do here for a while."

"Alright, if you're sure and Gene doesn't mind."

"Gene won't mind." Edna patted Susan's arm. "I'm sure he would love for you to go along, wouldn't you, Gene?"

"Ah—sure. You bet!" He tried to laugh as normally as possible as he took Susan's hand and walked to the car. "I won't be in there long, sweetheart. So you can wait in the car with Pogo."

"Alright, honey." She climbed in as Pogo slumped in the middle between the seats and forced a laugh. "Pogo, would you rather I sit in the middle?"

"No, I don't mind, really." Pogo stared at Scott. "We won't be all that long, will we Scott?"

"No, I can run in and pick it up." He started the motor and backed out of the driveway. "Susan, this baby handles real good."

"Yes, I think so." She reached across Pogo and patted Scott's knee. "What do you need to get in the hardware store?" She gazed from the window as the car sped along the highway.

Pogo glanced at Scott, then spoke up quickly. "A screwdiver."

"A screwdriver? Don't you have plenty of screwdrivers at the parsonage?" she laughed.

"This is a very rare and special screwdriver, Susan. It's made to tighten the screws in people's heads." Scott shook his head as his eyes caught those of the sheepish young man in the mirror. "Isn't that right, Pogo?"

"That is cute, real cute Scott!" Pogo smiled at Susan. "He's only pulling your leg, Susan. It's—well—a special kind of screwdriver for a rare kind of—square screw."

"I understand." She leaned past Pogo and kissed Scott before he climbed out. "Hurry back. Can't stand for you to be gone long."

"Wow! That's rough," Pogo said, "seeing as to how—"

Scott reached in and pulled Pogo out of the car before he could finish.

"On second thought, I think I might need you."

"Oh really, Gene, to carry out one little screwdriver?" Susan laughed. "What's the real reason? Don't you trust him in the car alone with me?"

"Yes, you could say that." He gave Pogo a shove once they were inside the hardware store. "Would you please watch what you say! Susan does not know I am leaving yet!"

"Why haven't you told her?" Pogo walked quickly behind him. "She is gonna have to know sooner or later."

"Right, but I will tell her when I am ready. Understand?" He looked at the clerk. "Do you have a piece of glass about eighteen by twenty?"

"Yes sir, sure do." He squinted his small, bitty eyes "Want me to wrap it up for you?"

"Hey, that would be great!" Pogo chuckled. "Could you make it look like a screwdriver maybe?"

"A what?" The clerk scratched his head.

"Never mind him. Just wrap it up." Scott slugged Pogo's arm "Will you keep still?"

"Well, it is going to be hard to explain why a srewdriver is shaped like a square."

"Rectangle! We will just tell Susan we saw something else we needed." Gene picked up an odd-looking screwdriver and laid it on the counter. "I'll take this too."

"Alrighty, that will be in all seven dollars and thirty-three cents."

Scott paid him and walked quickly back to the car.

Susan sat up and smiled. "Did you get it?"

"Sure did." Scott held up the screwdriver while Pogo slipped the package in behind the seats.

Susan smiled at him as he turned around. "What you got Pogo?"

"Oh, it is—a—well—a—"

"It is a piece of tile, sweetheart. John wanted me to pick it up." Scott started the motor and headed back toward the parsonage. He pulled the Corvette to a stop and handed Susan the keys as he helped her out. "Thanks, beautiful."

"You are welcome, handsome. I'll go see if Edna needs any more help with lunch, if you fellows have something to do." Susan reached up and kissed Scott's cheek and hurried to the house.

"Thanks hon," he called "We will be in soon." Scott walked swiftly over to the broken window "Pogo, go inside and see how much glass is on the floor."

"Right!"

Pogo started for the front of the church when Scott called, "And bring me some putty from the storeroom."

"Will do!" Pogo shouted and Scott grimaced. Pogo smiled through the broken window. "Hi there Scott, funny meeting this way."

"Yes, and we had better step on it before we get caught." He jerked the putty tube from Pogo's hand. "Now get a broom and start clearing away that broken glass."

"Okay, Scott." Pogo shrugged his shoulders in defeat and hurried off to find a broom.

Scott was finishing the window when he heard Poge whisling inside. "Be careful with that broom in there, Pogo. We wouldn't want you to break another—"

Before Scott could finish speaking, the broom handle came crashing through the freshly installed window glass.

Chapter 17

"Pogo! Get out here! Now!"

Pogo closed his eyes as he bit his lip, turned and walked quickly from the church and up to Scott. "Scott—I—I—"

"The next time I ask you to do a job, don't whistle while you work, damn it!" Scott shouted. "Now get in the car!" He turned and stormed into the parsonage and called out sweetly, "Susan, I need your keys again."

She came from the kitchen, dangling her keys. "Forget something?"

"Ah—yes, as a matter of fact." He kissed her tenderly. "I'll bring them back soon, darling."

"Just bring yourself back soon, Reverend Scott." She returned his kiss and waved from the door.

Scott frowned at Pogo.

"Pogo, if you had just caught that stupid ball we would not have to go through all this, and I could be with my girl."

"I am sorry, Scott, I just thought—"

"I don't want to hear what you think, pal." Scott's eyes went quickly to the rearview mirror at the sight of flashing blue lights. "Shit!" His eyes fell to the speedometer. "I was going seventy-five in a fifty zone."

"Caught by the fuzz! That's all we needed to finish up this day." Pogo slumped down in the seat as the officer looked in the window.

"What's the hurry, buddy?"

"Just give me the damn ticket." Scott pulled out his driver's license. "I've got work to do."

"Reverend?" The police officer gave Scott a puzzled look.

"Yes, that's right officer, he's got God's work to do." Pogo straightened up to get a better look. "We had an emergency call from one of our members. He is pretty sick, sir. Might not live. The family wanted Scott to get there as soon as possible."

"Oh, well, why didn't you say so, Reverend Scott." The officer handed the license back to him. "What is the address, sir. I'll escort you."

Scott frowned at Pogo as he gritted his teeth. "Riggles Hardware."

"Riggles Hardware?" The police officer shook his head.

"Alright, if you say so. Follow me."

Gene Scott followed along behind the police car. Pogo smiled sheepishly at his angry friend.

"Scott, I was·only trying to—"

Scott took a tight hold of his arm. "Just don't speak another word Pogo! I do not want to hear any thing else from you!"

At last they had the new piece of glass and headed back to the church. Scott handed Pogo Susan's keys and sent him to take them to her while he started on the window. After he finished putting it in, he hurried inside the church to clean up.

Susan took the keys back from Pogo and put them back in her pocket. "Thanks, Pogo. Where is my dear husband?"

"He's—ah—finishing that job we started. He'll be in soon."

As he walked to the door, Edna grabbed his arm. "Pogo, what kind of job have you fellows been doing?"

"Just something we've been meaning to get to." He laughed coyly and hurried from the room.

"That's funny. I cannot think of a thing those two could be doing. I think they're up to something."

"They got a screwdriver and a piece of tile in the hardware store, if that's any help," Susan said. "What could they possibly be up to?"

"A screwdriver and a piece of tile?" Edna scratched her head. "Didn't they go out at first to pitch a baseball?"

"Why yes, they did, didn't they?" Susan and Edna looked at one aother. They laughed.

"Edna, you don't suppose—?"

"I certainly do, Susan. The tile was probably a piece of glass." She dried her hands and walked to the back door. "It has to be a church window. I think we would have heard it if it had been the house."

"Shall we catch them with the evidence?"

Susan giggled as she and Edna slipped over to the church.

Pogo whispered emphatically through the window, "Scott! You had better get a move on. I think Edna is getting suspicious."

"Thanks, Pogo."

Scott stuck the putty tub in his pants and, gathering the broken glass into his handkerchief, started for the aisle. He heard the church door open, so he slid hurriedly under one of the pews. Slowly he tried to inch his way toward the back of the church, but found his big frame was completely stuck. The putty tub came open and putty covered the front of his pants. Taking the glass-filled handkerchief, he managed to push it out of harm's way. But the fact was still clear to him, Gene Scott was firmly stuck beneath the pew.

"Shit!" He mumbled to himself.

Susan and Edna looked at the newly installed window. Susan smiled to herself.

"Well now, what have we here?" She tossed the ball up and down in her hand. "Alright, Gene Scott, stop hiding! We know you're in here!"

Gene closed his eyes in defeat. He could not budge and they would, no doubt, find him sooner or later. He grimaced as he spoke.

"I am under here!"

Susan and Edna hurried to the sound of his voice and looked all around over the pews. Then Susan dropped onto her knees and gazed beneath the pews. Instantly she started laughing. "Ah ha! Caught cha! You can come out now!"

"Wanta bet?" He narrowed his eyes at her laughter. "I'm stuck under here."

"What?"

Susan and Edna laughed in unison, then crawled under the pew beside him. His body was wedged between the pew bottom and the floor.

"How in the world did you manage to get stuck here?" Edna tugged at his pant's leg. "And what is that white stuff flowing out of your pocket?"

"It would appear the pews are closer to the floor than they appear. And I put the tub of putty in my pants. The cap must have come off when I tried to roll over under this man-trap." He frowned at Susan for continuing to laugh.

"I'm sorry, Gene, but this is so funny." She grabbed the arm of Edna, who was still yanking on Gene's leg. "Wait! I have an idea!" She giggled girlishly and scrambled to her feet. "Stay here. I'm going to get the camera."

"Susan! Don't you dare!" Gene tried to free himself, but he was stuck fast.

"Oh, what a hilarious picture this will make!" Edna chuckled.

"I do not see anything funny, Edna!" Scott scolded.

"Oh Gene, where is your sense of humor?" Edna touched his face gently.

Susan was still laughing as she crawled back under the pew with the camera.

"Alright, honey, smile real big!" She pulled a srewdriver from her pocket and held it up. "Then we'll release you."

"Why not? What have I got to lose?" He forced a smile as the light flashed. "Now crawl out there and undo those screw, and free me, will you?"

"Alright, tiger."

Susan and Edna got up, undid the screws holding down the pew and lifted it so Gene could crawl out. Gene reached for the hankerchief with the glass shards, crawed out and rubbed his stiff back.

"Boy, it's great to stand up straight again." He looked at the two women with disgust as they stood laughing at him. "Laugh, by all means laugh."

"Susan, bring that big baby of yours inside and have him take off those pants before that stuff sets in." Edna punched his arm and walked back to the parsonage chuckling.

"Gene, you did look so funny lying under there. So helpless." She took his arm and walked slowly back to the parsonage.

Everyone sat silently watching the eight o'clock movie. Scott smiled at Susan and nodded toward the steps. She smiled and nodded her approval. Gene cleared his throat and stood up stretching.

"Susan. and I are going on up to bed."

"Oh? So early?" David picked up an apple and bit into it. "It's just eight thirty."

"Yeh Scott, and I thought you always enjoyed watching John Wayne." Pogo s looked mischievously down into his hands.

"I like Susan better." He took her hand and led her over to the steps. "Goodnight."

"Goodnight, lover boy." David hit Pogo's shoulder, laughing.

"Yeh, don't do anything that will get you into trouble." Pogo was trying so hard not to laught he could hardly talk.

"Will you two leave Gene alone!" Edna punched David's knee. "Now, get quiet!"

"The trouble with you guys is that you cannot keep a woman long enough to get into trouble with." Scott pulled Susam on up the steps callimg over his shoulder, "And believe me, you will never learn by watching John Wayne!"

Susan smiled at Scott as she walked with him. Her eyes fell to the bed and she giggled softly.

"There it is, our bed." She tossed her hair with her fingers then jumped across the bed laughing. 'Pull off those pants, mister, and come here."

"Glad to oblige, little darling."

He dropped his pants to the floor and walked to the bed. He gently undid her top and pulled it over her head. She reached up and pulled his sweater off. After they had undressed, Gene gathered Susan into his arms and kissed her passionately.

"Oh Susan, you have made me a happy happy man by becoming my wife."

"Not half as happy as you made me by becoming my husband, Gene darling." Her hand moved slowly up and down his strong back. "I love you so much, Gene, so very much."

"Susan, my Susan." He spoke softly as his tongue moved slowly down her neck and over her young round breast. "I love you, Susan."

His body found hers and in the soft still hours of the night, they made love.

At one o'clock in the morning, he rolled over exhaused. His hand found hers and held it tightly, knowing that in a few short hours he must slip out and leave her. Gene felt a tight, clutching pain in his heart for fear that he may never see her again. He slept fitfully and even those few minutes brought him no rest, filled with nightmares of Susan crying because he left her behind.

Looking at his watch, he saw clearly it was time to leave. He slipped from bed and· dressed quickly. Then he took a sheet of paper from his drawer. His hand shook as he wrote the words:

"Susan dearest, I have a mission I must complete. I am hoping of finishing it quickly, so I can return to you. Never forget how much I love you and it is because I love you so much that I could not tell you before hand. With all the love that is within me, yours forever, Gene."

He laid the letter down on his pillow and bent over to kiss her lips gently.

"I love you. I will love you for all my tomorrows." He whispered and, picking up his suitcase, rushed out of the room.

Chapter18

Scott made his way quickly to the airport and boarded the flight to Israel. His eyes filled with tears as the plane climbed through the dark morning sky.

"Oh Susan," he thought, "must we always be separated?" Closing his eyes tightly to shut out the staring eyes around him, he pictured Susan's face in his mind. "I love you," he whispered as he drifted into a restless sleep.

Susan opened her eyes slowly and looked beside her. She sat up when she realized she was alone. Her eyes fell to the letter folded neatly on Scott's pillow. With trembling fingers, she picked it up and opened it. Her heart began beating wildly in her throat as she read the words, over and over.

"Oh God, he can't be gone!" She leaped out of bed and threw on her clothes. Loudly from the top of the staircase she called, "Gene! Gene, please answer me!" She sat down slowly on the step, tears streaming from her eyes. "Please be there, Gene."

A hand touched her shoulder, causing her to jump. Edna tried to force a smile that came out weakly.

"Oh Edna, why did he have to go? Why?" She buried her head in Edna's lap when she joined her on the step.

"Oh that Bishop Weber and his precious Gloria! I wish all the Webers would kindly get lost!" She rubbed Susan's head gently. "There, there, Susan. Gene will be alright. He is so strong and brilliant? What could go wrong?"

"He needs me, Edna. Gene needs his wife." She looked up at Edna pleadingly. "Tell me where he is Edna. Please, you have to. You must!"

"Gene doesn't want you to know, Susan dear. Honest. It's for your own good, really."

Edna felt a lump growing in her throat. She knew Gene's location. She also knew the danger Susan could be in if the man named Stevens got his hands on her. "Oh, it's not fair, to either of you."

Pogo walked quickly up to the two women "Did Scott leave already? I was going with him!" He hit his hand on the wall and felt the sudden sting. "Shit! That Scott is the most stubborn person I have ever met! Goes off knowing he's in big danger and wouldn't even take his ole buddy here with him."

"Danger?" Susan stood and grabbed Pogo. "Do you know where he went, Pogo?"

"I sure do, and I am going whether he wants my help or not!"

"Take me with you." Susan took a deep breath as Edna grabbed her arm. "Don't say it, Edna. Don't say anything. I'm going and that's that!"

"Susan, you can't!" Pogo's eyes grew big. "If Scott found out I·was responsible for you finding out, he would probably kill me first then ask questions."

"I'll tell Gene I tricked you, Pogo, but I am going, so you might as well tell me where." She put her hands on her hips. "Well, we haven't got all year."

"Israel. He has gone to Rejila, Israel, wherever that place is." Pogo slumped in defeat and shook his head at Edna who looked ready to strangle him herself. "Sorry, Edna, I tried." He picked up his suitcase and glanced at Susan. "If you are going with me, you had better get a move on."

"I'm coming, just as soon as I get my suitcase."

"Susan, what about your parents? What are you going to tell them?" Edna rang·her hands together.

"I don't have the time to think of anything, Edna darling, but I am sure you can think of something good to tell them!" She kissed Edna's cheek and ran from the house calling over her shoulder. "As a big favor to Gene and me."

Scott arrived a day later in Rejila.The town was quiet and peaceful enough as he walked quickly into the hotel and rang the desk bell.

"Coming, coming!" a voice came from the back. A skinny, shaggy gray-haired man with a square jaw came hurriedly from the back room. "Yes, and what is your pleasure?"

"First, I would like a room. Second, I would like some information."

"A room I can give you and as for the information, it all depends on what it is." His narrow eyes sized up Scott. "You are a very big man."

"Am I? I hadn't noticed," Scott answered sarcastically. "I am Reverend Scott. I have been sent here by my bishop to help a fellow minister who is in danger. I am also to bring back four of your captives."

"Oh yes! Go across the street and the authorities will give you all the information you need." He pushed the register book around for Scott to sign and handed him a room key.

He signed and took the key. "Thank you. Would you see that my suitcase is taken to my room? I think I'll go on over to talk with your authorities now."

"Yes sir, I will see that your luggage is put in your room." He chuckled as he came around to get the suitcase. "By the way, they have one of Stevens' rats locked up in the jail. He might talk for a man your size."

"Thanks for the confidence."

He turned and walked across the street to the jail. Scott opened the door and stepped inside. Two men looked up from their card game, startled.

"I would like a few words with the one in charge."

"That would be me. I am in charge here." A heavy-set man on the far end stood up. "And what is it you would like to discuss with me? As you can see, I am a very busy man."

"I see." Scott eyed them disgustedly. "It appears to me you would be trying to recapture your women instead of wasting your time playing stupid card games."

"You must be that preacher they were going to send from the states." He leand back in his chair, a broad smile stretched across his mocking face as he settled back. "If you are as good as the last chicken they sent, we shall probably never see you again." He laughed and his men joined in.

Scott walked over and slammed his fist down on the card table, splitting it down the middle. The two men at the table scrambled to their feet and backed against the wall shaking while the third guard moved out of harm's way.

Fire blazed in Scott's eyes as his voice came out strong. "Now listen, I have got a job to do here and the faster I get finished the better I will like it! Now start talking damn it!"

"Ah—ah—your—ah—your Mr. Martin and four of our young citizens were captured by Stevens and his pack about one week ago. We wounded one of them and, knowing that he would rather kill himself than talk, they left him behind."

"Where is he now?" Scott stared at the empty cell.

"We put him in the dark room, hoping he would talk sooner or later." The heavy-set man turned his eyes to his partner. "Go get him and bring him here."

"But, captain, he ain't gonna talk! It ain't going to help none to walk all the way over there to get him." He yawned.

"Get a move on it!" Scott jerked him by the arm and shoved him out the door. "He is going to talk if I have to beat the hell out of him to make him open up!"

The shaken guardian ran quickly down the street, stumbling along the way as Scott watched.

"Some help you've got there, captain!" Scott turned to face the map on the wall "Is this your area?"

"Yeh, this is our town." The chubby finger pointed to a small mark on the map. "This guy we caught can probably take you right to the camp of Stevens." His finger made a wide sweep over the map. "He is somewhere out in this area."

Scott looked up when the door opened and a dark, long-haired man was being pushed in. "Here he is captain, the stinking rat." The guard's eyes fell on Scott. "And he is as quiet as a church mouse."

"Church mice can be made to squeal!" Scott grabbed the prisoner's arm. "If this rat knows what's good for him, he will talk and fast!" Scott's eyes burned into the frightened man's eyes. "What is your name mister?"

Silence fell upon the room as Scott's grip bit into the bare shoulders of the prisoner.

"You had better start talking or I will make your Stevens look like an angel compared to what I will give you!"

"His name is Horton, Jamar Hoton." The guard laughed. "Horton, the silent!"

"I'm going to silence you if you do not keep your smart-ass remarks to yourself." Scott pushed the guard to one side then jerked Horton up by the neck causing him to cough. "Now start talking, Horton. I will not kill you, but you certainly will wish I had when I get started breaking bones!"

"No, I—I can't! They will—ki—kill me for sure!" Horton tried to catch his breath. "Please, don't ma—make me!"

"Listen Horton, if you will cooperate with me, I will see to it that you get a lighter sentence compared to the rest of your gang."

"Alright, alright!" He gasped when Scott released him. "What do you want me to do?"

"Tell me anything I might do to get inside that camp, as one of you."

"Let me think." He pushed his black hair out of his eyes to get a better look at the man holding him. "Yes, I can think of one way, sir, if Smith has not got to Stevens yet."

"Who is this Smith? How is he involved with Stevens?" Scott released his grip, pulled a chair up and motioned for the prisoner to sit.

"Riffbone Smith. He is a real tough character Stevens has hired to set up raids and train robberies. He was coming from the states sometime soon, no definite date. Smith hadn't come yet when I was last with the gang." Horton cleared his throat. "Could I have a little drink? I'm as dry as a cottonball."

"Get this man some water." Scott pulled a chair up in front of him. "I want you to lead me to your camp. If Smith is there, you will probably know he is not one of your men."

"I am sure of it." He turned up his nose as he drank the water. "Do I have to go? I'm too weak to travel and Stevens will—"

"Stevens will never see you and we are leaving first thing in the morning!" Scott turned to the fat captain. "See that Horton has something to eat. Where could I borrow a Jeep around here?"

"Oh we will get you one, Scott!" His fat fingers circled Horton's wrist. "Get in that cell, Horton, and Vinny will go get you some grubb."

Scott went back to the hotel and ate a good meal before turning in. The morning would come early and he had a lot of acting ahead of him·if he was going to fool Jesse Stevens. He pulled his shirt and pants off and stretched his strong body across the bed. His thoughts were of Susan, wondering how she had taken his letter about leaving. What was she doing at that moment.

"Oh Susan," he thought as he unlatched his suitcase and held up her picture. "I love you, Susan darling, and I will always love as long as there is breath in me." He tenderly kissed the photo and closed his eyes and within minutes his tired body drifted off to sleep.

The next morning Scott made his way across the street to the jail for his prisoner. The Jeep was sitting right outside and Scott smiled to himself.

"I'm glad to see those men are finally moving things around here."

He walked inside and asked to have Horton releasted to him. They left the town of Rajila in a cloud of dust.

Chapter 19

Susan smiled at Pogo as they made their way slowly toward Rajila. "Surely it can 't be much further." She laid her head back on the seat of their rented Jeep. "I hope Gene is okay."

"I'm sure he is, Susan." Pogo tried to sound reassuring as he bounced over the roughly-made road. "If this map is correct, we should be in Rajila in about one hour."

"Good!" She took a deep breath. "I hope Gene is still there, but knowing him, he is already on his way to fight this Stevens creep all by himself!"

"Just hang in there, kid. I'm sure old Scott won't go doing anything foolish." He reached over and patted Susan's knee. "He has got too much going for him and that, bright eyes, is you."

Susan kissed Pogo's cheek.

"You are a pretty terrific guy yourself, Pogo, but then Gene would know the right kind of friends to pick."

"Thanks, Susan." Pogo smiled. "Keep your eyes open. In this country you can probably see a town for miles."

Scott glanced at Horton as he drove the Jeep quickly over the bumpy sand hills.

"This better not be a wild goose chase, Horton!"

"It's not, Scott," he spoke nervously. "This is the way, believe me."

"Well it better be!" He squinted against the glaring sun. "How much further?"

"When we come to that next hill." He pointed a shaky finger. "Better stop the Jeep and walk the rest of the way. It is safer on foot from here. You can slip up on them."

"Alright, get out!" Scott strapped the rifle on one shoulder and a water bag over the other. "Get your water, Horton, and let's go. If you make one sound so they can hear you, I will shoot you. Get it?"

"Don't worry, Scott. I'm not saying a word." Horton walked in front of Scott quickly. "If Stevens saw me, he would probably shoot me himself."

They slipped quietly up on the camp of thieves unseen. Horton searched over the group of men then shook his head at Scott and whispered.

"Smith can't be with them Mr. Scott. All I see are my so-called friends who took off and left me behind to rot in that stinking jail." He scanned the group of loud men until they landed on his leader. "That's Stevens over there with the red hair and the green floppy hat."

Scott stared at the creep who had brought him all this way, away from Susan. He looked. around the camp in hopes of spotting Martin. To his relief he saw him, locked securely in a cage.

"Where are the women captives held, Horton?" Gene whispered, looking down at the prisoner. "Are any of those women out there the girls taken from Rajila?"

"No, Scott. Those four broads are Stevens' women, although he shares them with the rest of the gang. The captive virgins are over there." He pointed at the hut behind Martin's caged prison. "As you see, your friend is caged like an animal, and in time, he will be slaughtered in a very distasteful manner."

"Let's get back to the Jeep." Scott gave Horton a light push. "I've got work to do and I want to finish up as soon as possible."

Susan and Pogo made their way into the Rajila Hotel. Pogo pointed to the shaggy gray-haired man then walked over, clearing his throat. The skinny clerk rose from where he had been sitting reading a paper.

"Boy, you kids sure know how to sneak up on a poor soul."

"We didn't mean to frighten you, sir." Pogo set down his suitcase and scratched through his brown hair. "We need a room, something to eat and some information."

"Everybody always wanting information. What sort are you kids after, way out here in Rajila?" His square jaw set into a stern look. "You are not up to no good, are you? You know, hanky-panky stuff?"

"No!" Susan tilted her head and frowned at the old man. "We happen to be looking for my husband. We know he is here or has been here."

He sized up the girl. "If you tell me what his name is, young lady, I might be of some service."

"Scott, Reverend Gene Scott, all strong and extremely handsome." Susan's heart beat wildly at the sound of his name. "Has he been here?"

"Yeh, just left after those crooks this morning." The old man scratched his chin and shook his head. "Can't imagine you and that Scott guy married up. He is so big and rough, and you—just a tender little peach."

159

"Do not let looks deceive you, sir. I am a pretty rough girl, especially when my man is in danger." She put her hands on her hips. "Can you tell me and my friend which direction he went this morning?"

"Captain Klamn across the street would be able to help you on that better than me, Mrs.Scott." He turned and pulled two room keys off the wall and handed them to. Susan. "The boy can sign for room 11. You can stay in your husband's room, number 12."

"Thank you." Pogo signed the register and raced out the door behind Susan. "It's getting dark fast. We will probably have to wait until morning."

"Only if I have to, Pogo." Susan knocked loudly on the jailhouse door. "Oh, come and answer!"

The door opened back and the captain's assistant smiled at Susan.

"Are you Captain Klamn?" She held tight to Pogo's hand.

"Naw! He's just inside." He stepped out of the way and motioned them in. "Hey, Cap, look what has come to visit us."

The captain looked up from his supper plate food. A smile stretched across his fat cheeks and he laughed loudly. "Well, bust my britches!"

"That wouldn't be hard for him." Pogo whispered in Susan's ear.

She smiled and cleared her throat. "I would like to know which way Reverend Scott went this morning, please."

"Scott?" Klamn leaned back in his chair and examined Susan's legs.

Pogo stepped in front of her and stared at the fat, mocking face. "Mrs.Scott just asked you where her husband went. I suggest you tell her."

"Husband? Scott is your husband, little lady?" His mouth dropped open as he sat up straight in his chair. "Ah—well, he went to find Stevens and rescue our women and that Martin guy."

"Yes, my husband went to rescue your women because you all are nothing but spineless, stinking lazy cowards!" Susan's face turned red in fury. "If anything happens to Gene, I will hold you personally responsible. Understand?"

"Oh yes, Mrs. Scott, I understand." He winked at his partner. "Make a pretty good couple. Just don't stand around picking bones. They tell you right out what is what."

"Where did he go, Klamn?" She clinched her teeth in disgust.

"Like I told you, Mrs. Scott, he went to find Stevens."

"You had to give him some kind of directions to go by." Susan put her hands on her hips "So stop beating around the bush and give me some straight answers."

"We had one of Stevens men locked up. Scott took him along to show him the way." He chuckled. "He's got more faith in that Horton than I would have, I grant you little lady."

"We could follow the Jeep tracks Pogo. They are our only hope." Susan looked up helplessly at him.

"We can't see them in the dark, Susan." He looked out at the darkening sky, then turn to the heavy captain. "Will those tracks still be there in the morning, Klamn?"

"If a sand storm doesn't blow up during the night, they'll stay right there." He picked his teeth with a broom straw. "But your friend is right, Mrs. Scott, the desert ain't no place to be at night. You could get lost real easy out there and die before anyone could find you."

"I am sure no one around here would even try to find us, Mr. Klamn." She turned and walked quickly from the jail, Pogo right behind her. "Pray for a calm night, Pogo. We have just got to have those tracks if we are ever going to find Gene."

Their eyes went up to the clear night sky and, taking each other's hand for security, they walked back to the hotel.

Scott tied Horton under the Jeep and placed a bag of water next to him. "You ain't going to leave me here, are you, Scott?" He twisted his head around to see what the preacher was doing.

"That's right, Horton." Scott checked his gun and slung it over his shoulder. "Stevens had to give Smith a password to use to make sure it was him. What is it Horton?"

"Ah—the ace of spades."

"You had better be telling me the truth, Horton, because if I don't come back, you can count on dying right there."

"I am, Scott, I am!" He swallowed nervously. "In my pocket, take it!" Scott felt in Horton's pocket and pulled out a playing card: the ace of spades. "He was to bring one, we all have one. It is our pass card."

"Is there anything else I need to know, Horton?" Scott stuck the card in his shirt pocket.

"It might be smart if you call Stevens 'lucky' once in a while. We all know him as that." Sweat ran from Horton's face. "Smith is a pretty rough talking character, Scott."

"Has anyone in the group ever seen him?" Scott wrinkled up his nose as he took a drink of the warm water.

"No, I don't think so." Horton swallowed. "Hurry back, Scott. This place ain't none too comfortable and there's varmints out here."

"Yeh, there sure are. Quite alot of two-legged varmints just over that hill."

Scott headed back toward the camp and within fifteen minutes he stepped up in front of Stevens, and smiled at his red head "Lucky Stevens, the ace of spades!" He flipped the card from his pocket.

Everyone stared silently, watching Stevens as he sized up Scott. "Smith! Riffbone Smith." He laughed, revealing a broken front tooth "How come you walked into camp? Don't you have a horse or a Jeep?"

"Had a horse." He crammed his hands in his pockets. "The stupid damn thing just keeled over and sat me on my ass."

"No wonder it keeled over! A big man like you, you should have been giving him a ride!" A heavy-set man walked around Scott looking him over.

The other men laughed at his remark.

"Well, they sure as hell aren't making horses like they use to." Scott grabbed the man's arm as he touched his shoulder. "Hey buddy, let's watch that, or maybe you would like a fat lip to go with that big gut of yours."

"Why you, I orda—"

Stevens yanked the man around and laughed mockingly in his face. "So Rip, there is someone who will stand up to you after all." He patted Scott's arm. "Riffbone, I can see that you and I are going to hit it off nicely."

"It might help things, since we will be working so close."

Scott looked over at Martin who was staring over at Gene Scott with his mouth open, as if he were tring to speak. Scott walked over to the cage and laughed. "What kind of animal do you call this? It is about the ugliest thing I have ever seen." As he continued to laugh he muttered between gritted teeth, "Just pretend like you don't know me, Martin, and I'll get you out of here."

Stevens walked over to where Scott stood. "Yeh Riff, that is what you might call a preaching bird or a missionary jackass!" He put his arm around Scott's broad shoulders "He is nothing but a praying coward, just sits there all day praying and praying."

"Coward is right, Lucky old pal. Does the stupid jackass think God is going to do his job for him?" Scott glared scornfully at Martin.

"God has answered my prayers, he sent—"

"Oh shut up!" Scott gritted his teeth. "I can't stand to hear a bunch of useless preaching." He walked away from the cage shaking his head.

A short bald-headed man came running up to Stevens. "Let's bring out the last virgin now, Lucky. She's the best, the very best of all."

"Why not?" Stevens slapped Scott on the back. "Come sit down over here with me, Riff. This little gal is the last of the four beauties we captured in Rajila." He grinned as the bald-headed man pushed the young girl down in front of him. "Cute, ain't she? She is the best of the crop. That's why we left her till last." He lifted her chin with the stick in his hand. "Look up here, sweetie."

Tears of fear streamed down her innocent face. Her body trembled when ever any of the men walked toward her.

"How would you like to break her in Riff?" Stevens smiled at Scott

"You want her?"

"She has got one hell of- a body." He feigned a laugh.

"Nothing doing, boss!" Rip put his meaty hand on the girl's shaking leg. "She is mine. You·said I could have her first."

"Shut up, Rip, I've changed my mind!" Stevens kicked his fat hand off her leg and looked at Scott, smiling. "Well, Riff, how about my offer?"

"Who could turn down such a great offer." He ran his hand up her leg and she jerked it away. "I like one with spirit! Hell, I will show her what makes life tick, by shit!"

Martin fell on his face mumbling. "God, oh God, forgive him! He must be insane, out of his mind."

Rip scrambled to his feet. "Smith can't come into our camp—a perfect stranger—and steal my virgin, Lucky!" His chubby cheeks shook with rage. "She is mine, damn it!"

"What makes you think you could tame her down, Rip?" Scott laughed scornfully. "You are nowhere near the man I am."

"What? I bet I am the biggest man!" He stood straight and shook his fist at Scott. "I know I'm the biggest man!"

"Drop your damn pants and we will find out who's biggest!" Scott stood up and unsnapped the hook on his pants. "Well, Rip, you fat slob, drop them."

"Oh God! God help him!" Martin cried out. "He knows not what he is doing!"

Scott glared at the cage. "Will you shut up, jackass!" Then standing seven inches above the six-foot Rip, Scott stared down. "Well Rip, big mouth, what the hell are you waiting for?"

"I—I—" He backed away as all the men began to chuckle. "I'll get you, Smith. You just wait." He turned and stormed into a tent.

Stevens punched Scott's arm. "She's all yours, Riff. Take her to the red tent and show her what a real man looks like."

"It is my damn pleasure." He yanked the girl up and pulled her into the red tent as he spoke loudly. "Alright, little virgin, get ready to be laid!"

Martin swallowed and fainted to the ground.

The girl screamed when Scott approached her. He held his forefinger across his lips and pulled out the cross from around his neck.

"Listen, I'm not going to touch you, trust me," he whispered. "I want you to do as I tell you. I am here to rescue you and the others, understand?"

She shook her head in relief "What do you want me to do?"

"I will rip part of your blouse. You scream, got it?"

She nodded.

"Alright you little sweetheart!" he called out loudly for those listening out side. "Let's see what I am getting!"

He ripped a sleeve off her blouse.

She screamed loudly and began shouting. "No! No, stop you pig! Get your filthy hands off me!"

Scott smiled and winked in approval. She gave him a relieved smile as he whipered, "Good girl. Now get in bed. Keep talking and screaming."

She climbed in the bed and jumped under the covers. "Stop, leave me along! Oh! Oh! It hurts, God help me! Oh, st—stop! Stop!"

Martin hit the ground and cried, "Forgive him, O God! Please have mercy on his sinful soul!"

"Shut up, you stupid jackass!" Stevens laughed and stood up pulled a blonde with big breasts into his arms. "Come on, bitch, let's go screw! That damn Riff has got me horny as hell!" He pulled the bleached blonde to his tent as his men grabbed a woman for the same action.

Scott peeked from the red tent door and smiled. "It worked, they have turned in for the night." He walked over and sat on the edge of the bed. "Get some sleep now, I will send them on a wild goose chase in the morning. It will give me time to get all of you safely out."

"Thank you very much." She smiled shyly from the covers. "What is your name?"

"Gene Scott." he smiled down at her "What is your name?"

"Rothia." She smiled at her hands. "I trust you, Mr. Scott, if you would like to lie down to sleep."

"I am sure Mrs.Scott would not like." He brushed her cheek. "Thanks anyway, Rothia. You get some sleep now. We have got a busy day tomorrow and maybe a lot of walking."

"Okay, Mr. Scott." She closed her eyes and went to sleep quickly.

"Poor kid," Scott thought as he sat down in a chair by the door. "Probably the only restful sleep she has had the whole time she has been with these lusty bastards."

He closed his eyes and pictured Susan's smiling face. "Soon, my darling," he whispered, "I'll be coming home to you."

Chapter 20

Scott walked out of the red tent the next morning smiling. He held Rothia tight around the waist. Stevens smiled up from his big plate of breakfast.

"Riff, looks like you tamed her down real good!" he laughed. "I think she is falling for you."

"Falling? Hell, she already fell." Scott laughed loudly and sat down next to Stevens. "Once a women has had Riffbone Smith, that is all they can think about."

"God, forgive him!" Martin hollered from the cage. He bowed his head and prayed aloud, "Help me to escape. I can put an end to this terror!"

Scott's eyes burned on Martin as he thought, "That stupid Martin is going to screw everything up if he doesn't stop praying out loud."

He scrambled to his feet and walked over to the cage. "How the hell are we suppose to enjoy our food with this stupid loud mouth animal sounding off all the damn time?"

"Scott, please, you mustn't—"

Scott's hand slung through the cage and knocked Martin out cold.

"That will teach you, son of a bitch!" He gritted his teeth as he rejoined Stevens "Let me finish that creep off while you guys are gone today collecting all that beautiful gold."

"Gold? What gold, Riff?" Stevens interest rose him to his knees "Where and how much?"

"The train running through Rajila today is carrying twenty boxes of pure solid gold. How's that, Lucky baby?" Scott looked up from his plate and winked.

"That is great Riff, but are you sure?" Stevens look was deadly serious. "I mean, if there is that much gold running through today, wow!"

"Hell no, Lucky! That cat can't be right!" Rip pounded his fist on the table. "You know good and well there ain't no damn train running today!"

"Hey Riffbone, Rip is right! There has never been a train run through on Wednesdays." Stevens looked upset as he slapped his knee.

"Man, are you all a bunch of stupid bastards!" Scott stood up, shaking his head. "That's exactly why they are running a special train through today. They know you idiots would not be out to rob them of all that beautiful gold! Do you think they are stupid enough to run it on a regular day?"

"That's it! Riff is right!" Stevens stood up "They have never had that much of anything on that train before! What time is it coming through Riff?"

"It will be passing through Rajila around 11 o'clock." He pulled a map from his pocket. "That means around 10:45 it will be passing through this gorge. You can block the rails and be waiting on your horses just the other side of the hills."

"That is a great set up Riff." Stevens patted Scott's back "Get ready to leave, men."

"I don't like it, Lucky." Rip's jaws shook as he spoke loudly. "Why ain't Smith coming with us?"

"'Cause I do the brain work, porky." Scott put his arm around Stevens' shoulder. "Besides, somebody has to stay behind and watch those captives. His eyes fell on Martin. "You never did answer me, Lucky. Can I shut up that loud mouth preacher once and for all?"

"The pleasure is yours, Riff, my friend!" he laughed as he mounted his black horse. "See you in about three hours, with gold for everyone!"

The men rode away, whooping and hollering.

Scott looked around the camp and noticed the five women belonging to the gang were watching him closely. He could handle them easy enough, he thought. The bleached blonde who hung around Stevens made her way slowly over to Scott. She eyed him up and down.

"Like what you see, bitch?" He wrinkled up his nose as he looked up into the sun-drenched sky. "Damn, it's getting hot."

"Tell me handsome, is it the sun or is it because I am standing so close?" Her hand ran down his arm as she looked below his waist. "Why don't we cool off in the tent, stud?"

"Why the hell not?" Scott took a tight grip on her wrist and pulled her into a tent.

Martin beat the ground with his fist and shook his head.

Inside the tent, Scott stared at the half naked blonde in disgust and pushed her back onto the bed, then tied her securely to the post.

"At least you'll stay cooler in here tied up. Just hope the insects don't find you."

Her body moved wildly as she struggled to free herself. "What the devil are you doing, big Riff?"

He looked around the messy tent for a cloth to gag her. She continued to jerk at her ropes.

"Riff, you screwball, untie me!" she whined.

"I don't approve of striking a women, but under the circumstances—" Scott's hand swung around and knocked her unconscious. He gagged her mouth with his handkerchief and went about fixing the other four women in the same manner.

After setting the four captive girls free his eyes fell on Martin shaking in the cage.

"Where is the key to this cage Martin?"

"—don't know!" His voice shook. "I—I think that Stevens·has it!"

"Shit!" Scott placed his hands firmly on the bars and, with a groan, started pushing them apart. The four girls smiled at one another as they watched their strong hero pull the preacher off the ground. George Martin stood up for a moment on shaky legs then made his way slowly through the open space.

"Hurry it up Martin! We haven't got all day." Scott saddled the remaining horses and helped the four girls and Martin up into the saddles. He looked quickly around the camp to make sure he had not forgotten anything.

"Alright, let's move!" He spurred his horse into the lead as the six riders made their way back to the Jeep.

Susan coughed as the dust from the Jeep filled her lungs. She spotted Scott's Jeep ahead. "Look, Pogo! It must be Gene's Jeep!"

"By George you're right!"

Pogo laughed as he pulled his Jeep to a stop behind Scott's. They jumped out to investigate it closely. Susan spotted Horton's feet and nudged Pogo's arm.

"There's someone under the Jeep."

Pogo fell to his knees and looked into the eyes of Horton. "Who are you fellow?"

"Untie me, boy! This villian came out of nowhere and tied me to my Jeep as he stole my money and took off with my goods!" Horton looked at his wrist "These ropes are about to cut me in two."

"Well, I can't let your hands drop off, can I?"

Pogo reached in his pocket for his knife. Susan grabbed his arm.

"Wait Pogo. Something is funny here." Susan frowned at the man under the Jeep. "That fat guy at the jail said Gene was the only one who left the town yesterday morning. That means the one set of tracks belong to Gene. This guy is lying."

"Yeh, you have got a good point there Susan." Pogo looked at the man closely and noticed the bag of water lying next to him. "Was this 'villian' that tied you up mean enough to kill you mister?"

"Why do you think he left me here like this? He wanted me to die slowly." Horton grunted.

"That's funny, a man wanting you to die leaving you plenty of water to drink." Pogo shook his head mockingly. "Not to mention the fact that he left you in the shade of your Jeep instead of stealing it too."

"Alright mister, where did Gene Scott go?" Susan's eyes burned with anger. "You had better tell us or we will tie you in the sun!"

"He—he went to the camp." He tried to point his finger. "That way."

"We better walk from here, Susan. Scott had to, so it would probably be safer." Pogo took a water bag and handed it to her. "Okay, let's go."

Pogo and Susan made their way slowly to the camp, not knowing Gene and his group were coming in their direction, just out of their sight.

Scott's eyes caught sight of the Jeeps. He felt his heart beat wildly in his throat. "Oh my God! It can't be!" He jumped from the horse and bent down to Horton "Whose Jeep is that, Horton?"

"Two crazy kids. They called each other Pogo and Susan." Horton took a deep breath "Scott, would you untie theses ropes? I'm hurting some kind of bad."

"Martin, come here!" Scott shouted over his shoulder as he untied Horton and pulled him out. "I want you to take the girls and Horton here back to Rajila. Do you think you can manage?"

"I will try." he stood slumped over.

"Rothia, can you drive a Jeep?" Scott pulled the keys from his pocket. "Yes Mr. Scott, I think so." She took the keys and climbed in behind the wheel.

"Horton, in the back." Scott tied the prisoner securily. "Martin, you ride in up front and keep a eye on Horton." Gene climbed back on the horse. "The rest of you girls take the horses and all of you go back to Rajila. Tell that captain to round up a posse and get here as soon as possible!"

"You bet we will, Scott!" Rothia waved from the Jeep. "Be careful!"

"Scott, you fool!" Martin stood up in the Jeep shouting "You cannot go back down there! When those crazy freaks find out you were lying to them, they'll kill you on sight.!"

"As if that never occurred to me, Martin? I am not going without Susan and Pogo! Now get a move on and tell that lazy Klamn to move his ass!" Scott turned his horse and headed back toward the camp.

Susan and Pogo looked around at the empty camp. She slumped down on a stump. "Oh darn, Pogo. Where is Gene?"

"I'll have a look around." He walked into a tent and came running right out. His face was a brilliant shade of pink. "There— there's a half-naked woman tied up in there!"

"Are you sure? Maybe it is one of the captives. Let me look."

Susan got up, but before she got near the tent Jesse Stevens jumped from his horse and grabbed her.

"Let me go!"

She kicked his leg, but he held her tight and gritted his teeth. "Where is he? I will kill that lying bastard!" Steven's eyes flashed fire.

"Hey boss, the girls are gone."

Rip's fat arms fell to his side when he noticed the bent cage bars. "And hell, look at this. Bent them damn bars like they were nothin."

"Ahhhh!" Stevens growled. "He tricked me. The son of bitch tricked me."

"Who are these two, Lucky?" The short, bald-headed man held tight to Pogo's left arm while another man gripped his other arm.

"He got away, didn't he?" Susan smiled at Pogo. "Gene got away."

"Which is more than you are going to do, sweetheart." Stevens smiled as he gazed at her body.

The bleached blonde twisted hurriedly over to him, whining, "Baby, Lucky baby!" She grabbed him around the neck. "That Riff was mean, real mean to little bitty me."

Stevens pushed her away. "Shut up bitch!" His eyes fell lustily on Susan. "I need something to take away this anger from my body."

"Take me, baby. That will ease your tention." The blonde grabbed at him again. He pushed her into Rip's fat arms.

"Lucky baby," she whimpered.

"What do you want me to do with her, boss?" Rip leered at the blonde.

"Why the hell should I care. She's yours," he laughed and grabbed Susan.

She stared kicking and screaming.

"Relax doll, Lucky baby ain't gonna hurt you."

"You're darn right you aren't! Gene will kill you if you lay one lousy finger on me!"

Her face was wet with tears of fear. Pogo tried to break free but the two men held on tight.

"Hey boss, what do you want us to do with this kid?" The bald-headed man jerked Pogo's arm tighter.

"Take him just outside the camp. Dig a hole and feed him to the worms," Stevens laughed. "If the worms don't finish him up, the sun will tomorrow."

"No! You can't do that to Pogo." Susan jerked her arm free only to have it grabbed again. "Pogo!" she called as she watched them drag him out of sight. "Oh God! Gene!" the words tore from her throat.

"He is probably miles away by now sweetie." Stevens pulled her toward his tent. "And if the traitor knows what's good for him, he'd better stay away!"

Scott watched from the rocks as Steven's men threw the dirt in on Pogo's body. He made a tight fist and gritted his teeth.

"Damn!"

He moved slowly from the rocks and smashed the two villians' heads together. They fell unconscious to the ground. Pogo closed his eyes and smiled.

"Oh Scott, thank God!"

Scott shoveled the dirt away and pulled Pogo from the place where he was buried. "Pogo, I should beat your ass but good! Why the devil did you come and bring Susan?" His attention turned to the camp "Where is she?"

"The last time I saw her, she was with. Stevens," he swallowed. "I think he was going to take her into his tent and rape her."

"I'll be damned if he does!" Scott's temper flared as he started toward the camp.

"Wait, Scott!" Pogo grabbed his arm. "You can't just go in. What about these two?"

Scott looked at the two unconscious men on the ground. He jerked off their shirts and tied them together.

"That should hold them until the authorities get here."

He made his way slowly toward the camp. The two men sitting

guard seemed to be the only ones outside and everyone else was occupied inside the tents. Scott motioned for Pogo to grab the smallest guard around the neck. With a quick reaction from both Scott and Pogo, each guard was held securely around the throat.

They tied them behind some boxes and checked to see if there was any they had missed outside. The camp lay empty, except for the noise coming from the tents. Scott's eyes burned on Stevens tent. He heard Susan scream out and, taking big steps, he raced over toward the sound.

Stevens had ripped off her pants and shirt. His lustful eyes stared down at her yellow underwear. A smile stretched across his weather-beaten face.

"A neat little dresser, yes you are, sweetie."

"You—you had better leave me a—alone!" She backed up against the back of the tent. "Gene will kill you!"

"What is he to you anyway?" He licked his lips as he grabbed her and jerked at her bra. She fought wildly, screaming.

"Gene! Gene!" As though her shouts were hopeless, she continued to cry out, "Gene, help me!"

Suddenly Scott's powerful arms locked around Jesse Stevens' throat, immobilizing him.

"You miserable son of a bitch!" Gene spat between gritted teeth. "I'll kill you for touching my woman, you damn bastard!"

"No—no—ple—please!" His voice came out weak as Scott was cutting off his supply of air.

"Beg all you like, Stevens. It won't do you any good!" Scott jerked at his left arm and it cracked. He covered Jesse Steven's mouth to muffle the scream. "Maybe you would like every bone in your body busted."

"Gene! You are going to kill him!" Susan grabbed at his arm "Don't kill him, Gene, please!"

"Shit!" He slung Stevens to the floor and tied him up. His arms held Susan in a close embrace. "Susan, are you alright?"

"Yes, now that you are here." She held on to him tightly. "Gene, I am sorry but I had to know that you were alright. "

"Yeh, right." He took her hand. "We will discuss what punishment you and Pogo deserve for following me later."

"Is Pogo alright?" she asked excitedly.

"Yes, for now." Scott and Susan walked outside where Pogo was waiting.

"Alright, there are five more men and five more women inside those tents." He looked down at Susan, who wore Gene's oversized turtle neck. "You stay here. Pogo, you come with me. We will get them while they are in action."

"Yeh, and they are probably getting pretty exhausted by now too." Pogo covered his mouth to hold back his laughter as he and Scott made their way to the front tent.

They slipped inside and with one blow from Gene Scott's fist, the lusty goon lay unconscious atop the naked girl. Pogo grabbed her mouth before she screamed. Scott grinned at her as he tied them together.

"If he comes to honey, maybe he can finish before the authorities get here."

"Pretty good, Scott." Pogo punched Scott's shoulder and laughed. "Pretty damn good."

"Yeh, sure! Let's get Rip next. He is one creep I have been wanting to plaster ever since I got here."

"Who is Rip?" Pogo frowned as Scott forced him into the next tent.

"There's the fat slob right there."

He laughed to himself as he watched the blonde trying to push the fat, limp body off. Gene suddenly grew pale when he saw the knife protruding from Rip's back.

"Oh my God. She killed him!" He pulled her from beneath him, locking her mouth shut with his other hand. "Well sister, you are in big trouble now." He tied her to the bed post and threw a sheet over her shoulders. "Better start praying you'll be tried for killing an animal instead of a low life slob."

He turned to see Rip's cold, empty eyes staring back at him. Grabbing Pogo's arm, Gene reached for the tent door.

"Come on. Pogo. This place is making me sick."

They were just finishing securing the last two when Klamn and about ten men road up. Scott shook his head and leaned over to Pogo.

"Why do they always manage to get here after all the action is over?"

Pogo laughed and walked out behind his big friend. Susan ran to Gene and threw her arms around him. He held on to her tight as he stared up at Klamn.

"I see you managed to get here, Klamn. I hope we didn't take you away from your supper or a rousing card game."

"As a matter of fact, Scott, you did." He laughed as he stepped down from his horse. "I was eating a delicious meal when that Martin and the four girls came barging in with Horton and some story about you needing help at once."

"As you can see, we got here as soon as we could." Vinni took in the three strangers, then smiled. "I must admit, at first I could not see how these two could help you round up Stevens and his cut-throat gang, but by the looks of things around here, your plan worked Scott."

"I'm with Vinni on this one." The sheriff shook his head in amazement. "I just knew you would come driving into town with that peacher and our girls and leave us in the mercy of Jesse Stevens!"

"Yeh Scott, we helped after all!" Pogo winked at Susan.

"Your plan really saved the day, darling." Susan smiled at his squinting eyes.

"That was just my back up plan, sweetheart." He turned to the officer in charge. "Do you really think I was just going to turn and run and leave your innocent citizens in your care?" His voice was practically a shout. "I was going to lay a trap for Stevens and lock him up once and for all." He turned to smile at his wife. "But since my back up team came to assist me, the gang has been captured and tied up."

Vinni turned his attention back to Susan. "I still cannot believe Scott is your husband."

"Well he is." She smiled into Gene's eyes proudly. "Every beautiful inch."

Pogo laughed and Scott punched his arm as he spoke, "Like I said, you will find all the crooks tied up. The tent is full, two over there behind boxes and just outside the camp, two more." Scott put Susan up on Klamn's horse, then climbed up behind her. "I am sure you can find a way back Klamn."

"But—?" Klamn looked down at his feet and chuckled. "Sure Scott, I'll take Vinni's horse." He smiled at his partner's frown. "Relax, Vinni. These crooks have plenty of horses we can ride."

"See you Klamn." Scott turned the horse around "Pogo, follow us. My horse is tied up just outside the camp. You can ride him."

Pogo climbed on and followed Scott and Susan as they made their way to Rajila.

Scott did not say a word until he shut the door to his hotel room. He looked, unsmiling, at Susan as she sat anxiously on the bed.

"Don't just stand there. Say something." She spoke softly. "Do you hate me for loving you, for wanting to be sure you were alright?"

"Hate you?" His voice shook. "Oh Susan, why did you come?

You could have been killed!" He went to her and drew her into his arms. "If anything ever happened to you, I would just die. You are my life. You are all I have, you and Pogo!"

"Oh Gene darling!" she cried. "What about your mom and dad? Where are they?"

"Who knows?" He shook his head and chuckled. "They didn't seem to want me. I was abandoned on the church steps in some humble community at the age of six months, they estimated. "

"Oh, my poor darling." Susan put her arms around his neck. "How could anyone do such an awful thing?"

"Must have been an ugly baby," he teased.

"Gene Scott, you were not anything of the kind!" She shook her head. "I hope our son looks just like you."

"Do you?" He took her face in his strong hands and kissed her lips gently. "Do you wish the poor kid such a tragic start?"

"Don't play the modest type. You know perfectly well you are a handsome, overly exciting man." She ran her fingers up his chest. "Did you think about me while we were apart?"

"Maybe a little bit," he teased as he pulled his shirt over his head. "A little more at night."

"Oh? Why then?" She unbuttoned her blouse slowly.

"My bed was cold and lonely." His fingers gently undid her bra. "I needed you there to get me warm."

"You could have brought me." Her fingers moved down to his pants and unsnapped them. "I would have made you hot—and gladly."

"You can do it now." His lips parted over hers as he picked her up and laid her back gently on the bed and filled her with his warm love.

Chapter 21

A bright smile lit Edna's face as Scott and Pogo stepped onto the parsonage porch. She grabbed Gene and wrapped her arms around him laughing.

"Oh thank God!" She pulled them inside and called, "John, David! They're home! Gene and Pogo are back safe!"

John and David came running down the steps.

"Gene, you had us scared stiff, you old rascal!" John slapped his big friend's shoulder. "Did Susan get home okay?"

"Oh yes, Gene, how is she?" Edna gazed anxiously into Scott's serious eyes. "She is alright?"

Gene Scott put his arm around her shoulders. "Yes, she is fine Edna."

"Is that Weber creep still here in TarSa?" Pogo picked out an apple from the fruit bowl and bit into it.

"Yes, old fatso is still here." Edna walked toward the kitchen door. "I can say one thing for TarSa, I am sure the candy stores are doing the business these days."

"Miss Weber is still here too, Scott." David flopped onto the sofa. "Gloria has been checking every day to see if you've gotten back."

"Well, as far as she or any of the Webers are concerned, I am still in Israel. Got it?" Scott followed Edna into the kitchen.

"You can count on us, Gene." She motioned for him to sit down and stuck her head out the door. "Pogo, come on in here and I will fix you a plate."

"Can't turn that down, Edna." Pogo laughed and sat across from Scott. "This is going to be fun, giving old Weber the slip!"

Scott stuck a spoonful of potatoes in his mouth. "Yeh! The whole Weber family is enough to turn your stomach."

"I don't think it is hurting you fellows' appetite too much." Edna chuckled as she watched them cramming down the home-cooked meal.

"If you had to eat that hotel food like we did, you would appreciate good food too." Pogo grinned broadly as he reached for another piece of warm bread. "This sure is great bread and chicken, Edna."

"Why thank you, Pogo." She smiled and pulled a cake from the cabinet. "Better save room for this cherry cake, fellows."

Gene smiled happily as he patted her behind. "Edna, you are my kind of woman! Damn, cherry cake!"

"Oh sure, sure!" She punched his arm "Just eat and shut up!"

Susan smiled at Jobi as he opened the door back.

"Where have you been, sis?" He took her hand and pulled her down the hallway. "Mom and Dad have been getting upset. "

"Didn't Edna call them?" She set down her suitcase. "She was supposed to call and explain."

"She did, sis." Jobi picked up her suitcase and carried it up to her room. "Only Edna can't lie so good, you know." He made a face. "I've been doing my best to cover for you."

"Thanks, Jobi!" She kissed his cheek. "I don't know what I would do without you."

"Yeh, you would stay in a mess!" He shook his head.

"Better fill me in on where I was supposed to be." She started unpacking her clothes.

"Edna told mom you had to help out in that children's handicap place." He flopped onto her bed. "After about three days, they decided to call you and see how you were. Mom was worried about you not having enough clothes."

"Oh great. She would!" Susan made a face "Go on."

"I think aunt Joanie put that bright ideal in mom's head. Then aunt Jewel decided she would try her luck again with Scott."

Susan gritted her teeth "Oh, really? They better stop chasing after my husband!"

"Yeh, well they don't know that juicy bit of information, sis." he said, his eyes wide. "When the nurse at that home told Mom you had not been there, she really lost her cool."

"That's just great!" Susan sat down next to her brother. "Then what?"

"Dad called Edna back because mom was total nerves. Edna managed to come up with another story quick. She told dad that the place you had gone was not the one on the island. Edna also told him not to worry because you had gone with Reverend Scott."

"Did she? How did dad take that?" She swallowed.

"He seemed to be relieved. Aunt Joanie and Aunt Jewel kept pouring on about how lucky you were." He sighed and laughed. "Boy, if they only knew the whole of it."

"Yeh!" Susan laughed in relief. "Oh Jobi. I am so happy! I only wish I could be with him all the time."

"With who, dear?" Shirley Andrews walked over and sat down beside her daughter.

Susan gaved her a shaky smile. "Hi, Mom!" Susan hugged her neck. "He—he's this guy I met."

"How serious is it dear?"

"It's very serious, Mom. I love him." Susan looked down at her hands.

"Susan dear, why don't you bring him home so we can meet him?" Shirley patted her daughter's hands. "He must be the same fellow Jewel was telling us about after poor Peter left so hurt and upset."

"Well Peter does not own me, Mom." Susan stood and brushed her hair back. "I will bring him home, when I think you and dad are ready to accept him."

Jobi looked at Susan warily when he saw Shirley's puzzled expression.

"Susan darling, I am afraid I do not understand. Is he one of those hippies you read about? One of these so-called love children who live in communes and don't believe in getting married?"

"Gosh no, Mom." Susan gave Jobi a sly smile. "He definitely believes in marriage. He is the most warm and gentle man I have ever known."

"Then why not bring him here, Susan? Why are you ashamed of him dear? Or are you ashamed of us?" Her mother put her arm around Susan's trembling shoulders.

"Of course I'm not ashamed of you. And I'm not ashamed of him. I could never be ashamed of him!" She pulled away from her mother. "It's just that you and dad would not understand our love."

"Oh Susan, he's not—not a different race, he is?" Shirley clutched her throat.

"Mom, I have many good friends who are of a different race! They are loving kind souls!" Susan knew her mother was not the prejudiced type, that she always loved and respected Mildred and was considered a permanent part of the Andrews' family.

"Susan, I have nothing against any race. I just ask you a plain question." Shirley stared down at her. "Is he or is he not of a different race?"

"Gosh no, Mom." Jobi said with a laugh.

Shirley Andrews twirled around and looked at her son. "Do you know who he is, Jobi?"

His face suddenly grew pale as he glanced at Susan and swallowed. "Yeh mom, I know, but I will not say a word."

"Jobi Andrews!" Shirley pulled her son to his feet. "Why won't you tell me, young man?"

"Gosh mom, we will tell you," he smiled sheepishly, "in time."

"Alright you two can play this little game now! Just you wait till your father gets home!"

She stormed out the door as Susan stared at her brother.

"Oh Jobi, why can't everyone just leave us alone?" She clutched her stomach "Oh, I feel sick."

"I can understand that, with all the nervous excitement." Jobi hugged his sister. "It'll be alright, you'll see."

"No Jobi, I feel sick, Real sick!" She ran to the bathroom and threw up.

An hour later, Owen Andrews pushed his way into Susan's bedroom. She lay quietly on her bed, a wet cloth over her forehead. Jobi stood up when he saw his father's confused, angry face.

"Susan, sit up young lady! I want to talk to you."

"Can't she lay still, Dad? She's sick," Jobi pleaded with his father. "She's been throwing up, sir."

"Went away and caught something, huh?" Owen called his wife into the room. "Your daughter is sick, or she is pretending to be!"

"Dad!" Susan forced herself to a sitting position. "If you want me up, I am up." She swallowed back the sickness rising in her throat.

"Owen, she does look sick." Shirley felt of Susan's forehead. "There doesn't seem to be a fever, although her skin is clammy and cool."

"Susan, your mother told me that you and Jobi have refuse to tell her who this boy is you are madly in love with. I suggest you tell us right now or I will dock you until you do!"

"Go ahead, dock me!" Susan stood on trembling legs. "But—but leave Jobi out of this! He is just an innocent bystander and is loyal. I made him promise to keep my secret."

"Innocent? Hardly. He knows who this boy is, and if he ever wants to play with his friends again, he will tell me this big secret!" Owen shouted.

Susan felt the room twirling and spinning in front of her as she felt her legs floating out from under her. Everything grew black as she slipped into unconsciousness.

"Oh Lord, Owen, she fainted!" Shirley bent down on the floor beside of Susan. "Go call the doctor, quick!"

Jobi began crying and cried out, "It's all your fault! Yours and dad's! If you hadn't kept harping on her, she would be alright!"

"Now, now Jobi dear, that just isn't true." Shirley looked up at Owen as he stepped back into the room when he heard Jobi's outburst.

"It's probably very true, dear, You know how easily Susan is to get upset." Owen picked up his limp daughter and laid her gently across her bed. "Mildred is calling the doctor."

Susan moved slowly and opened her eyes.

Her father smiled down at her. "It's alright, baby. You just passed out. The doctor is on his way."

"Oh, Dad, you didn't have to call the doctor." Susan was surprised at how weak her own voice sounded.

"Yes, my dear!" Shirley took her daughter's hands. "We just want to make sure you are alright."

"I am fine, Mom, really." She forced a smile. "I just need a little rest, that's all."

Mildred stepped into the room, wringing her hands anxiously. "The doctor is here, Mr. Owen."

"Good, Mildred." Owen stood. "Please show him in."

"Doctor, you may go in now." Mildred stood aside while Doctor James Warner walked quickly past her.

"Well, young lady, what seems to be your problem?" He gazed down at Susan's pale face with a smile.

"That's what we called you to find out," Jobi barked impatiently.

"Jobi!" Shirley gave an anxious chuckle laugh. "She fainted, Doctor Warner, and was complaining about being sick."

"She is sick, doc! Susan was throwing up in the bathroom!" Jobi looked at his sister helplessly. "Give her something, doc, to make her feel better."

"I will do everything I can for your sister, Jobi." He rubbed Jobi's head playfully. "You can count on that, son." He sat down on the edge of Susan's bed and open his black bag. "Would the rest of you step outside while I examine her? Mildred, you may stay to assist me."

"Yes, Doctor Warner, I'm here for Miss Susan." Mildred came to the bedside as the others walked from the room.

"Now Susan, you say you have been feeling sick. For how long?"

"Well actually, doctor, for the past few mornings. I have been waking up nauseated. I guess I have been coming down with this for several days now.

"Take a deep breath, Susan." He listened to her back and then her heart. "Sounds good." He took a needle from his bag and handed Mildred a stretch band. "Tie this on her upper arm, Mildred. I am going to take a blood test."

"Yes sir, doctor." Mildred did as he asked, then carressed Susan's face gently.

Susan smiled weakly up at her loving friend then turn to the doctor. "Do you have any idea yet, Dr. Warner?"

"I can't be positive young lady, but have you had sexual relations recently?"

"Dr. Warner!" Mildred said angrily. "What cause you got for saying such an awful thing to Miss Susan?"

"Because, it is very possible that Susan is pregnant." He gave her a serious look. "Is it possible, Susan?"

"Yes, yes, it is." She took Mildred's trembling hand. "Mildred, you must not tell Mom or Dad. Not yet Please. "

"But, Miss Susan, how did you go and get yourself pregnant? I know for a fact that you would never do anything foolish." Mildred's eyes were full of concern.

"Believe me Mildred, everything I did, I did it with a clear conscience." She gripped Mildred's hand. "Do you believe me dear friend?"

"How could I not?" She sat down on the bed. "Why, I helped raise you from a baby." Pulling her red handkerchief from her pocket, Mildred blew her nose loudly. "Who is the father of your baby, child?"

"My husband!" Her eyes sparkled as Mildred's became wide circles.

Chapter 22

"Did you say your husband?" Mildred could not believe her own ears.

"That is right, Mildred. My wonderful, darling husband." She held her stomach lightly. "A son, he wants a son."

"Who did you marry, Miss Susan? Was it this fellow you are so crazy about?" Mildred patted Susan's knee. "Well child, is it him?"

"Yes, it is." She swallowed nervously. "If you both promise me—and I mean promise you won't tell anyone, not a single soul— I will tell you."

"I promise, child! You can count on old Mildred."

Susan looked up at Dr. Warner, who had been taking in the conversation. "Well, Dr. Warner, will you keep my secret?"

"Now Susan, I—"

"He will keep it!" Mildred glared at him. "Or he'll wish he had!"

"I will keep it." He chuckled. "Couldn't have the best cook in the world mad at me."

"Then I will tell you," Susan laughed and took both their hands. "Reverend Gene Scott!" Excitement rang in her voice.

"You are kidding!" Mildred's mouth dropped open. "Reverend Scott! You are joking!"

"No I am not, Mildred. It's the God's honest truth." She pulled the hidden wedding ring out from around her neck. It dangled from the chain. "Oh Mildred, I love him so very much and he loves me. Me Mildred!"

Dr. Warner shook his head in confusement. "Susan, how is Reverend Scott going to take to having you pregnant?"

"Oh, I think after the shock wears off and he has finished yelling at me, he will embrace the idea." She bit her lip nervously and smiled. "Doc Warner, if I didn't feel so bad, I would get up and dance."

Mildred laughed and smiled at her. "You really are happy, aren't you child?"

"Oh yes, Mildred! The happiest girl in the entire world!"

"Now don't go getting your hopes up too much, Susan." Dr. Warner shut his black bag.

Mildred grunted as she gave the doctor a mean look.

"Mildred, brush down your hair. I was talking about the baby. I'll know for sure in a couple of days."

"Call me as soon as you find out, Dr. Warner." Susan clutched the ring tightly in her hand. "Promise?"

"I Promise," he laughed and walked to the door. "For a young woman who is in a tight squeeze like you are, you're taking this very well."

"Why wouldn't I, sir?" she responded joyfully. "I think giving Gene a baby is the happiest thing anyone could do."

Mildred stood and walked over to Doctor Warner. "I'll follow the good doctor out to make sure he explains everything properly to your folks."

"Take it easy, Susan. I will send you some pills to help with the nausea."

"Thanks, Dr. Warner, for everything." She lay back, smiling. "Oh Gene, will you be happy about us having a baby?" she whispered to herself. "A son."

"Well, James?" Owen Andrews met the doctor as he came down the steps. "How is she? What is the matter with our baby?"

"Miss Susan ain't no baby, sir," Mildred corrected him, her hands on her hips. "She's a grown up young lady."

"Mildred dear, this is no time to be debaiting the children's mental capacity." Shirley Andrews anxiously looked at the doctor. "How is she, doctor?"

"Susan is fine, really," he said with a shrug. "I suspect it's just a virus."

"See, nothing to worry about ma'am." Mildred pushed the doctor to the door. "I believe you said you had another call, Dr. Warner."

"Yes, I did actually. Thank you, Mildred, for reminding me." He waved at the Andrews. "I will send you my bill, Owen."

"Yes, please do." Owen closed the door and stared, puzzled, at Mildred. "Mildred, why did you practically push James out the door?"

"Cause, he had another patient to call on and there wasn't no cause for him standing around jawing with us." She turned and walked to the kitchen, calling back, "And don't go bothering Miss Susan. The doctor told her to rest."

Edna stared at Gene as he sat watching the television. He felt her gaze and turned to face her.

"Is something on your mind Edna?"

"Oh, it's probably nothing." She picked up her knitting.

"Alright, out with it." He turned toward her. "You look upset. Has Weber found something else for me to do?"

"No, it's not that. It is probably nothing at all." She forced a smile. "John would say it's just my imagination."

"It must really be something or it wouldn't bother you like this, Edna." Scott took her hand and smiled. "Tell me. I promise to listen with an open mind."

"It is probably nothing really, but Susan has been looking a little pale lately. She used to have such a bright glow in her cheeks. I could not help but wonder if she might be—" She looked around to see if anyone was listening.

"Might be what, Edna?" Scott frowned, suddenly concerned.

"Pregnant!" she whispered, and Scott's eyes fell to his hands, "Did you take any precausions to prevent it Gene?"

"No, no I didn't." He put his hand on Edna's. "I never thought for one minute I might get her pregnant. Boy, isn't that dumb."

"I am only guessing, Gene." She patted his knee reassuringly. "I am probably wrong."

"Shit, let's hope so." He forced a smile. "I would hate to start my family in secret too."

Suddenly there was a knock on the front door. Scott grabbed Pogo's arm and they raced up the steps. He turned as he reached the top and whispered down to Edna. "If it is you know who, I am not here." He closed the door to his bedroom quietly and fell silent.

Henry Weber stood smiling on the porch when Edna open back the door. Karolyn and Gloria stood silently behind him trying to see passed Edna.

"Henry, Karolyn, what a nice surprise." Edna forced a laugh. "Won't you come in?"

"Thank you, Edna dear, but we can only stay for a few minutes." Henry Weber walked past her and into the living room. "Hello, John. Where's Gene? I know he's here. "

"What ever gave you that idea, Bishop Weber?" David looked up from the television.

"George Martin phoned me earlier today and informed me that he and Scott had caught the entire gang." Weber opened the candy dish and grabbed a handful of chocolates. "Mmmm, delish! He said Scott was probably home by now."

Listening from from his bedroom door, Scott mumbled, "That

damn Martin. Might know he would screw up everything."

"Yeh, and having the nerve to take part of the credit for capturing those crooks." Pogo shook his head "The whole Weber family makes me sick!"

"You and me both, pal." Scott clenched his fist. "Shit."

"Did you say they were resting, Edna dear?" Gloria smiled toward the stairs. "Sounds a bit loud up there to me, not to mention Gene darling's bad language falling on one's ears."

"Maybe Scott is having a nightmare about you." David glanced at Gloria, unable to resist smiling.

"David!" John cleared his throat trying not to laugh. "You know how teenagers are, Miss Weber, always joking around."

"That is alright Reverend Crain. I think Davy is really cute." She winked at him. "Cute as a little button."

"If it would not be too much bother, Edna, could you go wake Gene up." Henry Weber crammed his mouth full of candy. "I really need to talk to him."

"Never mind, Edna, I am right here." Scott glared at the hefty bishop, who immediately tried to swallow his mouthful of candy. "I just got back, Bishop Weber. Surely you aren't going to send me somewhere else so soon?"

"No, Scott. Don't get all up in the air over nothing," Weber laughed. "Your new mission will be right here in TarSa. What do you have to say about that?"

"What sort of mission?" He sat down on the bottom step.

"Is there any danger involved, bishop?" Edna implored. "I mean, I think he has been through enough."

"Now, Edna." Henry Weber patted her shoulder. "Like most things, there is a small bit of danger involved, but nothing to any great extent."

"What is the mission, Weber?" Scott closed his eyes wearily.

"It's top secret, Scott. The fewer people who know about it, the safer it will be for you." Weber reached for another chocolate, licking his fingers.

"Boy, I hope he gets every drop." Pogo whispered in Scott's ear.

Gene Scott laughed and cleared his throat. "Alright, Henry. We'll talk in the library." He stood and walked to the study, Weber, Gloria and Pogo right behind him. Scott turned and spoke to Pogo and Gloria. "You two can go back to the living room."

"No way, Scott." Pogo sat down on the desk. "I want to hear what we have to do."

"No one said you, Pogo. It's me who has to do it." His voice was stern and loud.

"Calm down, Scott. Pogo will be helping you." Weber grinned at Scott's expression.

Pogo stood, laughing. "Ha ha, Scott! They want me too!"

"Shut up Pogo and sit down." Scott took the chair behind the desk. "Get on with it, Weber. What have I got to do?"

"We, Scott, we," Pogo said joyfully as he danced back and forth.

Gene grabbed his arm, causing him to stumble. He fired a glance toward the red head. "You. Out."

"No, Gene dear. I know everything. Don't I, Daddy?" She smiled triumphantly at her father.

"Yes, baby doll, you do." He winked at Scott. "She has to know everything that concerns you, Scott."

"I'm flattered. On with it, bishop. I'm losing my patience."

"Very well, Scott!" He pulled a candy bar from his pocket and unwrapped it. "Monday morning, you are to report down to the police headquarters. There will be a Detective Simus—Roy Simus—there to talk with you."

"Simus?" Scott sat up, recognizing the familiar name.

"Yes! He has been sent here by the FBI to crack down on a narcotics cartel that has been set up on the island." Weber chomped down on the candy bar. "You will be working beside a real pro, Scott."

"Yes, Gene darling. Mr. Simus is a detective lieutenant." Gloria smiled.

"Why do they want me to help?" Ignoring her, Scott changed positions. "I mean, why would they need a missionary?"

"They heard what a great job you have been doing in capturing those crooks, Scott. They were amazed at the good job you did." Weber chuckled. "Just think, the FBI wants one of my boys."

"I would rather not be considered as 'one of your boys,' Weber." Scott rose. "I will go down to the police headquarters Monday to see what this is all about."

"Of course you will, Scott. That's an order. I insist that you comply." Weber nodded as he stood and threw his wrapper in the trash can "Like the job or not, Scott, you will do it."

"Yes, I will do it." He turned and stormed out the door, muttering, "Shit."

"I just do not know why Gene gets so upset over these little things Pogo," Gloria said. "He always does so well."

"You had better go home now, Gloria, before your father has a sugar crash." Pogo shook his head as he watched Weber search his pockets furiously for some candy.

"Oh Polard, really!" Gloria turned toward the door "Daddy is not looking for candy, more like his car keys."

"Gloria dear," Weber walked through the hall toward the front door, "get your mother. I am starving for some of her home-made fudge."

Pogo grinned at Gloria and jogged up the steps to join his friend. He turned around when he reached the top laughing. "See Gloria, 'dear,' face it, your old man is a candyolic!" He turned triumphantly as she stomped her foot then he went into Scott's bedroom.

Chapter 23

Scott and Pogo walked into the TarSa Police Headquarter at 8:30 the following morning. The officer at the information desk stared up from his typewriter.

"Yes, could I do something for you?"

"Yes, you can. I am Reverend Scott, here with Pogo Goins. We are suppoee to meet with a Mr. Simus this morning." Scott looked around and discovered a heavy-set man staring at them from the doorway across from a water cooler.

"That's Detective Simus over there. I think he is waiting for you, by the looks of him." The man at the desk turned back to his typewriter without saying another word.

Scott walked over to the man in the door, Pogo close behind him. "Simus?" Scott offered his hand and Simus walked back into his office, calling over his shoulder, "Whoever is in charge out there, I do not want to be disturbed, understand?" He motioned for Pogo to shut the door behind him. "Well Scott, I have been waiting to meet you. The guys at the top think you're the right man for this job. They were impressed by all you've accomplished on your missionary journeys."

"What about you, Mr. Simus?" Scott smiled. "You do not seem to agree with them."

"I just know this, Reverend, I need men—good men—to do this job. It's no easy job, like building a church or making sinners believe, and I will not stand for any goofing off!" He pulled a cigar from the top drawer and lit it. "You are to do everything I tell you and we will do this job my way or you and your friend here are out of it, understand?"

"Suppose I think your way is not the best way, Simus?" Scott crossed his arms, feeling an intense dislike for this arrogant man.

"I will be the judge of how this is handled, Scott. I think I know this business a little better than you or that kid there." Simus stood up and walked to the window. "We are workin' with drug pushers, a big ring of them, and they are working mainly in the schools, targeting rich kids."

"What is our job?" Pogo slid into a chair.

"When I think you are ready, kid, I'll tell you what I want from you," Simus snapped. "Since you two are new at this sort of thing, I am giving you some books to read up on. It will help you understand what we are up against."

"Have you got undercover people set up to go into the schools?" Scott leaned back in his chair. "That's where the action is. Isn't that where you should grab them?"

"Thank you, Scott. I've already planned to do that," Simus mumbled. He pulled two books from his desk drawer. He handed them over to Scott and Pogo. "Alright, fellows, read and study up on these books."

"Do I work as an undercover agent in the school?" Pogo smiled broadly, knowing he was the right age.

Simus raised his voice. "Listen kid, I will tell you what I want you to do and when, get it? Now shut up and read the damn book like I told you."

"Mr. Simus, we are not just another one of your dummies you can push around. In my line of work, I take orders from no one." Scott stood, clutching the book tightly in his hand. "I will do everything I can to help in this assignment, but I will not have you pushing me or my friend around. I hope you understand."

"Oh I see. I got a tough ass to work with." Simus walked to the door and slung it open. "Stay here and read. I've got to go meet with a select group of students. We'll dicuss what you do later, after you've read those books." He turned and stormed out the door.

"Wow! Lovely person, isn't he?" Pogo flopped back onto the chair.

"We would have to get stuck with a smart-ass know-it-all." Scott gritted his teeth. "Start reading, Pogo! We don't want to upset the great Simus, do we?"

"Who cares?" Pogo opened the book and began reading.

Susan walked, half in a daze, up the steps to the school building. Dr. Warner had called her to confirm his diagnosis. She was pregnant with Gene's child. Her hands clutched tight to her stomach as her lips melted into a secret smile. She felt a hand on her arm and looking up, she saw Peter Simus.

"Peter! What on earth are you doing here at TarSa University?" She smiled.

"I'm going to attend college here this year. Dad's working on a case in TarSa." He shook his head, laughing. "You know, it's one of those cases that drag on and on."

"I hope it's nothing too serious." She sat down in the third row in the auditorium. "I hate to think that TarSa is troubled by some serious crime."

"It's dope, Susan. A big ring of drug pushers are working their way into this perfect little island of TarSa." Close to her ear, Peter whispered, "Dad is coming over today to choose some students to work as undercover agents for the Narcotics Division. We'll be young narcs," he chuckled.

"You said 'we.' Are you going to be one, Peter?" Susan studied his eyes with concern. "Is it dangerous?"

"Not if you are careful." He smiled reassuringly. "You see, Dad is going to have some pros working among us and they do the heavy work. We just sorta keep our eyes open and our ears peeled."

"Sounds heavy, Peter. Can I be one of these narcs?" She thought to herself, Gene would be proud of me for helping others. "Can I, Peter?"

"Father will be here shortly and has set up a meeting in the dean's office. Come with me Susan and he will check you out." Peter led the way.

Susan smiled up at Roy Simus as he recognized her. "Hello, Mr. Simus, how are you?"

"Susan Andrews, I can hardly believe my eyes." He smiled broadly. "You look the best I have ever seen you, and you were always beautiful."

"I am the happiest I have ever been, Mr. Simus." Her fingers clutched the hidden ring beneath her dress. "Your son tells me you are looking for students to help in this drug case you're investigating. I'm volunteering."

"Well! Spirit! That's what it takes, real spirit!" he laughed as he moved the cigar around in his mouth. "If you're sure."

"Oh yes, Mr. Simus." She bit her lip. "I will do anything to stop the drug movement."

"That a girl." He put his arm around her shoulder. "Of course, you can't tell anyone about this, Susan."

"Not even Mom and Dad?"

"Especially your mom and dad." He nodded, his expression serious. "No one at all, Susan. Understand?" Simus winked at his son.

"Right, sir!" She stood at attention. "I'm ready for duty, sir."

"It is good to know I can get a little co-operation from someone today." He put his hand on her shouder. "We're setting up agents in the TarSa High School and here at the university. Your job is to keep your eyes open at all times for any suspicious-looking characters that might be pushers. Don't attempt to do anything on your own. Report immediately to the officer in charge and he will handle matters from there. Clear enough?"

"It will be a breeze. You can count on me, Mr. Simus." Susan stood up, smiling. "Anything else? I'm late for class."

"No, dear, that is all for now." Simus walked to the door beside her. "Just remember, do not tell a soul."

"I won't. I promise." She opened the door. "And I'll keep my eyes open all the time."

"I know I can depend on you, Susan. Stay in the clear and keep your cool. You'll be given a code number. That's how you will be identified to the squad. Good luck.'If you have any questions, just ask Peter. He's helped before."

"Thank you, sir." Susan walked out the door and made her way down the hall to her first class.

Peter watched her disappear around the corner. "You can depend on Susan, Dad."

Scott and Pogo looked up as Roy Simus stormed into the room. "Well, have you finished reading those books?"

"Yeh, and it's a good thing." Pogo mumbled.

Simus slapped the desktop. "Speak up, boy! Can't stand a lot of mumbling. Have you finished the damn book?"

"Yes we have, Simus." Scott dropped the book on his desk "Three times. What do you take us for, morons? There are only twenty pages there."

Simus smirked. "I figure with your mental capacity, fellows, you could only read through the book once."

"You figured wrong, Simus." Scott stood. "Orders, Simus. What are they?"

"First of all, let me say as long as you will be working for us, you will be a cop. You'll have to put away the Bible and carry a gun."

Scott frowned. "Yes, go ahead."

"I will give you certain beats, Scott. You hang around those areas undercover. Do not try anything on your own. Just keep your eyes open for any thing that smells of dope, understand?"

"Yeh, I understand." Gene nodded toward Pogo. "What about my friend here?"

"He'll tag along with you. Four eyes are better thart two."

"Alright. When we see something that looks hot, we do what? Under your orders, that is." Scott raised his eyebrows.

"You get in touch with me immediately. I'll handle the process from that point." Simus shuffled some papers. "Any more questions?"

"Why can't we rack them up sir?" Pogo stood next to Scott.

"No racking up kid. That's my department. I don't want a couple of amateurs screwing up the whole works." Simus smiled mockingly.

Anger flared in Scott's eyes.

"We have reason to believe the big wheel heading this operation is here in TarSa. If we can wrap this little group up, I am sure the boys back home will be well pleased with us."

"With us, Simus, or are you thinking in terms of your own glory? We do the dirty work and you get the credit." Scott's voice was low, but powerful.

"You just do what you are told Reverend." Simus handed him a paper with a list of businesses and addresses. "This is where you and Goings hang out. Scott, your name will be Joe Bradon. Goings, you are Larry Dowell. Stay in the shadows, fellows and don't look like you're spying."

"When do we start?" Pogo asked. "Joe and me?"

"Tonight. Start hanging around those bars—and remember, do not try anything funny on your own." Simus looked down at his paperwork to avoid Scott's glare. "Get with it! Stop standing around here like a couple of goons."

Scott pushed the door opened and walked swiftly from the building. "That damn Simus is really asking for it!"

"Yeh, he really thinks he is one gold metal cop!" Pogo put his hand on Scott's back. "Well Joe, what's first?"

"Well Larry, first I am going to call Susan and see how she made out at college today." Gene winked at his friend.

"Hey, school did start today, didn't it?" Pogo climbed into the car and laid his head against the seat. "I'm glad I don't have to go."

"Yeh, bird brain, had to go and quit." Gene cranked the motor and sped off, leaving the police station and Simus in the background.

"Look who's talking. As I recall, Scott—I mean Bradon, you quit school too, correct?" Pogo laughed "Since I failed the twelfth grade, I thought what the heck!"

"You failed because you goofed off, Pogo! You should be starting college this year like my girl." Gene Scott kept his eyes on the road "Alright, maybe I did quit school at fifteen, but after I got out of the Marines, with the help of Uncle Sam, I finished my education and then went to college, Duke University."

"Yeh, well not everyone can be a gold metal preacher." Pogo chuckled until Scott reached over and punched his arm. "Ouch! Shit, Scott!" He rubbed the sting out of his arm. "Are you going to let Simus run over you?"

"Mr. Roy Simus has a big mouth." Scott stopped in front of the parsonage. "I think I'm perfectly capable of handling this case as well and probably better than that jackass. Should the opportunity arise, I'm going to take this baby over." He walked into the study and picked up the phone. Susan's number was busy. He sat down to wait a few minutes and try again.

Susan took the glass of milk from Mildred' s eager hand.

"And drink every drop of it young lady. We don't want to have a puny little baby Scott running around here."

"No, we do not," Susan said as she finished the glass. "I don't think Gene would take to letting his son be puny. He would work out with him until he took after his big, strong dad." She turned when she heard the phone ring. "I'll get it!" Susan yelled loudly enough for everyone in the house to hear. "Hello, Andrews' residence."

"Mrs. Scott, what are you doing at the Andrews' residence?" Gene laughed softly.

"Oh Gene," she whispered excitedly. "I can't talk long, darling. Mom and Dad will be home soon. I'm so glad you called."

"How did your first day of college go?" He wished he could crawl through the phone line and put his arms around her.

"Who cares about college? All I care about is when can I see you?" She clutched tightly to her stomach and smiled.

"Can you get out of the house Saturday night?" His heavy breathing over the phone intensified her desire to hold him.

"Is that the earliest, sweetheart?" She swallowed.

"Yes, darling, I am afraid it is. I have my hands full with work every night this week." He frowned at Pogo, who sat listening to every word. "What about Saturday? Can you make it?"

"Try and stop me!" She wanted desperately to feel his lips against hers. "I need a kiss, husband."

"A what?" he laughed softly.

"A kiss, Reverend Scott. Do I have to wait until Saturday for it?"

"Yes, but believe me, honey, I will give you more than enough to make up for lost time." Though he also had the desire to feel Susan's warm gentle lips against his, he knew he must control his emotions and wait. "The malt shop?"

"Alright, the malt shop. What time, Mr. Scott?" she smiled in anticipaton.

"As early as you can get there Saturday afternoon." He closed his eyes and took a deep breath.

"Five-thirty soon enough?" She felt her heart beating in her throat.

"That's fine, honey." He motioned for Pogo to leave the room, after which his voice lowered and became warm and romantic. "Susan, my darling, I love you."

"Oh Gene, and I love·you."

"Be a good girl for your old man, okay?"

"I will be a good girl, just for my man." She laughed softly. "You be good too."

Gene smiled. "I will certainly try, little darling. Fair enough?"

"Fair enough." She blew a kiss into the receiver. "That will have to do for now, Mr. Scott."

"Here is yours, Mrs. Scott." He kissed the receiver as well. "Did you get it?"

"Mmmm, I got it." She closed her eyes.

"Goodbye, Mrs. Scott."

"Goodbye, Mr. Scott." She hung the phone up softly and walked dreamily to her bedroom.

Scott heard a chuckle and turned to see Pogo peeking through the door.

"Scott old pal, do you always go around kissing telephones?"

"Pogo, if you know what is good for you, you had better take off—and fast. Get it?" Scott climbed the stairs to his room quickly and changed clothes.

Pogo followed him and asked curiously, "Hey, why the clothes change?"

"Because, Pogo, I am not going into that bar tonight as Reverend Scott. I so happen to be Joe Bradon, a worthless seazy bastard. I have to look the part to feel the part."

"I better change too then. I certainly don't feel like a Larry Dowell." Pogo pulled the blue shirt over his brown hair. "It's going to seem real funny, Joe, being called Larry."

"Why, pal, as far as they know you are Larry, my no-count friend. It will seem perfectly normal to strangers."

Scott opened his door and walked down to the study to leave a note for John and Edna, explaining that he and Pogo would be working all night. He placed the note on the kitchen table, then called up to Pogo.

"Hey, Larry! Come on if you are going for that beer with me."

Pogo came down the steps laughing. "Pretty good Joe, that sounded like a real low life."

"Shut up and get in that car before I low life your ass."

Scott drove the car to the front of Saddie's Bar and shut it off. "Well Larry, here we are. Good looking place, right?" He shook his head.

Pogo studied the shabby looking building. "Yeh Joe, a real classy night spot."

He got out of the car and followed Scott into the bar. They took a table in the corner and ordered two beers.

"This place is full of sneaky looking characters, Sc—Joe."

"Watch that, Larry. One little slip and good ol Simus will be breathing down our backs." Scott took a big gulp of beer. His attention was drawn to a young man about Susan's age sitting at the bar. His back was to Scott, who could not make out his face. The blonde-haired youth was busy conversing with two hippy-looking fellows. "There is a baby to watch, Larry," Gene whispered.

Pogo looked in the direction of the blonde boy as he handed one of the other men a small package. Pogo pulled excitedly at Scott's arm. "Hey, did you see that?"

"Cool it." Scott raised his hand and whistled to the waitress. "Hey, sweetheart, another round of beer this way."

"Coming up." She turned and twisted her way behind the bar.

"Larry, you must learn to say things without getting so excited." Scott paid for the beers and tipped the waitress a quarter. "Here you go honey."

She looked at the single coin in her palm and feigned a smile.

"Last of the big spenders, hey doll?" She mumbled and walked away lazily.

"He's leaving Sc—Joe!" Pogo stood and Scott pulled him back down. "What are you doing? He's getting away!"

"If you do not sit still and shut up, kid, I'm going to belt you," Scott whispered through gritted teeth. "Look, we cannot be sure if what he had was really the stuff."

"What difference does it make now?" Pogo slumped in his seat "He got away."

"Come on, we're leaving." He pulled Pogo to his feet and said nothing until they were in the car heading back to the parsonage. "Now listen Pogo, first we have to be dead sure the kid was selling dope. Then we get to know him, become steady customers."

"But, Scott, Simus told us not to act on our own. You're talking about a completely new plan. He'll kill us, lock us up, something terrible!" Pogo's voice shook.

"Now look, Pogo, I do not give a damn what Simus thinks. This is my baby—yours and mine—and I am going to handle her my way." Scott stopped the car when he reached the parsonage. "You can't just rush in on these cases, Pogo. You get yourself into them so you can get the main man, the big daddy. It's like that old Indian saying, 'Follow the cigar smoke. There you find the fat man. He is the one you bust. The others come down when he falls.'"

"And who is making up the rules, Scott, you or Simus?" Pogo's eyes grew wide.

"I am! Look, we're the ones taking all the risks and if Simus doesn't like it, well frankly, I don't give a good shit." Scott climbed out of the car and went quietly into the parsonage.

Chapter 24

Susan looked up from her lunch tray when she felt someone staring at her. A tall blonde young man with sunglasses smiled at her from across the busy lunchroom. She felt her stomach turn as he continued to stare. Peter Simus sat down beside her and bumped her arm.

"Hey young lady." He smiled down into her blue eyes "What's wrong? Don't like this great fantastic college food?"

"I've had better," she laughed and whispered softly, "See that blonde-headed boy standing over by the check out?"

Peter looked up casually as he picked up the salt. "There is no one over there now, Susan. What did he look like?"

Her eyes jumped to the empty space the stranger had occupied just seconds earlier. "He gave me the creeps, Peter. He was about your height, 6'1", blonde and he wore sunglasses. Black rims. I would guess a freshman like us."

"Well he probably just thought you were irresistible to look at." Peter chuckled. "That is easy to understand, Susan."

"Oh Peter," she giggled and shook her head. "It was not that. He was different, Peter. I can't explain it. Call it women's intuition if you like, but there is definitely something weird about him."

"If you spot him again let me, know Susan. It could be something." Peter stood and offered her his hand. "Now do not let your mind go thinking everyone you meet who is unusual is a dope pusher."

"I promise I won't." She picked up her tray and put it away then made her way quickly down the hall. She froze when she spotted the same boy standing by a locker across from hers. Their eyes met for a brief second and she could feel herself shake.

"What is it about this fellow?" she asked herself as she hurriedly got her books from her locker and, without another glance, made her way quickly to her next class.

In the nights that followed, Scott and Pogo made their rounds from place to place based on the list Simus had given them. They did not have as much luck as they had on the first night and they were about to chalk it up to beginner's luck when at last Scott saw the blonde entering Sally's bar. Scott bumped Pogo and nodded as they watched him order a beer and take a seat in the table next to them.

"This could be our go, Larry. Play along." Scott slapped the table with his fist and ran his hands through his hair. "Shit, if I don't get a fix soon, I will burst!"

"We tried everywhere, big Joe." Pogo swallowed his beer and called the waitress over. "Two more beers, cutie. My friend is having one hell of a go here, if you understand."

"Oh sure, kid. We get junkies in here all the time. I'll get your beer, but it won't help your friend none."

In a minute she was back with their drinks. "That's four bucks, honey."

Pogo paid her and tossed back a gulp. "Come on, Joe. Pull yourself together."

"Together? Damn stinking life!" He grabbed Pogo by the shoulders and shook him. "A guy can't get one lousy fix on this whole damn island!" He dropped his head onto the table and whispered to Pogo "Is he listening?"

"It's hard to say. He hasn 't looked up but he has edged over our way some."

"Good. Can't give up now." Scott slammed his fist against the table, cracking it down the middle. The waitress hurried over, the blonde headed boy close behind her. Her eyes flew open at the astonishing display of his power.

"Look, mister, you don't have to go taking all you damn troubles out on my furniture!"

"The man is uptight, lady." The stranger said calmly as he handed her a handful of cash. "Consider it cool, right chick?"

"Sure doll, as long as it's paid for." She pushed the money inside her blouse and went quietly to the bar.

"Hey, thanks for that." Pogo pulled out his wallet. "How much did you pay her?"

"It's paid for, buddy. Give it a rest." He pulled a chair up and gazed at the cracked table with a look of awe. "That's great strength you have there, mister."

"Strength? Ha! The hell of it is, it's all in my arms!" Scott rested his head in his hands. "My head, it feels like it's blowing off into outer space. Going, going, gone."

"Hey, buddy, you sound like you've got it bad. Real bad," the boy whispered, leaning his head down by Scott's. He looked around the room as he slipped his hand under the table. "You will find life better under the table my friend."

Scott's fingers felt the capsule. He forced a true-to-life smile as he pretended to swallow it.

"Thanks. You're a real pal." Scott's voice was full of relief. "How much do I owe you?"

"The first one is on the house." The boy nodded with a coy smile. "I can set you up as a steady customer if you like."

"If I like? Are you kidding!" Scott put his hand on the boy's shoulders. "You are a pal, yes sir! Damn good pal!" He looked warily around the room. "Where do we make the connection?"

"I work two bars, here and Foxhound. Which ever suits you, friend." He winked.

"Here will be fine, sonny boy." Scott swallowed a big gulp of beer and threw what remained against the wall. "Bombs away!"

"Hey, Joe, we better split!" Pogo stood and tried to pull his big friend to his feet. "Come on, Joe. Let's go!"

"I am a rock. You cannot move a rock and a rock cannot walk because he—or shall I say it—does not have feet." Scott laughed as he smiled at Pogo. "Hey Pal, have you ever heard of a talking rock, huh? I must be pretty damn special."

"What are your names, my friend?" The pusher ran his fingers through his blonde hair as he watched Pogo anxiously try to control his friend.

"I am Larry Dowell, and 'rock' here is Joe Bradon. He is not always like this. When he is working he's tough as shit and does twice as much as any other man on the job."

"What sort of work do you do?" The kid's eyes fell on Scott, taking his watch off and on.

"We work on the loading docks. The ships come in, the ships go out and we take off and put on hour after stinking hour until the whisle blows at six. It is a rotten lousy job, but hell, you got to eat, right?" Pogo pulled at Scott's arm again. "Come on, rock. If you are so damn special, move!"

"I will give her a try, old tree." He stood, nearly falling. Pogo grabbed for him and Scott extended his arm to hold him away. "Relax. This rock is steady." He laughed and put his hand on the stranger's arm. "What—what did you say your name was?"

"I didn't." He shook his head. "Randy Sumner. Hang in there, Joe. You know, my boss could use a big man like you."

The three walked outside, Randy helping Pogo get Scott into the car.

"I'll meet you here Saturday night, seven sharp." Randy said quietly and disappeared instantly into the dark.

Gene Scott pounded his hand against the car seat. "Damn!"

"What's wrong, Scott?" Pogo cranked up the car. "You didn't really swallow that stupid pill, did you?"

"No, damn it!" Scott gritted his teeth. "This job is interfering with my plans with Susan. I had a date with my wife on Saturday night!"

Pogo shrugged. "Well, duty before romance, old buddy."

"Just drive and keep your remarks to yourself, o buddy, old pal." Scott stared through the window. "I'll have to change our plans to Sunday instead.

When Scott could not reach Susan before Saturday, he decided to meet her at the malt shop long enough to explain why he had to break their date. Susan smiled at him as he approached the table.

"Reverend Scott, what kept you?" She giggled at his clothes. "And why are you dressed in those ridiculous clothes?"

He slid in next to her and took her hand under the table. "Susan honey, I can't go out with you tonight. I'm sorry."

"But why, Gene?" She gazed down in disappointment. "I was really looking forward to tonight."

"I've got to work, Susan. That is why I'm dressed like this. There was no way I could get out of it." He squeezed her hand. "Could you meet me tomorrow night instead?"

"Oh, Gene." Susan stared into his blue eyes. "I was really looking forward to being in your arms tonight. All night."

"And you think I wasn't?" He caressed her face with his fingertips. "I wanted nothing more than the weekend to get here, so I could—" He glanced around to be sure no one could hear him. "So I could make love to you, darling."

She snuggled next to him and feigned a weak smile. "What sort of job do you have to do?"

"I have been working on a secret task force here on TarSa. I can't tell you what it is because of the orders I've been given. But believe me, hon, I am in no danger."

"Secret job, huh?" She gave an ironic laugh. "There are a lot of those floating around."

"What does that mean?" He studied her face. "Susan, are you saying you have some sort of secret from me?"

"I guess everyone does, at one time or another." She gripped his hand tightly. "I promise to tell you one big secret tomorrow sweetheart."

"Why not now?" His voice was grave.

"Because, Gene Scott, this type of secret you don't just tell and then say, 'Okay, see you later.' I want to be with you longer when I tell you." She motioned for him to let her out. "Let's go outside. I feel like everyone is interested in our life as much as we are."

"You're right, it will be much more private outside." He paid the waitress for Susan's drink and they walked out to her car. "Susan, now you got me wondering what it is you're going to tell me. I hate secrets."

He turned to see if anyone was watching them, then bent over and parted his lips gently over hers. She locked her fingers around his neck.

"Now, husband, since you're going off to work rather than keeping your date with me, you have even more kisses to make up for."

"I had no other choice, sweetheart. You believe that, don't you?" He pulled her into his arms, holding her firmly against him.

"Judging by the way you feel," she said with a gentle laugh, running her fingers around his ears, "I'd say I had no other choice but to believe you."

"Very funny, young lady." He opened the car door for her. "I plan to make up for lost time tomorrow night. You can count on that, baby doll."

A smile of anticipation crossed her face as she climbed into her sports car.

"Then I shall be looking forward to tomorrow night." Holding his arm, she pulled him to her and their lips met in a burning kiss. She slipped her fingers down inside his pants. "Mummm. Can't wait."

"Susan!" He stepped away and closed the door. "Still my wicked little woman, Delilah."

"See you here same time tomorrow, Samson." As she drove away she blew him a kiss.

He climbed into his car and hurried back to the parsonage to pick up Pogo. They made their way quickly to Sally's Bar and Diner. Scott's immediately spotted Randy Sumner as he made his way through the door. Randy smiled and motioned them to his table.

"Hi Joe, Larry. Have a sit down." He motioned for the waitress. "Two more beers for my friends, Hazel."

"Are we late?" Scott asked as he turned the chair around and sat down, resting his arms on the back.

"Not really." Randy paid the waitress and casually slipped a small brown package from his pocket. "Here you are, Joe baby. There's enough here to keep you happy for a long time."

Scott slid the package into his pants pocket. "Thanks, buddy. How much?"

"Twenty singles, Joe baby." He took the money Scott handed him and stuffed it into his shirt. "Big Joe, I told Mr. Big about you. He's interested in you working for him, friend. Of course you will have to be checked out and run through the routine he has for new comers. But don't worry, Joe. I have faith in you." Randy leaned forward conspiratorially. "He really has been looking for someone just like you."

"Yeah. Well you can tell Mr. Big, if the pay is right, Old Joe baby will consider taking on the job." Scott guzzled his beer and whistled, "Another round, Hazel, sweety. Three glasses. Hell, I can't stand to drink alone."

Pogo chuckled as he finished his beer. "Good ol Joe, always thinking about his friends."

"Yeh, why not." Scott paid the waitress and slapped her on the back end. "That's your tip, honey!" He slipped a five down her blouse with a laugh.

"Thanks, handsome!" She twirled around. "I'm speechless."

"That's a switch," Scott said, lifting his glass. "A woman who's speechless."

Randy ran his fingers nervously through his long blonde hair. "Oh damn. Philmore Harrison."

"What's a Philmore Harrison?" Pogo asked, sitting back in his chair.

"May you feel more with Philmore." Scott chuckled. He realized Randy was trying to hide behind him. "Randy Baby, what's with the hide-and-seek?"

"That creep is always after me for a set up, but he never has the bread to pay for it. He goes total ape shit when I refuse to give him any."

"You supposing somebody tells him when you're here?" Pogo watched the big, well-built man in the faded green coat.

"Not unless he's threatened them. No one around here likes him. He's always stiring up trouble. Maybe Hazel will tell that crazy cat I've come and gone." Randy's hands trembled. "He is a sick, mad man!"

"Mad men can be handled, Randy," Scott said in a calm tone.

Scott watched as Philmore Harrison, his eyes wild, scanned the crowded room. A wicked smile broke across the mad man's face as he spotted Randy's jacket on the back of the unoccupied chair.

Gene Scott spoke calmly. "Prepare yourself, Randy baby. Your freako is headed this way."

"Stand by me, Joe, will you?" Randy's hand shook as he sat down in his chair.

Philmore smiling wickedly, loomed above him. "Randy, set me up dude! I need a fix. I need it bad. Real bad." He tugged at the scared pusher's arm. "I'll pay you back later, honest. Randy. You can trust me for the cash!"

"I can't do it. I am all out Philmore." Randy kept his eyes on his glass of beer.

"You are lying, Randy!" He jerked the boy's sleeve. "Now hand it over to me, quick!"

"I will give you one. Right between the eyes, if you don't shut up and get lost." Scott stood up and glared at the half-crazed man.

"And I'll kill you, mister? Do you hear me? Kill you!" His eyes shot fire at the preacher, then turned back to the pusher. "Give it to me, Randy, or I will send you to hell too!"

"I—I told you, I am all out of the stuff, Philmore!" Randy's voice shook.

"You're lying, you bastard! Lying!"

Philmore Harrison grabbed for Randy but before he could get a grip on him, Scott sent the wild man flying across the saloon. Before he could stand up, Scott grabbed him by the shirt and jerked him to his feet.

"Alright, buddy boy, let's go for a little walk." Scott pulled him out the door, Pogo and Randy close behind, "Now, I did not like the things you said to my friend in there, creep, so I suggest you apologize before I break you in two."

"I'm sorry man! Please, don't hu—hurt me!" Philmore Harrison shooked with fear as he begged. "Let me go, man. I'll leave"

"And you will never bother my little friend here again, right?"

"Sure, whatever you say, man."

He turned and ran like a wild animal when Scott released him. Randy bent over laughing.

"Wow Joe, that was something else! Old crazy Philmore ran like a bat out of hell."

"Randy, my little pal, I don't think that freak will give you any more trouble." Scott walked over and got in his car. "Be speaking to you. Let's go, Larry."

"You know it. I really dig you man." Randy waved as Scott pulled the car away from the curb.

"Wow, Scott, what were you thinking?" Pogo laid his head back. "That crazy junky could have knifed you or something."

"Yeh, well he didn't." Scott cut the windshield wipers on as the rain began to fall in small splatters against the glass. 'I hope Susan is home."

"Now, Scott, don't start worring about Susan while you're driving in the rain. You could make yourself crazy thinking on that."

"Susan is my life, Pogo. Everyone has something they are searching for and few ever find it." Scott's voice was solemn. "I finally found what I have been searching for and it took me thirty-six years."

"I knew Susan meant a lot to you, Scott, but I guess I never realized just how much." Pogo said quietly. He turned to his friend. "I'm glad you found her, Scott. You deserve to be happy."

"Happy!" He slid the car to a stop in front of the parsonage. "When I have Susan with me always, never to leave my side, then my joy will exceed all other joys I have ever known." As he reflected on his words, his face melted into a joyous smile. "Then I can shout—and I mean shout—my love, to the four corners of the world."

He climbed out and made his way slowly into the parsonage, his arm wrapped around Pogo's shoulder.

Chapter 25·

Scott waited impatiently outside Simus' office. Simus had phoned the parsonage at the crack of dawn and ordered Scott and Pogo to come to the station.

Pogo looked around nervously. "What do you think this is all about?"

"I don't know, Pogo, but it had better be good." Scott paced back and forth in the outer office. "If he causes me to miss church services, I will rack his head in his own file cabinet."

"I hope he don't have something planned for us tonight." Pogo squeezed the arm of his chair as he watched his friend's eyebrow arch.

"Well he can just forget it if he has." Scott said loudly with finality. "Tonight is Susan and my night and I'll be shit if anyone is going to screw that up."

"Hold it down, Scott." Simus stuck his head out of his office door. "Come on in and have a seat."

"What is this all about, Simus? I have a sermon to preach this morning. So make it fast." Scott remained on his feet.

"Just sit down and relax." Simus pulled a cigar from his desk drawer.

Scott sat down heavily. "Get on with it."

"I hear you fellows are chatting freely with the characters you have been watching."

"So you have a spy on your spies?" Scott gritted his teeth with disgust and turned to his friend. "Pogo, you don't suppose it was that tall, stupid looking jerk at the end of the bar. The one who looked like an undercover cop. Remember how he kept staring at us over his newspaper?"

"Yeh, some spy." Pogo grimaced. "He showed up at every bar we went to."

Sinus slammed his fist down on the desk. "I told you fellows frankly to remain silent and stay in the shadows! You two have disobeyed my orders."

Scott shrugged. "Look, Simus, I am going to handle this thing my way. As long as I'm sticking out my neck, I'll handle the risk my way. I guarantee you that." Scott stood up.

"Scott, neither you or this boy here know anything about dealing with pushers. They can get pretty deadly if you cast in your line and, instead of taking the bait, they find you're fishing." Simus chewed the end of his cigar nervously. "Now I demand cooperation from you two."

"You know what you can do with your cooperation." Scott stepped to the door. "Unlike your other Patsies, the church's involvement in this case is strictly free. No one makes or changes the rules for us. I play the game my way, not yours."

"Why the devil did you send in the request for documents to verify you've worked on the boat docks loading freight for the last year-and-a-half?" Simus walked along side of Scott as he made his way out of the building. "My boys said you ordered them to get it done immediately. What's this all about?"

"I'm surprised an investigator like you can't figure that out, Simus." Scott climbed in behind the wheel of his car. "Let's just say, I am not wasting my time sitting around on my ass drinking beer. When there is a job to do, I get it done." he slammed the door, causing the officer to jump back. He turned on the motor. "Got to go."

"Scott, you can't do—Scott!" Simus watched frustrated as the preacher sped away. He shook his head. "Damn that man—and everybody he loves!"

"You're late." John Crain whispered to Scott when he slipped into the seat next to him. "What did Simus want?"

The choir's loud anthem drowned Scott's reply as he bent over to talk with his friend. "He just wanted to bitch a little. Thinks I am handling the whole job badly." Gene's eyes fell on Susan's smiling face "Frankly, I could not care less what that jackass thinks." Before he realized where he was and what he was doing, he winked at his wife.

"Gene?" John touched his knee. "Better watch that kind of stuff in public."

The service went well and everyone listened quietly as Scott preached. Ever so often, Scott would glance down at Susan and their eyes would exchange unspoken words of love.

The last hymn was sung and Scott led the benediction. Susan placed her hand gently in his as she filed out of the church, following the rest of her family.

"I enjoyed the sermon very much this morning, Reverend Scott."

"Did you? I am glad you enjoyed it Susan." His gaze fastened on her. "You look quite lovely today, young lady."

"Why thank you, Reverend Scott. You're looking pretty good yourself." She smiled coyly as the lady behind her cleared her throat.

"Thank you. Coming from such a pretty girl, I find that a compliment." He smiled as he took Susan's arm and maneuvered her to his side. Reaching out, he took the older woman's hand. "Good to see you this morning, Mrs. Nelson. Where is Joe? I missed seeing him out in the congregation today."

"Bless you, Reverend Scott, Joe was not feeling up to par this morning. Up practically all night with his back." She twisted her pocket book handle.

"I'll keep him in my prayers for healing and I certainly hope he gets to feeling better, Mrs. Nelson. I'll try and drop in on Joe to see how he's doing." Scott gave her a broad smile, thinking to himself, "This is the way it should be, Susan, by my side, always."

"Susan dear, are you coming?" Shirley Andrews waved for her as Edna rushed to her. "Yes, Edna, is there something on your mind?"

"Shirley, my son David is too shy to ask you himself, but he would love to have Susan spend the day with him. You wouldn't mind, would you?"

"Of course not, Edna dear, if it will be no inconvenience for you."

Shirley smiled at her daughter. "Would you like that, dear?" Susan squeezed Scott's hand.

"Yes, Mom, I think that's a great idea. Thank you for inviting me, Edna."

"We love having Susan over. The young keep you so entertained." Gene smiled at Shirley.

"I wouldn't think you would have any problems keeping entertained, Reverend Scott." Shirley chuckled and pulled her sister Joan to her. "If you run out of something to do today, just pop over, Joan has absolutely nothing to do today, do you dear?"

"No, nothing, not a thing," she said, laughing sheepishly. "If you want more adult fun, I would love to have you come over."

"That's mighty sweet of you both, but I have got other plans for the day. Thank you anyway." He smiled and walked to the parsonage, Susan right behind him.

"Gene, this is much better. Now we'll have all day," Susan whispered excitedly.

"Yeh, that Edna is one wonderful little women." He laughed and slapped Susan's behind as they walked through the door. "Come here and kiss me, Mrs. Scott." He pulled her into his arms and kissed her tenderly.

"Mmmm, now that's what I have been waiting for." She ran her fingers along his neck. "You're one hell of a kisser, Mr. Scott."

"That's a funny way of describing a preacher's kiss." Pogo walked through the door, laughing.

"Well Pogo, this is no ordinary behind-the-pulpit preacher." Susan took his arm and held it tightly. "And he's all mine."

"I'll say one thing for you, Susan, you've got plenty of man, more than most," Pogo said wryly. "Actually more than one or two put together."

"Alright you two, enough of this. Knock it off." Scott sat on the sofa and pulled Susan down beside him. "Now tell me, what's that secret you were going to tell your old man."

"My—a secret." She looked up at Pogo and laughed sheepishly. "Could we be alone for a few seconds please. I know you will find out sooner or later, but I had rather we be alone when I tell him."

"Tell me what?" He slid his arm around her. "You've really got my curiosity up."

Susan waited until Pogo shut the door and they were alone. She cleared her throat and stood. "Gene sweetheart, prepare yourself for a shock. We—we are going to have a baby."

She swallowed as Gene leaped up and grabbed both her arms.

"Susan, are you saying 'a baby'?" His voice shook.

"Yes, yes, Mr. Scott. You and I are going to have a son." She closed her eyes as his fingers bit into her flesh. "Well, it's not all my fault, Reverend Scott."

"Damn! A baby is the last thing we need right now!" he practically yelled. Susan sat on the sofa and began to cry.

"I'm sorry you are not happy about our having a son, but I'm very happy about it, Mr. Scott."

"Susan," his voice grew tender as he sat next to her and wrapped his protective arms around her. "I never meant to shout, darling. I love you, Susan." Gene Scott's eyes lit up as he lifted her face. "A son? Do you really think it will be a son?"

"Oh yes my darling!" She threw her arms around his neck. "I want so much to give you a little boy."

"Shit!" He laughed and stood, picked Susan up in his arms and twirled her around. "We're having a baby!"

"Oh Gene, Gene! Then you are happy, I mean really happy." She kissed him. "You are, aren't you?"

"You bet I am, Susan. You bet I am." His lips parted over hers. "Hell, this might be just what we need to solve our problems. Not right away of course. I would not want your parents doing something stupid." He hugged her tightly. "But when our son gets here, they can't do a damn thing about it."

"Gene, did you say son?" Edna stood in the doorway, her eyes wide in shock.

"That's right, beautiful!" Scott squeezed Susan's hand "Susan and I are about to become parents. How's that for Sunday news?"

"Well, I don't know whether to laugh or cry." She pulled out a handkerchief from her pocket. "You seem to be pretty happy about it."

"I think it's terrific, Edna, really great!" Scott squeezed his arms around his young wife.

"What about your secret, Gene? It can't be kept much longer, I started showing a lot at five months with David." Edna's voice had a frantic tone. "You will have to tell sooner or later."

John walked up and put his hand on his wife's shoulder. "There, there, Edna. I'm sure Gene and Susan will work this thing out."

"You bet we will," Scott laughed joyfully. "After we have our son, they will think twice before trying to break us up."

"Gene is right Edna, Mom and Dad would not think of doing anything then." Susan rubbed her stomach. "I hate to sound pushy, Edna, but I think my son and I could use something to eat."

"Of course." Edna stuffed the handkerchief back into her pocket and smiled. "Food for the mother-to-be." She bussed Gene's cheek. "The father may have some too."

"Thanks, beautiful. Sometimes I don't know what we would do without you around." Scott caught sight of Pogo and David smiling from the stairs. "I guess you two nosy bodies heard the news?"

"Yes, daddy-O, as a matter of fact we did." David laughed and slapped Pogo on the shoulder. "Right, pal?"

"Right. So, papa bear, when is mama bear having baby bear?" Pogo asked with a grin.

Scott gazed at his young bride. "I don't know. Susan, when are you expecting the delivery of our baby?"

"In early spring, sweetheart. Dr. Warner said I was almost one month." Susan smiled as Gene put his hand on her stomach.

"I bet the little fellow is growing like a weed." He bent down and kissed her flat stomach. "Hang in there, little Scott."

Everyone was busy chattering around the table when Edna cleared her throat and waved her hands for silence. "I have an annoucement to make too."

Everyone grew quiet, looking toward her.

"Since the glad tidings this day, I think it is the right time to began plans on finding a permanent post for the Scott family."

"Now Edna, I—"

Edna waved for Scott to stay quiet.

"Chuck it, Gene, and kindly let me finish. Then you can comment." She ran her fingers through her short brown hair. "Now everyone knows how much this church is growing and the board has already suggested we start having two services on Sunday morning. The board also feels that this extra load could be too much for John to handle alone and wanted to know if Reverend Gene Scott would consider the post."

"Oh, Gene!" Susan took his hand. "That really would be wonderful!"

"The bishop would never see to it." Scott shook his head as he took a swallow of tea. "Edna, John, you know Henry Weber would rather die than have me take the easy way out."

"We do not intend to let Bishop Weber know anything about this little transaction, Gene." John leaned back in his chair. "We have drawn up a legal petition and have sent it off to the head of the Methodist board for approval. They in turn will read it, approve it and send it back for signatures from every member of our church."

"How long have you been working on this little project to save the Scott foundation?" Gene pulled Susan into his lap.

"I would say about two weeks, wouldn't you, dear?" John winked at Edna.

"At least two." She laughed triumphantly. "So old candy man will not know anything about our little transaction until the day that it comes through."

"Oh, Edna, John," Susan laughed, "a thousand blessings fall upon you! I certainly have been blessed when you became my friends! Blessed, truly truly blessed!" She smiled at her husband. "Haven't we been blessed, Gene?"

"You bet we have, little mother." He tickled her, causing her to cry out in laughter. "Isn't she a beautiful mother?"

"Oh Gene!" she giggled.

"I would say one of the prettiest little mothers I have seen." John

knew it wise not to say the prettiest with Edna sitting so close.
"Yeh, beautiful. Sexy little mother too." Pogo smiled broadly.
"But I guess she would have to be with old tiger here."
"Chuck it, Pogo." Scott held Susan tightly. "Mmmm, love you woman."
"Don't be squeezing her too much, Gene." Edna stood and began clearing the table. "She may look as slender as always, but you have got to remember she is carrying precious cargo."
"Oh, Edna," Susan laughed.
She stood up to help. Scott jumped up then and sat her back down.
"Gene, what are you doing? I am going to help Edna clean up this mess."
"Nothing doing, young lady." He rolled up his sleeves. "I'll help Edna. You just sit there and take it easy, young lady."
"Gene Scott," Susan said, "It's not going to hurt me to wash a little dish."
"Just stay put, little mother, we will take care of everything." David turned to Pogo. "Right?"
"You bet! Just let the menfolk take care of the heavy work. Can't let anything happen to our godchild." Pogo reached for an apron and tied it around him "Okay, dishwasher, let's move this assembly line."
"Fellows," Edna said, shaking her head, "I appreciate all this good help, but I think one of you will be plenty."
"You sit down too, Mom. Scott, take your lovely, pregnant wife and find a nice quiet corner to play in." David stuck his hands in the soapy dish water. "Let the old pros get to work on these dishes."
"I think he has a fever." Edna laughed and pulled John to his feet. "Better leave before he comes to his senses, dear."
Susan and Gene made their way slowly up to his bedroom. After they were privately locked inside, he pulled her into his arms and kissed her gently.
"I love you, Mrs. Scott."
"And I love you, Mr. Scott!" She slowly began pulling off his sweater. "I love your sexy chest too."
"Sexy chest?" he laughed and undid her dress and bra. His eyes fell on her round young breast. "I'm afraid there is no contest. You get first, second and third place."
Her fingers undid his zipper on his pants and gently slid them to the floor. Removing his boxers, she smiled down at his erection.
"There is certainly no contest on the babymaker department."

Joan Byrd

She pressed her warm body against his "My man wins far above the rest of all males."

"Susan, Susan." His hands moved over her shapely body in delight. "I love you, Susan. I love you so much."

"Gene, my darling, I love you." She melted under him as he found her body again in a heated embrace.

They lay quietly, held in each other's arms when a knock came on the door.

Scott raised up on his elbow. "Yes, what is it?" he asked softly.

"Gene, it's after ten. Better let David take Susan home now."

"Thank you, Edna. We'll be right down." He bent over and kissed her passionately. "That will have to last me for another long week."

"Darn!" Susan climbed out of bed and put her clothes on. "I hate leaving you, Gene. It's torture." She brushed through her long black hair. "I would rather have any excruciating punishment than to be separated from you, darling."

"It is agony for me too, sweetheart." He finished tying his shoestrings and stood, taking her into his arms. "Take good care of our baby, Mrs. Scott."

"Don't worry, that is one part of you I have got with me all the time." She touched her stomach gently. "Our little boy."

"Take good care of my girl too. She's the most important thing in my life." His lips parted over hers and his tongue moved slowly around in her mouth. "I love my girl with all my heart."

"Oh Gene!" She held him tightly "My heart is yours forever."

"Hey Susan," David called from outside the door, "are you ready?"

Scott opened the door. "See that you drive carefully, David. Okay?"

"Every inch of the way, Gene." He said with a smile and led the couple down the steps. "I guess you really made up for lost time, huh?"

"Just keep moving toward the car, David." Scott replied.

"I'm moving., I'm moving!" He laughed and opened the car door. "Hop in, honey."

"Watch that kind of talk and keep those dishwater hands off my girl." Scott touched Susan's cheek as he helped her into the car. "Be a good girl and don't be flirting with any of those cute college boys."

"Are you kidding, Scott? Susan doesn't have to flirt." David said wryly. "Those guys around campus think she is pretty heavy already, one neat chick!"

"Listen, they can look—can't blame them for that. But let them lay one finger on her and they better hope they have plenty of hospitalization insurance."

Susan laughed and kissed him.

Scott stood in the shadows of the parsonage and watched the car speed down the road. He lifted his head up to the heavens and took a breath of the cool night air.

"Thank you, God, for giving me the love of Susan. Let me be the kind of father to our children you would have me to be. Forgive me if I tend to care for their mother a little more, but she is inbedded deep within my heart and soul." He closed his eyes as his lips gently mouthed "amen" and, turning slowly, walked up to his lonesome bedroom.

The weeks dragged by as Scott and Pogo worked their 6:30 to 5:30 shift working on the loading docks. Scott only saw Susan a day or so over the weekends, which seemed to fly by for the love-starved couple.

Pogo lifted the large box and sat it on the loader. "Shit. This job is for the birds!"

"Yeh, it has been four lousy weeks and they still must be checking us out." Scott motioned to the loader operator. "Take her away."

"And the pay on this job is low. I mean for the hard work we put in, it's unfair." Pogo dropped onto a box and wiped the sweat off his neck. "Suppose Mr. Big just forgot about us, Scott, and we're doing this lousy work for nothing."

"It takes time, Pogo. Those bastards don't take any chances."

"That's just great, Scott." Pogo shook his head. "Mr. Big and his gang don't take chances. The police department doesn't take chances. But good old Pogo and Scott—well they're just a couple of stool pigeons."

"The trouble with you, Pogo, is that you let things upset you too much." Scott patted his friend's shoulder. "Just relax, things will start shaping up." His eyes followed the loader as it was lowered before them. "They just have to."

Susan had been keeping a sharp eye out for the blonde-headed boy ever since the day in the cafeteria. She had found out his name was Randy Sumner, a freshman with low average ratings. She had noticed he was always huddled with some of the wilder types. Remembering what Simus had told her, she didn't. want to do anything without talking with him first. She dailed his number and left a message that she had something important to discuss with him.

"Susan, please come in." Roy Simus pulled a chair from the desk as he smiled at the bright girl. "Now I believe you said you had something you wanted to discuss."

"Yes, Mr. Simus, it's about my job, sir."

"What is it, Susan? Are you wanting out?" he asked. "I can understand."

"Oh no, Mr. Simus." Susan sat up excitedly. "It's right the opposite, really."

"You don't say." He gave her a puzzled look. "I am afraid you will have to explain, my dear."

"Sir, I have been observing one particular boy very closely for the past few weeks and I think he is one of the big pushers at college." she leaned toward the desk. "As a matter of fact, Mr. Simus, I think he is the main leader there."

"What's his name, Susan?" Roy Simus pulled a pencil from behind his ear.

"If I tell you sir, will you listen to my plan? I just know it will work." She spoke excitedly.

"Plan?" The detective moved the pencil around nervously in his hand. "Alright, Susan, what do you have on your mind?"

"Well sir, from the reports we have been getting, most of the cases hit by the drugs have been rich students."

"Yes, that is true. They hit where they will be sure of the payoffs." He shifted in his seat. "Go on."

"This boy has been asking a lot of questions about me. I think, if I played along with him, we might find out something."

"Susan, this thing you are asking could be extremly dangerous." Simus admired the girl's strong will.

"Not if I'm careful. You see, I pretend to fall for the gum trick, where the pusher offers you a stick of gum which has been drugged. I don't really chew it because I have a regular stick hidden in my hand, and that is the stick I really chew."

"You've really thought this out, young lady." He scratched his head. "I guess it would not hurt if you found out if the kid's a pusher, but that's as far as you take it Susan. After he gives you the gum and tries to make a sale, then you report it and stay out of it from there on."

"But chief, if I hang in there, I may find out who is the big man behind the scenes," she pleaded. "Please, Mr. Simus, I know it sounds ridiculous to you, but if I started hanging around this fellow, he might open up."

"You mean, sorta like a girlfriend?" His eyes brightened up at her idea.

"Exactly!" she exclaimed. "Please sir, just let me give it a try. We must put an end to these low down dirty drug devils."

"Susan, it sounds like a pretty winning idea, but if anything happened to you and I gave you the go ahead, well I could never forgive myself." He scratched his head. "Susan, if I agree to this plan of yours and you see for one second you may be in danger, will you promise me that you will withdraw at once?"

"It's a deal, chief!" Susan shook his chubby hand and stood up. "Thank you very much, Mr. Simus. I won't let you or TarSa down."

Roy Simus stood beside her. "Susan, just for the record, what's this boy's name?"

"Randy Sumner." She replied. "Six foot-one inches tall, long blonde hair, blue eyes, a freshman with C average grades."

"You seem to know quite a bit about this fellow," Simus said with a laugh.

"Well Cap, I'm off, to do my duty to God and my country!" She started whistling as she danced merrily out the door.

Scott and Pogo had been sitting in Sally's for almost two hours before Randy Sumner finally came over smiling.

"Hi, Joe baby. Thought I was lost I bet, huh?"

"Yeh, I was beginning to wonder." Scott pulled a chair up for the late arrival. "Take the load off your feet, pal."

"Mr. Big don't like any of his cats talking to new prospects until they are check out clean." Randy smiled.

"I guess by your talking to me, I am considered clean then." Scott turned to Pogo. "Can you imagine that chum, me clean?"

"You clean? Now that is a slam on your outrageous reputation, Joe." Laughing, Pogo slapped the table. "Clean. Right. Hey Hazel, bring us a round of beer, will you? We got some celebrating to do. Dirty old Joe here is clean."

"Clean? You're kidding, right?" She laughed aloud. "Joe baby, nothing personal but let's face it, there is not one clean bone in your dirty body. From the top of your handsome dirty mind to the middle of your sexy darling legs."

"Well, sweetheart, I did not know you observed me so closely." Scott raised his full glass. "I wish to purpose a toast."

"Get with it then, daddy-O." Randy held up his glass smiling.

"To Hazel, the evilest little waitress on this side of hell."

"I'll drink to that!" Pogo winked at the big busted waitress as he took a big gulp of beer and almost choked.

Scott slapped his friend's back as he turned his attention back on Randy. "What did Mr. Big Rat have to say about me kid?"

"He likes the way you're built, Joe, and your strength. There's no question about how much he likes it, man." Randy moved closer to him and whispered, "You'll get the final test Friday night, baby."

"What sort of damn test?" Scott swallowed the rest of his beer. "I despise tests, kid, and I will not be taken for some stooge, get it?"

"Cool down, friend. It's not so bad. Before Mr. Big meets you face to face, he has the final touches checked out by one of his really close associates." Randy elbowed Scott and winked. "His steady girl, Candy Carmel, a real dish, Joe! You and her, all alone, in her fancy little apartment. Dig it, man?"

"Hey. Joe, now that is interesting." Pogo said, leaning toward them.

"Yeh, isn't it?" Scott glared at him. "What kind of test exactly is this little candy dish going to give me?"

"Don't worry, Joe baby. When Candy gets a look at you and sees what she has to test, believe me, your night will not be wasted." He smiled, arching his eyebrows. "Old Mr. Big sure trusts his little Candy."

"And I take it you don't?" Pogo's head drooped toward the table as he thought about how Susan had to trust her man as well.

"Candy knows men and can spot a phony miles away. She's always the last word as far as the men Mr. Big hires, dig?"

"I'm sure old Joe here can give little Miss Candy a real man treat." Pogo slapped Scott's back. "Right, Joe baby?"

"You are damn right, Larry baby!" he returned the slap, knocking Pogo out of his chair. Gene reached down and pulled him up. "Sorry, Larry. Didn't mean to dump you like that."

"Sure thing, Joe." Pogo dusted off his pants "Anything for a laugh."

"You can tell Candy dish I will see her Friday night, if she is lucky." Scott smiled and stood. "What's the chick's address, kid? I'm no damn mind reader."

"1411 Sunrise Lane, apartment 12." Randy stood and socked Scott's arm. He shook his fist and made a painful face. "Shit, Joe! Show Candy what a real man is like."

"You bet I will." He walked out into the night air. "Old Joe always satisfies his women." Opening the car door, he climbed behind the wheel. "See you around, kid."

"Sure thing, Joe baby." Randy waved as the car sped out of sight. He shook his head. "I hope Candy is a smart enough chick to tell Joe to buy another car. That is one ugly sled. It looks like something a preacher man would drive, not a hip guy like Joe."

Susan watched as Randy Sumner walked into the library. She had been disappointed the previous night when Gene called to tell her he was working Friday evening. She knew he was on a secret mission and could not reveal any information requarding his work. Still she knew one thing for sure: she could trust him with all her heart.

Susan decided to make her move with the blonde prospect. She made her way slowly into the library and deliberately walked up to him. As she pulled a book from the shelf, she could feel his blue eyes focused intently on her.

"Like what you see, Randy Sumner?" Her voice was teasing.

He gave her a surprised smile. "How do you know my name, sweetheart?"

"Well, honey, when someone watches me for weeks, I ask around to find out just who he is." She took his hand and walked over to a table "Why are you so interested in me, Randy?"

"'Cause you are my kind of chick. You are about the prettiest girl in this whole dumb college." He put his hand on her knee and gazed into her eyes. "No, I would say you are definitely the prettiest."

"Thank you." She eased his hand off her knee. "You wouldn't have a stick of gum would you, Randy?"

A sparkle came to his eyes. "Are you a mind reader beautiful? I was just going to ask you if you would like some." He pulled out a stick of gum in a plain wrapper. "This is a new brand. I hope you like the flavor."

"I sure could use something. I'll give it a try." She took the gum and pretended to unwrap it under the table. She hid it in her skirt pocket and pulled out the piece she brought from home. "Have to be careful," she whispered. "If that old battle ax Harper sees me chewing gum in the library she'll boot me out of here."

"Yeh, she is a pain in the ass." He glanced toward the librarian. "What is it with librarians? They all look alike."

"Who knows, I think they must come off an assembly line."

Susan touched his arm. "Say, this is different. What's the name of it? It has a funny kick to it."

"There is no real name for it, baby, but I can get you all you want, anytime." He winked at her as he looked at his watch, which was obviously gold. "History time."

"English time for me." She stood up and walked down the hall, turning toward him to smile. "Thanks for the gum, Randy. It's a blast."

"What about tonight? It's Friday. No classes tomorrow. How about a date?"

She looked up into his eyes, which were full of excitement and anticipation. "Well it's sorta short notice, Randy. Oh, but what the heck. Sure. Pick me up at my house around seven. Know where I live?"

"Susan Andrews, who doesn't?" He grinned broadly and hurried down the hall.

As he disappeared from her sight, she muttered, "That's one up for the good guys." She snapped her fingers and walked down the hall whistling.

Gene Scott walked up to apartment 12 and rang the bell. A bleached blonde wearing pink tights opened the door. Unabashed, her eyes ran up and down on Scott's body. A smile of approval spread across her red lips.

"Well Joe! You're even better than Randy or Mr. Big described you!" She took his hand and pulled him into her apartment.

"You ain't so bad yourself Candy!" he said, as he thought to himself, "Susan would kill me if she knew I was alone with an obvious whore."

"Please make yourself comfortable, sugar. But remember, your future depends on what I tell Mr. Big." She twisted her way behind a black bar. "What is your pleasure?"

"Gin and Candy." He smiled slyly from the sofa when she raised her eyes to his. "In that order."

"You sound like my kind of man." She made her way to him with a slow, provocative walk, handing him one of the two glasses of gin. "Here you go, lamby."

"Thanks, babe." He took the glass from her hand and pulled her down beside him. "How come this Mr. Big lets you spend your nights with other guys? If you were my women, damn, I would never allow anyone to touch you."

"That's because you're different, Joe." She smiled and took a sip from her glass. "I like you. I like you a lot, lamby."

Scott tossed the drink back in a single gulp. He realized Candy had been drinking long before he arrived.

"Well that makes two of us," he said. "I like me too." He laughed, then pulled her closer. "How about a refill sweetheart?"

"Honey lamb, I will give you anything you damn want." She hopped up and took his glass to the bar. "Gin really makes me feel good you know, Joe?" she said as she sat back down beside him and finished her drink. "It really warms my soul."

"That makes you every kind of hot," he said, then thought to himself, "If I get her drunk, she'll believe anything."

"You know so—something, hon—honey lamb, I think little Can—Candy kisses is getting—" She laughed in a high-pitched tone. "Tip—tippsy!"

"Is there any other way to be baby? Everything is better. Singing, sex, dancing." Scott smiled as he whirled her around the floor. "Come dance with me until I fall on my tired ass."

"And pass out from the sexy gin." She laid her spinning head against Scott's chest. "Floating into darkness and never to re—mem—ber, a what the hell, who cares?" she giggled. "Joe, Joe is the man for me—" she sang off key.

"Now—now that is what I call bea—ful, beaut—i—ful singing!" He pretended to be as drunk as she was.

She slid from his arms to the floor, out cold. He picked her up and carried her to her bed, then slipped out the door laughing softly to himself.

Susan fought Randy off all night and finally she felt safe on her front porch.

"My, my Randy Sumner, you sure are fresh on your first date with a girl."

"Well I figure there is no reason to goof around with a chick. I prefer getting right to the old one, two, three." He tried to take her in his arms, but she pulled away "Hey baby, what gives with you?"

"Randy, love, I never neck, hug or kiss on my front porch. Why if my daddy saw us? He would never let me date you again, not ever!" She looked nervously at the door "He is very old fashioned, Randy. He hates for me to even go out on a date. I had to lie to him tonight just to date you."

"How come?" Randy asked, puzzled, never having been faced

with this situation before.

"If he knew you just asked me today, Randy, he would've put his foot down. I told him you asked me last week." She looked down. "I especially wanted to go out with you this evening."

"Oh?" He took her hand, glancing at the door. "I'll see you at college Monday then."

"I hope so." She waved to him as he drove away. Taking a deep breath of night air, Susan sighed with relief. "Boy, the things we cops have to go through, all for duty." She walked silently into the house.

The weeks continued to go by. Susan was winning Randy's confidence and Gene Scott was certainly winning Miss Candy Carmel's. The married twosome rarely got to see one another, but at those times when they did, their love-starved bodies met in welcoming embraces. Simus was after Scott for answers, but until Scott was ready to supply any, the detective would just have to wait. Gene and Susan kept hiding the secret from one another they were working for the police. So, unknowing of Susan's involvement, Scott finally decided on a plan to bring Mr. Big out in the open and put an end to the reign of his drug pushers.

Scott stood smiling in Candy Carmel's doorway.

"Hi baby!" He grabbed her and twirled her around. "Have I got an idea that will knock you flat on your sweet ass!"

"What, Joe baby? Tell your lover."

Scott had convinced her that they had made love on various occasions when he would get her drunk and she would pass out. She had swallowed his lie.

"Let me and you knock off Mr. Big and keep all the dough for ourselves."

"Joe baby!" She flopped onto the sofa laughing, then sat up as it suddenly struck her that Scott was serious and realized what the plan would mean to her. She would be free of Big and have Joe, the man she wanted. "You know," she said quietly, "I actually think we could do it."

"You bet we can do it baby." He fixed them both a drink "What do you say we do it this Saturday night. You invite him over for dinner. I will be waiting for the knock off."

"Joe baby, you're terrific." She held up her glass. "To my wonderful smart, sexy Joe!"

"I'll drink to that." He took a sip and sat at the table. "You can ask him tomorrow. Tell him you feel sexy and you need a real man."

"But Joe baby, you are the only real man I've ever had." She ran her fingers in his hair. "Why should I tell that pig he is?"

"If Mr. Big is anything like I think, he'll eat flattery up with a shovel, a snow shovel." He pushed his empty glass into her hand "Fix me up, will you?"

"Then you will be waiting behind the bedroom door. And when the right time comes, pow!" She finished her drink and fell onto the sofa. "Wake me later, sugar."

Gene Scott stood and smiled at the drunk woman, fast asleep. "Sleep it off, you poor dumb blonde."

He walked out the door smiling to himself and patted Pogo on the back as he got into the car.

"Well, friend, Saturday night we get our answers."

His hands on the steering wheel, Pogo smiled. "She fell for it?"

"Did she ever." Scott shook his head. "Drive on and stop by the coffee shop at the corner. I could use a stiff black cup."

Susan poured Randy another glass of gin.

"Are you trying to make me—drunk—sweetheart?"

"But of course," she teased. "How else do I get answers."

"Maybe by asking questions, doll." He shook his head. "I'm crazy about you, you know."

"Are you Randy Sumner?" She ran her finger along his forehead. "Then why won't you tell me what kind of work you do? You wear expensive jewelry and drive a really cool car."

He chuckled. "Do you reallywant to know that bad baby?" He tossed back the last of the gin. "I sell D-O-P-E!" He pulled her to him and kissed her. "Now that you know, doll, you going to have to meet Mr. Big."

"Is Mr. Big your boss, honey?" She poured a little more into his glass and a dash into a glass for herself to make him believe she was joining him."

"Mr. Big himself! He is the biggest jerk in   these   parts!" He winked at her. "But he's far from being the biggest man, or the best."

"Then is someone even higher over him?" She sat up, ears peeled. "Randy?" She shook his dropping shoulders. 'Who is the bigger fish? Who else do you work for?"

"Work for? Oh! I—work—no, don't work for him." He laughed. "He's just my big friend, my buddy! Joe, good old Joe!"

"When can I meet Big Randy?" She tried to hold his head up. "You said you would introduce me, Randy. When?"

"Saturday night!"

He fell over onto her. She squirmed out from under him, and walked to the corner to flag down a taxi.

Chapter 27

On Saturday morning Susan sat nervously in Simus's office.

He cleared his throat. "Well, Susan, is this Sumner a pusher?"

"I am sure to know tonight, Mr. Simus."

"Susan, you have been working on this boy for a month. Surely you know something by now. You are a smart girl." He chewed on his cigar nervously.

"Alright, so maybe I do sir, but after tonight I will know plenty more," she said excitedly.

"Susan, have you been getting too deep in this case?" He·tapped·his pencil lightly on his desk. "You know what I told you."

"Yes sir, I remember, Mr. Simus, but do you or don't you want to catch these crooks?" She sat up in her chair. "Tonight I get to meet the leader of the drug ring, Mr. Big himself."

"Mr. Big?" Simus frowned. "Is that the man's name?"

"I think it is a nickname, sir. I'm sure Randy knows better than to say his real name."

"What makes you think you will get to meet this Mr. Big?" The detective had mixed emotions about this revelation.

"Randy is taking me to meet his boss tonight and he told me last night he's a pusher." She smiled triumphantly. "Pretty good detective work, wouldn't you say sir?"

"Pretty good, Susan," he laughed. "I would say, damn good. Compared to the rest of the men I have working on this case, you are a genius."

"Then tonight is all set, right?" She stood up.

"Susan, sit down." He ran his fingers through his hair. "This is no game you are playing. These men are dangerous. You'll be in big danger tonight, Susan."

"That is why your men will follow from a safe distance," she said, nodding. "Randy will lead us right to Mr. Big himself."

"I wish that damn Scott and Pogo were as smart as you, my dear."

"Scott!" Susan's eyes grew huge as she stood. "I—I guess I better go get ready for tonight."

"Susan, is there something wrong dear?" He followed her to the door.

"No sir, I'm fine." She feigned a laugh.

"I'll have my men stake out your house tonight. The rest is up to you, dear." He put his hand on her shoulder. "And be careful."

"I will do my best." She walked down the street to her car in a daze, unaware she was being watched from across the street. Randy Sumner stared at Susan silently as she walked away from the police station. Susan was a spy and he had fallen for the trap.

"Tonight," he thought, "I'll make her pay for betraying me."

Each time Scott had tried to reach Susan she had not been at home. The last time he called was around seven o'clock and was told by Shirley Andrews that Susan had gone out on a date. He tried to reason it out as he knocked on Candy Carmel's door. She opened it and pulled him inside nervously.

"It's about time! Where have you been Joe? I was afraid the big pig would beat you here!" She looked into his serious eyes, unaware he had his mind on his wife rather than on killing someone he had never met. "Just calm down, Joe. Is this your first knock off?"

"What?" He snapped back to his surroundings and the reason he was there.

"I said, is this the first time you have killed anybody?" Her hand trembled as she lit a cigarette. "Well, is it?"

"Yeh." He looked out the window. "Give me a damn cigarette." He snatched it from her, stuck it in the corner of his mouth and lit it. "Why don't that bastard come on?"

"Joe baby, relax." She pulled him to her bathroom. "Wash your face with some cold water. I'll let you know when Big gets here."

"You're right, baby. I've got to get a hold of myself." Scott walked over to the sink, making sure to keep his ears open.

Susan jerked when Randy forced her into his car. She tried to guess why he had done it. Probably because she had left him last night after he had passed out. He climbed in next to her and without saying a word, sped down the street. She feigned a laugh.

"Hey Randy, what is with you tonight?"

Suddenly she grew anxious when he turned down a dark road and switched off the headlights. "Randy, why in the world did you do that?"

"We are being followed!" he said ominously. "I gave them the slip."

"Followed?" She swallowed. "Why do you think that, Randy? I never saw anyone."

"I don't think baby, I know!" He grabbed her arm "You little traitor! Squeal on me, will you!"

"Randy, I would never squeal on you." She tried to pull free, but his grip was too tight "Randy, I didn't!"

"I saw you Susan. This morning at the police station." His eyes burned with fury. "Why, Susan, why?"

"Randy, drugs are bad. You should know that. You don't take them." She spoke softly, trying not to show her fear. "If you tell the police everything about your gang, they'll give·you a break. I will see to it."

"Mr. Big will judge your punishment." He turned the motor on and backed the car off of the side road.

"I will not go!"

She tried to get out, but he slapped her hard across the head, sending·her into unconsciousness.

Scott stood silently inside the bedroom door listened to Mr. Big and Candy talking just outside. He wiped the sweat from his forehead and took a firm hold on the doorknob. Slowly it turned under his hand. He could see an over-dressed male standing with his back to him. The man's hair was gray around the temples and along the back. Scott moved slowly from his hiding place and slipped behind Big. Raising his fists high over the drug king's head, Scott brought both hands down, knocking the creep to the floor.

Instantly relieved, Candy stood smiling at the limp, heavy form on the floor. "So, finally the giant Mr Big finally met his match!" she laughed and took Scott's hand. "Finish him off, Sugar. Give him the knife, Joe, right in his fat gut."

Scott pushed Candy down in a chair. "Stay out of my way, baby." He walked to the closet and grabbed several pairs of hose.

"Hey, sugar lamb, what are you going to do with my stockings?" She started to stand up, but Scott pushed her back down. "Joe·baby, that ain't no way to treat a lady."

"I don't treat ladies like that." He pulled her arms behind her and tied them together securily.

"Joe baby? What the devil are you doing?" She tried to break free, but the hose bound her firmly.

"Just relax, sweetheart. I'll take them off soon enough." He turned to Mr. Big and tied his arms and legs together "Alright, Candy, on your feet. We are going for a little ride."

"Where are we going, Joe·baby?" she whined. "Untie me. These knots are cutting off my circulation."

"Get in the car. Move it!" he shoved her out the door and pushed her into his car. Taking Mr. Big by the arms, he threw him over his shoulders and dragged him out the door. "Now to take you both for a little ride."

"Joe, will·you please answer your Candy! What do you think you are doing?" She looked pleadingly into his silent face as he sped down the road. "Now I get it. You plan to knock us both off so you get all loot. Joe baby, you need me. You know nothing about our operation."

"Here we are." He pulled·to a stop in front of the police headquarters.

"Joe, are you crazy?" She squirmed in her seat. "You'll get us all locked up!"

"Just shut up and get out Miss Carmel." He pulled her out and pushed her up the steps. "Now when you get inside, I want you list every single person working for you, get it?"

"But, Joe baby, you can't mean it!" she whined. "No! I will not do it, I refuse!"

Gene Scott took a firm hold on her arm sending jolts of pains through her body. "Now listen, Miss Carmel, you either talk or I'll start breaking bones," he said throught gritted his teeth. "So what's it going to be?"

"Alright!" she cried out. "I'll tell you everything you want to know. Just stop hurting me, you big brut!"

"Right decision, Miss Carmel. Just remember to tell us everything when we get inside."

Once inside the station, Scott shouted, "Simus, get your ass out here!" Scott turned to the two police officers who stood staring at him. "There's a guy tied up out in my car. Bring him in."

They turned and hurried toward the street.

"What is going on out here?" Roy Simus came quickly from his office and watched as his men brought Big into the room. "Scott, who are these people?"

"The leaders of the drug ring, Simus! Mr. Big and his partner Miss Candy Carmel." Scott shoved her down into a chair. "Miss Carmel has agreed to write down all the names of those persons working for them." He placed his hands firmly on the back of her neck. "Isn't that right, Miss Carmel?"

"Yes, yes!" She breathed heavily. "Just bring me something to write on."

"Sir!" The phone operator stared up from the switch board. "It is a report on the Sumner kid."

Scott stared at Simus as he grabbed the phone.

"Simus here. Go ahead, forty-six."

"We lost them, sir. We were waiting for Sumner at Miss Andrews like we were ordered. We followed them to West Forty-Seventh and lost them. The kid must have caught wind of us or something."

Scott's breathing began to come in short bursts as he listened to the sickening news.

"Miss Andrews, was she with him?" Simus chewed on his cigar.

"Yes sir! Sumner pushed her into the car. I think, from his behavior, he was mad at her."

"Well, keep looking forty-six. We have to find them." He hung up the phone down and slammed his fist onto the counter. "I knew I should not have listened to that wild idea of Susan's."

"Susan!" Scott grabbed Simus by the collar. "What the hell has Susan got to do with this case, Simus?"

"You know Miss Andrews?" He pulled himself loose and stuck his cigar back in his mouth.

Scott knocked it out and jerked him up so their faces were inches apart. "I know her very well, Simus, and if anything happens to her, I will personally see to it that you are held responsible. Where were they going and why was Susan with Sumner?"

"He was taking her to meet his boss, Mr. Big. They never got to him because you did."

"Randy must've caught on. He must've found out Susan was tricking him!" Gene Scott brought his fist down on the desktop. "Damn it!"

"Calm down, Scott. We must talk this out," Simus said as he gazed at his undercover agent. "Are you a friend of the Andrews family?"

"That is not the point here, Simus! The point is, some crazy, scared kid has Susan and we've got to find them! Talking it out is not going to help! We have got to start moving!" He turned and stormed out the door.

Gene Scott hurried as quickly as he could to Sally's bar where Pogo was waiting. He rushed in and grabbed his friend's arm.

"Whats up?" Pogo's face grew white when he saw Scott's expression. "You didn't really kill him, did you?"

"Good heavens, Pogo!" He pulled him up from his chair. "Have you heard from Randy?"

"No. Why?"

"He has Susan. She was working for the cops and he knows it!" Scott took a deep breath.·

"Susan?" Pogo's eyes grew big. "But—but how can that be?"

"I can't explain now, Pogo, and I don't know exactly what she was up to. Only we got to find her—and fast!"

Scott turned when he heard a familar voice call his name. Randy Sumner waved him over. Gene noticed Susan was not with him.

"What's wrong, man?" Scott stared at him as he thought to himself, "What have you done with my woman, you little creep?"

"We're in·danger, Joe! The cops are getting close—real close!" He looked around wildly.

Scott's heart was beating in his throat "God!" He thought, "Is Susan alright?" He looked down at the frightened boy. "Let's go outside to talk in private, Randy."

"I have a broad hidden that knows about me! She knows, Joe!" he shook with fear. "I can't reach Mr. Big or Miss Candy anywhere! I'm scared, Joe, real scared!"

"Just try to calm down, Randy." Scott put his arm on the boy's shoulder. "Where is this chick? Let me talk to her."

"I have her hid real well, Joe. Can't nobody find her. She can just die there and no one will ever find her."

Scott grabbed him around the neck, causing him to choke as he tried to speak. "Joe! What's wrong with you, man?"

"Where have you hidden Susan?" His voice was fierce, ominous.

"How—how do you know her name?" He swallowed and shook his head. "You're a cop, aren't you? A damn, stinking cop?"

"Give it up, Randy! It's over. The whole game is over!" Scott's voice shook. "Mr. Big, along with the rest of your gang, is in jail. We have them all kid."

"I don't believe you, Joe—or who ever you are." Sweat rolled off the scared young man's face. "Well·you'll never find the girl. You'll never find Susan. Never!"

"For God's sake, Randy, tell me!" Scott shook him by his shoulders.

"Take your hands off me, copper!" Randy yelled, "You dirty, stinking pig!"

"He is not a cop, Randy. He's a preacher." Pogo's voice was soft as spoke. "Please tell us where she is."

"Then start praying for her soul, preacher, 'cause she is going to die!" Randy shouted. "Die, do you her me?"

"Kid, tell me where she is now!" Scott's fingers bit into the boy's arm.

"I will never tell you, preacher man." He shook his head in defiance.

"That is not the right answer." Scott struggled to look upon the boy with compassion. "Randy, why the hell are you doing this to Susan? She has done nothing to you, son."

"She tricked me, man! I fell in love with her, I think." His eyes fell. "And you, Joe, I never loved anyone like I did you. I looked up to you."

"Randy, if you ever loved Susan, please tell me where she is." Scott's lip quivered. "Susan is my whole life. If—if she dies, Randy, my life is useless."

"Why is she so important to you?" He stared up into Scott's tear-filled eyes. "Surely she's not your daughter."

"Susan is my wife, Randy." Scott closed his eyes to hold back his tears. "I do not want to hurt you, Randy, but damn it, if you don't tell me where Susan is, I—I—" He jerked him off the ground. "Tell me!"

"And me? What happens to me?"

"We'll do everything we can," Pogo said. "Won't we, Scott?"

"Scott?" Randy swallowed. "What did Susan mean when she said, 'Please don't hurt little Scott'?"

"Did you hit Susan?" Scott held him tightly. "Tell me, damn it! If you've killed my baby, I will—"

"Baby!" Randy choked. "I'll tell you, but we better hurry, man!" Tears ran down the young man's face. "I thought she was just scared. I didn't understand what she was saying."

"Where is she, please for God's sake, Randy!" Scott's voice rang out.

"At the docks, in a box!" He climbed into Scott's car. "Hurry, east gate!"

"Scott, drive this thing," Pogo said. "I'm scared shitless!" Pogo jumped into the back seat.

Leaving black marks on the pavement, Scott sped toward the ship loading docks. In less than ten minutes they were out of the car, following Randy Sumner at a run. Randy stopped in front of a wooden box nailed shut.

"Oh God!" he mumbled. "My toolbox is in my car."

"Don't need one." Scott wedged his hand in between the jointed top and pulled back hard in the lid. The nails cracked out of their buried places and Gene pulled out his limp wife.

"Susan, honey, speak to me!" He slapped her cheeks lightly. "Susan! Please, God, oh God!" Tears blinded his sight as he dropped his face to her neck. "Susan, darling, wake up," he whispered.

She opened her eyes slowly and with a weak hand touched the curls on his neck. "Gene. You came for me."

"Oh Susan!" He held her tightly. "Thank God you're alive. Thank God."

He lifted her carefully and put her in the car. Pogo drove quickly to the police headquarters. Simus and his son, along with most of the staff came out to meet them.

"Oh, thank God you found them Reverend Scott!" Peter Simus started to take Susan from Scott's arms, but Scott kept him away. "Reverend Scott, could I please have her sir?"

"No you may not!" he snapped. "I'm taking her home!" He looked down at Randy. "This boy gave himself up and I have a statement to make on his behalf when the time comes." He turned, got back into the car and drove to the Andrews.

Chapter 28

Susan sat smiling up at Gene Scott on the sofa in the Andrew's living room. The rest of her family had given them some time to talk.

"Gene Scott, I'm a very lucky girl to have you."

"I am the lucky one, Susan Scott." He smiled.

They looked up when the door opened. Shirley and Owen Andrews came into the room smiling.

"Well, Reverend Scott, have you helped our little girl with her problem?" Susan's mother kissed her daughter's cheek.

"Yes, I think so." Scott's eyes met Susan's, knowing the lie they had told her parents about Susan breaking off with her mysterious love was why she was so upset the night he had brought her home from the station. "Susan is a remarkable young lady, Shirley. I don t think you will have to worry about her."

"That is good news." Shirley smiled up at her husband. "Now we have some good news for you, my dear."

"What good news, Mom?" she looked up, puzzled.

"You know how much you have always wanted art lessons in Paris? Well, your father has managed to get you into a six-month course. How's that?" Her mother's voice was filled with excitement.

Susan stood up quickly. "No! I will not go!"

"Go, Susan." Gene looked deeply into her eyes.

"Go—Reverend Scott? Why?" She felt tears forming.

"It will take your mind off things." He took her hand and looked down.

"What things Scott?" She squeezed his hand and he looked into her eyes. "Have you got another mission from that creep Weber?"

"Susan dear, is that any way to talk about the bishop?" Owen Andrews smiled sheepishly at Scott. "Children today are so outspoken."

"She is right, Owen. Weber is a creep." Gene took Susan's other hand. "I was going to tell you anyway. It is nothing dangerous but it will keep me away for several months."

"What and where and for how long?" Susan's eyes filled with sadness and more tears.

"Africa. My mission is to lead a group of men to build a hospital and church over there. It was your grandfather who suggested me for the job."

"Granddad?" Susan's mouth flew open.

"Father knows a good man when he sees one." Shirley smiled at Scott.

"Will you be working with my father, Reverend Scott?"

"Yes I will." He gazed at Susan. "There will be no danger involved. I'll be over there about six or seven months."

"Oh!" Susan turned as she pulled her hands free and ran from the room.

Scott walked quickly to the door behind her as he cleared his throat.

"I think I better go explain something to your daughter. Excuse me." He walked quickly after her and caught her just outside the gate. "Susan, I have to go."

"But what about Sand Palms? They wanted you. We could have been together some anyway." She laid her head over on him "I can't stand being without you that long."

"Don't you think I will be going through hell too!" He took her face in his hands. "Susan, while we are apart I will be only half alive. My heart, soul and love will be with you."

"Will they always send you away from me, Gene?" she asked, clinging to him.

"The Methodist board is considering my job for Sand Palms. I think they liked the idea pretty good. They want me back behind the pulpit." He kissed her nose. "I'm going to write them and inform them about my being married and that this mission will be my last. If they don't give me the post at Sand Palms or one like it, I will turn in my Bible."

"Gene Scott! You could never do that!" She touched his cheek. "It is as much a part of you as breathing."

"My Susan." He touched her lips. "They probably will agree to it, but to be with you, I would give up everything." his lips parted over hers "I love you so much."

Susan and Gene lay wrapped up in each other's arms. They were exhaused from making love and now just satisfied to hold on to each other for their last few minutes together. His fingers gently brushed through her long black hair.

"I am going to miss you, Mrs. Scott."

"Write me everyday." She looked into his eyes. "Promise."

"I promise to write you every day, my darling." He bent over and kissed her. "Sealed with a kiss."

"And I promise to write you." She squeezed her arms around him. "Oh Gene, I am going to miss you dreadfully!"

"You will be so busy with those art brushes you won't have time to miss me." He teased.

"Ha! That's what you think!" She looked down and laughed softly. "At least there is one good thing about taking art lessions."

"What is that honey?"

"I can keep little Scott a secret easily by wearing smocks all the time. Pretty clever wife, huh?"

"Clever and beautiful." He kissed her passionately.

A knock came at the door and Edna spoke softly. "Hey you two, it's time for your planes to leave. You both have to be at the airport in forty minutes."

"We know Edna, we are coming." Susan's voice grew shaky as tears began to flow from her blue eyes. She grabbed Gene around the neck. "Oh Gene, I love you!"

"Susan, my Susan." He kissed her and lifted her to her feet.

Quickly they took a bath and, getting Pogo on the way down, they were off to the TarSa airport.

Getting one last kiss in the car, Susan and Gene walked quickly inside. Shirley, Owen and Jobi Andrews stood up from where they had been nervously waiting. Shirley hugged her daughter, tears staining her face.

"Oh Susan, you be careful."

"I will, Mom." Susan winked at Scott.

"Did Reverend Scott solve your last minute problems, dear?" Owen put his arm around his beautiful daughter.

"Yes, Dad, he did." She took Gene's hand. "How much longer before I leave, Dad?"

"About five minutes, baby." He kissed her cheek.

Susan hugged her father, then her mother. She gave Jobi a kiss on the forehead. She walked slowly back over to Gene Scott and took his hand again.

They held onto each other tightly as her lips whispered, "I love you Mr. Scott."

Fighting his own tears, Gene's fingers tightened around hers as a voice came over the intercom.

"Flight to Paris, France, leaving now at gate seven. Passingers must board now."

"Take care of yourself, Susan." Scott's eyes grew misty as he added softly, "And little Scott."

She reached up and kissed his cheek. Turning, she ran swiftly to the gate crying. Scott told the Andrews goodbye and he and Pogo went to their rented airplane.

The waiting was hard and the days seem to crawl by for Susan and Gene. But nevertheless the letters never stopped coming. Susan marveled at how well she hid little Scott and no one ever mentioned her looking heavy. After her long six months in Paris, she found herself waiting in TarSa.

"Only a few more weeks," she told Jobi as they played catch. The spring flowers were just beginning to bloom and she could feel little Scott active within her. "Hold on in there little Scott," she laughed. "You are rowdy enough for two little Scotts."

"Hey, sis, what if you and Scott have twins?" Jobi laughed "Wouldn't that be neat?"

"Hold on there, Jobi," she laughed. "I think taking care of one little Scott and one big Scott will be enough for me to handle."

"Ah shucks, sis, twins are so sweet." He pitched the ball gently to her. "When is Scott coming home?"

"Sometime this week, I hope." She rubbed her stomach. "I hope so. I don't think I am going to keep little Scott a secret much longer."

Mildred stuck her head out the door and yelled, "Miss Susan, Reverend Scott is on his way over, child."

Susan grabbed Jobi. "He is back, Jobi! Gene is back!"

She ran in quickly to get ready for him and was waiting outside when he drove up. Not caring who saw him, Scott jumped out and took Susan up in his arms.

"Susan, my darling, I've missed you! Damn, how I missed you!" His lips parted over hers as she held him tightly.

"Oh Gene, Gene!" She took a deep breath "Oh!"

"Honey, what is wrong? Something hurt you?" He gazed at her anxiously. "Is it little Scott?"

"Yes!" she laughed. "The little rascal just kicked me again."

"Sporty little fellow, isn't he?" Scott put his arm around her. "Hasn't anyone noticed."

"No, it is so funny, Gene." She laid her head on his strong chest. "He's due in less than two weeks and nobody has even suspected my being pregnant."

Shirley and Owen Andrews drove up and got out smiling.

"Reverend Scott, nice to see you got home safe." Shirley took his hand. "Joan was just asking this morning, saying, 'I wonder if

Gene will be back today'.'"

Just then Joan and Jewel came running from the house calling Gene's name. Susan gritted her teeth.

"Speak of the little devils," she mumbled.

Scott laughed. "Hello, ladies. You are both looking great. Got a date tonight?"

"I don't know, Gene, have I?" Jewel took his arm. "You are looking extra good yourself. Who'd you get dolled up for?"

"Well it certainly wasn't you, Jewel." Joan batted her eyelashes and brushed Owen's sister aside. "You've been away far too long, Gene."

"Joan, why don't you go out and play—in the freeway!" Jewel slapped her hand off Gene's shoulder. "Maybe a man will pick you up and take you out!"

"Why don't you both go jump in the refrigerator? That's where you live half your time anyway," Susan snapped.

"Susan!" Shirley's mouth flew open.

"It's true madam, they eat like two over grown sows. I can't serve leftovers anymore cause there ain't any left anymore." Mildred put her arm around Susan as Jewel and Joan let out little cries of pain. "Miss Susan was only telling the truth."

"Hello everybody!" Gloria Weber came twisting around the corner with her parents. "We were out for a little walk when we spotted Gene's car parked in front of your house."

"So we thought we would drop by to say hello." Henry Weber chomped on a candy bar.

"Hello!" Susan said loudly. "Now you said it and I said it, so goodbye!"

"What?" Henry Weber nearly swallowed the whole Baby Ruth.

"Susan!" Shirley Andrews laughed sheepishly. "Susan has not been herself lately, bishop. You must excuse her."

"For what?"

Susan put her hands on her hips, but Scott took them in his. "I promised Susan I would have a little talk with her. Excuse us."

"Hold on there, Gene." Gloria walked over and grabbed his hand. "Daddy said, if you do not marry me, he's going to send you off this time to a place so dangerous that even an animal would not feel safe." She smiled. "And that poor mysterious girl in your life, well I do not happen to believe there is one. I think you made the whole thing up."

"Why don't you go jump in the lake, Gloria Ann Weber!" Susan pushed her arm off Gene's. "And keep your witchy hands off of Scott!"

"Susan!" Shirley looked over at her husband. "Owen, can't you talk to your daughter?"

"Thanks, dear." he mumbled "Now Susan—"

"Dad, she is always flirting after Reverend Scott! He cannot stand it! Besides—" She glared at the fat bishop. "Old Bishop Weber is always sending him away just to satisfy his precious spoiled little witch!"

"Ohhhh!" Gloria whined. "I orda knock you off your feet!"

"Touch her, Gloria, and I will send you flying!" Scott warned the red head through clenched teeth.

"Oh Daddy, do something!" Gloria backed away, confused and frustrated.

"Now listen, Scott, that is my baby you're threating." Henry Weber's neck grew red.

"And that is exactly what she is, a big baby!" Edna walked up and hung an arm around Scott's shoulder. "It came through, Gene. You'll be preaching at Sand Palms for as long as you like."

"What?" Weber looked shocked. "How is that when Scott has chosen the mission field?"

"The members of the church voted one hundred percent on Scott." John Crain slapped Weber on the back. "We sorta went behind your back, sir. We knew it would be the only way."

"Daddy, do something! There must be something you can do." Gloria tossed her red hair.

"There is nothing your father can do, Gloria." Edna laughed victoriously. "Everything was done legally. It took months to complete, but we did it!"

"Daddy, don't just stand there, do something!" Gloria took his arm.

"Just shut up, Gloria!" Karolyn Weber grabbed her daughter's arm. "Now behave."

"I know now, Susan!" Peter Simus came running up the walkway "I have figured it out. Mr. and Mrs.Andrews, your daughter has been having an affair with an older man."

"What?" Shirley's face grew white. "But, Peter, how, who?"

"Shirley is right, Peter. How can you know such a thing—much less believe it to be true?" Owen looked over at his daughter to read any guilt. "Did you see her with someone?"

"No, not exactly sir, but by what I have put together, it has to be."

"Oh Peter, shut up!" Susan took Scott's arm and squeezed it.

"Was it your art instructor?" Jewel sighed. "Oh how romantic, and a Frenchman at that."

"Get real, Aunt Jewel! Peter does not know what he is saying! He has no proof because I am not having an affair!" She spat out the words. "Peter is just trying to win me for himself!"

"Well he cannot have you!" Scott spoke loudly. Everyone looked at him. "She does not love this pushy young man!"·

"How do you know so much about her, Gene?" Gloria demanded.

"Because Gene has beem counseling Susan,·Miss Weber." Joan gave the red head a distasteful smile.

"Gene, it's time." Susan whispered up at him, but he was too busy listening to all the auguments around him.

"If you want my opinion, I think Miss Susan is old enough to make up her own mind." Mildred spoke up

"Me too!" Jobi shouted. "She acts a lot more grown up than you, Miss High-Nose Weber.

"Jobi!" Shirley choked back a laugh "What is going on? I think I am dreaming and having a nightmare."

"Gene!"

Susan tugged at his arm. He patted her hand as he listened to the group discussion.

"Well, one thing is for sure," he said. "Susan has brains and knows how to use them, unlike some people I know."

"Oh really!" Gloria yelled "And just who are referring too, Gene Scott, me?"

"You said it, not me," he laughed.

"Gene! Somebody!" Susan yelled to the top of her lungs. "Gene!"

He looked down at her as everyone stared at them.

"She called him 'Gene'," Joan swallowed.

"That—is his name, is it not?" Mildred turned up her lip and looked over at Susan; worried she might be in labor.

"What is it, Susan?" Scott's voice rang with excitement.

"It's time Gene. It is time!" She took a deep breath.

"Time for what?" Shirley walked over to her daughter.

"My baby, Mom." She tried to smile.

"Baby?" Shirley's legs fell from under her as Joan and Jewel slapped the shocked Owen on the back.

"Someone get Shirley a chair!" Edna shouted.

Pogo grabbed a lawn chair and hurried over. "Here you go Mrs. Andrews." He swallowed, wondering what would come next.

"Thank—thank you Pogo." Shirley closed her eyes, then opened them widely. "A baby?"

"Scott!" Owen stared angrily into the preacher's eyes. "You were supposed to be helping my daughter! How could you have led her to think this tragic thing was alright for her?"

"Do you have something against babies, sir?" Mildred smiled, then realized from the look Owen Andrews gave her that she had better remain still. "Sorry, Mr. Owen. I will keep my opinions to myself, sir." She could not resist a smile.

"Who is the father, Susan?" Owen took a step toward her.

"Gene, I have got to go!" She squeezed his hand.

"We can talk at the hospital. Susan is going to have this baby right here if we don't move!"

Scott started to walk but Owen stopped him

"Just hold on there, Scott! Susan is my daughter, I will take her! I think your advice is not needed anymore!"

"Yes Gene, why should you want to go so badly?" Gloria whined.

"Because it is my baby, damn it!"

"Oh!" Shirley sighed "My baby has been having a love affair with Reverend Scott! My Lord!"

"Oh, how lucky can one girl get!" Joan hit Jewel's arm.

"Yeh, some people get all the luck," Jewel sighed.

"Gene!" Susan cried out in pain.

"Step aside, Owen. I am taking Susan to the hospital!"

"Now look, Scott, giving my baby a baby does·not mean you can just go prancing into the hospital and sign her in! It takes a relative."

"Is 'husband' close enough?" Scott asked as he scooped Susan up in his arms. "Now move, damn it, before I have to deliver my own baby."

"Did he say married—they were married?" Shirley looked up sickly·at her husband. "Well, thank God they're married."

"Lucky! Shit how lucky can one girl get?" Jewel shook her head as she climbed into Owen's car.

The entire party drove quickly to the hospital. They sat nervously in the waiting room. Scott walked back and forth, twisting the wedding band he at last had happily put on. Gloria walked up to him and took his arm.

"Gene, how could you marry a little girl? I would be glad to have given you babies."

"You, Miss Gloria?" Mildred laughed. "Why you are too much a baby yourself to go around birthing babies."

"Oh shut up! What would a servant know?" Gloria turned back to Gene. "I'm the right woman for you Gene. Why can 't you see that?"

"Why don't you take your hands off, Gene?" Edna walked over and pushed Gloria's hand away.

She tossed her red hair around. "Daddy, do something!"

"I am going to do something I have wanted to do for a long time!" Edna slung her arm around knocking Gloria Ann Weber to the floor. "There!" She clapped her hands together.

Henry Weber helped his blushing daughter to her feet and stared at Gene. "Think you're real tough, marrying an eighteen-year-old." He pulled a small box of candy from his pocket. "The church won't like it, a man your age taking such a young woman and when I get through with my report—"

Scott knocked the candy from Weber's hand. "That's enough, Henry. I've heard everything I want to from you. Just shut up."

Weber hurried over to his wife and sat down, red faced.

Gloria looked over at her father. "Daddy, do something! Don't just sit there!"

Weber cleared his throat. "Maybe Scott is right. He deserves to live his own life the way he sees fit."

"Daddy!" Gloria whimpered, then looked at her mother for help. "Mommy?"

"Just shut up, Gloria, and sit down before I hit you myself!" Karolyn Weber rubbed her fresh headache.

"Ohhhh !"

Gloria started crying as the nurse walked in smiling. "Reverend Scott?"

Gene stood up from where he had just sat down nervously. "Yes!" he swallowed.

"Your wife just had two beautiful twins." The nurse beamed.

"Twins?" He closed his eyes. "Susan, how is my Susan?"

"Could not be better!" She put her hand on his arm. "You have got a very brave little wife, sir. She wanted to stay awake for the whole thing."

"Can I see her now?" he twisted his ring.

"I think you should before she climbs out of bed to come see you." The nurse started out the door. "Oh by the way! One girl and one boy."

Scott followed the nurse out the door. Jobi jumped straight up. "Yippee! I told Susan it was going to be twins!"

Shirley's jaw dropped open. "You mean you knew all along, you little rascal.?"

"They certainly are in love, Shirley." Edna put her arm around the new grandmother. "I have never seen two people as much in love as those two."

"You can say that again." Pogo said, beaming. "Scott thinks nothing that breathes is better than his woman."

"And I help bring them together," Jobi said proudly. "The best brother-in-law I could have ever got."

"You are absolutely right, son." Shirley stood up, a grateful smile across her face. "Gene, my son."

"At least I think he and I will get along great." Owen shrugged. "We are in the same generation after all."

"Lucky Susan," Joan sighed.

"Yeh, one lucky girl."

Gene took Susan's hand and kissed it. "How do you feel Mrs. Scott?"

"Like I have just had two little Scotts." She laughed and pulled him down and kissed him. His lips parted over hers as his tongue gently rolled within her sweet mouth. "Too bad we have to wait a few more weeks before I can have that sexy body of ·yours."

"Believe me, when I can, I am gonna make up for all that lost time," he said, pushing her hair back from her eyes. "A son and ·a daughter. Pretty good work there Mrs. Scott."

"You put them there, Mr. Scott. Our love found a way to tell everyone! What shall we name them Gene?"

"Samson and Delilah!" he laughed. "A part of us in a part of them."

"Oh Gene, I love that." She pretended to write in the air. "Samson and Delilah Scott."

His lips melted over hers as his fingers gently embraced her.

"I love you, Susan. All of our secret meetings are over. When you leave here, you will be with me. We will walk out of here like any married couple who just had babies. Love did find a way, darling!" He took her face·in his hands.

"And together we will be happy forever."

"I certainly will, for I will have you, my darling Susan, for all my tomorrows."

Author's Notes

The Scott's stationary life in TarSa is short-lived when Reverend Gene Scott is called once again on an unusual mission involving prostitutes and drugs. Not wanting Susan to follow him, Scott only tells her parts of the mission. But with a visit from Gloria Anne Weber, Susan learns everything. Pogo makes a date with a mysterious girl and refuses to tell Scott who she is, knowing he would not approve.

Book # 3:

Today, Tomorrow and Always

in the

All My Tomorrows series.

www.ingramcontent.com/pod-product-compliance
Lightning Source LLC
Chambersburg PA
CBHW060424180626
46817CB00007B/2662